praise for the bir

"Modern medicine clashes with folk remedies in *The Birth House*, McKay's stirring saga of midwifery in Nova Scotia. . . . This is an impressive novel, laced with quirky research and rippling with muscular poetry." —*The Observer* (UK)

"An unusual, vigorous and disciplined novel." —*The Irish Times*

"By turns lyrical and gripping, brimming with historical detail and with a touching love story at the core, *The Birth House* brings to life a time, place and traditions long forgotten." —*The Irish Post*

"*The Birth House* has a spirited momentum and it is difficult not to be swept along by it. McKay's writing is often beautiful, with colourful turns of phrase that mirror the earthiness of her setting, and her protagonist." —*Sunday Business Post* (UK)

"[McKay's] writing is . . . injected with a sly sense of humour and chockablock with vivid images. . . . *The Birth House* is deeply infused with Maritime lyricism and more than a dash of its salty roots." —*CBC Arts Online*

"McKay has done her research . . . and along with her lyrical prose and deft storytelling, she cements the historical context with clippings of advertisements, news articles and correspondence among the characters." —*Chicago Sun-Times*

"Fresh as a loaf of homemade bread just out of the oven, *The Birth House*, a tale of sex, birth, love and pain, will more than satisfy the hungry reader." —Joan Clark, author of *An Audience of Chairs*

"The moon over Nova Scotia must have extra magic in it to have fostered a writer of Ami McKay's lyrical sway and grace. She retrieves our social history and lays it out before us in a collage of vivid, compelling detail. In McKay's depiction of Dora Rare, an early twentieth century midwife, attention is paid to the day-to-day moments of love and tending that enable humans to endure. And we the readers get to witness the emergence of a powerful new voice in Canadian writing."

—Marjorie Anderson, editor of the Dropped Threads series

"Ami McKay is a marvellous storyteller who writes with a haunting and evocative voice. The novel offers a world of mystery and wisdom, a world where tradition collides with science, where life and death meet under the moon. With a startling sense of time and place *The Birth House* travels through a landscape that is at once deeply tender and exquisitely harsh. McKay is possessed with a brilliant narrative gift."

—Christy Ann Conlin, author of *Heave*

"Reading Ami McKay's first novel is like rummaging through a sea-chest found in a Nova Scotian attic. Steeped in lore and landscape, peppered with journal entries, newspaper clippings and advertisements, this marvellous 'literary scrapbook' captures the harsh realities of the seacoast community of Scots Bay, Nova Scotia, during WWI. With meticulous detail and visceral description, McKay weaves a compelling story of a woman who fights to preserve the art of midwifery, reminding us of the need, in changing times, for acts of bravery, kindness and clear-sightedness."

—Beth Powning, author of *The Hatbox Letters*

the birth house

a novel by

AMI MCKAY

VINTAGE CANADA

VINTAGE CANADA EDITION, 2007

Published in Canada by Vintage Canada, a division of Random House of Canada Limited, Toronto, in 2007. Originally published in hardcover in Canada by Alfred A. Knopf Canada, a division of Random House of Canada Limited, Toronto, in 2006. Distributed by Random House of Canada Limited, Toronto.

Vintage Canada and colophon are registered trademarks of Random House of Canada Limited.

www.randomhouse.ca

This is a work of fiction. Any references to herbal remedies and/or midwifery techniques are not meant to be considered as a substitute for professional advice. They are not to be considered as viable treatments.

Excepts from the following songs are included in the book:

P. 94 "I Don't Want to Play in Your Yard" (Wingate & Petrie) copyright Petrie Music Co., Chicago, 1894; P. 106 "Waltz Me Around Again Willie" (Cobb, Shields) copyright F.A. Mills, N.Y., 1906; P. 242 "Little Bessie" (J.M. Barringer) copyright P.W. Search 1876; P. 309 "A Good Man is Hard to Find" (Eddie Green) copyright Handy Brothers Music Co. 1918; P. 333 "Come All Ye Old Comrades" traditional Nova Scotian folksong based on the Scottish folksong "The Donside Emigrant's Farewell."

Library and Archives Canada Cataloguing in Publication
McKay, Ami, 1968–
The birth house : a novel / by Ami Mckay.
ISBN 978-0-676-97773-8
I. Title.
PS8625.K387B57 2007   C813'.6   C2006-904703-0

Text design: Kelly Hill

Printed and bound in Canada

6 8 9 7 5

For my husband, Ian
My heart, my love, my home

prologue

MY HOUSE STANDS at the edge of the earth. Together, the house and I have held strong against the churning tides of Fundy. Two sisters, stubborn in our bones.

My father, Judah Rare, built this farmhouse in 1917. It was my wedding gift. *A strong house for a Rare woman,* he said. I was eighteen. He and his five brothers, shipbuilders by trade, raised her worthy from timbers born on my grandfather's land. Oak for stability and certainty, yellow birch for new life and change, spruce for protection from the world outside. Father was an intuitive carpenter, carrying out his work like holy ritual. His callused hands, veined with pride, had a memory for measure and a knowing of what it takes to withstand the sea.

Strength and a sense of knowing, that's what you have to have to live in the Bay. Each morning you set your sights on the tasks ahead and hope that when the day is done you're farther along than when you started. Our little village, perched on the crook of God's finger, has always been ruled by storm and season. The men did whatever they had to do to get by. They joked with one another in fire-warmed kitchens after sunset, smoking their pipes, someone bringing out a fiddle . . . laughing as they chorused, *no matter how rough, we can take it.* The seasons were reflected in their faces, and in the movement of their bodies. When it was time for the shad, herring and cod to come in, they were fishermen, dark with tiresome wet from the sea. When the deer began to huddle on the back of the mountain, they became hunters and woodsmen. When spring came, they worked the green-scented earth, planting crops that would keep, potatoes, cabbage, carrots, turnips. Summer saw their weathered hands building ships and haying fields, and sunsets that ribboned over the water, daring the skies to turn night. The long days were filled with pride and ceremony as mighty sailing ships were launched from the shore. *The Lauretta, The Reward, The Nordica, The Bluebird, The Huntley.* My father said he'd scour two hundred acres of forest just to find the perfect trees to build a three-masted schooner. Tall yellow birch, gently arched by northwesterly winds, was highly prized. He could spot the keel in a tree's curve and shadow, the return of the tide set in the grain.

Men wagered their lives with the sea for the honour of these vessels. Each morning they watched for the signs. *Red skies in morning, sailors take warning.* Each night they looked to the heavens, spotting starry creatures, or the point of a dragon's tail. They told themselves that these were promises from God, that He would keep the wiry cold fingers of the sea from grabbing at them, from taking their lives. Sometimes men were taken. On those dark days the men who were left behind sat down together and made conversation of every detail, hitching truth to wives' tales while mending their nets.

As the men bargained with the elements, the women tended to matters at home. They bartered with each other to fill their pantries and clothe their children. Grandmothers, aunts and sisters taught one another to stitch and cook and spin. On Sunday mornings mothers bent their knees between the stalwart pews at the Union Church, praying they would have enough. With hymnals clutched against their breasts, they told the Lord they would be ever faithful if their husbands were spared.

When husbands, fathers and sons were kept out in the fog longer than was safe, the women stood at their windows, holding their lamps, a chorus of lady moons beckoning their lovers back to shore. Waiting, they hushed their children to sleep and listened for the voice of the moon in the crashing waves. In the secret of the night, mothers whispered to their daughters that only the moon could force the waters to submit. It was the moon's voice that called the men home, her voice that turned the tides of womanhood, her voice that pulled their babies into the light of birth.

My house became the birth house. That's what the women came to call it, knocking on the door, ripe with child, water breaking on the porch. First-time mothers full of questions, young girls in trouble and seasoned women with a brood already at home. (I called those babies "toesies," because they were more than their mamas could count on their fingers.) They all came to the house, wailing and keening their babies into the world. I wiped their feverish necks with cool, moist cloths, spooned porridge and hot tea into their tired bodies, talked them back from outside of themselves.

Ginny, she had two . . .

Sadie Loomer, she had a girl here.

Precious, she had twins . . . twice.

Celia had six boys, but she was married to my brother Albert . . . Rare men always have boys.

Iris Rose, she had Wrennie . . .

All I ever wanted was to keep them safe.

part one

Around the year 1760, a ship of Scotch immigrants came to be wrecked on the shores of this place. Although the vessel was lost, her passengers and crew managed to find shelter here. They struggled through the winter—many taking ill, the women losing their children, the men making the difficult journey down North Mountain to the valley below, carrying sacks of potatoes and other goods back to their temporary home, now called Scots Bay.

In the spring, when all who had been stranded chose to make their way to more established communities, the daughter of the ship's captain, Annie MacIssac, stayed behind. She had fallen in love with a Mi'kmaq man she called Silent Rare.

On the evening of a full moon in June, Silent went out in his canoe to catch the shad that were spawning around the tip of Cape Split. As the night wore on, Annie began to worry that some ill had befallen her love. She looked across the water for signs of him but found nothing. She walked to the cove where they had first met and began to call out to him, promising her heart, her fidelity and a thousand sons to his name. The moon, seeing Annie's sadness, began to sing, forcing the waves inland, strong and fast, bringing Silent safely back to his lover.

Since that time, every child born from the Rare name has been male, and even now, when the moon is full, you can hear her voice, the voice of the moon, singing the sailors home.

A RARE FAMILY HISTORY, 1850

I

EVER SINCE I CAN REMEMBER, people have had more than enough to say about me. As the only daughter in five generations of Rares, most figure I was changed by faeries or not my father's child. Mother works and prays too hard to have anyone but those with the cruellest of tongues doubt her devotion to my father. When there's no good explanation for something, people of the Bay find it easier to believe in mermaids and moss babies, to call it witchery and be done with it. Long after the New England Planters' seed wore the Mi'kmaq out of my family's blood, I was born with coal black hair, cinnamon skin and a caul over my face. *A foretelling. A sign.* A gift that supposedly allows me to talk to animals, see people's deaths and hear the whisperings of spirits. A charm for protection against drowning.

When one of Laird Jessup's Highland heifers gave birth to a three-legged albino calf, talk followed and people tried to guess what could have made such a creature. In the end, most people blamed me for it. I had witnessed the cow bawling her calf onto the ground. I had been the one who ran to the Jessups' to tell the young farmer about the strange thing that had happened. *Dora talked to ghosts, Dora ate bat soup, Dora slit the Devil's throat and flew over the chicken coop.* My classmates chanted that verse between the slats of the garden gate, along with all the other words their parents taught them not to say. Of course, there are plenty of schoolyard stories about Miss B. too, most of them ending with, *if your cat or your baby goes missing, you'll know where to find the bones.* It's talk like that that's made us such good friends. Miss B. says she's glad for gossip. "It keep folks from comin' to places they don't belong."

Most days I wake up and say a prayer. *I want, I wish, I wait for something to happen to me.* While I thank God for all good things, I don't say this verse to Him, or to Jesus or even to Mary. They are far too busy to be worrying about the affairs and wishes of my heart. No, I say my prayer more to the air than anything else, hoping it might catch on the wind and find its way to anything, to something that's mine. Mother says, *a young lady should take care with what she wishes for.* I'm beginning to think she's right.

Yesterday was fair for a Saturday in October—warm, with no wind and clear skies—what most people call *fool's blue.* It's the kind of sky that begs you to sit and look at it all day. Once it's got you, you'll soon forget whatever chores need to be done, and before you know it, the day's gone and you've forgotten the luck that's to be lost when you don't get your laundry and yourself in out of the cold. Mother must not have noticed it . . . before breakfast was over, she'd already washed and hung two baskets of laundry and gotten a bushel of turnips ready for Charlie and me to take to Aunt Fran's. On the way home, I spotted a buggy tearing up the road. Before the thing could run us over, the driver pulled the horses to a stop, kicking up rocks and dust all over the place. Tom Ketch was driving, and Miss Babineau sat in the seat next to him. She called out to me, "Goin' out to Deer Glen to catch a baby and I needs an extra pair of hands. Come on, Dora."

Even though I'd been visiting her since I was a little girl (stopping by to talk to her while she gardened, or bringing her packages up from the post), I was surprised she'd asked me to come along. When my younger brothers were born and Miss B. came to the house, I begged to stay, but my parents sent me to Aunt Fran's instead. Outside of watching farmyard animals and a few litters of pups, I didn't have much experience with birthing. I shook my head and refused. "You should ask someone else. I've never attended a birth . . ."

She scowled at me. "How old are you now, fifteen, sixteen?"

"Seventeen."

She laughed and reached out her wrinkled hand to me. "Mary-be. I was half your age when I first started helpin' to catch babies. You've been pesterin' me about everything under the sun since you were old enough to talk. You'll do just fine."

Marie Babineau's voice carries the sound of two places: the dancing, Cajun truth of her Louisiana past and the quiet-steady way of talk that comes from always working at something, from living in the Bay. Some say she's a witch, others say she's more of an angel. Either way, most of the girls in the Bay (including me) have the middle initial of M, for Marie. She's not a blood relative to anyone here, but we've always done our part to help take care of her. My brothers chop her firewood and put it up for the winter while Father makes sure her windows and the roof on her cabin are sound. Whenever we have extra preserves, or a loaf of bread, or a basket of apples, Mother sends me to deliver them to Miss B. "She helped bring all you children into this world, and she saved your life, Dora. Brought your fever down when there was nothing else I could do. Anything we have is hers. Anything she asks, we do."

As I pulled myself up to sit next to her, she turned and shouted to Charlie, "Tell your mama not to worry, I'll have Dora home for supper tomorrow." We sat tight, three across the driver's seat, with a falling-down wagon dragging behind.

Miss B. began to question Tom, her voice calm and steady. "How's your mama sound?"

"Moanin' a lot. Then every once in a while she'll hold her belly and squeal like a stuck pig."

"How long she been that way?"

"It started first thing this morning. She was moonin' around, sayin' she couldn't squat to milk the goat, that it hurt too much. Father made her do it anyways, said she was being lazy . . . then he made her muck the stalls too."

"Is she bleedin'?"

Tom kept his eyes on the road ahead. "Not sure. All I know is, one minute she was standin' in the kitchen, peelin' potatoes, and then all of a sudden she was doubled right over. Father got angry with her, said he was hungry and she'd better get on with what she was doin'. When she didn't, he shoves her down to the floor. After that, hard as she tried, she couldn't stand on her own, so she just curled up and cried." He gave a sharp whistle to the horses to keep them in the middle of the rutted road, his jaw set hard, like someone waiting to get punched in the gut. "She didn't want me to bother you with it, said she'd be alright, but I never seen her hurtin' so bad before. I came as soon as I could, as soon as he left to go down to my uncle's place."

"Will he stay out long?"

"More'n likely all night. Especially if they gets t'drinkin', which they always do."

Tom's the oldest of the twelve Ketch children. He's fifteen, maybe sixteen, I'd guess. I think about Tom from time to time, when I run out of dreams about the fine gentlemen in Jane Austen's novels. He's got a kind face, even when it's filthy, and Mother always says she hopes he'll find a way to make something of himself instead of turning out to be like his father, Brady. I can tell she prefers I not mention the Ketches at all. I think it makes her scared that I'll not make something of myself and turn out to be like Tom's mother, Experience.

The Ketch family has always lived in Deer Glen. It's a crooked, narrow hollow, just outside of the Bay, twisting right through the mountain until you can see the red cliffs of Blomidon. No one here would claim it to be anything more than the dip in the road that lets you know you're almost home. The land is too rocky and steep for farming and too far from the shore for making a life as a fisherman or a shipbuilder. Too far for a pleasant walk. The Ketches suffer along, selling homebrew from a still in the woods and making whatever they can from the hunters who come from away, men who hope to kill the white doe that's said to live in the Glen. In deer season they block off the road, Brady at one end, his brother Garrett at the other. They stand, shotguns strapped to their backs, waiting to escort the trophy hunters who come from Halifax, the Annapolis Valley, and faraway places like New York and Boston. The Ketch brothers charge a pretty penny for their services, especially since they're selling lies. It's true, there's been a white doe spotted on North Mountain, but it doesn't live in Deer Glen. It lives in the woods behind Miss B.'s cabin, where she feeds it out of her hand, like a pet. I've never seen it, but I've heard her call to it on occasion, walking through the trees singing, *Lait-Lait, Lune-Lune.* Father said he saw it once, that she's the colour of sweet Guernsey cream, with one corner of her rump faintly speckled. He came home with nothing that day and told Mother, "It would have been wrong to take it." Shortly after, at a Sons of Temperance meeting, the men of the Bay all pledged never to kill it. They all agreed that there's sin in taking the life of something so pure.

It was nearly dark when we got to the Ketch house, its clapboards loose and wanting for paint, the screen door left hanging. The inside wasn't much better. A picked-over loaf of bread, along with pots, pans and empty canning jars were crowded together on the table, all needing to be cleared. Attempts had been made at keeping a proper house, but somehow the efforts had gone wrong, every time. The curtains were bright at the top, still showing white, with a cheerful flowered print. Halfway to the floor, little hands had worn stains into the fabric, and the ends were frayed from the tug and pull of cats' claws. No matter how fresh and clean a start they may have had, the towels in the kitchen, the wallpaper and rugs, even the dress on the little girl who greeted us at the door, all showed the same pattern, their middles stained, their edges worn and dirty. The entire house smelled sour and neglected.

Experience Ketch was hunched over in her bed, clutching her belly. Her oldest daughter, Iris Rose, was standing next to her, dipping a rag in a bucket of water then offering it to her mother. Mrs. Ketch took the worn cloth and clenched it between her teeth, sucking and spitting while she rocked back and forth.

Miss B. sat on the edge of the bed and held Mrs. Ketch's hand. She talked the woman through her pains enough to get her to sit up and drink some tea. The midwife wrapped her wrinkled fingers around Mrs. Ketch's wrist, closed her eyes and counted in French. She pinched the ends of Mrs. Ketch's fingertips and then pulled her eyelids away from her pink, teary eyes. "Your blood's weak." Miss B. pushed the blankets back and pulled up Mrs. Ketch's bloodstained skirts. Her hands kneaded their way around the tired woman's swollen belly, feeling over her stretched skin, making the sign of the cross. After washing her hands several times, she slipped her fingers between Mrs. Ketch's legs and shook her head. "This baby has to come today."

Mrs. Ketch moaned. "It's too soon."

"Your pains is too far gone and I can't turn you back. If you don't birth this child today, all your other babies don't gonna have a mama."

"I don't want it."

Iris Rose knelt by the bed and pleaded with her mother. "Please, Mama, do what she says."

The girl's much younger than me, twelve at the most, but she's as much mother as she is child. From time to time she'll show up at the schoolhouse, dragging as many of her brothers and sisters behind her as she can. She barks at the boys to take off their hats, scolds the girls as she tugs on their braids, making her voice as big and rough as an old granny's. For all her trying, it always turns out the same. By the time the snow flies, the desks of the Ketch children are empty again.

Mrs. Ketch needs them home, I guess. I've heard that each of the older ones is assigned a little one to bathe, dress, feed and look after, so they don't get lost in the clutter of a house filled with dirty dishes and barn cats. With six brothers of my own, I think I can say there's such a thing as *too many*.

When Mrs. Ketch's wailing went on, Tom and the older boys disappeared out to the barn. With Iris Rose's help, I tucked the rest of the children into an upstairs room. She stood in the doorway with her arms folded across her chest. "Now don't you make another sound, or Daddy'll come running through the hollow and up these stairs with an alder switch!" The room went quiet. Six small greasy heads went to the floor, six bellies breathed shallow and scared.

"Can I watch?" Iris Rose asked.

"If you promise not to say anything."

"I'll be silent. I swear."

I left her on the stairs, peeking through the broken, crooked pickets of the banister.

Miss B. and I turned back the straw mattress and tied sheets to the bedposts. She tugged hard at them. "See now, Mrs. Ketch, you know what's to do . . . when the time comes, you gots to hold on for dear life and push that baby out." Miss B. motioned for me to steady Mrs. Ketch's shaking knees. "And it's comin' fast and hard as high tide on a full moon. *Pousser!*"

Mrs. Ketch bent her chin to her chest, the veins on her neck throbbing. "Let me die, dear Lord. Please let me die."

Miss B. laughed. "How many times you been through this, thirteen, fourteen? You should know by now, the Lord ain't like most men, He ain't gonna just take you home when you ask for it . . ."

Just last Sunday Reverend Norton went on and on about the trespasses of Eve, pounding his fist on the pulpit, his face all red and puffed up as he spit to the side between the words *original* and *sin*. While he talked at good length about the evils of temptation and the curse Eve had brought upon all women, he never mentioned the stink of it. I never imagined that "the woman's tithe for the civilized world" would smell so rusted, so bitter.

I kept the fire in the stove going, unpacked clean sheets from Miss B.'s bag, did whatever she told me to do, but no matter how busy I made myself, my stomach ached and my hands felt heavy and useless. I don't think my nervousness came from it being my first birth, or even from seeing such pain and struggle in a woman, but more from hearing the sadness, the wanting, in Mrs. Ketch's cries. Nothing we did seemed to help. She sobbed and cursed, her wailing and Miss B.'s coaxing going on for an hour or more, I'd guess, or at least long enough for Mrs. Ketch to give up on a miracle and have a baby boy.

He was a sad, tiny thing. His flesh was like onion skin; the blue of his veins showed right through. If I had looked any harder at his weak little body, I think I might have seen his heart. Miss B. bundled him up in flannel sheets and handed him to Mrs. Ketch. "Hold him, now, put your chest to his so he knows what it's like to be alive." But Experience Ketch didn't want her baby. She didn't want to hold him or look at him or have him anywhere near. "Get that thing away from me. I got twelve more than I can handle anyways."

I couldn't stand it. I took him from Miss B. and pulled him close. I whispered in his ear, "I'll take you home with me. I'll take you for my own." Out of the corner of my eye

I saw Iris Rose run up the stairs. I turned to Miss B. "He's looking so blue, his arms, his legs, his chest. His breath is barely there."

"He's born too soon." She made the sign of the cross on his wrinkled brow. "If he'd been born three, four weeks later, I could spoon alder tea with brandy in his mouth, make a bed for him in the warmin' box of the cookstove and hope he pinked up, but as it is . . ."

I stopped her from going on. "Tell me what to do. I have to try."

Miss B. shook her head. "If you can't see him through to the other side, then you should just go on home. Mary and the angels will soon take care of him. I have to see to his mama."

I sat in the corner and held tight to the dying child.

Miss B. wrapped a blanket around us. "Some babies ain't meant for this world. All you can do is keep him safe until his angel comes."

"There's nothing else I can do?"

She leaned over and whispered in my ear. "Pray for him, and pray for this house too."

2

ETWEEN MY PRAYERS and Miss B.'s spooning porridge into Mrs. Ketch's mouth, the baby died. It was almost dawn when Brady Ketch came home. He stomped through the house, drunk and demanding to be fed. "Experience Ketch, get outta that bed and get me some food." The poor woman tried to get up, as if nothing had troubled her at all, but Miss B. held her down. "You need rest. Lobelia tea and rest, then more tea and more rest. At least three days to get your strength, but a week would be best. If you don't, you gonna bleed 'til you're dead."

Mr. Ketch staggered, reaching for the bundle of blankets I was holding in my arms. "Let me have a look-see there, girl. What'd we get this time, wife? Another boy, I hope. Girls don't eat as much, but they take their toll everyways else. I don't trust nothin' that can't piss standin' up." He pinned me against the wall, his dark mouth leaving the skunky smell of his breath in my face. "Ain't you pretty . . . you Judah Rare's girl, right?"

"Yes, sir."

"Your daddy's got the right idea. How'd he manage to get all boys and just one pretty little thing like you? Bet you come in handy when your mama gets tired. He's one lucky son of a bitch, I'd say."

Mrs. Ketch hissed at her husband. "Leave her be, Brady."

He pulled back the blankets to look at the child. "I'm just lookin' at what's mine."

I stood still while he pinched at the baby's thin, blue cheeks. "Hey there, little critter, ain't you gonna say 'hello' to your—" He stopped and pulled his hand away, his curiosity giving way to confusion and then to anger. He turned and stared at Miss B. "What'd you do to it?" Before she could answer, he grabbed her by her shoulders. "Looks to me like you killed my child and put my wife half-dead on her back." Brady Ketch slid his hands around Miss B.'s throat, slipping his fingers through her rosary beads. "What's to keep me from taking you back in the glen and snappin' your wattled old witch's neck?"

An iron skillet lay on the floor by the cookstove. A doorstop shaped like a dog sat in the corner, one ear and the snout of its nose chipped away. I could've killed Brady Ketch and not felt a minute's worth of guilt. "God sees what you do, Mr. Ketch."

He let go of Miss B. and made his way back to me, smiling, leaning into my body and stroking my hair. "Now, don't you worry, little girl, Miss Babineau knows I'd never mean her any real harm. It's just sometimes a woman needs a man to set her right. Says so in the Bible."

Miss B. started packing up her bag. "See that she gets her rest. Three days off her feet, no less." She moved towards the door. "Come on, Dora."

"That won't do." Mr. Ketch stood in front of the door. "She can't just take to bed for days whenever she feels like it. There's things that need to get done around here. You gotta *fix* her. Now."

Miss B. stared at him. "I told you, she needs bedrest. Three days and she'll be good as new."

He crossed his arms in front of his chest. "That Dr. Thomas, down Canning way, he'd know how to make her right. When Tommy snapped his wrist, the doc fixed it up so he could use it right away. Tied it up nice and clean, give him a few pills, and Tom was chopping wood that afternoon."

"And you can afford a fancy doctor always runnin' up the mountain to *fix* your family?"

Brady pretended to hold a rifle in his arms, pointing his finger past Miss B. and out the window. He clucked his tongue in his mouth and moved his hands as if to cock the gun. "Let's just say the doc and I . . . we have a *gentleman's* agreement when it comes to that sweet white doe everyone's always lookin' to bag." He grinned as he slowly changed position, now pointing at Miss B.'s heart, squinting one eye to take aim. "And don't think I don't know where to find her."

Miss B. pushed his arm away and started again for the door. "Well, ain't that fine."

Brady opened the door and shoved Miss B. onto the stoop. As I started to hand the child's body to him, Miss B. called out to Mrs. Ketch.

"You send Tom to get me if the bleeding gets any worse."

Mrs. Ketch rolled over, her voice sounding tired and sad. "I can take care of myself . . . Just get out now, and take the baby with you. I don't want that ugly thing in my house."

Miss B. sang little French prayers to the dead baby boy and wrapped him in one of the lace kerchiefs she's always tatting on her lap. We laid him in a butter box, tucked October's last blossoms from the pot marigolds and asters all around him and nailed the tiny coffin shut. She vanished between the alders in back of her cabin. I walked behind, following the sound of her voice, cradling the box in my arms, trying to make up for his mother not loving him. If only my love had been able to raise him from the dead.

Miss B. whispered. "Shhhh. *Le jardin des morts,* the garden of the dead, the garden of lost souls." In the centre of a mossy grove of spruce was a tall tree stump. The likeness of a woman had been carved into it . . . the Virgin Mary, standing on a crescent moon, her face, her breasts, her hands, all delicate and sweet. All around her, strings of hollowed-out whelks and moon shells hung with tattered bits of lace from the branches, like the wings of angels.

Grandmothers and old fishermen have long said that the woods of Scots Bay have cold, secret spots, places of fox-fire and spirits. "Never chase a shadow in the trees. You can't be sure it's not your own." Charlie must have chased me a thousand times down the old logging road in back of our land, both of us running into the woods behind Miss B.'s place, shouting, *witched away, witched away, today's the day we'll be witched away.* We'd spent hours weaving crowns from alder twigs, feathers, porcupine quills and curled bits of birch bark. We'd imagined faerie houses and gnome caves in the tangled roots of a spruce that had been brought down by the wind. We'd come home, tired and hungry, declaring we'd found the hidden treasure of Amethyst Cove but had lost it (yet again) to a wicked band of thieves. In all our time spent in the forest we never found or imagined anything like this.

Miss B. took off her shoes. "Can't let no outside world touch Mary's ground."

She began to make her way around the grove, tracing crosses in the air, circling closer and closer to the Mary tree. I slipped off my boots and followed. When Miss B. was finished, she knelt at the base of the tree and began to dig at the moss. Beneath the dirt and stones was a thick handle of braided rope. Together we pulled up a heavy wooden door that was covering a deep hole in the ground. "Our Lady will watch over him now." She took the tiny coffin, tied a length of rope around it and lowered it into the dark grave. "Holy Mother, Star of the Sea, take this little soul with thee." She let go of the rope and took my hands. "You gots to give him a name. Just say it once, so he knows he's been born."

I closed my eyes and whispered "*Darcy*," after Elizabeth Bennett's sweetheart in *Pride and Prejudice*. Because he should have lived; he should have been loved.

I've seen the runt of a litter die. When there are too many kittens or too many piglets, the mother can't keep up with them all. The runt gets shoved out by the others and the mother acts as if she doesn't even know it's there. Maybe Mrs. Ketch knew Darcy wouldn't live from the start, maybe she pushed him away so she wouldn't love him, so she wouldn't hurt.

It's a disgusting mess we come through to be born, the sticky-wet of blood and afterbirth, mother wailing, child crying . . . the helpless soft spot at the top of its head pulsing, waiting to be kissed. Our parents and teachers say it's a miracle, but it's not. It's going to happen no matter what, there's no choice in the matter. To my mind, a miracle is something that could go one way or another. The fact that something happens, when by all rights it shouldn't, is what makes us take notice, it's what saints are made of, it takes the breath away. How a mother comes to love her child, her caring at all for this thing that's made her heavy, lopsided and slow, this thing that made her wish she were dead . . . that's the miracle.

3

LATE IN NOVEMBER we bank the house, always on a Saturday. Even with all nine of us stuffing baskets of eelgrass around the house's foundation, it still takes a good part of the day to get it done.

Just after high tide, I went down to the marsh with Father and my two older brothers, Albert and Borden, to pitch the tangled heaps of grass onto the wagon. Mother stayed behind with the rest of the boys to pound stakes and build a short stay fence that would hold the grass in tight to the stones. By December, when most families have finished the job, it looks like all the houses in the Bay have settled in giant bird's nests, ready to roost for the winter. Uncle Irwin and Aunt Fran pay to have neat, tight bales stacked around their house. Others swear by spruce bows all heaped up on the west side, facing the water. Father says he's too smart to waste good hay and that the porcupines'll clean the needles off the spruce in one meal, so we're stuck doing things the hard way.

At least the twins, Forest and Gord, are big enough to help this year. Even though they've turned eight, they still act like whimpering puppies, forever tugging at my sleeves, following me, calling my name. Every day we walk the Three Brooks Road, the same round loop. Past Laird Jessup's place, then down along the pastures and the deep little spot where the brooks all meet, then on around to school. Sometimes we go down to the beach to play, or out to the wharf to fetch Father, who always takes us back on the other side, the *Sunday side* of the loop. Up to the church, then on past Aunt Fran's place, up to Spider Hill and home again. Boys ahead and boys behind. I'm the only girl stuck in the middle of six boys who spend most of their days poking, laughing and wrestling together as they trip and drag their muddy boots through my life.

Mother says I shouldn't complain. She's got her own rounds to make. Up before dawn, down to the kitchen, out to the barn, back to the kitchen, down to Aunt Fran's, over to the church, back to her kitchen. She holds the boys close to her every chance she gets. They wiggle and roll their eyes as she kisses the tops of their messy heads. She sighs as she lets them go, watching them run off to play. "Things aren't as certain as they used to be." She's not talking about their age or the fact that they're always outgrowing their shoes. *It's the war*, she means to say, but won't. It's the war that she's afraid of, that's got her wondering how long she can keep her boys at home, that has us listening to gossip and reading headlines and moving in circles, as if we might cast a spell of sameness to keep the rest of the world away.

Banking the house took so long that I was late getting to Miss B.'s. I have been visiting her every Saturday since we buried dear little Darcy. It's a relief to get to her door, to sit at her kitchen table, to be able to breathe and sigh and even weep over my small, blue memory of him. I've told the tale only once, to Mother. When I came to the part where Mrs. Ketch refused the child, it was all she could do not to shake and cry all over me. Instead, she held her breath, closed her eyes and whispered, "God forgive, God bless." Although I can still feel the weight of his body in the crook of my arm, I won't put her through hearing of it again. She wasn't there; she doesn't need to know how much it still comes to my mind. And now there's no one else to tell. Father wouldn't know what to say. He'd be angry with me for bringing it up at all. My dear cousin, Precious, though she hangs on every word of a good story, is still Aunt Fran's child . . . any news that's ugly or sad is not allowed in their house: *words of sensation and death leave a sinful mark on the walls of a good Christian home.* (Aunt Fran prefers to carry her gossip under her hat and deliver it to everyone else's door.)

I'm Miss B.'s only guest on Saturdays, or any other day of the week. I'm the only person in all of Scots Bay who dares make a friendly call to the old midwife. As a child, I was always happy when Mother had reason to send me to Miss B.'s cabin, happy to walk down the old logging road, away from Three Brooks Road and our house full of boys, happy just to sit with her in her garden, or in her kitchen filled with, as she says, "things to make you wonder." A tarnished, round looking-glass hangs by the door. Jars and bottles of herbs, salves and tinctures line her cupboards. Feathered wings are tacked up over the door and every window. Crow, sparrow, dove, hawk, owl. One large, dark wooden crucifix hangs over her bed, while the rest of the two-room log cabin—every wall, shelf or tabletop—is covered with tallow candles and a thousand Marys. I did my best not to ask questions, but if she spotted me staring at something, she'd be quick to recite a verse or sing a song about whatever it was. (Although sometimes she'd just smile and say, "Never mind that just now, Dora. If I told you, you'd never believe.")

It's long been understood that, unless you're a woman who's expecting, or you've got an ailment that can't be cured, you're better off not to bother with her. *Never break bread with midwives or witches; your skin'll soon crawl with boils, hives and itches.* I don't know who's worse about spreading such rumours, schoolyard tattletales or the ladies who run the White Rose Temperance Society. Those women never give Marie Babineau more than three words about the weather, *some cold today, fog comin' in, strong south wind . . .* They're careful not to form their words into a question or to invite her into their conversations. They ignore her gap-toothed smile and never look twice at her brown, wrinkled face. They spread loud-mouthed gossip about the *green stink* they say comes from her breath and "out every wine-soaked pore of her body." Aunt Fran says it's like soured, mouldy cabbage. Mrs. Trude Hutner argues, "I'd say it's more like a wet dog that's been nosing around a skunk." Most of the Ladies of the White Rose don't have babies underfoot anymore, so they feel they haven't any need for Miss B. Along with their age, *comfortable* size and the scattered prickly hairs sticking from their chins, they've forgotten Miss B.'s sweetness and everything she's done for them. They forget that when you're close to her, eye to eye, she smells as honest and kind as the better parts of hand-picked herbs and fresh-ground spices. Her sighs are full of lavender, ginger and fresh-brewed coffee . . . her laughter leaves hints of chicory, pepper and clove.

Always keep at least three pots on the stove. One for tea, one for the simples and one for coffee with blue sailors. "You know I never touch the coffee but my one cup that gets me goin' of a morning. Any more'n that and I gets the jumps," she says as she bounces in her rocking chair. "I only lets it go on simmerin' 'cause I like the black, grumbling smell of it. Brings a man to mind, it does."

She makes a great show when I visit—fussing over her iron pots and teacups, serving lavender tea and beignets, each one a plump, warm square of sugar-coated heaven melting on my tongue. I'm grateful (in the most selfish way) that no other fingers are pinching at the chipped, yellowing edge of Miss B.'s best serving plate every Saturday afternoon. No, the Ladies of the White Rose, who once called on her to birth their babies and cure their ills, politely ignore the river of stories that sit ready on her every breath. They are deaf to her wise, loose chatter, peppered with lazy French and the *diddle diddle dees* of Acadian folk songs.

Miss Babineau's great-grandfather Louis Faire LeBlanc was the last baby to be born before the British drove his family and the rest of the Acadians from their settlement along the dyke lands of Grand Pre. Miss B. sighs and clutches the mass of rosary beads twisted around her neck whenever she speaks of it. "The precious seeds of Acadie were scattered across the earth, the names LeBlanc, Babineau, Landry, Comeau, all planted along the bayous with bayonets, ashes and blood." Many died on the difficult journey to Louisiana, but little Louis Faire lived. "He grew to be a strong, fine man. Blessed by the Spirit. Called of angels, he was. The sick, the weary, them that was gone out of their heads . . . they all come to Louis Faire. A *traiteur,* he was. He put his hands on their heads and their bodies—lettin' the prayers come down, right through his mouth, healin' them. Thank you, Mary. Thank you, Baby Jesus. Thank the Father in Heaven. Amen."

At seventeen (the same age I am now), Miss B. was visited by Louis Faire in a dream. He spoke to her, telling her that God had chosen her to take the sacred gifts of the *traiteurs* back to his homeland. The dream lasted all through the night and into the next morning, her great-grandfather's spirit whispering secret remedies and prayers of healing in her ears. When it was over, she began walking, leaving her family behind as she made her way from Louisiana to Acadie. No one is quite certain of how she ended up in Scots Bay instead of the fertile valley of her ancestors. All she will say is, "It was for Louis Faire that I came back to his homeland, but only God could make me live in Scots Bay."

Mother says Granny Mae once told her that Miss B. had had a vision, a visit from an angel, right here in the Bay. "When Marie Babineau got to Grand Pre and saw the beautiful orchards, fields and dyke lands that had once belonged to her family, she was so overwhelmed with sadness that she ran, crying, up North Mountain and all the way to the end of Cape Split. While she sat at the edge of the cliffs, weeping, an angel appeared, comforting her, reminding her of her dream and of the gifts Louis Faire had given her before her journey. The angel explained that, in fact, she was the spirit of St. Brigit, the woman who had served as midwife to the Virgin Mary at the birth of Christ, and that she had been sent to bless Marie and ask her if she would dedicate her hands to bringing forth the children of this place. Grateful for the angel's tender care, Marie vowed to do what God had asked of her." You can't say no to something like that.

Aunt Fran says it's more likely that she took up with a sailor, and when he got tired of her talking, he dropped her here on his way home to his wife. It doesn't matter. I'd guess she's so old now that nobody cares about the whens, whys or hows of it, as long as she's got "the gift" whenever they need it.

Miss B. never asks for payment from those who come to her. She says a true *traiteur* never does. Grandmothers who still believe in her ways and thankful new mothers leave coffee tins, heavy with coins that have been collected after Sunday service. In season, families bring baskets of potatoes, carrots, cabbage and anything else she might need to get by. They hide them in the milk box by the side door, with folded notes of blessings and thanks, but never stay for tea.

It was starting to get dark by the time we settled in for beignets and conversation. Not long after, I heard an odd stuttering sound from the road. I looked out the window and could just make out that there was an automobile coming towards the cabin, the evening sun glowing gold on its windshield. No one in the Bay owns even a work truck, let alone a shiny new car like that. Most men call them "red devils," believing that just the sound of one is a sure sign that their horses will bolt and their cows will dry up for the day. No one comes out here from away unless they're lost or looking for someone. No one comes down the old logging road unless they need to see Miss B. There's one road in and one road out . . . and it's the same one.

Miss B. took her teacup from the table, dumped what was left into a pot on the stove and stared into it, shaking her head. "Get up to the loft and hide behind the apple baskets. I think there's some quilts you can pull over your head.

Don't you let out a peep." The sound of the car was outside the cabin now, slowing and then sputtering to a stop in the dooryard. I started to question Miss B., wondering why she was acting so alarmed. She frowned. "Trouble's come, I'm sure of it. I seen it in my leaves just yesterday and didn't believe it, but now it's here in this cup too. A bat in the tea, two days in a row . . . says someone's out for me. I'd better take care in what I say and do. Shame on me for not trusting my tea. Go on now, get up there, before it comes for you too." To please her, I climbed the old apple ladder that was fixed to the wall, pushed at the square lid that covered the small opening to the loft and crawled up into the space above the kitchen. Hiding under a worn wool blanket, I lay flat on my belly, peering through the loose boards into the kitchen below. Miss B. was squinting, looking in my direction. I whispered down to her, "I'm safe." She smiled and nodded, then put her finger to her lips and turned to answer the knock at the door.

A tall, serious-looking man stood in the doorway. He introduced himself as, "Dr. Gilbert Thomas." Miss B. invited him in, took his long overcoat and hat, and wouldn't let him speak again until he was settled at the kitchen table with a cup of coffee. She patted his shoulder and then smoothed the slight wrinkle she'd made in his dark suit coat. "Well, ain't you tied up proper, like every day was Sunday?" Taken by her kindness, his voice halted and stuttered each time he tried to say *shouldn't* and *don't,* as if the words were too painful to get out. He sat cockeyed to the table, his knees too high to tuck under it, his fine, long fingers shyly wringing the pair of driving gloves that were sitting in his lap. Except for the hints of grey in his hair that shone silver when he turned his head, Dr. Gilbert Thomas looked as if someone had kept him clean and quiet and neatly placed in the corner of a parlour since the day he was born.

In a slow, steady tone, the doctor began what sounded like a well-rehearsed speech. "As a practitioner of obstetrics, I am bound by an oath to my profession to come to the aid of child-bearing women whenever possible." He winced back a sip of Miss B.'s strong coffee and continued. "You, as well as other generous women in communities throughout Kings County and across the Dominion have had to serve in place of science for too long."

Miss B. smiled and pushed the sugar bowl and creamer in front of him. "A little sugar there, dear?"

"Thank you." He spooned in the sugar and doused the coffee with a large splash of cream. "Imagine the benefits that modern medicine can offer women who are in a compromised condition . . . a sterile environment, surgical procedures, timely intervention and pain-free births. The suffering that women have endured in childbirth can be a thing of the past—"

Miss B. interrupted him, catching his eyes with her gaze. "What you sellin'?"

Dr. Thomas's stutter returned. "I, I . . . I'm just trying to tell you, inform you of—"

"No. You ain't tellin', you sellin' . . . if you gonna come here, drummin' up my door like you got pots in your pants, then you best get to it and we'll be done with it."

She waved her hand in the air as if to shoo him away. "Oh, and by the way, whatever it is, I ain't buyin'. I figure if I tell you that right now, you'll either pack up and leave or tell me the truth."

Dr. Thomas continued. "The truth is, Miss Babineau, I need your help."

She settled back in her chair. "Now we're gettin' some-wheres. Go on."

"We're building a maternity home down the mountain, in Canning."

Miss B. interrupted him. "One of those butcher shops they calls a hospital?"

Dr. Thomas answered. "A place where women can come and have their babies in a clean, sterile environment, with the finest obstetrical care."

She scowled at him. "Who's this 'we'?"

"Myself and the Farmer's Assurance Company of Kings County."

"How much the mamas got to pay you?"

He shook his head and smiled. "Nothing."

Miss B. snorted. "You're a liar."

"I won't charge them a thing. I won't have to, we—"

"You got a wife?"

"Yes."

"And she's a good girl, a lady who deserves the finer things?"

"Well, of course. But I don't see—"

"How you expect to keep her if you don't make no money?"

He laughed. "I get paid by the assurance company." He lowered his voice and smiled. "And you could get paid too . . . if you participate in the program. They'll give you five dollars for every woman you send to the maternity home."

Miss B. got up from the table. "What I gots, I *give*, and the Lord, He takes care of the rest. There's no talk of money in my house, Dr. Thomas." She held his coat and hat out to him. "I gots all I need."

Dr. Thomas took his belongings from her, but motioned towards the table. "Please, I didn't mean to offend you. Let me at least have my say and then I'll go."

She poured the doctor another cup of coffee and sat back down at the table. "You got 'til your coffee's gone or it turns cold."

Dr. Thomas quickly made his case. "Many families in Kings County, Scots Bay included, already own policies with Farmer's Assurance. A small fee, paid each month, gives these families the security of knowing that if something happened to the man of the house, he could get the medical attention he needed and they could still go on." He spooned more sugar into his cup. "As you well know, the mother is just as important as the father; she's the heart of the home, she's what keeps everything moving."

Miss B. nodded. "I always say, if the mama ain't happy, ain't nobody happy."

Dr. Thomas grinned. "Exactly! For the price of what most households spend on coffee or tea each month, a husband can buy a Mother's Share from Farmer's Assurance. This guarantees his wife the happiness of a clean, safe birth and the comfort of having her babies at a Farmer's Assurance Maternity Home. The family can rest well knowing that 'Mother' will be well cared for during her confinement."

Miss B. stared at him. "What if a mama wants to have her baby at home?"

Dr. Thomas looked confused. "Why would she want to do that when there's a beautiful new facility waiting for her?" He tried again to convince Miss B. "You are a brave woman, Miss Babineau, taking on this responsibility all these years. Everyone I talk to has said how skilled you are, how blessed, but with new obstetrical techniques available, women can rely on more than faith to see them through the grave dangers of childbirth."

Miss B. sat there, humming and knitting, looking up at him every so often as if to see how much longer he was going to stay.

Frustrated, Dr. Thomas tried to further the conversation. "Do you know Mrs. Experience Ketch?"

Miss B. took a sip of tea. "Some."

"Her husband, Mr. Brady Ketch, came to my offices about a month ago with some disturbing news. Since you've had your hands on so many babies in this area, I wonder if you might be able to make some sense of what he told me."

Miss Babineau smiled. "I'll certainly do whatever I can."

The doctor's tone grew serious. "Mr. Ketch was quite distressed. He said that his wife was bedridden and too weak to stand. He was afraid she might die. I followed him to their home and found her to be in poor health. She was pale and wouldn't speak."

Miss B. shook her head. "Well, that's just some awful. I hope you could help her."

"I made her as comfortable as I could under such circumstances, but there's one thing I still don't understand. When I asked Mr. Ketch what had brought about his wife's illness, he said that she had just given birth the day before, and that you and a young girl were there to attend it." Dr. Thomas stared at Miss B. "Was there *nothing* you could do to keep her from falling into such poor condition?"

Miss B. completed her row of knitting and shook her head. "Did you happen to catch wind of the man's breath?"

Sugar spilled from the doctor's spoon before he could get it to his cup. "Pardon?"

"I'm sorry to say so, Doctor, but the only truth Mr. Brady Ketch is good for, is in tellin' the innkeeper when he's reached the bottom of a whiskey barrel. If his wife's in trouble it's 'cause he can't keep his hands from her one way or another. If he's not puttin' a bun in her oven, he's slapping her black and blue. If I've ever given Experience Ketch a thing, it's been to tell her she's workin' herself to death."

"Are you telling me that you don't know anything about her having a baby?"

Miss B. pulled on the ball of yarn in her lap. "Did you see one there?"

"No, Mr. Ketch said it was a stillbirth."

Miss B. rolled her eyes. "Why, I'd guess we'd both know it if she'd just had a birth, as I'm sure you gave her a thorough examination."

He drummed his fingers on the table, staring at his cup. My handkerchief was sitting near it, the one that Precious had given me for my last birthday, my initials embroidered in a ring of daisies. "Mr. Ketch said Mr. Judah Rare's daughter might be able to shed some light on the matter."

"Miss Rare is a proper young lady who's kind enough to keep company with a wretched, feeble granny like myself. She's also wise enough to know better than to find herself in Brady Ketch's part of the wood. Nothin' there but lies and brew. Either one you choose, you're askin' for trouble."

Dr. Thomas picked up the folded square of cloth and looked it over. "Dora's her name, isn't it? I stopped by her house and spoke with her mother before I came to call on you. What a kind woman she is. She guessed that I might even find her daughter here, with you."

Miss B. calmly put out her hand, reaching for the handkerchief. "Left this behind last time she was here. You know how forgetful them young girls can be. Can't tell you what they done that same mornin', never mind yesterday, or last week. Some flighty too, never know when she'll show her face at my door."

Dr. Thomas frowned as he chewed on the inside of his cheek. It's the same thing Father does when he knows something he's planned on paper isn't going to work with hammer and nails. "Maybe I'd better visit Mrs. Ketch again and see if she can remember anything now that she's back on her feet."

Miss B. gave a cheerful response. "No need for that, my dear. Brady Ketch may well forget he ever knew you and shoot you on sight. It's best you leave the women of the Bay to me."

The doctor mumbled under his breath. "Leave them to have their babies in fishing shacks and barns."

Miss B. scowled. "What's that?"

"I think you should be made aware that the Criminal Code of 1892 states: 'Failing to obtain reasonable assistance during childbirth is a crime.'"

Miss B. ignored him and said, "I'm wonderin', Doctor, how many babies you brought into this world?"

"During my residency in medical school, I observed at least a hundred or more births—"

"How many children you caught, right as they slipped out of their mama's body?"

"Well, I—"

Miss B. stopped him from answering. "It don't matter . . ." She pulled at the tangled mass of beads around her neck. "See these? That's a bead for every sweet little baby." She pulled the longest strand out from the neck of her blouse. "See this?" A tarnished silver crucifix dangled from her fingers. "As you've probably heard tell . . . this child's mama 'give it up' in a manger." She let it fall to her chest. "So's next time you come out here, tryin' to save the *barn-babies* of Scots Bay, you remember who watches over them." She stood up from her seat. "I believe your coffee done got cold, Dr. Thomas. I'd ask you to stay for supper, but I know you'll want to get back down the mountain to your dear wife. The road has more twists when it's dark."

Mother didn't wait long to ask me what it was Dr. Thomas wanted. "Did he find you at Miss B.'s? He seemed nice enough. Quite the thing to come way out here. Your brothers couldn't get over that automobile of his. What'd he want, anyway?"

"He just wanted to find out how many babies were born in the Bay last year. Part of some records they keep for the county, or something like that."

"That's interesting. How many babies were there?"

"When?"

"Last year. How many babies were born in the Bay last year? I can think of three, at least. There was Mrs. Fannie Bartlett, and—"

"Oh, you know, I can't recall. I think she just laughed and said, 'the usual.' You know Miss B."

Mother went back to stirring a big pot of beans on the stove, wiping her brow as she inhaled the word *yes*.

~ *November 16, 1916*

Never have I had so many things I couldn't say out loud. At least my journal listens to the scribbling of my pen.

When Dr. Thomas left Miss B.'s, his face was all flushed, looking like he wouldn't be happy until he'd found a way to make Miss B. say she was wrong and he was right. I told her that I couldn't bear to see her locked up behind bars, that maybe she should consider asking the women of the Bay to seek Dr. Thomas's care from now on, but she just smiled and strung a single bead of jet on a string and hung it around my neck. "He ain't gonna come back. There's nothin' out here for him. All the money's down in town. Them people down there come to doctors with every little ache and pain. They empty their pockets right on the examinin' table. Why'd he want cabbages and potatoes for pay, instead? Besides, a man who can't drink my coffee straight ain't got nerve enough to do me harm."

She's probably right, but it hasn't kept the nightmares away. It's been the same one for the past three nights. First I'm dreaming I'm with Tom Ketch, and he's looking down on me, gentle and sweet, like he might even kiss me. I close my eyes, but when I open them, Brady Ketch is holding me tight, his unkempt beard scratching against my cheek, his foul tongue pushing into my mouth. I try to scream and my voice won't sound. I try to get away and my body goes limp, like I've got no bones, and then I'm falling, falling into the ground, into the dark, wet hole under the Mary tree. There's moss and bones, leaves and skulls, potato bugs and worms. I can hear a baby crying. I dig through the muck until I find it. It's Darcy, only this time he looks like the most perfect baby in the world. He's pink and beautiful, plump and whole, his clear blue eyes staring up at me, waiting for me to take him home. When I go to reach for him, the Mary tree comes to life, her roots turning to arms as she pulls the baby up from under the moss. I call out to her, "I'll take care of him this time, I promise." She doesn't speak; she just takes Darcy and starts to walk away. I cry out again, "Please, bring him back. I'll take care of him." I follow her, hoping that at least she'll take him up to heaven, but she just keeps on going, walking out of the woods and down the mountain, until she's standing at Dr. Thomas's door.

~ *November 20, 1916*

Tonight we strung apples to dry and made coltsfoot cough drops. Miss B. pulled what looked to be an old recipe book from the shelf and placed it on the table in front of me. "This here's the Willow Book." She closed her eyes and stroked its cracked leather cover. "For every home in Acadie that was burnt to the ground, there's a willow what stands and remembers. *By the Rivers of Babylon, there we sat down, yea we wept, when we remembered Zion. We hanged our harps upon the willows in the midst thereof.* We put things here we don't want to forget. The moon owns the Willow." She untied the thick piece of twine that was holding its loose, yellowed pages together, thumbing through until she found what she was looking for. "Thank you, Sweet Mary. Here it is: coltsfoot. Some likes to call it the son-before-the-father 'cause it sends up its flowers before the leaves. Just the thing for an angry throat. You write your name down in the corner of the page, Dora. So's you remember to remember."

From the last apple, she made a charm, grinning and singing as she pared the peel away to form a long curling ribbon of red. "The snake told Eve to give Adam her apple, oooh, Dora, who gonna get yours?" She threw the peel over my left shoulder and then stooped on her hands and knees to study it. She crossed her chest, then drew a cross in the air. "Look at that . . . I sees a pretty little house, a fat silk purse and the strength of a hunter's bow."

I bent down to join her. "What does it mean?"

"Nothin'—not right now, anyways." She patted my hand as I helped her to her feet. "You'll knows it when it do."

I'd beg her to tell me more, but there's no use in bothering Miss B. with questions. She's said all she wanted to say. I suppose Tom Ketch is a hunter; he's got to have a bow, living in Deer Glen and all . . . but there's no pretty little house and not enough money to fill a thimble, let alone a silk purse. Miss B.'s never wrong about these things. She can tell a woman that she's with child before the woman knows it herself. She can tell if it's a boy or a girl, and the week the baby will arrive, most times getting it right down to the day. She can touch a person's forehead, or hold their hand, and tell them what's making them sick. So, even though she never said *who,* or even *when,* I can't stop guessing at her clues and thinking over each word.

4

THINKING IS SOMETHING that Father says I do entirely too much of: "You think on things too long, especially for a woman." At first I thought it was just something that fathers tell their daughters, but he's not alone in this; Aunt Fran never seems to tire of carrying her journals of medical findings to the house and reading aloud from them during tea with Mother and me. Her latest is *The Science of a New Life* by Dr. John Cowan, M.D. "It's right here, Charlotte, see? Oh, never mind your trying to read it just now, I want Dora to hear it too. I'll just read this bit out loud. It won't take but a minute. Let's see . . . here it is . . . the esteemed Dr. Cowan states, 'Closely allied to food and dress, in woman, as a producer of evil thoughts, is idleness and novel-reading. It is almost impossible for a woman to read the current "love-and-murder" literature of the day and have pure thoughts, and when the reading of such literature is associated with idleness—as it almost invariably is—a woman's thoughts and feelings *cannot be other than impure and sensual*.' There now, Charlotte. There it is in black and white. Overthinking and novel-reading causes, at the very least, fretting, nightmares and a bad complexion."

This past autumn she was convinced that my bout with a cold and cough was brought on by my constant attention to *Wuthering Heights.* She even scolded Mother for letting me read it. "Lottie, whenever I see that daughter of yours, she always has a book under her nose! It would be one thing if she was studying psalms or even a verse or two of poetry . . . no wonder her health's been compromised by the slightest change in the weather."

Mother laughed. "Oh, Fran, with all your talk, you'd think Dora's caught her death just by reading about the God-forsaken moors of Yorkshire."

She turned to me and asked, "This is the one about the moors, isn't it, Dorrie?"

"Yes, Mother."

"And then there's the one about that poor woman whose husband kept her locked in the attic . . . I always get them confused. Of course, I've got no time to read them myself, I'm so slow at it and all, but Dora's kind enough to tell me about them from time to time. Don't you worry about her, she'll be back to feeling right in no time at all."

Aunt Fran lowered her voice. "Her cold is just the start of a greater sickness. These 'stories,' as you call them, will only lead her to more pain."

"Fran, talk plain, will you?"

"I'm talking about *derangement.*"

"Don't be silly!"

She whispered. "And deviant behaviours."

Aunt Fran decided it was best to give Mother her copy of *The Science of a New Life.* "Normally, I wouldn't lend this out. But I'll make an exception in Dora's case. You can't put this sort of thing off and expect it to cure itself." She patted

Mother's hand. "I've marked several pages for you. The ones that apply to her *condition*."

Mother smiled and nodded. She no sooner put it on the dresser next to her bed than Father was ordering me to "Gather up those books of yours, Dora. Bring them out to the brush pile." I acted as if I didn't hear him and walked out to the pen to feed the sow. Before long I could hear the crackle of the fire, smell the smoke from dried twigs, *Wuthering Heights, Pride and Prejudice* and all the rest. I leaned against the fence and cried. There's no point in arguing with him. There never is. *I'll say one thing for the boys: at least they don't cry. I'll never understand you, Dora.*

Last night was the first night of bunking down. When I was little, I looked forward to cold December winds and the first snow, to Father closing off the upstairs and all of us children dragging our pillows, blankets and feather mattresses down to the front room. Each night we lay piled together, Mother kissing our cheeks in the order of our births—Albert, Borden, Charlie, Dora, Ezekiel, Forest and Gord—cozy and snug until the grass turned green in the spring. Although our winter sleeping arrangement has become crowded and a bit smelly in the last few years, I still love listening to Borden's late-night storytelling: the time old Bobby One Eye paddled the riptides off Cape Split, how he and Hart Bigelow came to invent pig bladder baseball, the tale of the hidden treasure that's never been found on Isle Haute, and the ghost of Old Cove Fisher's lost foot.

This year, Father didn't seem to know what to do with me. I heard him arguing with Mother over it after breakfast.

"Maybe she could stay at Fran's for the winter."

Mother sounded upset. "Why would we send her away? Surely there's enough room for sleeping."

Father lowered his voice. "She needs to act like a proper young lady."

"And she doesn't?"

"It's just that with six boys . . ."

"Judah Rare, you're being foolish."

"She's getting to the age where she might be considered, someone might think . . ."

"That she's a sweet girl who cares for her brothers?"

"She and Charlie still hold hands whenever they walk down the road, and no matter how many times I've scolded her, she insists on getting in the middle of the boys when they wrestle or fight."

"Stop worrying over her. She's got a pure and innocent heart. I'm almost certain she's never even been kissed."

"That's the trouble. No man wants a girl who's always tied to her brothers. The longer we let this go on, the more people will think there's something odd about it. Let's send her to Fran's. I'm sure your sister would be happy to—"

"Yes, I'm sure Fran would be happy to make a housemaid out of my daughter. How we raise the children is our business and no one else's. We'll put Dora on the end after the twins, or lay her longways down by their feet, but she's staying home and that's that."

Father's right in supposing I've lost my innocence, but it wasn't by having my rose plucked in the middle of a field that hasn't been hayed. (I can still look forward to a bit of blood on the sheets on my wedding night.) Still, a girl can lose her heart long before she gives it away. Mother's never mentioned it, or maybe she was too busy to notice, but I remember exactly how it happened. It was the day Father showed me I was no longer a child.

Before that day, I belonged with my brothers, I was one of them. If Borden or Albert teased me, I'd tease them right back. If Charlie put mud in my shoes, he'd find a toad under his sheets that same night. For every shove one of them gave me, I'd pinch two bruises into the fleshy part of a thigh or the back of an arm. Then Father put a stop to it. On a warm, sunny day (about the same time I started to bleed and my breasts began to feel heavy when I ran), Albert, Borden, Charlie and I snuck off to Lady's Cove after school. The tide was just going out, the rocks were filled with pools of warm seawater, and a long strip of clay lay glistening at the edge of the shore. In the shelter of the cove, we did as we always had done: we stripped off our clothes and began throwing wet, heavy balls of mud and clay at each other. We must have been quite a sight, laughing and screaming, our bodies streaked with sloppy trails of brown and grey, but *my* name was the only name Father called out when he found us. It was a slow, angry insisting, *Dora Marie Rare.* I pulled my clothes over my dirty, crusty skin and he pulled me by my arm all the way home. I shouldn't have argued with him, but it didn't seem fair that I should be singled out. After all, it was Borden's idea to go to the cove, it was Albert's idea to wade in the water, it was Charlie who threw the first mud ball. Father didn't care. He turned, took both my arms and shook me as he spoke. "I never want to see you behaving like that again."

"But, Father, I—"

"Don't make me cut an alder and take it to your skin, Dora."

When we got to the house, Mother greeted us on the porch, looking concerned. She must have spotted us coming up the road and seen from Father's stride that he was angry. He ordered me to pump a bucket of water from the well. "Get yourself cleaned up before supper, and I'd better not find a speck of clay behind your ears." When I came back into the house, I heard him complaining to Mother. "She's too old to fall in with the boys, and she's gotten some smart with her mouth too. Talk to her, Lottie, tell her she'll never get a husband if she keeps it up. No man around here wants a wife who talks back."

He acted as if it made him sick just to look at me. He shook me so hard he put his fears right into my body. He let go of every nasty thought, every father's nightmare, and put them in my head—the desire to watch animals mate in the spring, the thoughts of wanting to be touched, the need for men to notice me. I couldn't have stayed innocent, even if I'd wanted to. I guess he finally realized that there's no way to stop a girl from becoming a woman.

At least I'm not as far gone as Grace Hutner. She has a way of speaking, putting her finger to her chin and rolling her eyes while she giggles . . . it's as sly as any county-fair magician or snake oil salesman. There's always a slight dip to the front of her blouse and an impatient turn to her ankle as she sticks her leg out to the side of her desk or into the aisle of the sanctuary at church. The lightness of her hair and the blue of her eyes fool most everyone into thinking she's perfection walking. Her one-dimpled smile pulls everyone into her path, boys, girls, men. They fall right to her side: "Do you need help carrying those books, Grace?" "Tell us about your new dress, Grace." "A young thing like you shouldn't walk alone." Every churchgoing boy in the

Bay, including both Albert and Borden, has rolled her in the hayloft. The only time I've ever seen the two of them come to blows was over her. She had them each believing her heart belonged to him. Even though they made peace and forgave each other when she took up with Archer Bigelow, she can still get them to argue over which one of them gets to walk her home from church. All the boys want her, and every little girl wants to be her. Grace Hutner could make a man want to go blind, just so he could better hear her lies.

I've "borrowed" a few books from a dusty, forgotten cupboard at the schoolhouse, Charles Dickens and Jane Austen among them. Miss B. lets me keep them at her cabin as long as I read them aloud to her while she makes clay pipes with her willy-nilly fingers. She teases me, holding my wrist before and after each reading, counting my heartbeats. "Your heart's not changed a flit, your skin's not hot . . . you sure you're alright?" We have formed a reading circle for two, *un veille du mot,* as Miss B. calls it, and have begun with Jane Austen's *Northanger Abbey.* The heroine, Catherine Moreland, is falling in love with the dashing, yet passive, Henry Tilney. She is seventeen.

Once I figured Aunt Fran's copy of *The Science of a New Life* had been forgotten, I stole it too and hid it between my mattress and the boards of my bed. Dr. John Cowan and I have gotten to be on quite intimate terms.

Let us glance at some of the results of masturbation,
as affecting the health and character of the individual;
the array is altogether an undesirable one: headaches,

dyspepsia, costiveness, spinal disease, epilepsy, impaired eyesight, palpitations of the heart, pain in the side, incontinence of urine, hysteria, paralysis, involuntary seminal emissions, impotency, consumption, insanity, etc.

The female, diseased here, loses proportionably the amiableness and gracefulness of her sex, her sweetness of voice, disposition and manner, her native enthusiasm, her beauty of face and form, her gracefulness and elegance of carriage, her looks of love and interest in man and to him, and becomes merged into a mongrel, neither male nor female, but marred by the defects of both, without possessing the virtues of either.

Dr. Cowan may go on to call it *self-abuse,* but I like to refer to it as *practising patience.* What's the harm in thinking of love? Is bringing around little heartaches under my covers any different from mouthing the words of the Brownings or Keats or Christina Rosetti? Just yesterday I took another book from Miss Coffill's library at the schoolhouse, this time a poetry collection. *Come to me in the silence of the night; Come in the speaking silence of a dream.* I've marked my favourites with bits of string. Like my hands down between my legs, the words are sweet, and nothing but wishes.

~ December 1916

Dr. Thomas has not been back to bother Miss B., but Aunt Fran reported the other day that the maternity home in Canning is nearly finished and there's to be a "Ladies Tea" for the women of Scots Bay. She's encouraging all "the fine ladies of the Bay" to attend. Of course, she gets herself excited over any occasion that calls for her to wear a new hat and lift her pinky. She was also quick to inform me, "Dr. Thomas will be presenting a lecture on 'Morality and Women's Health,' something I think you'd quite enjoy, Dora."

The more I learn about them, the more I realize I'm not much for doctors.

5

Dr. and Mrs. Gilbert Thomas
Invite the ladies of Scots Bay to attend a special afternoon of
Tea and conversation
at
The Canning Maternity Home of Kings County
Saturday, December 7, 1916
Transportation to and from Canning will be provided
from the Seaside Centre.

THREE TEAMS OF STURDY horses hitched to three beautiful new sleighs were waiting at the Seaside Centre. Courtesy of Dr. Thomas.

Mother said I would have to take her place in representing the Rare family, since she had far too much work to do at home. I tried to convince Miss B. she should come along for the ride, but she refused, saying, "I ain't been down North Mountain since the day I arrived. It's been so long now, I guess I'd up and turn to dust if I set as much as one toe outside the Bay."

Aunt Fran told Mother not to worry. "I'm already going, in an *official capacity* as secretary of the White Rose Temperance Society, so it's no trouble to watch over my dear young niece. I'll see that she minds her *p*'s and *q*'s." Precious had begged her mother to include her as well, but Aunt Fran put her off, explaining, "You know how you suffer in the cold. Who knows what state you'd be in after riding down the mountain and back?" She smoothed Precious's hair and retied the bow at the end of her braid. "What do we always say?"

Precious chimed in with a reluctant sigh. "Think of yourself, think of your health."

Aunt Fran smiled and popped a lemon drop in Precious's mouth. "Well done, dear, well done."

Poor Precious waved us off and began to make her way home, but not before she made me promise to tell her "every little thing that happens."

Aunt Fran was dressed in her Sunday best. When Mrs. Trude Hutner made a fuss over Fran's new rabbit fur muff, Aunt Fran insisted that Mrs. Hutner and Grace ride opposite so they could continue their conversation. She handed the muff to Mrs. Hutner for a proper inspection. "It arrived yesterday. Irwin said I should pick out an early Christmas gift from the Eaton's catalogue. At first he suggested that I might like a new coat, but I told him 'no,' of course, what with the war on and all. This is all I need. I was going to wait until church tomorrow to use it for the first time, but this seemed like the perfect occasion."

Mrs. Hutner nodded as she stroked the soft white fur. "Like a little bit of heaven, I'd say . . . but practical too." She slipped her hands inside the muff and grinned. "I think it's time I had a new one myself. Perhaps I'll give Grace my old one and mail in my order to Eaton's this week."

Aunt Fran tried her best to fight the disapproving look from her face. The two women are friends, but only because they are both in the position of having much more than most women in the Bay. Evidently, it takes equally thin parts of kindness and sincerity to marry well. "There was a lovely one made from beaver, pictured right next to this one. You'd certainly look smart in such a dark colour, if I do say so myself."

Mrs. Hutner pouted and handed the muff back to Aunt Fran. "I'll keep that in mind."

Most of Aunt Fran's time (and much of Uncle Irwin's family fortune) goes towards her need for *having*. Last Christmas it was Irish linens, after that, French lace table runners, and then it was figurines made from Italian porcelain . . . mostly birds, insects and fruit. These days, her fancy's gone towards collecting spoons, hundreds of them, engraved with the faces of royalty and the great wonders of the world, the likes of which Aunt Fran would never dream of leaving her comfortable home in the Bay to see. She faithfully polishes them, singing hymns all the while, grinning as her reflection turns in the bowl, *right side up, upside down, right side up, upside down.* They line her parlour wall, each one a useless droplet of silver, but delicate enough not to offend God or any of the good Christian ladies of the Bay.

Mother always smiles to herself whenever we visit Aunt Fran. "A woman's got to have something to set her clocks by . . . Fran's cuckoo sings somewhere between spouting off Bible verses and rubbing those spoons." I've never heard her complain about Fran's treasures or how little she has for herself. She spends day after day sweeping dust and dirt out the door, one mealtime running into the next, her heavy, tired feet shuffling in front of the hot cookstove. Her back aches from wringing clothes over the washtub and tugging milk from the Guernsey's udders. She was the pretty one who married for love. Seven children later, I hope she holds tight to that thought, as she tucks our dreams safely under our pillows and kisses Father good night.

I watched the trees go by, birch branches sparkling in the sun, spruces flocked white with fresh, wet snow from the night before. The horses kept a brisk pace, the sleigh cutting a clean path as we made our way down the mountain, winter-brisk air rushing past our faces. Fran shouted above the jangling of the sleigh bells. "I also got three new spoons . . . Buckingham Palace, the Pyramids of Giza and the Taj Mahal. You should come to tea next week and see them, they are glorious, simply glorious!"

Mrs. Hutner paused and buttoned the collar of Grace's coat to the very top. "Only if you'll come and see my newest pretties . . ." Grace smacked her mother's hand away and pulled the button loose again.

Aunt Fran clapped her hands together. "Oh, Trude, did you get it already?"

Mrs. Hutner reached for Grace's hand and squeezed it, tight. "Yes, the box arrived three days ago." She spoke at a fast, excited pitch. "The Gilded Lotus. Rose medallion pattern, covered with flowers and gilt, and the charming face of an empress looks back at you from the bottom of each cup. They're so small and delightful, each one with its own little rounded cover, like a tiny Chinaman's hat. *Guywan* they call it, a covered cup." Grace wormed her hand away from her mother's grasp and then slowly dug her heel into the toe of her mother's boot. Mrs. Hutner's eyes began to water. "They have no handles, you know."

Aunt Fran handed her a handkerchief. "How very odd."

Mrs. Hutner dabbed the corners of her eyes. "You'll have to excuse me, I've been feeling under the weather."

Aunt Fran nodded in sympathy. "Something's going around. The Widow Bigelow started off with a slight cough, but wound up in bed for a week. I guess it's a good thing we're going to see the doctor."

The Canning Maternity Home sits at the top of Pleasant Street. The tall, straight house looks as if it sprang up, white and clean, from nowhere. A stranger to the area would never guess that the place was once the rundown, forgotten house of Captain Robert Dowell, an English ship's captain who had a wife in London and an extra wife right here in Canning, Nova Scotia. His tombstone in the Habitant Cemetery reads:

Captain Robert Dowell
1836–1883
Who gave up his life
to his one true love,
the sea.

Most people might take those words to mean that he drowned, but the fact of the matter is, Captain Dowell met a more sinister fate. After Emily Dowell, wife number two, received a letter from Lucinda Dowell, wife number one, the two women made an agreement. They vowed that the Mrs. Dowell who saw darling "Robbie" next would take a butcher's knife and run it deep into his unfaithful heart.

It was Emily who met him first. It was Emily who waited in the dark of the wharf, Emily Elizabeth Dowell, née Trublood, the fair-faced daughter of the Honourable Judge Kingston Trublood. It was Emily who stabbed Captain Dowell, shoved him in the water and made good on the chance to right a wrong. Sadly enough, Emily couldn't live with the consequences. She couldn't bear to think that her own father might have to put her head in a noose. When she was done, she turned the knife on herself. Her marker is set next to her husband's. Underneath a carved hand that points to heaven, it reads:

Emily Elizabeth Trublood Dowell
1858–1883
Faithful consort
True of heart

The mystery of their two bloody bodies floating in the Habitant River might never have been solved, except for a letter that the Canning postmaster received after their deaths.

Manchester
England

October 25, 1883

Attention: Postmaster
The Village of Canning
Kings County, Nova Scotia
Canada

Dear Postmaster,
It has been many months since I have heard from my dear
friend, Mrs. Emily Dowell. Does she still reside there? Is she
well? Please tell me, have she and her dear husband settled
their differences? I wouldn't trouble you, but it isn't like her
not to send word. We are relatives of a sort, through marriage,
and I am most anxious to hear news of her.

Awaiting your kind response,
Mrs. Lucy Dowell

The postmaster, a Mr. Martin deGroot, sent a quick response to Lucy Dowell. Even after the gruesome details were explained, they continued to exchange letters, Lucy telling of the lonely damp weather of Manchester and Martin cursing the long Nova Scotia winter. It wasn't long before the postmaster realized it was the perfect match, Lucy being a widow, and he being in need of a wife. In the spring he sent for her, and Lucy Dowell became Mrs. Lucy deGroot.

Mother and Aunt Fran's side of the family is connected to the deGroots through their great-great-grandmother's sister. She left the Bay to marry into the strong Dutch family and never returned. Mother always points out the deGroot orchards on the way to Canning. "There's the finest apples in Kings County." They are round and plump with a red blush, just like the rest of our deGroot cousins, not at all like the small, tart fruit that grows in the Bay. We see the apples and the cousins once a year, in the autumn. Father brings new barrels down the mountain, and in return we get our share of apples and cider.

It was because of that simple tradition between our two families that Charlie and I always felt we had the "rights" to crawl through the broken cellar door of Captain Dowell's house. Despite the boarded windows and the faded "no trespassing" sign, we figured (through murder, marriage and loose blood ties) that the house was ours. We'd sneak off to the house whenever Father let us tag along on his Saturday trips to Canning. To clean out the ghosts, we'd run up and down the stairs, howling and screaming. After that, we'd sit in the attic, silent and still, to see if they'd return. Even the ghosts wouldn't recognize the place now.

Mrs. Dr. Thomas is a sweet woman, and although I found her to be kind enough, she seemed almost giddy with hospitality. She bounced as she led us from room to room, her expectant belly pushing forward, her hair piled in girlish ringlets atop her head. She rested her hands on her round stomach. "It's our first, and hopefully one of the many babies to be born at the Canning Maternity Home." She winked at Aunt Fran. "We ladies of Kings County are lucky to be in such good hands."

We followed her through the first floor, touring a small sitting room, Dr. Thomas's examination room, a large kitchen and sleeping quarters for two nurses.

The second floor had been turned into one large room. The white walls were lined with neat, square cupboards filled with folded towels and blankets. Under the far window were three large washbasins. Straight down the middle of the room were two long rows of empty white bassinettes. This was the nursery.

Dr. Thomas greeted us as we approached the third floor. "Welcome to the delivery room, ladies." The top post of the banister, once dark with carved sea serpents and sailing ships, had been painted over, whitewashed like everything else. The dreary attic was now a wide, ample space. Ten spare beds with tight white sheets lined the walls. In the centre of it all was a large table, set with candles, finger sandwiches and fine china. Dr. Thomas motioned for us to be seated. "Please, won't you join me for tea?"

He took each of the ladies' hands as they entered the room, complimenting their dresses and hats, commenting on mutual acquaintances, distant relatives and the weather. He paused when he came to me, repeating my name after I said it. "Miss Dora Rare. A lovely name."

We sipped our tea as Dr. Thomas explained "the advantages of modern childbirth." He pulled on a sheet that was hanging from the ceiling and let it fall down as a partition between two beds. "At the Canning Maternity Home we have both privacy and efficiency. Up to ten women can labour at once and still have the best in obstetrical care." He pushed the sheet back and tied it to the wall. "And more beds can be added as needed." He stood at the end of a bed and turned a crank. The head of the bed rose and lowered and then rose again. "The new mother can labour and rest in the same bed." He bent down and yanked a metal footing from either side of the end of the bed, smacking them into place with a hard jolt. "Stirrups. For support during birthing."

The ladies all smiled and nodded. While they continued to eat their tiny sandwiches, Dr. Thomas wheeled over a metal cart. It was draped with a sheet and looked something like a caddy for tea and sweets. Aunt Fran gasped when he revealed the contents of the tray. The doctor chuckled. "It may look ominous, but I assure you, it's all part of progress." The tray was cluttered with shining silver knives, scissors and other medical instruments. Stored in the compartment beneath were jars of every shape and size. He took two medicine bottles and nestled them around the flower arrangement in the centre of the table. "Pituitrin and chloroform, a mother's two best friends." He then held up a pair of large wide tongs. "Forceps, the obstetrical physician's best friend." He passed them around the table. "I brought out all these things—the surgical knives, the scissors, the needles, the bottles of ergot and ether—not to frighten you, but to show you the path of modern medicine. These things *hasten* childbirth and put the labour process in the doctor's hands. He has complete control. The faster the birth, the less chance for infection, and the less time the mother has to suffer. I'm sure you'd all agree, the less a woman has to suffer, the better."

The women whispered and nodded, Trude Hutner adding, "Two days of labour it was with my Grace." She patted Grace's hand. "Can you imagine? Two whole days."

Dr. Thomas sat down at the head of the table. "Late last week I was called to a birth in the village of Baxter's Harbour. The local midwife attended the young mother's birth, but as the labour progressed, it was clear that the mother was in much distress. The father, having been sent away from his home by the midwife, had sense enough to come to Canning to enlist my help. When I arrived, the mother was in a state of utter exhaustion and was too weak to deliver the child. It was too late for her to get any relief from the medicine I administered, too late for the use of forceps." He shook his head. "That poor mother and her child are not alive today." He took the forceps and placed them back on the cart. "Every time I recall that tragedy, I realize that there are more occasions than any of us care to think when a physician's hand is the only saving grace."

While the ladies were all shaking their heads in silence, Dr. Thomas continued, looking in my direction. "I don't think that young mother was much older than your dear Miss Rare." The ladies all turned and looked at me. "She's the perfect example of one of Scots Bay's fine young ladies who will be needing my assistance in the future." He smiled and then winked at me, as if he knew me, as if we shared a secret (or as if he might have known I was hiding at Miss B.'s the day he called on her). My face, my ears, the back of my neck went hot. "It's never too soon to start thinking about the day she'll be a bride, a wife, a mother."

As the ladies all agreed with Dr. Thomas, Grace choked on a petit four. Mrs. Hutner poured more tea in her daughter's cup and encouraged her to drink (or at least hold her cup to her face to stifle her laughter).

Dr. Thomas placed a small booklet next to each place setting around the table. "A Mother's Share from the Farmer's Assurance Company would make a wonderful gift for a new bride."

Mrs. Thomas added, "For any woman, really."

The doctor stood behind his wife and placed his hand on her shoulder. "It gives a woman the peace of mind of knowing that she has a safe, clean place to have her babies."

Although impeccable with his manners and polite at every turn, it was clear to me that Dr. Thomas was less concerned with a woman's circumstances and more concerned with selling his services. *You ain't tellin'. You sellin'.* Thinking of Miss B., I raised my hand to speak, my voice wavering as I questioned Dr. Thomas. "What about the cost? I don't know many families in Scots Bay who can afford what you're asking."

Aunt Fran hissed at me. "Dora, don't be rude."

Mrs. Thomas smiled. "What a family spends on coffee and tea each month could easily buy a share."

Not feeling as if I'd had a proper answer, or that Mrs. Thomas had the slightest notion of what the word *cost* means to most families in the Bay, I ignored Aunt Fran's scolding and held up the back of the pamphlet. "But it says right here, 'A Mother's Share costs twenty-five dollars for one year.' That's an awful lot of coffee beans."

Aunt Fran snatched the pamphlet from my hand and whispered, "I won't hear another word from you."

Dr. Thomas interrupted. "No, she's right, not every woman may be able to afford her own share, but that's why I've brought you ladies here today. This is a wonderful chance for women's organizations like the White Rose Temperance Society to help the ladies of their community. What price, I ask you, is greater than life?"

Although she was all politeness and smiles, when the tea was over, Aunt Fran was the first to head to the door, pulling me along and muttering under her breath as she went. "For heaven's sake, my own niece. If I've told Lottie once, I've told her a thousand times, you've got to keep an eye on that girl. Keep her away from books and those boys."

Dr. Thomas followed close behind. "Mrs. Jeffers, a word, if you please?"

She turned, forcing her angry grimace into a pleasant smile. "Certainly, Doctor, although we've already taken up so much of your time today."

He took her hand in his. "I wanted to thank you for coming and for bringing your niece along with you. It's a pleasure to see such thoughtfulness in a young lady, don't you agree?"

Aunt Fran blushed. "Why, yes, how kind of you to say so. I'm always telling Dora that she needs to speak up more, open that dear mouth of hers on occasion."

Dr. Thomas looked at me. "So good to see you, Miss Rare. Please give Miss Babineau my best, will you?"

I nodded. "Yes, I certainly will."

Aunt Fran interrupted. "Dora, dear, you neglected to tell me that you had already made Dr. Thomas's acquaintance."

Before I could insist that we'd never met, Dr. Thomas looked at me and grinned. "I imagine that Miss Rare is *hiding* all sorts of surprises."

6

MY SATURDAY VISIT with Miss Babineau the following week was spent at Mabel Thorpe's place. Miss B. had her birthing bag packed and was ready to go as soon as I walked through the door. "Turn yourself around. Mabel's bornin' her third, so we'd best get over to the house and lend a hand." I thought of Mrs. Ketch and of baby Darcy and how I held him until his breath was gone, his body cold. In the time that had passed since his birth, my nightmares had disappeared only to be replaced with the thought that perhaps I had caused his death, that Laird Jessup had been right to blame his calf's misfortunes on me, that my presence at any birth somehow brought on ugliness—pale misshaped bodies, weak hearts and eventually death. "I don't think I'd be much help. Maybe I should go back home."

Miss B. took my hand, pulled me out of the house and started walking down the road. "It's gonna be just fine. Don't you worry."

I should know by now, once Marie Babineau's mind's made up, there's no saying no.

The walk was cold and long. By mid-December the trees are naked, the Bay has turned the colour of lead and the winds have changed, pushing the grass down, ignoring our lives as it cuts the breath short and shallow, forcing us to move from fire to fire. Mabel's house sits along the main road where it branches off towards Cape Split, just after the shipyard and Hardy Tupper's blacksmith shop. It's no different than all the other Thorpe houses in the Bay, framed straight and square like a saltbox, with one chimney poking up through the middle of the roof. This is how the Thorpes are too, plain living and dependable, every last one.

Once inside, Miss B. was quick to push Mabel's husband, Porter, and their two small children out the door and off to stay with his sister's family down the road. "That wife of yours has to think on this baby now. The little ones won't know why she's not actin' herself, and dear Mabel can't do what she needs to if she's frettin' over givin' them a fright."

Her belly almost too wide between them, Mabel leaned towards her shy, quiet husband, giving him an awkward kiss on the cheek. She tousled the hair on her little girls' heads saying, "You be some good for your auntie. Mind your daddy and say your pleases and thank-yous." Two little strawberry-blond heads nodded together as they looked up at their mother, smiling, reaching out their hands to rub the roundness of her one last time. At four and five they are perfect stair steps, both freckle-faced and as sweet-natured as their mother. Big as a barn and nearly ready to drop, Mabel Thorpe still made motherhood look easy. Miss B. says, "It's a mama's faith what keeps her children right. I'm not talkin' 'bout the churchgoin' kind, neither. Miss Mabel's got faith in goodness. Tell me you can't help but believe in it too just by lookin' at her."

Soon after they left, two of Mabel's neighbours, Bertine Tupper and Sadie Loomer, arrived. Miss B. greeted them by kissing their cheeks and teasing them about the difference in their heights. "Well, if it ain't the broom and the bucket." Bertine's as tall and sturdy as you'd expect a blacksmith's wife to be, while Sadie, though wiry and rough as a sailor with her talk, isn't much taller than my youngest brothers. They came through the door cradling baskets filled with tiny quilts, cradle blankets and baked goods. Miss B. cooed over Bertine's knitting, smoothing the folds with her blue-lined hands. "*L'amour de maman.* A mother's love." Then she set us all to work, even Mabel. "It's too early to be puttin' yourself to bed, little mama. You know right well you gots to keep on movin' so's you can open up them bones." Mabel didn't argue. She busied herself with her friends, moving back and forth between sifting flour and gripping the edge of the kitchen table when her pains grew too hard.

From three different outports in Newfoundland, Mabel, Bertine and Sadie all came to the Bay about the same time. They're what Aunt Fran calls *women from away.* She says it means they couldn't find husbands in their own villages, so they had to find a way to get "hitched" to men from somewhere else. "Newfoundland may as well be the moon the way those women act sometimes. When you've got no family to speak of, no one knows who you *really* are. I suppose that's what they want, running off like that from home, like they've got something to hide." I think they're wonderful, and even brave, sitting together at church socials, laughing louder than Aunt Fran thinks they should. They seem more like sisters (or at least how I imagine sisters might be).

Miss B. called to me. "Dora, go out and fetch us some fresh eggs. It's time to make the groanin' cake."

Some say the groaning cake, or *kimbly,* brings good fortune to the new child. These days, most people save the tradition for when the mother's churched. The first Sunday she can get out of bed and take the baby to services, the father stands outside the church door and hands each mother in the community a little cake wrapped in brown paper and red ribbon. Mabel wanted to do it the old way, where the mother breaks the eggs and mixes the batter herself just before the baby comes. "It fills the house right up with sweetness. That's the way my mother and all her sisters did it back home."

Bertine nodded in agreement. "My granny always said just the smell of it baking cuts the pain."

Sadie added, "As soon as you think a baby's coming, it's time to tie lavender to the bedposts, put an axe under the bed and a cake in the oven."

Miss B. smiled as she lifted the cozy off the teapot. "The scent of a good groanin' cake, a cuppa hot Mother's Tea and *time*. Most times that's all a mama needs on the day her baby comes." She handed Mabel a cup. "Plenty of time to do whatever she needs, tell whatever story's on her mind, time enough to say all her prayers."

As the afternoon wore on, Mabel became more and more quiet, stopping every once in a while to hold her stomach and let out a groan. After her water broke all down her legs and she got to where she couldn't hold a spoon in her hands or a smile on her face, Miss B. led her back to the bedroom. She unpacked three glass jars from her bag, sterilized scissors, scorched muslin and castor oil. She sang and prayed over them, and after that, over anything else she touched. It was getting dark now, so I lit a few lamps and brought them into the room.

Sadie and Bertine took turns telling Mabel gossip as they pulled a clean nightdress over Mabel's round belly.

"And then Bertine gots her foot tappin'. You know the way she does when she thinks she's been lied to, says, 'well, isn't that interesting'—an' all that."

Mabel paced back and forth, trying to keep her mind from her pain.

"I just thought it was awful interesting that Mrs. Trude Hutner would say she already knew whats how to thrum a pair of mitts when you know right well she's never knitted a proper mitt, nor sock, nor a bloody thimble for her thumb. These women around here like to think they know it all . . . she wouldn't have to stuff the *Canning Register* down her husband's boots if she knew to make a proper sock."

Sadie's half Bertine's size, but it didn't stop her from teasing. "Shut it now, Bertine, and let me tell it right. No one wants to hear about your blessed wonderful socks . . . again."

Mabel reached for the bedpost, groaning with pain. "Here it comes."

Miss B. clutched at the rosary beads around her neck. "Hold on to it, don't you go pushin' just yet." Sadie and Bertine rushed to their friend, holding her up on either side. With every moan Mabel let out, they did their best to comfort her, saying, "You'll be fine, just a little while longer, you'll be fine," but when her pains came in waves, each one following on top of the next, they gave up their words. Miss B. closed her eyes and listened. "There's a sound that creeps up . . . it's like no other sound I ever heard. When it pulls at the hairs on the back of your neck, that's how you knows it's time."

Miss B. asked me to bring in a bowl of warm water and a clean towel. She spread blankets on the floor, making a soft nest at Mabel's feet. "You gotta get on your knees now, dear, it's time you gonna push." Bertine and Sadie got down on the floor with her, giving Mabel their shoulders to hold on to. Miss B. sprinkled a few drops of castor oil in the water, prayed over the bowl, wrang out the steaming cloth and placed it against the red, bulging skin between Mabel's legs. She looked at me and motioned to a small stool beside her bag. "Bring that stool and come hold this for me. Keep it close and warm so she don't tear."

Mabel cried out as the next pains began. Miss B. knelt beside me. I started to move to change places with her, but she whispered in my ear, "You stay put." She looked up at Mabel. "Now we push, little mama, now we push."

It was tight and round where I held the cloth, and as I pulled my hand away, I could see the dark of the baby's hair. As she pushed, Mabel's body seemed to open up as wide and full as her wailing. When the baby's head moved out into the light, I saw that its face was starting to turn blue. Miss B. whispered in my ear, her voice calm and steady. "It's just a corded birth. You gonna get him loose so he can breathe." I held my breath as Miss B. went on. "Feel your fingers 'round the neck. Can you slip the cord over the baby's head?" The wet bumpy cord was taut and pulsing. There was barely a finger's width of space to hook my fingers underneath. Not wanting to frighten Mabel, I turned my head towards Miss B. and mouthed the word *no*. Miss B. called out to her, "God knows you're tired, dear, as do all the angels in heaven, so on this next push they're gonna help you get that baby out."

Mabel whimpered, her body shaking and weak. "I don't know if I can."

Miss B.'s voice was firm. "You ain't got no choice . . . now here we go. Mother Mary, help this mama, help this baby, Mother Mary, Blessed Virgin, Our Lady of the Moon and Star of the Sea, *Ave Maria Stellas . . . un, deux, trois . . .*"

Mabel closed her eyes and let out a long, anguished wail. Bertine and Sadie cried out loud beside her, moaning right along with her, all three women letting out heavy groans. As the baby slipped out, all milky-looking and wet, I pulled the cord free from its neck. Miss B. scooped the baby up, opening its tiny mouth with her fingers. She held her mouth to the infant's, her cheeks puffing with gentle breaths, then made the sign of the cross over and over as the baby gave its first cry.

It was late by the time we finished tending to Mabel and her new baby, clearing away the bloodstained sheets, spooning fennel broth between Mabel's tired lips. Miss B. squeezed drops of watery red alder tea into the infant's mouth "to clear the liver and cut the hives." When mother and child were sleeping, we left them to Sadie and Bertine's care. I recorded the day's events in the Willow Book, still amazed at the way it felt to be the first person to bring her hands to a child's life. While it cannot replace the sadness I feel over Darcy, it has changed me, somehow opening my heart again.

December 8, 1916. Evening, about half-past eight.
Mabel Thorpe has another beautiful baby girl.
Her name is Violet.

Not wanting to wake up my family, I stayed over at Miss B.'s cabin and slept in her rocking chair until dawn. I woke to find Miss B. standing beside the rocker, praying over me.

She whispered, "You believe in spirits of the dead?"

Thinking I was dreaming, I whispered back. "Yes."

"You know where they lives?"

"Right here. Right where we are. Everywhere we are."

"How you know this?"

"I just do."

7

EACH SUNDAY AT the Union Church we recite the Apostles' Creed. The voices of the congregation rise up together in holy-mouthed repetition, saying, "*I believe in the Holy Ghost.*" When my Auntie Hannah June died, she came to me in spirit. She told me she'd forgotten to do something before she left. She'd forgotten to write down her mother's recipe for brown bread. Hannah June was always the one to make the bread, for every social and family picnic. She guarded the secret with her life and never bothered to write it down. I guess she thought it was the one thing that meant she was needed. Maybe she was right.

At family gatherings, everyone always waited for her arrival, anticipating the basket of warm, doughy sweetness she would bring. Once, before a Women's Institute bake sale, I saw her standing just outside an open window at the Seaside Centre, as if she was waiting for someone to say her name. No sooner had Aunt Fran said, "Where's that Hannah June and her brown bread?" then in she came, flour still clinging in the wrinkles of her hands, smelling like yeast and molasses.

The Sunday after she died, there in the middle of church, while everyone else was saying, "*To thee all angels cry aloud; The heavens, and all the powers therein; To thee cherubim and seraphim continually do cry.*" Auntie Hannah June's ghost settled down beside me and led my pencil across the inside of the back cover of the hymnal. *To my dear sister Maude, 1/4 cup molasses, 1/2 cup oats, 2 egg yolks . . .* I passed the book behind me to Aunt Maude. She cried, right there in the pew, trembling and dropping wet tears all over the place.

The morning after Mabel's birth, Miss B. had gone on about her thoughts of the dead, sitting down in a chair next to me in her kitchen, clutching my hand. "Wherever them spirits lives, up or down or in the treetops, hidin' behind gravestones or under my bed, I'm goin' there soon. Goin' to meet with Mary and the angels, my *maman* and my grandpapa Louis Faire." She opened her eyes wide and stuck her face in front of mine. "See? The brown of my skin and the bright of my eyes is all muddy with clouds . . . my knittin' needles been playin' waltzes instead of jigs."

I started to speak, but she put her finger to my lips. "Shh . . . I gots to give it up and it's *you* that's got to follow." She pulled at the tangle of beads around her neck, her bony fingers tugging apart the strands of pearl, jet, coral and wood. A single black strand came away from the rest, weighted with a silver crucifix, a long brass key and a small leather pouch. "Keeps the gris-gris, the evil eye and the voodoo away." She held the rosary beads to her lips. "I remember the day you arrived."

"The day I was born?"

"Oh no, long before that . . . I'm talkin' about the day your spirit came down and started flutterin' around in your mama's belly like a pair of butterfly's wings."

She slipped the beads through her fingers, one after another, as she spoke. "Your mama had come to me crying, convinced that the baby in her belly was dead. She'd had a dream, a vision of a beautiful lady with hair as dark as night and sparklin' green eyes. She done thought it were an angel from God, come to tell her that the baby had gone to heaven."

"I just knew that weren't the way it was, so I sat her down, brewed her some raspberry tea and began talkin' to her belly. It wasn't but a minute later that she felt you beginnin' to move." Miss B. laughed. "I told your mama not to worry, that her dream was showin' her that she was gonna have a fine baby girl. Oh, she could hardly believe it, the wife of a Rare man havin' a *girl*. But after you started kickin' her in the ribs, she trusted me, she knew it was true, not like your father . . . he wouldn't hear it, no matter how many times I grabbed him after church and swore on the reverend's Protestant excuse for a Bible. Why your daddy almost went and fainted when you didn't have a piddler danglin' between your legs." She placed the crucifix, key and pouch in the palm of her hand, the beads trailing down in her lap. "I knew from the start who you was, Dora Rare. You's what I call *lagniappe,* a little something extra."

"Miss B., I'm not sure what you mean by all this."

She went on, stroking the crucifix as she spoke. "I know most folks think what I do ain't nothin' but a bunch of witchery, but everything gots a reason, I promise you that." She looked up at me. "It's the things *they* can't see, the things they're afraid to get an understandin' of that I gots to pass on to you." She laid the strand of beads in my lap. "It's time I gave this to you." She put her finger to the pouch and made the sign of the cross. "This holds the veil, the caul that covered your eyes at your birth." She untied the ribbon that held the pouch shut and gently fished out the contents. It was a homely little thing, unremarkable, looking much like the withered red bits of Irish moss I often find in the twins' coat pockets. Once considered a treasure, now forgotten and left behind.

"Seein' how he couldn't brag you was a boy, your daddy bragged over that caul. As any good sailor knows, a caul's as good as any blessing of St. Christopher, it brings fair wind and plenty of it, and it'll save 'em from drownin' too. You weren't even a day old, and the men were all fightin' over it. A letter even come from as far away as Halifax, offerin' great sums of money, but your *maman* thought better of it and give it to me to keep safe. It couldn't get no safer than hangin' 'round my neck, burnin' next to my heart while I whispered to it, day on day, night on night. I give it all the words of Louis Faire, all the secrets of the simples, all my prayers to Mother Mary, all what's written in the Willow Book. *This* is how I knows that you are my follow, the next *traiteur*." She hung the strand of beads around my neck, her hands shaking, her eyes pleading and haunted. "You have to take it from me, Dora, take the prayers, the secrets. If you don't, they'll be lost, and I'll never have a moment's peace on the other side. Stay with me 'til I cross over. It won't be long; the grave's not too far off now. I know I won't see another winter."

I tried to calm her. "You're just tired, Miss B. A good night's sleep and you'll be fine."

"You proved yourself with Mabel's little one. The women here, they'll need someone. They'll need you."

I laughed and teased her, hoping she would leave it alone for now. "By the time you die, Dr. Thomas'll have built one of his fancy maternity homes right here in Scots Bay. Maybe even two."

She grabbed my arm and held tight, muttering a stream of prayers in French. "They need you."

Frightened, I twisted away from her, making my way to the kitchen to put on my coat and boots. "Mother needs me at home. I'm too young. I'm sorry . . ." I left the caul and Miss B.'s beads on the table and ran to the door.

She called out after me. "You must take it. It's what God means for you. It is your *destinée* . . ."

8

I SPOKE WITH MOTHER about what went on at Miss B.'s. We were doing the mending after breakfast, pushing darning eggs down into the heels of Father's socks, hoping to make them last another winter. The only time words come easy between us is when we're busy. Everything I've learned from Mother, every bit of her truth, has been said while her hands were moving.

When I finished telling her of Miss Babineau's offer, she paused and looked up from her knitting. "And what did you say?"

"I told her no, of course. I can't leave you to take care of the boys alone."

Returning to her handwork, she looped the yarn into a tight knot. "I know you don't think I know much about the world, but I hear what's going on. Newspapers get here often enough, and God knows Fran tells me what's fashionable and so on." She cut the end loose with Father's old pocketknife. "Things are changing for women. They want a say in things, to be their own persons. Some girls are working at jobs where they make their own way. If we lived in a bigger place, there might be more opportunity for you. I've heard that out west and even in some towns down towards Halifax, girls your age are doing men's jobs, working on farms while the men are away . . . but here in the Bay there isn't room for it, the men's pride won't have it. You know how it is, a girl lives with her parents until she gets married, and then she spends the rest of her life raising babies, cooking, cleaning, waiting on her husband. Do you really want to go from helping me take care of all these boys to taking care of another man?" She was fishing for a small white button in the bottom of a canning jar. "I know Marie Babineau doesn't have much, but she's got one thing I've never had, and that's quiet. I can only imagine having moments all to myself that no one else knows about." Her eyes squinted and narrowed as she guided the end of her thread through a small, shiny needle. "Your father wants you to stay with Aunt Fran."

"I thought he'd given up on that."

"He spoke about it again just yesterday morning. He said you've been breaking the rules."

"What rules?"

"He saw you sleeping next to Charlie again, Dora."

"It was cold, the twins stole my blankets, and Charlie offered to share. I don't see why he thinks it's so wrong."

"He just does."

"So he thinks I'm some sort of . . ."

"He's your father and he wants what's best for you."

"He doesn't know the first thing about me, let alone what's best for me."

"Your father . . ." She lowered her voice to an angry whisper. "Your father is a good and honest man whose only weakness is having pride in his work and his family. You'll not speak that way about him again."

"Mother. I'm sorry, I—"

"The truth is, we've barely enough for the winter this year. Albert and Borden are going off to join the war. They want to do their part. I know you don't want to go to Fran's, but now with Miss B. . . . you could stay with her." She stitched a patch on the knee of Father's overalls. "I don't think it's much to ask, considering . . . just for a little while."

I tried to find a way out of it. "We could sell my caul. Miss B. said people offered money for it when I was born."

Mother shook her head. "That was a long time ago. No one believes in that sort of thing these days."

"But I don't want to leave home. I don't want to leave you."

She took my hands in hers. "My gram always said, *Each day brings another handful of opportunities. It's up to you to make the best of what you're given.* And that's just what you're going to do. With all the young men going off to fight in the war, who knows what will happen to them. You've got to think of a future for yourself, just in case."

Every summer, for "Mary's day," Miss B. makes a gift, a Lady Moon for each of the girls in the Bay who's turned eight in the past year. They're simple little things, rag dolls wrapped in blue dresses, stitched with crescent moons and stars, hands sewn together in prayer, bodies stuffed with dried seaweed, rose petals and lavender. Mothers, too polite to refuse them, turn their heads when their daughters leave them behind, tucked behind the headstones in the cemetery beside the church or fallen into a puddle alongside the road.

There have been few things in my life that I've called mine. Anything that was important or special disappeared soon after it came to my hands. No matter how well hidden, my dolls and their tea sets were eventually found, lined up on the fence and destroyed. Smooth beach stones flew from my brothers' slingshots, knocking my treasures into the pigpen. Father tried talking to them, but he never blamed them, never punished them for it. *That's what boys do.* This is why I set my Lady Moon free. And not just my Lady Moon, but all of the other forgotten dolls as well. Some years I've found only a single doll lying on the beach, other years there have been as many as five sweet faces crowded into a round-bottomed basket, trimmed with a torn piece of cotton for a sail. I tell them all a secret and set them afloat from Lady's Cove as the tide goes out. They bob and bounce on the waves as I send them away, hoping they'll get to a place where they'll be loved. It's for their own good.

Destiny or "just in case," it's two weeks to Christmas, and then I'll be staying with Miss B. I've come to know her enough that it shouldn't scare me, but it does. I don't know that I'll ever have her kind of wisdom, or the courage it takes to live like her—to be given such little respect, to be alone. I'm scared of what it means to take a step, any step, that's not in the direction I dreamed I'd go. But I'm seventeen, never been kissed, and there's no one in sight for love, let alone marriage, and there's nothing else to do.

9

NGELS AND SHEPHERDS, three Wise Men and a Virgin all paraded through the sanctuary, put on their play and paraded out. Aside from the trail of dung left behind by my brother Gord's pet lamb, Woolly, the Scots Bay Christmas Eve Pageant of 1916 was the same as always . . . ordinary, somewhat smelly, and more or less a success.

Just as she has for the past ten years, Aunt Fran acted as Madame Director. I had suggested that this year we put on Dickens' *A Christmas Carol* instead of the usual nativity play, but Fran scowled and argued, "The Christmas season is for celebrating the birth of Christ, not some cripple named Tom."

"It's Tim."

"What?"

"The child in *A Christmas Carol* is Tiny Tim."

"Fine. Christmas is about Christ, not crippled Tiny *Tim*. It's too late to choose a different play. We already have all the costumes, and I've chosen the music. Besides, aren't there ghosts in the Dickens play? It would be more than dreadful to frighten the small children of our community on Christmas Eve. May I assign the parts now, Dora?"

My cousin Precious made a fine but forgetful Virgin Mary. She'd open her mouth wide each time she lost her lines, waiting for Aunt Fran to clear her throat and bellow out Mary's words while crouched behind the pulpit. The stuffed bird perched in the mass of feathers on Fran's new Christmas hat seemed to peer out to the audience as she cupped her hand aside her mouth and announced, "Behold, I am the handmaid of the Laaaard." Precious-Mary would then repeat, as if she'd just remembered a forgotten item from a grocery list, "Oh yes, that's right . . . I am the hand-maid of the Lord."

The only other excitement came when Grace Hutner, leader of the chorus of angels, presented her solo. Two young shepherds stood behind her, leaning on their crooks, holding their long wool beards to their faces, trying (not quite hard enough) to hide their snorts of laughter each time she sang out the word *purity*.

As tradition holds, the narrator wasn't to be revealed until after the play ended. Aunt Fran pointed up to the choir loft and proudly announced, "This year, our own dear Reverend Covert Norton agreed to wear the star-singer crown. I'm sure you'll all agree that it was as if God himself were speaking to us from heaven."

Most of the congregation seems to enjoy the reverend, but I find his Free Will Baptist preaching overbearing and vulgar. He's got a sore, narrow-eyed look from the pulpit and is always lapping his tongue at the pocket of his left cheek. What's worse is the way he's prone to shout and spit, spray-ing hellfire and tobacco every time he shakes his fist. Aunt Fran has been generous enough to pay for him to stay through Christmas. "His boldness is just what the Bay needs. He's a man of God who speaks the truth 'til it hurts." What was supposed to be a temporary post until a new Methodist minister could arrive has gone on for nearly a year. After what I witnessed tonight, I'm afraid he'll never leave.

Halfway home, mother noticed that she had forgotten her Bible. She tried to make light of her forgetfulness by saying, "I suppose there's no safer place for it than in our dear little church," but I could tell she felt lost without it. I volunteered to go back and fetch it for her, welcoming the chance to walk alone, snow crunching under my feet, surrounded by stars and the woody-sweet smell of chimney smoke.

The main doors to the meeting house were locked, but I managed to clear the snow away from the half-door in the back of the church. When I was small, Albert warned that the tiny door facing the cemetery was a coal chute that led straight to hell. I would laugh and say, "God wouldn't put such a thing in a church!" Albert would just smile and shake his head. "Of course he would, Dorrie, that's where the reverend puts the bad children who keep their eyes open during prayer." After that I kept my eyes pinched shut, right through the sermon and on to the end of the benediction with its "*God be with you 'til we meet again.*" Perhaps Albert would be interested to know that his coal chute to Satan is merely an opening to the staircase that leads to the bell tower.

On the opposite side of the stairwell was a second door, an opening to the back of the sanctuary. As I pulled the heavy door towards me, I found that the doorway was covered with a large tapestry. The wide, purple banner embroidered with crown and cross was a recent donation by the Ladies of the White Rose Temperance Society. Candles and lamps still flickered in the sanctuary. Peering from behind the folds of cloth, I spotted two people moving in and out of the shadows of the choir loft. A woman was bent over the railing, her skirts and petticoats lifted high on her back, bouncing. Reverend Norton stood behind her, grasping her hips, shoving his half-naked body hard against hers over and over again. His voice was quiet at first, and though I couldn't catch what he was saying, it was clear he had control of the woman, leading her along with his heavy-breathed talk.

I'm familiar with the muffled sounds of my parents "stretching the ropes" of their bed. It usually starts with Father's low voice mumbling, followed by hints of Mother's laughter. It's hard to ignore the rhythm and thump of it, but somehow it comes faint to our ears and just shy of embarrassment. There in the church I had found something quite different. I knew I was trespassing on a secret.

Reverend Norton's face was determined, his voice growing loud and commanding, the words *want, come* and *give* grunting out from his mouth. For the longest time the woman was silent, and I wondered if he was forcing her to take him. Just as I had made up my mind to yell out for him to stop, the woman cried out, moaning, "Oh God, oh, oh!" Reverend Norton pressed himself tight to her, her petticoat now falling quiet around her, his face groaning and shiny with sweat.

He grinned as she turned to face him. He kissed her lips, then her cheek, and whispered something in her ear. She nodded while she tugged at her skirts and hastily pinned on a feather-laden hat . . . Aunt Fran's glass-eyed phoebe winked back at me in the candlelight.

~ *December 25, 1916*

Stockings for all, filled with saltwater taffy, peppermint sticks and an orange in each toe. Mother had sewn two new white aprons for me to wear when I'm helping Miss B. When Father wasn't looking, she handed me a well-worn edition of *A Tale of Two Cities.* "I found this in Fran's cupboard the other day. She'll never miss it."

It was a fine enough Christmas, but I haven't been able to stop thinking about last night, how I stood like a statue while they laughed and pecked at each other with no remorse. I've never thought of Reverend Norton as anything but foul, but Aunt Fran! She flitted about all Christmas evening as if nothing were wrong. I had to excuse myself halfway through dinner. Mother felt my forehead and reminded me to thank Fran for the lovely new diary and pen set she'd given me. (If she could only see what I'm writing in it!) I can't tell Precious. I shouldn't tell Miss B. I'd like to tell Mother, but I'm not certain it would do any good. And if she told Father and he told Uncle Irwin . . . that would put a stop to it. But then I think it might put a stop to everything about Aunt Fran. Uncle Irwin's a quiet man as it is, and when he's mad, he stops speaking altogether. Word of his wife's infidelity might leave him silent for at least a month, maybe three, maybe six, maybe forever, and that's the worst thing anyone could ever do to Fran. If Uncle Irwin didn't listen to her chatter, didn't notice her dress, her hair, or whatever little thing she's going on about, I think she'd just shrivel up and disappear. Maybe that's what did it in the first place. Reverend Norton's always coming for Sunday supper, always making a point of thanking Fran for her contributions to the missionary effort. He's been *seeing* her. He's noticed her so much that now she's his. "Sold to the highest bidder," as Miss B. says. If he leaves by spring, I won't tell. If not, I don't know what I'll do.

10

Tales from New Zealand

A delightful gathering was held Saturday-last at the home of the Widow Simone Bigelow in Scots Bay. Residents of the Bay included Mr. and Mrs. Irwin Jeffers and their daughter, Precious, Miss Marie Babineau and Miss Dora Rare, as well as Masters Archer and Hart Bigelow, sons of the gracious hostess. As the highlight of the evening, Professor John Payzant, brother of Mrs. Bigelow, shared tales and treasures from his days in New Zealand. He has been visiting from Halifax during the winter holidays. Special guests from Canning were the Reverend Covert Norton and Dr. and Mrs. Gilbert Thomas, who were happy to say that the weather was quite fine and the sleighing good for their visit to the Bay.

The Canning Register,
January 15, 1917

AUNT FRAN MAY HAVE married into her share of money, but the Widow Simone Bigelow is by far the wealthiest woman in the Bay, and in many ways the saddest. Descended from Marie Payzant, the

Widow Bigelow inherited the legendary Huguenot woman's poor luck in keeping husbands. Married first at fifteen, she lost Mr. James Rafuse within one month of their wedding. He fell off the roof of a neighbour's barn. Another suitor, a Mr. Samuel Huntley, was thrown from his horse on his way to the Union church only minutes before they were to be wed. At twenty, she married Captain William Bigelow. They settled down in the grandest house in the town of Parrsboro, where she soon after gave birth to a son, Hart Payzant Bigelow. Three years later, Captain William Bigelow sailed to the West Indies on the schooner *Fidelity* and never returned. As luck would have it, William Bigelow had a brother, a Captain Fitzgerald Bigelow, who was in need of a wife. At twenty-four, Simone married again. The new Captain Bigelow, however, was not about to live in his brother's house, in his brother's town, with his brother's wife, no matter how remarkable she proved to be. Since *all things being equal* was Simone's family motto, and since this marriage did not require her to change her name, she didn't feel that she should have to change her standard of living either. The day after the wedding, she locked her child and herself inside the house in Parrsboro until her new husband agreed that he would have it pulled from its foundation and sailed across the water to Scots Bay.

They were happy in the Bay. So happy, in fact, that the Captain, Simone and young Hart were soon joined by a new son, Archer Fales Bigelow. Of course, not more than a few years passed before Captain Fitzgerald Bigelow's ship, *Beautiful Dreamer,* was raided by a band of pirates and his body was left hanging from a mast. Simone Bigelow gave up on marriage after that.

She stays in her giant Cyclops of a house, all warty with Lunenburg bumps, while her son Hart spends much of every summer struggling to keep the clapboards covered in his mother's favourite colour, a gaudy rooster red. Every evening she perches herself on the balcony, standing in front of a great round window, talking to herself and looking out to sea. Some say she goes out there to cry, others say it's to curse her ancestors. Miss B. says, "That poor woman's got her share of *haints*. She knows better than anybody, if you don't talk to your ghosts from time to time, they'll make you crazy."

Although the widow would say it's her rheumatism that's brought her to know the midwife, Miss B. says otherwise. On more than one occasion she's been called over to the Bigelow place to clean it out. "Miss Simone may put on a good show at church, clutching the hymnal, singing them hymns louder than everybody, but I'm not the only one who hangs a colander over her keyhole, or keeps a needle jar in the window and a crow's wing over the door." The two women often argue over religion or how to make a decent roux, but they agree that they have no choice but to get along. "We'd lose all but the foulest words of our mother tongue, our *maman français,* if we weren't civil to each other. Our blood both come from people who suffered for God, and that make our hearts almost the same. When she needs me, I be there."

This time, Miss B.'s invitation to the dinner party seemed more for show than anything else. The widow made quite a fuss over our arrival, kissing Marie on the cheeks and starting all her sentences with *quoi qu'il en soit,* "be that as it may," her loud and pointed overuse of French brought on by her brother's visit. She can't be blamed for this of course, since it comes from what most residents of the Bay call "feelin' fussy." A person tends to get the fussies when someone visits from away, especially if it's someone like Professor Payzant, who left the Bay to live abroad, vowing to "make his mark." The person with the fussies insists on acting as if they haven't missed a thing, that they've kept a keen eye on the whole world through newspapers, or friends of friends, or letters from faraway places, or perhaps even something as exotic as a crystal ball.

Over dinner, Professor Payzant explained that he felt it was his duty to come back to the Bay to share his adventures with us. "I'm happy to do it; in fact, I consider it a calling of sorts, bringing the best parts of the world to my dear sister in Scots Bay.

"I thought long and hard about this evening's gathering. Would it be the pigmies of Papua New Guinea, the Inca of Peru, the mighty Zulu? In the end, the decision was clear: tonight you shall meet the Maoris of New Zealand!"

We retired to the parlour, where Professor Payzant brought out several artifacts from a large steamer trunk. Intricate carvings of whalebone and greenstone, spearheads and small wooden flutes, a long, sweeping cloak made from dog skin, feathers and flax. He passed around a book of photographs as he described the tribal life of the Maori. "They look quite menacing with their wild eyes and their tattooed faces, but I can assure you that it's the higher classes who have their bodies pierced and pricked in such fashion." He held up a crude tool. "A simple process, done with bone chisels and blue pigment. The more important the man, the more intricate his *moko,* or tattoo. Dare I say, the highest-ranking chiefs even have their buttocks covered. The women are more modest with their adornment, only having it on their lips and chin."

The reverend popped a pastry in his mouth, licking powdered sugar from his fingers as he stared at the photo album, glancing every so often at Aunt Fran. "What lascivious-looking creatures. They must be mad with lust over their constant nakedness."

Professor Payzant responded, "What seems sordid to some is quite natural for others. For all our differences, they were hospitable to me, taking me into their homes and even teaching me to cook food in the hot springs by dipping skin pouches into the steaming water. Quite ingenious, the Maori." He walked around the room, putting out all the lamps but one. "Now I'll tell you one of their legends.

"Te Rauparaha, chief of the Ngati Toa tribe, is perhaps one of the most famous of all the Maori chiefs. Once, while this great warrior was fleeing his enemies, a local chief assisted him by hiding him in a kumara store under the earth." Professor Payzant's voice fell to a low whisper. "Te Rauparaha sat silent in the darkness, barely wanting to breathe, waiting for his death.

"When at last the store was opened and the sun shone in, it was not the spear points of his enemies he saw, but the smiling face of the gracious and famously hairy chief! When Te Rauparaha came up from the pit and was once again standing in the sun, he performed a wild and victorious *haka*."

Professor Payzant removed his shoes and began to chant, his eyes bulging, tongue stuck out, fists beating at the sides of his head, stamping and grinding his bare white feet on the floor. Uncle Irwin was asleep, snoring in a chair in the corner of the room.

Professor Payzant motioned for the rest of us to join him as he continued to stomp his feet. "Imagine their tattooed faces." He stuck his tongue out at Widow Bigelow. "Imagine their wild eyes!" Aunt Fran, Reverend Norton, Dr. Thomas and Precious lined up next to him. They repeated the chant, stumbling over the words, Dr. Thomas scowling as he tried hard to get every gesture right, Precious, laughing and giggling. Professor Payzant instructed, "Now turn, single file, your left hand grabbing hold of the left ankle of the person in front of you, your right hand on the small of their back to steady yourself!" Reverend Norton's hand slipped, grabbing at Aunt Fran's behind. She turned and winked at him. He grinned with delight.

Instead of joining them, I chose to look further into the contents of the professor's trunk, wishing I could crawl inside and sail off to anywhere but here. Not that I don't care for the Bay, but sometimes I feel tethered to this place, by what's always been. So many of the men, my father included, have sailed away from here. They come home with globe-shaped bottles, giant seashells or sailor's valentines for their wives. And after all that, they still swear that "there's no prettier sunsets then right here in the Bay." I hope they're right, because it seems the women will always have to wait and wonder.

I picked up one of the headpieces, ran my fingers over the intricate carvings, held it to my face and breathed in its woody scent of hot sun and warm sea. Through the mask (the face of a snarling, bloodthirsty monster), I could see Miss B. sitting next to Mrs. Thomas, her eyes closed, hands stroking the woman's round belly. I couldn't hear what was being said, but I could see tears falling down Mrs. Thomas's face. Before I could put the mask away, the young mother-to-be caught sight of me. She screeched and then fainted into Miss B.'s lap. Dr. Thomas broke free from his place in line, Precious falling to the floor, Reverend Norton catching Aunt Fran in his arms.

The doctor knelt at Miss B.'s feet, giving little smacks to his wife's cheeks. "Lydia, Liddie . . . wake up, dear . . . are you alright?" He glared at Miss B. "I should have known better than to leave her side."

Mrs. Thomas's eyes fluttered as Dr. Thomas helped her to sit up. "Oh, Gilbert, don't be silly. It's my own fault. I should have taken care to wear a different dress; this one is too confining and hot. Besides, you should be thanking Miss Babineau rather than scolding her. She was giving me good news." She grinned at Miss B., then squeezed her husband's hand. "We're expecting a boy."

Dr. Thomas patted his wife's hand. "Shh now, Lydia, you should stay quiet." He held the back of his hand to her forehead. "I know you're anxious, but let's not give in to foolishness. I've told you before, there's no way to predict the sex of a fetus."

"Ain't never been wrong yet," Miss B. argued as she offered Mrs. Thomas a cup of tea.

The doctor's face grew red, his voice flustered. "Superstition and wives' tales may prove true some of the time, but they can't be trusted. Belief in such practices in today's day and age does nothing but halt the progress of science. No wonder so many of the women out here won't come to their senses."

Arms folded across his chest, eyes still closed, Uncle Irwin said, "I can't recall a time she's been wrong. Not once."

"That's all fine and good, sir, but I'm afraid that's impossible." Dr. Thomas fanned his wife with one of the feathered Maori masks. "Counting on that sort of thinking is ignorant, dangerous even."

"The danger's in forgettin' who's really in charge. Science don't know kindness. It don't know kindness from cabbage," Miss B. interrupted.

The doctor raised his voice. "Science is neither kind nor unkind, Miss Babineau. Science is exact."

"*Exact?* Exact don't do a woman no good when she's wailin' for her mama."

He pulled out a handful of coins from his pocket and dropped them in Miss B.'s lap. "Which reminds me, I owe you a little something, Miss Babineau."

She looked at him and scowled. "What's that for?"

"Mr. Laird Jessup brought his wife, Ginny, to me last week. Mrs. Jessup will be the first woman from Scots Bay to have her baby under my care."

Ginny Jessup is the most recent *woman from away* to come to the Bay, having married Laird Jessup last summer after he brought her across the Bay of Fundy from New Brunswick. She's much younger than Laird (not much older than me, I'd guess), and his second wife in five years. He lost his first wife when she ran off to Halifax with a picture frame salesman. Of course, Aunt Fran blamed it on the fact that Laird's first wife had also come from away. "You'd think he'd have learned his lesson the first time. If he'd just waited a bit longer, he might have taken Dora's hand. The man's got good land and such nice cattle. Can't ask for much more than that." Not that I would ever have married him, but Ginny's a better match by far. She speaks so soft you barely know she's there, and it's clear she'd just about throw herself in front of a wagon if she thought it would please her husband, always following after him, whispering yeses.

The Widow Bigelow reached over and put her hand around Miss B.'s clenched fists. "That's wonderful news, especially for you, Marie." She grinned at Mrs. Thomas. "I've been trying for the longest while to convince our dear Miss Babineau that it was high time she gave up nursing all those mothers and let the rest of us take care of her."

Miss B. pulled her hands away from the Widow Bigelow. "We been through this before, Simone. I ain't done 'til the good Lord shows me the way home." She held the coins out to Dr. Thomas. "And I told you, I don't take no money."

Aunt Fran interrupted. "The White Rose Society would be happy to put the money in a Mother's Fund, as you once suggested, Doctor. The women of the Bay can choose for themselves as to how they want to have their babies." Dr. Thomas handed Aunt Fran the money, and she put it in her purse, pulling the strings tight. "After seeing the maternity home for myself, I'd say it makes good sense." She gave Miss B. a sympathetic look. "After all, we won't have our dear Miss B. forever."

Miss B. scolded Aunt Fran. "Don't look at me like I was already dead and gone, Fran Jeffers. I gots help when I need it. I got Dora now, and she does just fine."

I smiled at Miss B. "Dr. Thomas, the maternity home is nice enough and all, but I do wonder about the safety in getting there. Going down North Mountain in the winter can be difficult."

"I'm glad you mentioned that, Miss Rare. Perhaps you would be willing to act as an escort for Mrs. Jessup when the time comes. You could see what goes on, even lend a hand, reassure Miss Babineau. I'd compensate you for your troubles, of course."

Miss B. answered for me. "We'll have to see about that."

Archer Bigelow was in the kitchen when I went to put another pot of tea on the stove for Mrs. Thomas. He sat there, legs lazy and wide, with one arm draped over the back of the chair. I could feel the dark of his eyes staring at my back, creeping up my spine.

Grace Hutner and the rest of the card-party girls bicker over who'll sit next to Archer at church, at pie socials, at Temperance picnics down to Lady's Cove. It's not lost on me that he's handsome, and not like a boy, but as a man who's nearly thirty. Even his work clothes cling to him like they want something, his pants folded tight in his boots, his thick wool vest buttoned neat. He stood and steadied my waist as I climbed on top of a stool to reach a bag of sugar in the cabinet. He wrapped his arms around me as I came back down, lingering long enough for me to smell pipe tobacco and pomade, ginger beer and shaving soap. I felt the warmth of his breath as he whispered in my ear, "You're lovely."

Before I could respond, Archer's brother, Hart, stomped through the doorway, leaving loose trails of snow on the kitchen floor. "Beware old Archie there, Dorrie, he's some careless with his affections." My face blushed with embarrassment as I pushed Archer aside and gave my attention to the kettle, now whistling and spitting on the stove.

My two oldest brothers, Albert and Borden, along with Hart, have long called themselves the "Holy Terrors of the Bay," always pulling pranks to make me or Mother scream. Father even calls Hart his seventh son. On my thirteenth birthday, Hart hog-tied me while Albert and Borden threatened to lower me into the pigpen. Hart was over six feet tall by the time he was twelve. He started working for Father in the shipyard shortly after. He'd been on less than a month when he caught his left hand between a rope and a pulley and lost three fingers. Miss B. tried her best to save them, but they were a ragged mess. If it weren't for that, he'd be off to the war with Albert and Borden. Instead, he's stuck in the Bay, breaking his back, watching his ten-fingered brother sweet-talk and grab all the girls.

Precious came into the kitchen. "Mrs. Bigelow wants to know if you've run into trouble."

Flustered, I answered, "Trouble?"

"With the tea?"

I set the pot, sugar and creamer on a tray and hurried out of the kitchen. "No, no trouble at all."

The rest of the night I thought of Archer, wished he would come into the room, or that I'd find some excuse to get back to the kitchen. Maybe I'd ask him to tell me what he meant, or say that I wasn't sure of what it was he had said and could he say it again? Maybe he'd come close, this time staying long enough that the smell of him would linger on my clothes, just long enough so I could go on thinking of him whenever I breathed, without having to mean to, without having to try.

By the time I got back to the kitchen, Grace Hutner was standing at the back door, pulling on Archer's arm. "Lovely night for a walk, wouldn't you agree, Dora?"

~ *January 20, 1917*

We have finished *Northanger Abbey*. Despite the meddling of Isabelle Thorpe, all has ended well. Catherine marries Henry Tilney.

Miss B. has gone on, night after night, complaining about Dr. Thomas. "*Exact* . . . How *exact* gonna do her anythin'? Ain't no *exact* way to have a baby . . . like catchin' snowflakes, she's gone before you got it figured out . . . *exact,* in all my life . . ." Most of the time she follows these rants with her thoughts on "how we gots to handle him" and why. Her constant fretting makes me wonder if maybe she'd be better off if she just gave up.

I've cleared out the loft over the kitchen. With my old feather bed, wool blankets and a quilt, it makes for cozy sleeping. I had been sharing Miss B.'s bed, but it's too small for the both of us, and if she's indulged in a nip or two, she's prone to rattle and snore. Now, with a lamp and my books (rather than hiding from Dr. Thomas), I like it up here, tucked away with strings of wrinkled apples and bundles of sage, catnip, raspberry leaves and rosehips. As in all the other nooks and crannies of her cabin, Miss B.'s got a picture of the Virgin Mary tucked away in the corner. It's pasted on top of the horsehair plaster, along with crumbling wallpaper and old sections of newspaper. I look at her each night before I sleep, my own way of praying, I suppose. There, in the flickering light of my oil lamp, the Holy Mother smiles at me, her face framed in white roses, her hands cradling a small white dove with a glowing red heart. She stares at me, looking like she knows something I don't.

Never mind what she knows. Never mind Dr. Thomas or Miss B. All I can think of is the word Archer Bigelow whispered in my ear, the word that sits in my wishes, working with the Devil to get me to believe that it might just be true. He said it. I didn't imagine it. *Lovely.*

II

PRECIOUS HAS BROUGHT a new book, Dr. A.W. Chase's *Information for Everybody,* to my attention. She smuggled it in the bottom of an egg basket and was panting with excitement by the time she reached Miss B.'s door. It's not nearly as interesting as when she brought me Aunt Fran's copy of *Sexual Secrets,* with its nine hundred pages of Dr. O. S. Fowler's commentary on the "electric currents" shared between men and women and how they are "especially regulated and deranged by sexual intercourse." Sadly, today, the topic on Precious's mind was not sexual relations, but rather a question of blood. My dear cousin is only fourteen and not yet having her courses, so the following passage put her in a panic.

> Allow me here to give a word of caution about taking cold at this period. It is very dangerous. I knew a young girl, who had not been instructed by her mother upon this subject, to be so afraid of being found with this show upon her apparel, which she did not know the meaning of, that she went to a

brook and washed herself and her clothes—took cold, and immediately went insane.

Her sweet, round face turned pale as she pointed to the words on the page. "The thought of that young girl thrashing around in a creek, shivering and mad! Can you imagine?"

I explained the menstrual processes as best I could and assured her that I would never let her go mad from bleeding or exposure. I then made her promise she'd come to me as soon as she even suspected one drop of blood. It was a difficult conversation, since her mother has never spoken a single word to her about the facts of life. Storks and faeries have more to do with Precious's idea of "where babies come from" than anything else. It won't be long before I'll have to explain that too, although I'm not sure how to go about it. The poor girl can hardly keep herself from fainting to the floor when she reads the words *blood, death* or *naked.* Aunt Fran does her no favours, always treating her like a baby. Precious never has any chores to speak of, and she gets every new thing she desires, dresses from Halifax, satin ribbons for her hair, sweets before supper. I only wish she clamoured after literature the way I do. I've now stolen nearly all the novels Miss Coffill keeps tucked away at the schoolhouse, and Aunt Fran's collection of almanacs and journals of health is outdated, no matter how entertaining they may be.

I'm surprised Precious spends any time with me at all, now that she's become one of the "proper young ladies" of the Bay. About the same time Sam Gower stopped pulling at Precious's braids and started walking her home from school, Grace Hutner invited her to her first card party.

I can't say how many more times we'll comb each other's hair, share brown bread and cream or sing the refrain, "I don't want to play in your yard; I don't like you anymore. You'll be sorry when you see me, sliding down our cellar door." Each day she becomes more and more like her name, her golden hair twirling into ringlets around my fingers, her eyes and thoughts bright with privilege. I keep more and more of my thoughts from her, knowing I can't explain why they've grown so dark. My skin's never washed as pale as hers. When I blush, it never shows. I feel dirty when I sit next to her.

When we were young, the other girls forgave Precious for staying at my side. When we were finished playing, she'd turn and run to them, explaining it away as a cousin's duty. I understood. Now I see them wanting her, the pretty-mouthed girls pulling her into their teasing and gossip. It's only gotten worse since I've been living with Miss Babineau. They bend their heads together, whispering in the back pews of the church, "The old midwife is teaching her to spin, so's she can be a witch." "I heard she's learning to tip tables and teacups." Like anything else in this world, some of it's true; most of it's not. Sooner than later, they'll make Precious choose.

She begged to stay for a cup of tea. It's not that she especially cares for Miss B., it's more as if she wanted to leave with something to tell her magpie friends . . . as if they'd dared her to sit in the rickety two-room shack of a Cajun witch and have her tea leaves read. I forgive her for it. She hasn't yet learned the difference between acting out of kindness and acting for herself. Judging by her mother's actions, I'm not sure she ever will.

"Please, Dora . . ."

I scolded her, imitating Aunt Fran. "It's not long 'til dark, dear. You know that walking in the night air causes a young lady nothing but illness and poor complexion."

Miss B., who had stayed silent until now, laughed out loud. "Get home now, Precious. Your *maman* will have your lily-white hide if she finds out you been sittin' 'round my fire."

12

Aunt Fran poked her head through the door of the cabin and called out a cheerful "Anyone home?" Miss B. invited her in and directed me to set another cup and saucer on the kitchen table. The best I could find was an old tin mug and a biscuit plate. Aunt Fran ran her fingers around the cold metal rim, her face pinched in disapproval. I forced a polite smile and exchanged my usual chintz-ware demitasse for her mismatched set.

"Why thank you, Dora. How very thoughtful of you." She lifted up the sugar bowl, looking all around, searching for a pair of tongs, no doubt thinking of the heavy silver ones that came with the sterling tea service she had inherited from Uncle Irwin's mother. I wiped my teaspoon with a clean tea towel, and placed it in the mouth of the bowl. If she couldn't bring herself to use her fingers to pick out her sugar cubes, she would have to make do with that.

Miss B. barrelled through to more practical matters. "Nice to see you knows your way to this part of the Bay, Fran." She pulled the curtain away from the kitchen window and looked out to the dooryard. "I sees you come alone too . . . didn't know you had it in you to mind a horse like that. What brings you here in such terrible cold? No one's sick, I hope?"

I thought of Father being kicked by a horse while hitching up the sleigh, Mother with a fever, one of the boys sick with measles or mumps.

Aunt Fran chuckled, blowing streams of air over the edge of her cup, steam wetting her nervous lips. "No, no, no one's sick. No bad news. Everything's fine. Just fine." She took a sip of tea from the tiny cup, pinky finger high and proud. "Actually, I'd like to speak to you alone, Marie . . . you understand, don't you, Dora? It's a *female* concern."

Miss B. tsked and shook her head. "You a female, Dora?"

I smiled. "Last time I checked."

"Well then, it concerns you too . . . don't go anywheres."

Aunt Fran tried again. "But, Marie, this is a delicate matter." Her voice fell into a hissing whisper. "It's about my *courses*."

The old woman hissed back, making light of Aunt Fran's seriousness. "What's the matter, Frannie, ain't the Redcoats a landin' on your shores no more?"

Fran picked up the teapot and poured more for each of us, trying not to shake as she did so. "I said I was fine." She offered Miss B. sugar and milk. "I was just wondering . . ." Her voice trailed off. "I was wondering if there's something to make sure they come on. The courses, I mean."

Miss B. kept at her. "What's that? I didn't hear what you said."

"It's almost time, three, maybe four days away at the most. Can you, is it possible . . . to make sure they come, on time?"

"You worried they won't come at all? What's got you doubtin' the moon? You ain't *expectin'* otherwise, are you?"

Fran sighed with frustration, digging into the pocket bag in her lap. "I'll pay you for your trouble, Marie. Do you have something or not?"

Without blinking, Miss B. snatched up the salt and sprinkled it over the table. "Put your filthy money away, Fran Jeffers." She tossed a handful of salt in Aunt Fran's face. "I gots a mind to ask you to leave, makin' such *sacrilege* at my table . . . if you think you can buy honest help, then I'd say you're best off gettin' back on your rig and goin' down to Canning to pay your Dr. Thomas a visit."

Miss B. closed her eyes, clasped her hands together and began mumbling to herself, her grey hair falling out of its topknot and down around her face, looking as old as a thousand prayers. "Perfect Mary, Mother of all, bless this house. Save this home from evil. From greed, from sin. Bless this poor, wretched woman, come to me with her pockets and heart lined with sinnin', bless her, Lady, bless this house." Aunt Fran shook her head, looking impatient and tired all at once.

I leaned towards Miss B. and whispered in her ear.

Aunt Fran sighed. "Stop telling secrets, Dora."

Pulling a strand of beads loose from around her neck, Miss B. began to finger her way through the rosary. "Hail Mary, full of Grace—"

"Marie Babineau, are you going to help me, or not?"

Aunt Fran's face was red. It wasn't a blush of embarrassment or even anger, but more from the kind of heat that rushes through your whole body when you're helpless, when you know you've done something that can't easily be made right. My aunt, who had always made everything about her life seem grand and important, now looked scared and small.

I put my hands on Miss B.'s. "Please help her."

She stopped praying and fell silent, as if she were listening for an answer. When she opened her eyes, she looked only at me. "Alright, then." She walked to the cupboard and pulled out three jars of herbs and the Willow Book. "High Tide Tea—it's all right there . . . give her enough herbs for a week's worth. That should do her fine." *Three days before her courses are due, a woman should start drinking this tea. Twice daily, at high tide. Keeps the courses regular.*

Patting the quilts on her bed, Miss B. called to Aunt Fran. "Come on now, pull down your bloomers and I'll see if I can't give you some extra help in callin' the angel down." Aunt Fran lay down, her face turned up, staring at the ceiling. Miss B. took a thin, white candle from a trunk at the end of the bed, and rubbed oil up and down the length of it. She turned and whispered to me, "Slippery elm. This'll get her goin'." Holding the candle, she made the sign of the cross over and over again above Aunt Fran's body. She pulled back her skirts and slipped the tip of the candle between Fran's legs. Aunt Fran let out a whimper. Miss B. stopped and looked at her. "You gots to let me in, Frannie. All the way to your Holy of Holies."

Aunt Fran took a deep breath. "Just be done with it."

Miss B. went on, Aunt Fran letting out a short groan. Miss B. said more prayers as she removed the candle and placed it in Aunt Fran's hands. "If not tonight, then surely by morning you gonna start to bleed, and be havin' some pains too. Nothin' too bad. Just take to your bed like you're not feelin' well. Make sure you light that candle for the next three nights. Say a prayer to Mary, thank her for her kindness, thank her for the moon, thank her for the tides. You'll be good as new." She helped Aunt Fran get her things together and sent her out the door. "Don't forget to take your tea."

Miss B. didn't say anything for the longest time after Aunt Fran left. It wasn't until after supper that she broke her silence. "What you gots to know is this . . ." Her fingers circled one of the strands of beads around her neck. "It don't matter one way or another. I ain't God. No matter how hard you try, it's always gonna be between she and Him, whoever *she* might be. I'm here to deliver women from their pain. Simple as that."

She busied herself, lighting candles and putting them all around a statue of the Virgin Mary. "Woman's got every right to look after herself. She's got every right to be scared, too. She can feel the rope gettin' tight, even if her husband or some other man don't pay no mind. If he forces his self on her, it's simple enough for me to make it right, and I can't believe that it's no accident." She tied dried herbs together in a bundle, dipped it in lavender water and shook droplets all around the cabin. "If she's the one who made the mistake . . . well, she's probably just tired. Tired of looking after herself, too tired to get after her man about it, or thinkin' she'll lose him if she does. Only the woman knows if she's got enough love to make a life. It's *love* that's gots to make the choice. No matter what anybody says, no matter how much money or fancy this and that you think she has to her name, only the heart knows what it's got to lose, one way or another. Understand?"

My Dear Dora,
I am grateful to both you and Miss Babineau for your recent
hospitality. It is my fondest wish that our pleasant visit will
stay in our memories only.

You are a dear niece and a wise young lady. Never forget
the values of loyalty and family.

Your adoring Auntie Fran

Aunt Fran was smiling and happy at church today, bringing Guernsey cream for Miss B. and extra kisses for everyone else. Miss B. ignored Fran's twittering and stared at Ginny Jessup.

What Miss B. calls her "occasional" limp, a slight dragging of her left foot led by her cockeyed hip, forced her to reach into the aisle for support. Ginny's arm just happened to be near by. "Well, look at you, Missy. Ain't that a fine, round belly you gots there."

Ginny gave a polite nod. "You alright there, Miss B.?"

Miss B. put her arm through Ginny's and patted her hand. "My bones is just tryin' to run off without me again. Other than that, I'm fine. Don't you worry about me."

Laird Jessup came up behind his wife. "Let's get you settled in the pew."

Ginny gave an apologetic look as Laird pulled her away from Miss B. "He worries over me, especially since it's getting so close and he's back logging in the woods most every day."

Miss B. nodded. "And so he should . . . so he should."

The congregation bid farewell to a small group of boys, some headed for Camp Aldershot, others to Halifax, before leaving to join the fight. I am sad to say that my brothers

Albert and Borden will be among them. Reverend Norton assured them that God would be smiling on their efforts. *William Cooke, Guy Jessup, Avery Morris, Samuel Morris, Albert Rare, Borden Rare, Byron Wallis, Tom Ketch.* "The good Christians of the world have endured far too many tragic stories these last two years. Every newspaper carries the accounts of vicious acts by a barbaric enemy. They have taken innocent lives, they have slashed the throats of nuns, they have destroyed farmlands and homes . . . and let us not forget the *Lusitania.* Our enemies have no remorse." He leaned forward, his hands grasping the edges of the pulpit. "But we can take comfort in knowing that the Almighty Lord has no patience for the wicked . . . and these fine men will see to His reckoning."

He seemed almost anxious to see them go, sending them off with prayers for their safe return, for *victory.* Victory isn't anywhere near the same as peace. Surely there are mothers, sisters and lovers in Russia and France, Belgium, England and even Germany who feel the same. Scores of men on both sides are already dead. *Glen Ells, lost at Corselette, age 19. Alfred Hiltz, lost at St. Eloi, age 26. Carey Tupper, lost at Ypres, age 38.* They will never see home again.

Most husbands and fathers in the Bay have stayed behind to take care of their families and their fields, to work in the woods, to hunt and to fish, to carry on with life the same as always. It's the younger men who will go, those without wives, those with dreams of seeing someplace far away from here, those who feel the weight of duty and guilt. After the service ended, the boys stood outside, holding their heads high and proud. Mothers, aunts, sisters and grandmothers filed past, kissing their cheeks, slipping coins in their hands, filling their pockets with wishes and prayers.

When the line ended, the card-party girls circled around, twisting their curls, pretending to ignore the flirtatious teasing of the new recruits.

Tom Ketch, whom I hadn't seen since the day his mother lost her baby, stood to the side, watching. No one had come for him, not his father, or any of his brothers or sisters, or even his mother. He'd made his way up from Deer Glen, up the long road with only the hard, bitter February winds off the Bay beside him. His arm brushed past my shoulder as he started for home.

"Dora."

"Tom?"

He said nothing else and walked away.

As I tried to hide the tears that came each time I thought of my brothers leaving home, I watched the rest of them, their parted lips and turned shoulders, coy smiles on either side, pulling one another in for a closer look. It's a sad thing to see the boys begging for kisses and letters from home, sad to think I am not one of those girls.

13

"GET UP! WE'RE GOIN' to see Miss Ginny. I got a feelin'."

We went down Three Brooks Road to Ginny Jessup's in the cold pink of morning, uninvited. Miss B. offered no gifts and made no excuses, she just pushed her way into Ginny's house and sat herself down in the parlour. She looked Ginny up and down. "Ooooh, I knew it. I knowed it last Sunday at the church." She pointed at Ginny's belly. "He's way out front there, fixin' to settle down. Get yourself flat on the couch, Miss Ginny, and let me have a feel." Miss B. closed her eyes and blew warm air into her hands, then began to feel her way around Ginny's taut belly, talking and cooing to the baby. "Sweet baby, you got to get yourself turned around. You can't be settlin' yourself so your mama sees you is a boy before she sees your pretty face." She looked up at Ginny as she continued. "See, up here, almost under your ribs . . . that's his head. And this . . ." She rubbed her hand over a round lump, low in Ginny's belly, and shook her head. "This here's his bum."

Ginny, who had willingly gone along with Miss B.'s orders, spoke, her voice quiet and scared. "That's bad?"

"It ain't good. A breech baby's just waitin' on trouble."

Ginny sat up and straightened her clothes. "Well, I'll be sure to let Dr. Thomas know of your concerns."

Miss B. took Ginny's hand. "Too late for that, unless you plan on tellin' him today. When's the last time you seen him?"

Ginny paused.

Miss B. went on. "'Cause if he don't have wits enough to notice, then I knows he don't know how to fix it."

"Early January. He said he'd come up and check on me, since I'm a little nervous to travel in the snow, but he's busy, with the maternity home and all. I'm sure he'll be up any day now, though."

"It's too late for that. If that baby gets his bum down there good, ain't no turning back. Next time you see Dr. Thomas, you can tell him we done him a little favour, see?" She smiled at Ginny. "Don't you worry, we gonna turn this child around. Just have to talk some sense what he can understand."

After a dose of Mother's Tea with pasque flower, Miss B. instructed Ginny to get down on the floor. "You gonna walk like the elephant do. Hands and feet. No knees like a baby now, hands and feet, hands and feet." It was a sight to see the old woman leading the young mother-to-be around the room, Ginny breathing heavy, moving slow and cautious between footstool and plant stand, then following the edge and fringe of a dusty hooked rug. When Ginny was too tired to keep up, Miss B. helped her right herself and get back to the sofa. "Let's sit you down."

Miss B. looked at me. "I need three things—an ironing board, a towel and a bucket of snow."

I ran back and forth, asking Ginny where to find

things, rifling through the pantry, scooping wet, slushy snow from the dooryard.

Miss B. placed the board on its end, leaning the other end against the cushions of the sofa. She rapped the board with her knuckles, as if to test its strength. "Pull your skirts up, girl . . . All aboard!" Ginny hiked her skirts up over her belly and started to straddle the contraption like she was getting on a horse. "No, no, my dear, we lay you down, head towards the ground. I'll make sure you don't gonna slip." Once Ginny was positioned with her feet above her head, Miss B. filled the centre of the towel with snow. Ginny squirmed as the midwife placed the icy towel on the ridge of her belly. "I'll hold that steady while Miss Dora has a word with the wee one."

I looked at Miss B.

"Everybody knows you come down from the girl who called the tide in. You gots songs in your blood. Besides, your voice is sweet and young like his mama's, not all woolly and broken like mine." She pulled Ginny's legs wide. "Now, rest your chin on her thigh and sing somethin' pretty."

I started in with the first song that came into my head. The only one that Precious can play on Aunt Fran's piano without making a mistake.

Waltz me around again, Willie, around,
    around, around;
The music is dreamy, it's peaches and creamy,
Oh! Don't let my feet touch the ground.
I feel like a ship on the ocean of joy,
I just want to holler out loud, "Ship Ahoy!"
Oh! Waltz me around again, Willie, around,
    around, around.

Before the end of the second verse, Ginny was giggling with excitement, the taut skin of her stomach quaking with elbows and knees. Miss B. nodded and smiled. "He wants to see the sun just as much as you want him to, only we have to show him where it shines."

Once Ginny was upright and comfortable, she thanked both Miss B. and me for our visit. "I wanted you to be the one, Miss Babineau, to catch my baby, but Laird . . . he wouldn't hear it. I know he doesn't mean anything by it . . . he says he just wants the best for me."

Miss B. stopped packing up her bag and put her hands on Ginny's belly once more. "Ten days or less I'd say. You'll have no troubles now. You're almost there."

Ginny rubbed the sides of her stomach, staring at it as if she could see the child inside. "My mother died having me. I guess Laird's worried it runs in the family. He just thought about it too long, and the next thing I knew we were down in Canning, signing the papers. You understand, don't you?"

Miss B. patted Ginny's hand. "You're gonna be fine. Dr. Thomas said to send Miss Dora down with you. She'll be right there, holdin' your hand. She knows what to do."

"I'm glad you're going with me, Dora." She looked up at me. "Laird thought too hard about that too, said no at first. He had some crazy story about your witchin' one of his cows when you were young, but I insisted and said I wouldn't go down that mountain without another woman's help, and if I couldn't have Miss B. then I'd better have you." She smiled, looking a little bit proud of herself. "At least I got him to agree on that much."

~ February 25, 1917

Canning Maternity Home
Ginny Jessup's first birth

I can tell Ginny's nervous, scared. It's her first baby, after all. *Laird worries so.*

You're a good girl, Ginny. You'll be a good mother.

Dr. Thomas says he can make it easier. He can take the pain away. Twilight Sleep, scopolamine and morphine. She won't remember a thing.

She's breathing heavy, here it comes. *Yes, yes. Make it go away.*

Count back from one hundred, relax, all will be well.

She's propped up, heels settled in the stirrups, knees falling limp to either side. The body keeps working while she's gone, quaking, twitching.

He's silent as he works down there, between Ginny's legs.

There's another woman in the delivery room. She's angry, howling every complaint she's ever had against her husband. *Bastard. Son of a bitch. Lazy. Stupid. Yellow no-account bucket-mouthed ass.*

I wonder if there's pain, even if she's not aware of it. Will it come back in a dream tonight, tomorrow? He tells me the method he's using gives him complete control. A clean slice to the tight red skin, this allows for the outlet forceps to enter without lacerations, it allows for a clean, accurate repair when all is said and done.

The other woman is groaning, weeping, asking for her mother.

Ginny's child is *extracted.* His head misshaped, a little bruised, breathing like he's exhausted and can't catch any air.

Twilight Sleep leaves them a little short of breath, nothing that a hot bath in the nursery won't cure.

The other mother is quiet now. I can hear her breathing on the other side of the curtain pulled around her bed.

Ginny's eyes open and her hand reaches out to me. The rest of her body is still, as if she's afraid to question what's just happened. There was no moment of celebration at the end. She's feeling left behind, unsure.

You're a good girl, Ginny. You'll be a wonderful mother.

The doctor sees this as normal. A kind of bliss. He's happy when he greets her and tells her everything went smoothly, splendid. A healthy baby boy. *Can you recall what happened?*

Not much. No, nothing, actually.

Good. Good.

She's weak on her feet. She can't keep food down. She thanks him for his accomplishment. She waits to hold her child.

The Just Cause
Pier 19
Halifax, Nova Scotia

February 26, 1917

Mr. and Mrs. Judah Rare
Scots Bay, Nova Scotia

Dear Family,
After arriving in Halifax, Albert and I were lucky enough to
join up with Skipper Rupert Flynn, who was fast to say,
"Never met a Rare man who wasn't a right-good sailor."
Because of our experience with schooners, he has invited us to
join the crew of The Just Cause. *Right now she looks "like a*
proper goddamn mess." (Sorry, Mother, those are the skipper's
words, not mine!) The galley's range is rusted out and held
together with bits of wire. She's missing blocks, shackles and any
good lengths of rope, but I'm sure that when we're finished with
her, she'll be a sound and worthy, three-masted topsail schooner.
Skipper says they're even set to fit her with 12-pdr guns, as she's
to be numbered as one of the "mystery ships" that are being used
to tease out the German U-boats for stealth attacks.

The crew is a challenging and crazy lot. As Flynn puts it,
"We're sailors who don't mind living on a whim and a prayer."
Perfect for us, I'd say! Albert and I will be part of the "Panic
Crew." Mostly we'll be posing as innocent fishermen and
passengers standing on deck. Our cook, George "Hefty"
Wages, who served three months on a Q ship in the North
Sea, has been known to go so far as to don a dress and hat and
cradle a sack of potatoes in his arms like a baby. When a
U-boat comes close enough to fire, we're to scramble, throw

out the lifeboats and shout, "Abandon ship, abandon ship!" If the Fritzies move in for a closer look, to see if the ship's worth looting, the second crew comes up from below, raises the White Ensign and gives them a good blasting!

Here's to a fisherman's life on The Just Cause. I suppose it beats wading through the trenches like the rest of the boys from the Bay have set off to do. With any luck, this time next month we'll be on our way to Sydney, Cape Breton Island.

Will write again soon.

Love, Borden

P.S. I am sending this letter with Fred Steele. We have been advised to keep our poking around the coast to ourselves, so Fred's been kind enough to say he'll put my scribbling in his pocket and deliver it on his way back to the Bay after working the docks in Halifax.

Miss Dora Rare
Scots Bay, Nova Scotia

March 3, 1917

Mr. Borden Rare
The Just Cause
Pier 19
Halifax, Nova Scotia

Dear Borden (and Albert too),
It sounds as if you are looking forward to life on the high seas.

Life in the Bay moves along as usual. Last I was at the house, Father was curing venison. I know he missed your help in getting the beast home, as Charlie is no match for the two of you.

Mother misses you every hour of every day. You'd think she'd feel she had a son or two to spare, but on the contrary, she thinks of both of you often, and Gord says she still calls your names through the house at suppertime. She has placed a Food Control poster in the kitchen at the Seaside Centre and stands in the foyer after church reminding the ladies to "Eat less meat, fight with food!" You would be proud of her, indeed.

I'm getting on fine at Miss B.'s, and my education in midwifing is going well. Just last week, I went with Ginny Jessup down to Dr. Thomas's. She and Laird have a baby boy.

Safe journey and wind in your sails.

Your adoring sister,
Dora, spinster midwife in training

14

REVEREND PINEO ARRIVED this week, his first sermon titled, "Forgive and Forget." I took this as a sign that I need not do anything more when it comes to Aunt Fran's indiscretions with the now absent Reverend Norton.

Archer Bigelow came in late for Sunday service. There's room at the end of our pew now that Albert and Borden are away, so he sat next to me. I swear I heard several girls catch their breath as we stood for the hymn, Archer's shoulder touching mine, his hands holding the hymnal steady between us. I felt as though the entire congregation was staring at me during the fellowship greeting. As I turned and reached over the back of the pew to take Grace Hutner's hand, my polite gesture was met with sharp fingernails digging into my palm. All the while, she smiled sweetly, "Greetings in Christ, Dora." I managed a painful reply. "Greetings in Christ, Grace."

After church was over, Precious scampered through the meeting house, handing out invitations for her upcoming card party.

The Queen of Hearts is baking tarts,
and I'm as giddy as an old March Hare!
I should be so pleased if you would dine with me
Friday, March 9, at half past seven
Mad Hatter tea and card party to follow
Yours sincerely,
Miss Precious Jeffers

Hart came up to Archer and plucked the envelope from his hands. "A little old for tea parties, aren't we, brother?"

Archer grabbed the invitation and shoved it in his breast pocket. "Speak for yourself, brother."

Hart snorted and shook his head. "You should be up to your knees in mud at Ypres instead of playing hearts with little girls."

Archer replied with loose laughter in his voice. "At least I can hold my cards in one hand and a girl in the other."

I've never seen brothers more different than those two, or more at odds. My brothers argue, but not over anything that matters—who gets the last of the mashed potatoes, who has to feed the cows this week, who forgot to shut the barn door. Sooner than not, they lose sight of their bickering and get back to their usual jabber and jokes. If it ever came right down to it, I've no doubt they'd defend one another life and limb. Archer must not think about how easy it would be for his brother to beat him senseless or he wouldn't come back with such nasty responses. He has charm, but Hart's easily got twenty more pounds and a half foot of height on him, neither of which care much about a winning smile or quick wit. I tried my best to think of something clever to say to keep them from arguing, but

Grace Hutner stole the chance, her eyes knowing and bright as she snugged the knot of Archer's tie up to the top of his collar.

"Archer's got no choice in the matter. He's by far the best partner I've ever had . . . I couldn't possibly play a single hand without him."

Hart sulked away, and Archer's attention turned towards Grace. She continued on, her voice lilting, swinging up and down with giggles and sighs, her body leaning into his, pulling at his sleeve, owning him.

I dreaded going to Precious's party. I even found myself wishing that Miss B. might have a *feelin'* come on, or that Ginny Jessup's baby might catch a little cold, so I could decline the invitation. When the evening arrived, Charlie came with the sleigh and Miss B. pushed me out the door.

Precious already had pairings in mind, directing us after dinner to our places at the card tables set up in the parlour. I had hoped I could keep Charlie as my partner. We make a feisty brother–sister match when it comes to partnership hearts, whist or 120's. Unfortunately, Precious placed him with Anna Rogers, who was more than happy to follow his lead.

Table one, Precious and Sam Gower, Anna and Charlie. Table two, Florence Jessup and Esther Pineo, Clara and Irene Newcomb. Table three, Grace Hutner with Archer Bigelow, and me with Oscar Foley. Everything about Oscar is round and slow, his eyes, his face, his body, his wit. Losing is a painful and tortuous affair with Oscar as a partner. He's never quite sure who has won or lost until someone announces it to him.

After four miserable rounds, Archer suggested we switch partners. "For variety and friendship." Oscar agreed, I agreed, and Grace, after forcing a cheerful grin, agreed. Archer and I made an interesting pair, my quiet, unassuming face never balking at his loud exclamations every time he picked up a new card. What an actor he is! There aren't enough spades in three decks of cards to bring on all that moaning. Poor Grace tried her best to direct Oscar through the game, but without success. When it was time to switch tables, Archer took my arm and escorted me towards Charlie and Anna. Grace stomped upstairs to pout.

A good hour must have passed before I realized that our table was the only foursome still playing. The other girls had gathered near the fireplace, circled in serious conversation. Grace broke from the group and approached Archer, flourishing a large white ostrich plume that must have come from one of Aunt Fran's hatboxes. "As President of the Scots Bay Chapter of the White Feather Brigade, I present this token to you, for your undying dedication to being a traitor, a menace and a coward. May all the starving orphans of Europe curse your name."

I'd read newspaper accounts of men being heckled and "feathered" by young women in the streets of London, but never thought such rudeness would happen here in the Bay. Not much had been said about the men who had chosen to stay home, as most people feel that many of them have good reason. Not long after Albert and Borden left, Father mentioned Archer's name, wondering why he hadn't signed on. Mother, who always tries her best to see the good in others, said that maybe the Widow Bigelow had asked him not to go, that she couldn't bear to see another man taken from her life, or that perhaps Archer didn't want to make

Hart feel poorly, or that their mother needed both of them to look after her big house. The longer she went on, the more Father was inclined to say that her reasons made no sense. She ended it by saying. "Talking ill of Archer Bigelow won't bring our boys home any sooner."

Archer took Grace's actions for a joke, tucking the feather through the buttonhole of his shirt and puffing up his chest. "As the only member of the Scots Bay Order Against Young and Tragic Deaths, I accept this honour and will wear it proudly."

Outraged, Grace pulled Precious next to her and pointed at the door. "I think I speak for all the young ladies in this room when I say that you are truly not a man, but a snake and a coward. You are not welcome here."

I couldn't hold my tongue. "You don't speak for me."

Precious was frantic. "Dora, how could you?"

I continued, "You have no right to question his decision not to go to war."

Grace was fuming. "If I could, I'd march through Europe myself, killing Huns right and left, gutting them with a bayonet and crushing their skulls with the heel of my boot. But I can't, and neither can any other woman who might wish for victory over evil . . . and neither can these boys who are too young to serve their king." She glared at Archer. "But you can."

I interrupted her again. "What about wishing for peace? Isn't Archer entitled to that?"

She spat back at me. "You can wish for peace and still fight in the war."

I glared at her. "Can you?"

Archer stood up. "Ladies, I'd love to stay and debate the vices and virtues of war, but it seems my time has come.

Miss Rare, would you be so kind as to help me find my way home?"

Precious stood in the doorway, whimpering about ruined foursomes and leftover tarts. Grace and the other girls consoled her. They were on to a game of charades before we got out the door.

I've never been afraid to talk to boys. Growing up with so many brothers, I always felt my thoughts could stand on their own (much to Father's concern), that because we had all grown up together in the Bay, we were on equal footing. I've no skill at playing foolish like Grace, no moneyed fairness like Precious, and therefore no reason to keep my mouth shut. But as Archer and I walked down the empty road, led by the near-full moon, I fell silent, aware of everything I might say, but couldn't. Older than Albert and Borden by far, he's never seemed the least bit boyish to me. He's been clean-shaven and clever for as long as I can remember, and he's the only person who could make me feel I'd nothing to say.

Sometimes I think that if I lived in another town, if I had no brothers, or if I ran away to a city like Toronto or Boston or even New York, I'd have been bought and paid for by now. It's no secret that men in big places have a serious affection for the unknown. But here, where life is small and thoughts are even smaller, they stare at my face and the darkness of my hair, my skin. They stare and stare but never touch.

He said he didn't want to go home. I didn't want to curl up in my loft at Miss B.'s alone, so I led him to the only place I knew that was empty and out of the cold, through the tiny bell tower door, down the aisle of the sanctuary and up to the choir loft. We huddled together in the last pew, sharing sips of rum from a battered old flask, talking and laughing.

"I always thought you were a good little teetotalling girl, Dora."

"And I always thought you were too good to talk to the likes of me."

He took a long drink and wiped his mouth with the end of his scarf. "You know why women are so keen on their almighty temperance societies and this war?"

I shook my dizzy head, thinking that anything he had to say would prove to be important.

"Because it gives 'em an excuse to scold their husbands in public!" He offered me the flask. "Think on it, Dora, it's the only time women have been given the right to call themselves superior to men. And what's more, they can get on their high horses and say that God's backing them on it." He stared at me, his face serious and sad. "Do you suppose all the poor and homeless children of the world were put that way because of drunk and cowardly men like me?"

I stared back into his eyes. "There's nothing cowardly in being a pacifist. It's perfectly fine to call yourself a conscientious objector."

He took the large feather from his lapel and leaned towards me, stroking it under my chin. "Alright, then. Dora Rare, will you kiss this conscientious objector?"

In our little church, dark and holy, his breath heavy with salty-sweet rum, he kissed me. Before long, he was pulling me into his lap, tugging apart the buttons of my blouse, his cold hands on my breasts. I straddled my legs around him, giving in to him, rubbing my body against his, hoping that he might always choose me instead of Grace Hutner. *Choose me. Choose this lonely girl who's never been touched. Choose me, and all the things I've kept to myself, in the dark of my bed, are yours.* I felt my way to his pants as he helped me slip the end of his belt out of its buckle.

"That was my first kiss, you know."

He took my hands and pulled them away, then started fastening up the buttons at the top of my blouse. My fingers followed behind his, undoing his work. I began kissing him again, guiding his hands back to my breasts. "Don't stop, please."

He buckled his pants and scolded me. "Never beg, Dora. Patience never begs."

I tried to kiss him again, but he wouldn't have it. He pushed me away and left without another word.

~ March 11, 1917

This is what Precious's stolen copy of *Sexual Science* has to say about matters between men and women.

> Electricity is undoubtedly the instrumentality and measure of all life, action and enjoyment, and originates that galvanic action which establishes it. The male is positive and the female negative, and like two oppositely charged galvanic batteries coming in contact, their sexual conjunction restores an equilibrium by each imparting and receiving his and her magnetism.

A woman needs to see the weakness of a man before she can love him. This is how it happens in novels, anyway. It isn't that Archer, or any man, is truly beautiful. Not like the sad last fiddle tune at a dance, or the scent of roses through an open window. No, the attraction lies in finding the flaw, seeing it set right next to his confident swagger. Maybe that's what all the girls love about Archer: his talent for telling lies and having them sound like the truest thing ever said. Until he pushed me away, he had me believing I was his only weakness. I guess when the rum wore off, Archer Bigelow realized not every girl's worth taking home from the party. If he only knew how well versed I've become at practising patience.

To the
YOUNG WOMEN OF CANADA

Is your "Best Boy" wearing Khaki?
If not, don't YOU THINK he should be?

If he does not think
you and your country are worth fighting for,
Do you think he is WORTHY of you?

Don't pity the girl who is alone –
her young man is probably a soldier,
fighting for her and her country –
and for YOU.

If your young man neglects his duty to his
King and Country, the time may come when
he will NEGLECT YOU.

Think it over – then ask him to

JOIN THE ARMY TODAY

Miss Dora Rare
Scots Bay, Nova Scotia

March 20, 1917

Pvt. Thos. Ketch
B. Co. 112 Bn West NSR
CEF Overseas

Dear Tom,
*I don't know if this letter will reach you, but if it does, I hope
that it finds you well. Reverend Pineo has encouraged all of
the girls in the Bay to send out a letter to at least one young
man outside of our families who is fighting in the war.
Although I don't know what I might say by way of encouragement, I chose you.*

*Your mother and sisters must miss you, I'm sure. Even
though my brothers have sent a letter, telling us not to worry,
I miss them. Before he left, Borden said, "If I die, at least I'll
have died a hero." I suppose he's right. But I have to wonder
which is the greater death, dying a hero in a war that you
didn't start, or staying here, going on as if the other side of the
world doesn't exist.*

*I'm afraid that while I'm all for the boys from the Bay, I
am not for the war. If you wrote back with the usual argu-
ments, I wouldn't hear them. I am decidedly a pacifist in the
camp of Julia Grace Wales or Sylvia Pankhurst, although I'm
not brave enough to do anything but keep my thoughts to
myself. Can you imagine if I dressed in white and wore a
"Women's Peace Army" banner to the Scots Bay Union
Church? (I hope this thought makes you laugh.) Sometimes I
think that if I had any skills at all I would run away and join*

with these fine women as they picket in the streets of London or New York.

Instead I am here, learning to be a midwife, expecting never to see you again. Not that I think you will die . . . it's more that I'm hoping that, when it's over, you'll see something better over there, you'll find something that's yours and never look back.

Why I'm saying all this I don't know, but the thought of my words reaching you somewhere across a wide blue ocean is enough to make them real and worth so much more than if I had shared them with anyone else.

God bless you, Tom,
Dora

"I ask myself, is it just a wild flight of imagination to conceive of a world without war . . . but someone must try . . ."

Julia Grace Wales

15

*The Ladies of the White Rose Temperance Society
Cordially invite you to attend an afternoon
of Tea and conversation
Sunday, April 15, 1917
2 p.m.
Seaside Centre
Please join us in welcoming our honoured guest,
Dr. Gilbert Thomas, doctor of obstetrics
of the Canning Maternity Home*

*Dr. Thomas will be sharing his thoughts on
Keeping Our Babies Safe*

AUNT FRAN HAD BUILT a fire in the kitchen
stove at the Seaside Centre that morning, for tea,
of course. "What kind of secretary of the White
Rose Temperance Society would I be if there wasn't any
tea? No proper ladies' social is held without it." She hadn't

thought about it being the middle of April, hadn't remembered that the afternoon sun comes streaming into the
meeting room, bright and hot off the Bay. "Last year we had
snow on the ground until May. How was I to know?"

She bristled as Bertine Tupper, Sadie Loomer and
Mabel Thorpe arrived, none of them wearing hats, their
dresses bearing stains and signs of small children and
Sunday lunch. Fran mouthed to Mrs. Trude Hutner, *Women
from away.* Bertine complained about the heat as soon as she
walked through the door, her wide, round cheeks flushing
red, her eyes fluttering in a false swoon. "Some hot in here,
I'd say." She went back outside and returned a moment
later, wrestling a large stone in front of the door to hold it
open. Sadie, her small body now showing with a pregnant
belly, waddled around the room, tugging open any window
that wasn't stuck shut.

"Seems someone thinks it's still winter, eh, Dora?"
Mabel came to me, her voice singsong and soft as she
rocked her baby girl, Violet, in her arms. "Look here, Vi.
Say hello to the girl that first caught you."

I made a wide smile at the baby. "Hello, Miss Violet."

Aunt Fran scowled as the pages of her songbook fluttered out of place. The Widow Bigelow, Madame President
and founder of the White Rose Temperance Society of
Scots Bay, waited until Bertine and Sadie had settled in their
seats to explain, "Oh dear, you know I'm prone to chills
when there's a draft. After my terrible bout with rheumatism this past winter, well, I'm just afraid, you understand,
ladies? Fran, if you'd be so kind . . ." Fran hurried around the
room, muttering to herself about "those women thinking
they can," "come from a God-forsaken climate," "what with
their Newfoundland blood and all," as she closed the place

up tight. Miss B. and Bertine sat on either side of me, their knitting needles clacking as they talked.

We sat like roasting hens in flowered cotton dresses, clucking and pecking at tea biscuits, twenty women circled together, suffering through the heat and the sweet-sick smell of face powder and rosewater. After a few minutes of business and Aunt Fran leading all four verses of "'Twas Rum That Spoiled My Boy," she introduced Dr. Thomas. "We are so very pleased to have Dr. Gilbert Thomas with us. It's a great honour to host such an upstanding citizen of Kings County."

Dr. Thomas greeted Aunt Fran and changed places with her behind the crooked old music stand. "Thank you, Mrs. Jeffers, and thank you, ladies." He pulled at the top of the stand, turning it round and round until it matched his height. "I've come here today with a message of great importance. The women of Scots Bay and women all across rural Canada are paying the debt of ignorance. Your children are being neglected in the womb and born in the poorest of conditions." The doctor looked past the glasses perched on the end of his nose, perspiration rolling down the sides of his face. "Your children deserve better. You deserve better."

Aunt Fran fished through the cabinet over the piano and tugged out a large basket of hand fans. Hidden away behind songbooks and leftover programs, the fans are rarely, if ever, used. When she ordered them years ago, Fran must have argued that "they would be the perfect thing in a pinch, for an afternoon tea, an evening temperance meeting, perhaps a wedding reception." She handles them as if they were priceless relics, tsking softly at the image pictured on them, the yellowing face of Frances E.

Willard, 1839–1898. *God rest the good woman's soul, the founding mother of temperance.* The foggy image of Miss Willard, her proper-pinned bun, her buttoned lace collar, flickered and jittered in our hands. Her words cooled our sweaty necks and our moist breasts as they blurred past our heat-weary faces. *It will be like dynamite under the saloon if, just where he is, the minister will begin active work against it; if just where he is, the teacher will instruct his pupils; if just where he is, the voter will dedicate his ballot to this movement.*

Dr. Thomas continued, "I am gravely concerned and convinced that the women of this community are not getting adequate health care. This is indeed a crime. Why should you ladies continue to suffer, most notably the trials of childbirth, when there are safe, modern alternatives available to you? You should seek out the best care you can afford as soon as you suspect you are in the family way. You should count yourselves fortunate to have a fine institution like the Canning Maternity Home so close at hand." He glanced at a note in his hand, adding, "A clean, modern facility."

Cradling baby Violet in her arms, Mabel spoke. "Pardon me, Dr. Thomas, but we already have a midwife right here in the Bay." She smiled at Miss B. "Miss Babineau seems to do just fine."

Bertine nodded in agreement. "Why should we go all the way to Canning to have our babies?" She reached over and placed a hand on Sadie's pregnant, round belly. "Especially a woman who's had two or three already, like Sadie here . . . I can't imagine that she'd make it down the mountain before the baby arrived." Bertine's voice is strong and loud, and if you didn't know better you might think she was an angry woman, prone to argument and meanness. Really it's nothing more than habit, since she's always having to shout to her husband, Hardy, over the pounding of his blacksmith hammer and the constant ringing in his ears.

Dr. Thomas ran a handkerchief across his wide brow and along the back of his neck. A pinched smile accompanied his words. "Ladies, I understand your concerns. Let me assure you that if you were in a situation where you needed a doctor to come to you, I would do my best to get here."

Bertine moved to the edge of her chair, her cheeks pinking to red from the overheated room, her foot lightly tapping at the floor. "By the time you got word and got yourself up the mountain and around to the Bay, you'd be lucky to get here in time to catch the baby."

Mabel raised her hand. "Miss Babineau and Dora Rare brought my last child into the world and never asked for a thing. People give Miss B. what they can . . . potatoes, apples, firewood, butter and eggs, a little money if they have it." She stuck her pinky in the baby's mouth to quiet its fussing. "Are you willing to do that?"

Aunt Fran shook her head and rolled her eyes at Trude Hutner.

Dr. Thomas's face fell into a concerned pout. "Please, ladies, let's not be so quick to place judgements." He cleared his throat as Bertine settled back in her seat. "In this day and age, a doctor's care should be the rule, not the exception. The Farmer's Assurance program allows for just that, and I'm pleased to announce that your own Mrs. Francine Jeffers has graciously agreed to start a fund for young mothers who may not have the means to pay into the program." He walked over to Bertine and Sadie. "I'm presenting you with a recipe for healthy babies and happy homes. If I gave you the recipe for the world's best chocolate cake, wouldn't you want to share it with all your friends and relatives?"

Soft whispers from the rest of the women stuttered over the edges of their cabbage rose teacups.

"Most homes, even the nicest, cleanest of homes, do not meet today's medical standards for childbirth, and as caring as Miss Babineau is, there's proper training to be considered. The laws of science and of this country no longer allow for guessing. We must leave nothing to chance. The training program for obstetricians is rigorous and complete. I'm sure you would agree that knowledge is essential, wouldn't you, Miss Babineau . . . wouldn't you, ladies?"

The Widow Bigelow started nodding, then Aunt Fran and the rest of the ladies, their heads wobbling in silent, unthinking agreement. Medical training, scientific method, modern knowledge . . . these things have never been part of their daily lives, they have no use for them . . . but heaven forbid they show it. Some even turned their heads in an effort to avoid Miss Babineau's eyes, their chins dipping downward with the weight of their implied ignorance. Mother had said she would try to attend but hadn't made it. She must have gotten caught up with the boys at home. *I'm all finished having babies, Dora. What would they need me there for, anyway?* I'm glad she wasn't there to see her sister and the others trying so hard to please, giving away their pride, their sense, as if they had some reason to be ashamed.

Miss B., who had sat silent until now, spoke. "Where was you born, Dr. Thomas?"

"In Kentville."

"No, I mean *where* was you born? *Exactly.*"

"I believe I was born in my parents' home, but—"

"Yes, indeed. I'm sure you was, and every woman here was born in someone's home, whether it be their child-hood home, their aunt's, their neighbour's or whatever. I'm always here when they need me, and I'm not asking them to go any farther than my dooryard. I don't ask them to risk their lives on washed-out or snow-drifted roads. I don't ask the impossible. And I don't *never* ask them to wait . . ."

"That's all fine and good, Miss Babineau, but I should think you'd be relieved to have a doctor willing to take on this tiresome responsibility for your community . . ." Dr. Thomas moved close to Mabel, staring at her baby as if he were looking to find something wrong with her. "You are a lucky woman to have such a healthy, dear child."

Mabel stared back at him. "I couldn't have done it without Miss B. and Dora. No offence, but I don't think any doctor could have done better."

Dr. Thomas raised his eyebrows. "Was it a painful birth?"

Mabel smiled at me. "It was a wonderful day. Miss B. made me as comfortable as possible."

"So you did experience pain, then?"

"Well, yes, but isn't there always pain in childbirth?"

Dr. Thomas walked back behind the music stand. "I suppose there's pain for those who limit their care by choosing the assistance of a midwife over a trained physician. Home remedies and wives' tales only go so far. As a responsible doctor, I can promise you the finest care and a pain-free birth. These days, women all across North America and Europe are having their babies with little or no pain. Why should you allow yourselves anything less?"

The women gasped their approval, practically choking on inhaled yeses and disbelief.

"The latest methods of obstetrics—chloroform, ether, chloral, opium, morphine, the use of forceps—these things can make birthing the joyful experience it was meant to be. I can even administer Twilight Sleep if desired."

Bertine gave a puzzled look. "Twilight Sleep?"

"Twilight Sleep allows the mother to fall into peaceful rest while her muscles continue to do the work. The doctor delivers the baby, and the mother wakes feeling rested, with no memory of hardship or pain."

Mrs. Hutner fanned herself with vigour. "I wish I'd had Twilight Sleep! If some doctor could have kept me from the two days of agony I had lying in with my daughter, I'd have given him the family farm and Gracie along with it." The women chuckled and laughed.

Ginny Jessup had come in late. She was sitting at the back of the room, her new baby in her lap. Dr. Thomas walked to her and put his hand on her shoulder. "Mrs. Jessup benefited greatly from Twilight Sleep." He smiled down at the tiny infant in her lap. "What was your first birthing like, Mrs. Jessup?"

Ginny gave a shy, awkward answer. "I wouldn't know."

"You can't remember any of it? The pain and suffering, the exhaustive hours of waiting?"

"No, sir. I cannot."

He grinned. "And that's how it should be for every woman."

I interrupted. "I'm sure one thing Mrs. Jessup won't forget is how much she's had to pay for her *forgetting*. I'm afraid most of the women in our community can't afford to employ that kind of expertise, even after giving up their fattest hog or their best milking cow."

Aunt Fran scolded me. "Dora, you've no right to talk to the doctor like that. If you speak out of turn again, I'll have to ask you to leave."

Bertine's foot began to tap again. "She's just having her say, and I for one don't mind hearing it."

Dr. Thomas went on, his voice even and calm. "Children are innocent, perfect beings. We should do whatever it takes to keep them safe, regardless of the cost. Even the law says so . . . the Criminal Code of 1892 states, 'Failing to obtain reasonable assistance during childbirth is a crime.'" He looked at me with concern. "You wouldn't want to drag all of these upstanding ladies to prison with you, would you, Miss Rare?"

"No, but I don't think the women here fully understand—"

"It seems to me—" Mrs. Trude Hutner cleared her throat and started again. "It seems to me that what the kind doctor is trying to say is—it's high time we put our backwoods thinking to rest. I'm sorry, Miss B., I know you mean well, but don't you think it's time you stepped aside and let the doctor do what he's trained to do?"

The Widow Bigelow agreed. "I've been trying to tell her—"

Other voices joined in from around the room. *"It's for the best."*

"Should've given it up years ago."

"How old do you suppose she is?"

"Now that there's a doctor nearby."

"She should."

"She should."

"She should."

"Yes, she should."

Bertine's foot was now stomping on the floor. Miss B.'s needles were flying as she whispered a little prayer. "Dear Mary and sweet baby Jesus, bless us all."

Raising his voice, Dr. Thomas continued, trying his best to keep his words from stuttering. "I'm afraid, no matter how hard we might wish it weren't so, the law no longer considers a country midwife's care to be 'reasonable assistance.' It's only a matter of time before anyone who insists on taking up the practice of obstetrics without proper authority will be held accountable by a higher court than common opinion. It's only a matter of time before something dreadful happens."

Miss B. rose from her seat, standing as straight and tall as she could. "Strappin' ladies down and tyin' 'em up like hogs to have their babies, now that's dreadful!"

Aunt Fran, whose social sensibility won't tolerate an argument, reached for the gavel that was always present at these meetings but never used. Her face flushed red as she gripped the handle. "Thank you, Miss Babineau. Please be seated." Fran gave a thankful sigh as Miss B. returned to her seat. Placing the gavel back on the table, she announced, "We'll be singing our closing hymn from *Triumphant Songs,* number one-eleven, 'Send Me a Lifeboat,' all three verses." She sat on the piano stool and started pumping her feet, the harmonium wheezing as she began to sing.

~ *April 15, 1917*

Miss B. came home and went right to bed—without complaining about Dr. Thomas, without having her afternoon tea, without saying her prayers. It seems a line has been drawn in this little place between the women who know what's important and the women who don't but pretend that they do.

16

NOT LONG AFTER (or perhaps because of) the mess at the White Rose meeting, the Widow Bigelow invited Miss B. and me for Saturday tea. I was surprised to find Mother leaving as we arrived, the widow calling after her, "I'm sure we'll have much more to talk about in the days to come!"

Mother gave a cheerful wave to the widow and called back to me, "Sorry to miss you, dear, but I'd best get back to my work at home."

Once the widow and Miss B. were settled in the parlour, I went to the kitchen to make the tea and set out a plate of biscuits. My understanding of French may be poor, but I was certain I heard my name mentioned several times throughout their conversation, the widow's voice sounding earnest, Miss B.'s attitude growing sour. To make matters worse, Archer wasn't home the entire visit. I hadn't expected him to be there, but I had hoped.

Although he hasn't asked to see me outside of church or called on me at Miss B.'s, Archer has become a permanent visitor in my family's pew. After Precious's party, he replaced Grace's spiteful ostrich plume with a simple white dove's feather pinned to his lapel. He wears it with a smirk and pride everywhere he goes, even to Sunday services. Grace and her court of card-party maids hiss and spit at him as he makes his way through the sanctuary. (This is likely the true reason he sits next to me.) Quite simply, unless he wants to sit next to his doting, chatty mother, he has no place else to go. I have warned him that he should be careful not to flaunt his political sentiments. While Grace may be fairly harmless in her taunting, others, like Father and the rest of the men in the Bay, may find his actions offensive.

Instead of Archer, it was Hart who came grumbling into the kitchen, smelling of turned earth and sweat, the legs of his overalls covered in dirt and sawdust, his filthy, chapped knuckles grabbing at the biscuits.

I slapped his hand away from the plate. "Those are for your mother and Miss B."

He laughed as he held my wrists together with his good hand and pinched up three biscuits with the scarred, knobby fingers of his other hand. "Aren't we a proper little Mrs. Bigelow?"

Miss B. came storming into the kitchen. "We're leaving."

I pulled away from Hart. "But you haven't had your tea . . ."

Miss B. grumbled, already halfway out the door. "I got no patience left for that woman."

During the walk home, Miss B. carried on, mumbling and swearing in French. Thinking that Mrs. Bigelow may have tried to use her influence as the president of the White Rose Society, I asked, "Did she tell you to give it up? Being a midwife?"

"No, that ain't it. She knows that's gonna happen all on its own, sooner than later." She went back to cursing under her breath. "Who does she think she is? Talkin' 'bout my girl like that."

"I thought I overheard my name back there. Did I do something to upset Widow Bigelow? Is that why you're so angry?"

"No, no . . . *you* done nothin' wrong. That's the thing, see?"

"I don't understand."

"Maybe you better go by your mama's house for some answers. She knows more about this than me."

Mother had acted strange at dinner last Sunday. While spooning out the boiled dinner, she began asking all sorts of questions about Archer. Did I find him to be a nice fellow? Did I think we should invite him to Sunday dinner? Did Charlie find him to be a hard worker, a loyal companion, a fair sport?

Charlie responded, laughing and spitting over his plate. "He's some *quick,* that's for sure."

Mother's brow wrinkled and narrowed. "What do you mean?"

He mumbled, his mouth full of food. "When you're fast with your words, you have to be fast on your feet." He swallowed, adding, "I've heard he's fast with his hands too. Isn't that right, Dorrie?"

I blushed as I tried to ignore his comments.

Mother didn't let it go. "Dora?"

"I suppose." I kicked Charlie's shin under the table. "At least as far as playing cards goes . . . yes, he's very quick-witted."

What Mother had to say

"This isn't the way you were supposed to find out. I wanted Archer to be the one to tell you. The Widow Bigelow is wanting, is *hoping* for you and Archer to be wed. In expressing her wishes for her son, she has made a generous offer. If your father will find a spot on Grampy Rare's land, she will pay for him to build you a house. She will pay for it all, Dora. The windows, the shingles, the timber, as well as everything in it. All the finest draperies, linens, china . . ."

"And you agreed?"

"Yes."

"But Archer hardly knows me. I don't think he even cares for me, not like he does most other girls. Are you sure you heard right? If the Widow Bigelow wants to see anyone married, it's Hart. She carries on after him all the time, reminding him that he's well past thirty and still acting like a boy, asking him when he's going to settle down. He can't go off to the war, and most girls won't look twice at him with his hand the way it is . . . you know what a mean tease he can be . . . maybe he was tired of her nagging and said, 'Careful, Mother, or I'll leave you and marry Dora Rare,' and she thought he meant it. Besides, what about all the things you said to get me to leave home? What about 'the peace and quiet of not having a husband too soon'? Who will look after Miss B.?"

"I said those things before I knew. I never thought . . ."

She never thought I'd get married, at least not until some old broken-toothed widower came over in a skiff from Advocate or Parrsboro, looking to take some new blood back to his village. That's how Sadie Loomer got here. Wes didn't have anybody but his cousins who'd marry him, so when he heard the news that Hardy Tupper had gotten himself a wife from Newfoundland, he set sail the next day and came back a month later with Sadie.

What Miss B. had to say

"It's not that I take to feelin' sore for myself. I can get along without you if I has to . . . but she thinks she got the rights t'buy you for her son, that's what's wrong with it. And I'll tell you the truth, you should know it's 'cause you a good girl, you a pure girl. What got me goin' was when she asked me if I could *check on you, just to be sure* . . . like I'd need to sneak up on you in your sleep and feel for it. It's plain to me you ain't been run around, and don't tell me you have: I see you blushin', I see you bitin' your lip when he sits too close in the pew, he ain't had you. But that's the ugly thing of it, see? It's an old thought, what comes from the word of the Lord all turned wrong . . . that somehow a girl's sweetness can make up for all the sour in a man. And I'm shakin' my head over your mother. Not askin' you before. You're a woman now, and a woman has rights to her own person, or at least she should nowadays. But if you love him, or you think you could, now that's another thing . . ."

What Archer had to say

"Oh, that?" He was holding his hat in his hands, one eye fat and circled with purple, green and black. "My dear brother lost control of his fist again. Nothing new there."

We sat at Lady's Cove, the warmth of the day still held in the rocks, the tide lapping its way out from the shore, the sunset turning everything to gold. Archer's voice turned quiet and sincere. "I suppose by now you know what my mother wants. I'm sorry for that. She gets it in her head what she thinks is best and expects that everyone else will agree."

"I figured there must have been a misunderstanding. Do you agree with it? Because you don't have to, I mean, we don't have to . . . I'd understand if you didn't want . . ."

"What do *you* want, Dora?"

"I don't know."

He took my hand. "I feel like I've been waiting all my life to get started, to find the right girl, to make a life. I don't want to spend the rest of my days painting my mother's house, wondering why I don't care about the price of a barrel of herring. Mother's got money set aside for me, for us. I'll take dear old Captain Bigelow's gold and invest it in the railroad, or automobiles, or maybe the electric company down in the Annapolis Valley." He leaned his face close to mine. "Haven't you ever thought you might like something more? More of the finer things, more from life, all the things no one ever expected you'd have, not even you? Because that's what's waiting for you." Kissing me between his words, he asked again, "What do you want?"

"Love."

He whispered in my ear, "Love takes care of herself. Love does what she wants."

What I have to say

No one's ever asked me what I wanted, not for Christmas, or birthdays, or for any reason at all. It never bothered me. I knew that whatever it was, no matter how small, it probably couldn't be gotten, at least not without making hardship for someone I loved. So today, when someone finally asked, his lips begging against mine for an answer, I said the first word in my mind, a thing that costs nothing and everything to give.

Archer's affection and feelings are as romantic as can be for this place, I'd guess. I can spend my time wishing for the "true love" I've only read about, but it's impractical at best. I've never seen one gesture of poetic adoration in the

Bay, not one *how do I love thee,* or a single *shall I compare thee to a summer's day?* There's no time for sonnets or words like *darling* or *beloved.* A love affair in Scots Bay would just look foolish and somewhat sad. He, smelling of salt herring and cutting himself on brambles to gather a bouquet of simple wild roses; she, looking tired, patting the flour out of her hair, hands stained blue from dying wool. In our plain corner of the world, romance is nothing but awkward. Better to leave it between the pages of books.

I sees a pretty little house, a fat silk purse and the strength of a hunter's bow. That's what Miss B. had said the night she peeled the last apple for drying. She said nothing about love. We'll get on with the wedding and hope that Archer is right about the rest. I will marry him. I cannot refuse it.

FATHER ASKED ME to help him choose the spot for the house. It seemed as good a time as any. Everything is green now, pushing up from the ground, all of us breathing right along with the wet earth. People are glad to meet one another along the road again, spring caught in their talk, ready to make plans and promises. The first swallows of May turned and raced low, chattering over the fields as we walked to Spider Hill. From the top you can see all of the land that was passed down to my grampy . . . the six houses of Father and his brothers, the brooks cutting their way down the mountain, through the hollow and down to the Bay. It's one of the prettiest spots in the Bay, in sight of North Mountain, Cape Split and the sea. There's pieces of an old foundation here, moss-covered stones sticking out of the earth. It's what's left of the cabin where my grandfather Darius Rare grew up. Eventually, the empty homestead fell down around itself and rotted into the ground.

Each year on my birthday, when I was still small enough to sit in his lap, Father would tell the story of Spider Hill.

"Don't know why I walked the Sunday way that morning. Maybe it was the pinch in your mother's voice when

I went out the door, saying today would be the day for a new baby, 'some special, this baby,' she said.

"It was a warm morning, and the fields were wet, the sky clear. There was a heavy dew on most things, but when I looked ahead to the pasture, the hill seemed to be covered with frost. Frost in May isn't unheard of—I've seen it once or twice, as a boy, but it was always in the low spots. That hill's the first thing that sees the sun of a morning. Any frost that had settled there would have been long gone by the time I came by."

"But when you got there, you saw different . . ."

"Now stop your wiggling and let me tell it, birthday girl."

"When you got there . . ."

"I could see it wasn't frost at all. Thousands on thousands of spiderwebs were covering the hill, all worked together like patches of a quilt. The fence posts were buried so thick I had to cut through the webs with a pocketknife. I could throw rocks in the middle of the thing and they bounced right back like they was India rubber. Everything, three acres of your grampy's land in all, was covered with the busy work of those little brown-backed spiders. The same ones that crawl into the corners of your room to say that winter's not far off."

"I'm not scared of them."

"I know, Dora. You're a brave little girl."

"What made them do it, Daddy?"

"No one had ever seen such a thing, so no one could say for certain. Some said the spiders sailed in on a warm south wind, others said they came up from the ground, from all the bones that rest up there, from your grampy putting the remains of his butchering out for the fishers, the coyotes, ravens and crows. He'd send us boys to drag them up there. *You give the scavengers a little something from time to time and they'll leave the rest alone.* People came from all around to see it. They even sent some smart professor over from Wolfville. After looking at them all over and writing lots of things down, he still couldn't figure those little crawlers out."

"I know why they did it."

"You do?"

"Oh, yes."

"Will you tell me?"

"I can't, Daddy. It's a secret."

After a couple of years of starting, *Don't know why I walked the Sunday way that morning* . . . and me rolling my eyes at him, saying, "I know it already," he gave up. Standing there, it seemed like he should tell it again, but I knew he wouldn't. I couldn't ask. I didn't want to see the years of my "acting smart" in his disappointed blue eyes. I don't know what he thinks of any of this, of Archer, the wedding. It's another thing he won't say and I won't ask, both of us satisfied with knowing that the house is a gift neither one of us can afford to turn away.

He pointed out a place near the church, but I felt it was too near to the road, and it bordered on the burial ground. He pointed out another, with an open, rolling meadow, but it was too near Aunt Fran's for my taste. The longer we stayed on the hill, the more I realized there was no better place for me to make a home than right where I was standing.

Spider Hill has always been my high ground, my safe corner of the Bay. Only once had anyone, outside of Charlie, dared to follow me there. When I was ten, a handful of girls had chased me from the schoolyard, throwing rocks and calling me names. I ran to the top of the hill,

Grace Hutner close behind. She grabbed my braids and held tight, threatening to drag me back down the hill and to blacken both my eyes. In our tussle I managed to grab a handful of dirt and throw it in her face. She let go of my hair and began to shriek, tugging at her dress and pulling at her hair. She was crawling with spiders. (Or at least that's what she was convinced of . . . I never did see a single one.) She hurried away, waving her arms in the air, crying, "Witch, witch, Dora's a witch!"

Across the other side of North Mountain is Cape Blomidon, the great throne of the Mi'kmaq god, Glooscap. Cape Split is what's left of his jewelled hand, scarred and torn by the thrashing tail of a giant beaver. Isle Haute, distant and floating out in the Bay, was once a moose, born from the beaver's dam at Cape Chignecto and chased into the Bay by Glooscap's hungry dogs. Although I have never read it anywhere, and have never been told as much, I've often imagined that Spider Hill is Glooscap's eye, and that if he were to come alive again and crane his neck up from this spot, he could see the entire Bay of Fundy from all sides. On summer evenings I'd climb to the top of the tallest spruce tree on the hill and pretend I was Glooscap's watcher, a little brown-backed spider, studying the lives of the people below. I'd stay there for hours as the men made their way across the mudflats, following the retreating tide to gather fish from the seine, as children circled the school-house playing tag, as their mothers pulled clothing and sheets into baskets, as the moon rose opposite the last pink breath of the sun.

"Here," I said, as I held my eyes from blinking so I wouldn't miss the sun disappearing under the edge of the Bay. "I want the house to be here."

Father nodded. "This always was your spot, wasn't it, Dorrie?"

"Yes."

~ *May 20, 1917*

A letter came from Borden, thanking me for the sailor's comforts I sent him late this past winter (wool socks, a knit cap and two pairs of mitts). He says they've seen no sign of the Fritzies, so he's been keeping himself busy by mending sails, fishing, playing hearts and playing pranks on the rest of the members of the crew. He sounds the same as always.

Seems when he passed around an old family photo Mother had sent him, one of his mates, Hefty the cook, became "quite smitten" with me. Borden thinks I should write him, as Hefty's younger brother was recently lost at Beaumont Hamel. I guess he hasn't gotten the news of my engagement to Archer.

Miss Dora Rare
Scots Bay, Nova Scotia

May 22, 1917

Mr. Borden "Chips" Rare
Ship's Carpenter
The Just Cause
Sydney, Cape Breton Island

Dear Borden (and Albert too),
Your letter was a welcome surprise. I know you are kept busy on board the ship, so I'm happy enough to read the letters and cards you send to Mother.

I'm afraid your cook will have to find another if he wants a steady girl. I will write him a note of condolence, but that will have to be all. I am engaged to marry Archer Bigelow. What do you think of that?

Most everyone is happy about the arrangement, except perhaps Grace Hutner, who long had her sights set on Archer (and his mother's money). She's decided that he wasn't good enough for her anyway, since he agrees with me in thinking the war is unjust. Instead, she's taken to chasing after our dear brother Charlie! He assures me that "Grace Hutner isn't the kind of girl you take to church." He volunteered to tell me exactly what he thinks she's good for, but I refused to hear it. From the way she's been grabbing at his arm and bringing butter tarts to the house, I can only imagine. Wait until she hears he has no intention of signing on. She'll have to feather him as well. (Although I'm sure she's thinking twice about that game, since there are so few boys left in the Bay.)

I know you have never liked Archer half as much as Hart, but please be happy for me. He's been nothing but a gentleman and more than worth his weight in kindness and compliments. Despite his charm with the ladies, I feel he is devoted. I think we are a good match.

Your soon-to-be-wed sister,
Dora

18

"GET ME TWO long-handled spoons and grease 'em up good with tallow, Dora." Miss B. was sitting on a chair by the bed, one hand slid up between Grace Hutner's thighs. "What the devil you got stuck in there, anyways?"

Grace held her breath as Miss B. inserted the spoons and gently pried the object out of Grace's body. "Look at that! Look who was grinnin' back at me." Miss B. held up a small, rounded piece of porcelain painted with pink flowers and the smiling image of a Chinese empress, one of the teacup covers from Mrs. Hutner's prized Gilded Lotus set. "That must have been some tea party you went to, Gracie."

Grace grabbed the teacup cover from Miss B. "I'll take that. It belongs to my mother."

Miss B. scolded her. "It sure don't belong up in your little sweet spot. Don't be puttin' things up there that don't belong, no matter how handsome he is."

Grace sat on the edge of the bed and sighed. "Some men just won't take no for an answer." She smiled at me, fluttering her eyelashes. "And then there's some you just don't *want* to say no to, isn't that right, Dora?"

I clenched my teeth. "It never hurts a man to wait."

She laughed as she pulled up her stockings and fastened them to her garters. "Really? They always tell me different."

Miss B. called out from the kitchen. "You gonna be a little sore for a couple of days, then you're good as new." I followed Miss B. and watched as she got into the cupboard and brought down a heavy jar filled with what looked like steeped brown roots. The label read: *Beaver Brew.*

"I'll give you somethin' that'll keep you clean 'til your next moon time, so you don't have to worry 'bout your little princess there. Just this once."

I stood next to Miss B. and hissed at her. "What are you doing?"

She strained some of the mixture into a small jar. "I'm makin' you a weddin' present. Now leave it alone 'til she's gone."

Grace looked into the canning jar that Miss B. had handed to her. "What's in it?"

"No concern of yours."

"It smells awful."

"Make sure you drink it all, now, or it don't do no good."

She whispered to Miss B. "It really works? I can't get a bun in the oven?"

"Drink it down."

Grace took a sip and nearly gagged it back up. Miss B. laughed at her. "It's easier if you just take it in one go."

She took the rest and left, grinning and smirking at me as she went out the door. "See you at church, ladies."

I sat at the kitchen table with Miss B., hot, angry tears coming down my face. "How could you give her something like that? You know she'll go after Archer."

"No matter what I done, you know she gonna go after him and anybody else who'll look at her twice."

I stared at the floor. "Do you hate me that much for leaving you? Don't you want me to be happy?"

She came up behind me and put her arms around me. "You'd be hurtin' a lot more if Gracie went and got herself knocked up with your man's child."

Miss B.'s gotten slow, her back looking more hunched and broken every day. She complains in the morning, says she can't taste her coffee, can't smell it, can't feel its bite. "Don't know whys I bother drinkin' it."

She still says she won't give up tending to the women of the Bay until she's dead in the ground, but since Dr. Thomas's lecture to the White Rose Temperance Society, the women in the Bay have all but given up on Miss B. Once in a while, they'll ask her to mix up a remedy to ease their courses or come looking for a bottle of her cough syrup to soothe a child's sore throat, but more often than not they avoid her, busying themselves with false chatter whenever she comes close.

The women from away are still faithful to her. Mabel Thorpe, Bertine Tupper and Sadie Loomer have been leaving baskets on the doorstep every other day, loaves of brown bread, pints of cream, applesauce, pickles. This morning I watched Sadie waddle down the road, her belly heavy with child, turning every so often to see if Miss B. had come out to collect her offerings. Miss B. left the jars lined up on the kitchen counter. "Some pretty, ain't they? I'm almost afraid to eats 'em, 'fraid I'd be swallowin' that poor little mama's guilt into my gut." She shook her head and clutched her rosary. "She's some small, that Sadie. And

her babies are some big. I pray to Mary and sweet baby
Jesus that Mister Doctor know what he's doin'."

Not long after he addressed the ladies of the Bay, Dr.
Thomas became a full member of the Sons of Temperance,
lending his brotherhood and advice to the men of the
order. Many men from the Bay attend (most in name only):
Father, Uncle Irwin, Mr. Hutner, Laird Jessup. As Laird did
with Ginny, Sadie's husband, Wes, has made it clear that
Sadie will be going down to the Canning Maternity Home
to have her baby. It's become a point of pride with these
men, to be able to pay for the "proper" things in life. If you
want the best saddle for your horse, you go to Pauley's tack
shop in Canning; if you want the best axe, it'd better be a
Blenkhorn; and if you want your children born "right some
strong," then Dr. Thomas is your man.

More and more of Miss B.'s days are spent sleeping.
When she's not praying for Sadie, she's praying for "Louis
Faire to guide me to my home-goin'." Sometimes she'll wake
in a fright, calling to me to help her "Bring the child out,
Dorrie. Sing her down through her mama's bones. Sing the
moon down. Sing her on down." She's forever reminding me
of things that need to be done, roots to be harvested before
the new moon, which herbs bloom in June, July and August.
She even insisted on teaching me to collect the first dew of
May. "Livin' here it might come as snow, frost or fog . . . you
never know, but no matter how it comes, you gots to gather
Mary's Tears, puts 'em in a bottle and save 'em for blessing
the sick." Under her watchful eye, I stretched a large piece of
sailcloth between four apple trees, tying the ends low to the
trunks. She handed me a heavy, smooth stone. "Roll this in
the centre there, so's the dew can runs down the middle."
Then she took her wide wooden bread bowl and crept under

the shallow canopy, leaving it just under where the rock was hanging so it could catch the dewdrops.

She fretted over me while I put in a garden at Spider Hill. Aside from peas, cabbage and other vegetables, there is now a start from every herb in Miss B.'s garden. *Blue-eyed Mary, Lady's keys, Our Lady's bedstraw, Mary's slippers, Mary's gold, Mary's nettle, Mary's bouquet, Mary's bed, Mary's tears, Mary's washing plant, Mary's sword of sorrow, Sweet Mary, Jesus wort, Lady's modesty.* "And don't you forget to collect the seeds before autumn. You'd think the fruit was the prize, or the leaves, or even the roots . . . but it's the seeds that keeps the secrets. Like any other mother, the plant done spent all her life learnin' the earth. It's her seeds that does the rememberin' for her. It's all right there in the seed."

While we worked, at least a dozen men were circling the new cellar that Father and Uncle Irwin had dug at Spider Hill. Laird Jessup's wagon was filled with stones he'd gathered during his spring plowing, and one by one the men carried them to the top of the hill. Even though the ship-yard is busy with the men working hard to build the skeleton of their next schooner, they have been spending their evenings and Sundays gathered at the hill, while Father maps out the plans with his footsteps. The men stand together, nodding in agreement, clutching the bowls of their pipes or scratching and pulling at their beards.

Un coup de main, Miss B. calls it. "Men come together, first for one and then the other. This house is some special, bringin' us together when the world has done split apart."

She's forgiven the Widow Bigelow and seems resigned, but not entirely happy about my upcoming marriage to Archer. She read my tea leaves for my eighteenth birthday, telling the future of my new home. "I sees all the things a house should hold . . . laughter, songs, but some tears too. And babies . . . lots and lots of babies to hold." This made me happy. More than being in love, or being a wife, I have wanted to be a mother.

I promised her that I'd continue to assist her with her midwifing as long as in return she promises to live forever, so she can be there to catch all my babies, and their babies, and their babies after that. She pouted when I said it.

"Don't you lie. I knows you're givin' up on me, just like everybody else." I told her she was wrong, but she went on. "Now, now . . . I've almost given up on me too. Might as well . . . no sense hangin' my dreams on these bones. Ain't nothin' gonna stop this old body from makin' her way to the grave. Time has its way and that's that."

I couldn't bring myself to tell her that Archer's already insisting I stop midwifing once we're married. "A husband needs the attentions of his wife. You can't be distracting yourself with the work of spinsters and old grannies and expect me to be happy about it. Besides, Dr. Thomas is more than ready to take it over from Miss B., you said so yourself." I didn't say what I'd do one way or the other. I didn't say anything at all.

~ *July 1, 1917*

This afternoon, Archer and I went out to Lady's Cove for a picnic lunch. The tide was stretched out away from the shore, leaving the mud flats bare and shining in the sun. I walked barefoot, collecting mussels and a few clams, the warm, heavy sand giving way up to my ankles. Archer built a fire, his happy whistling echoing in and around the tide pools and cliffs.

After we ate, he pulled a locket from his shirt pocket (a beautiful gold thing engraved with a circle of lilies) and handed it to me. He said his mother wanted me to have it for our wedding day.

When I said I thought it was too generous a gesture, he stood and loosened his belt, his trousers dropping down past his knees. He grinned as he stared at me, touching and putting himself on display, asking me for a little thank you for the groom-to-be.

This way of my giving thanks started the night after Grace Hutner's visit to Miss B.'s. I hadn't expected to have him standing in front of me, half-dressed, before our wedding night, but it seemed the only way to keep my virtue (a welcome requirement for Archer's inheritance) while keeping him away from Grace. I've been meeting him at the church or down in the shallow caves at Lady's Cove as often as I can.

I've seen my brothers naked many times, running down to the brook with their parts dangling down, three sheets to the wind, innocent and laughing. But Archer never laughs, and what he's got between his legs is far from innocent. *Come on, Dorrie. Just get on your knees. It won't take long, no one needs to know. Now open up that sweet mouth of yours and take me in.* I wonder if this is the way love starts for most girls. Not out of devotion, but from the need to make a man happy. *Sometimes it takes more than kisses to say thank you. Just think of it as my way of saying I trust you. That I want you more than anyone else. I'm at your mercy, my love.*

He's particular about the way it's done. *Always, always on your knees.* Hair pulled back away from my face, his hands tugging at my braids, guiding me . . . slow at first, then *faster, faster.* Despite the way it makes my jaw ache, and the bitter, salty taste it leaves in my mouth, it does change him. There's a gentleness he shows that isn't there at any other time. *Little girl, you're my sweet little girl.* He coaxes and groans as if he's the one giving in. I just hope it's enough.

Just as he was stroking my cheek, bringing my face close to him, and to the stale, musky smell of his body, Hart's voice rang out from the edge of the cliffs above us. As Archer scrambled to pull his clothing back together, Hart made his way down to the cove. Archer's face was red with anger.

"Save something for the wedding night Archie, or Mother'll disown ya . . ."

I got to my feet and busied myself with throwing sand on the fire, not looking in Hart's direction. I wish he hadn't seen us like that. It's not that I fear the fires of hell for what I've been doing, or even that Hart might judge me to be no different from Grace. It's just that when I kneel in front of Archer, I feel as if God will be disappointed if I don't let him have his way, that I should thank heaven he wants me at all. Having someone witness it makes it that much worse. My only comfort is in something Miss B. told me long ago: "It's been proved over and over again, right as rain—The Lord made men so they just can't help themselves."

~ *July 5, 1917*

All the contents for the house arrived today. Five wagons were lined up in the road, and dozens of men were moving boxes and crates up the hill. The women were all there, the Widow Bigelow directing the men as to where to put the furniture, Aunt Fran gossiping to Mrs. Hutner. "My cousin, Clara, in Halifax, she bought the makings of an entire house right out of the Sears catalogue. The Aladdin Built in a Day House. The entire house came by train. An *entire* house, clapboards, shingles, doorknobs and all!"

Archer winked at me as he dragged the iron frame for our bed into the house. There's no turning back now.

19

Rare-Bigelow Nuptials

Mr. and Mrs. Judah Rare of Scots Bay are pleased to announce the wedding of their daughter, Dora Marie, to Mr. Archer Bigelow. The Reverend Claude Pineo performed afternoon nuptials at the Scots Bay Union Church, Friday, July 11. The bride was attended by her cousin, Miss Precious Jeffers. The groom was attended by his brother, Mr. Hart Bigelow. Mrs. Francine Jeffers, aunt of the bride, offered her talents in song by singing a fine rendition of "Oh Promise Me." The ladies of the White Rose Temperance Society, along with the Widow Simone Bigelow, mother of the groom, hosted an evening celebration at Lady's Cove, with many residents from far and near in attendance. The happy couple will make their residence at Spider Hill and will receive well-wishers at once.

The Canning Register,
July 25, 1917

EMBROIDERED SILK ILLUSION. Seed pearls and blown glass beads. Fine tatted lace made from Aunt Althea's sleight of hand, turned into roses and forget-me-nots.

Three weeks before, the ladies of the church auxiliary had sung a song and said their pledge, and Aunt Pauline Rare had read the minutes from the last meeting. Then, to my surprise, she announced that the next order of business concerned "the wedding of Dora Rare to Archer Bigelow." The women smiled and stared at me. Mother patted me on the knee and grinned.

For the next few hours they bickered and laughed, arguing over who makes the tastiest buttercream frosting and who has the finest voice to sing "I Love You Truly." In the end it was decided that July 11 was the luckiest day for a wedding (as the men won't set sail on a Friday). It would be a sunset service at the Union church, Reverend Pineo to officiate, and bonfires with baked lobster and mussels at Lady's Cove to follow.

Aunt Fran asked, "And what will we do about the rum? You know the men insist on bringing it out for weddings and funerals . . ."

Mother nodded. "I say, none 'til sunset and done by dawn. And no man to touch a torch or a fire or we'll lose at least one boat, barn or even a house."

A round of "ayes" went through the room. Bertine Tupper added, "Each wife tends to her own, too. I'm not having anyone else's husband lying in my garden when I wake up. Hardy makes a fine mess between the cabbage and peas all on his own."

After the laughter fell away, Aunt Fran raised her voice again, this time sounding quite serious. "And what about a wedding gown?" She looked at my mother. "Charlotte, is she wearing yours?"

Mother sighed. "That's a concern . . ." She busied her hands with darning a sock as she spoke. "When I married Judah, I never thought I'd have a daughter. You all know the saying, *Rare men bring Rare sons.* In hundreds of years of living in the Bay, it's held true . . . until Dora." She looked at me with sadness. "I used my dress to make christening gowns for your brothers. I'm so sorry, dear."

Aunt Fran shook her head, her voice filled with disgust. "Well, I suppose she could wear mine."

Mother made a quick reply. "She'd swim in your gown, Frannie . . . and besides, you'd be the first to admit, it's rather old-fashioned looking nowadays."

Aunt Althea tried to comfort Mother. "You know, Charlotte, I did the same thing with my dress."

The other wives of my father's brothers chimed in. Aunt Irene, Aunt Lil, Aunt Pauline and Aunt Tilly all admitted to taking apart their wedding gowns and piecing them into baptismal dresses. Aunt Lil giggled and added, "I made some beautiful pillow shams from part of the train too. The satin's so nice to sleep on. Who could have guessed you'd be needing it for anything else?"

Aunt Althea turned to Aunt Fran. "Did you bring any of those ladies magazines with you?"

Aunt Fran reached under her chair and handed a stack of *Ladies' Home Journals* and *Butterick* pattern books to me.

"What are these for?" I asked.

Aunt Althea smiled. "Pick a dress you like, and we'll find a way to make it for you. Pauline and Tilly are the finest seamstresses around; they'll make silk from a sow's ear if they has to."

On my wedding day my feet danced under the scalloped hems of fourteen delicate christening gowns. Crowned with wax orange blossoms and waves of silk tulle, I married Archer Bigelow.

At sunset, we made our way down to the cove. Hart, Charlie, Sam Gower and Uncle Web carried me on a piece of sailcloth as if I were the Queen of Sheba. Archer chased after them, threatening to steal their share of rum if they tried to steal his wife.

He fed me roasted lobster tails, raspberries and wedding cake. He held my waist tight as we danced. He told me he would always love me, and I said I'd never doubt his word. Between two fiddles and a wheezy concertina, I watched my parents at the end of the reel, Mother smiling as they met, Father bending a bit as their hands joined to form the arch. Their love is an easy, well-worn fit. Where did it come from? As a new bride, did she enjoy at least one day of bliss? A day, or two, or even a week when she was required to think of nothing else but her fragile little world of two, of husband and of wife.

Father was about to make his fifth or sixth toast of the evening when Bertine Tupper came running down the cliffs, shouting my name. "Dora, you gotta help. Sadie's in trouble, says the baby's comin' right quick."

"Where's Wes?"

"He went to get Dr. Thomas. Sadie wouldn't go down to Canning, said she'd never make it."

"Where's Miss B.?" I asked.

"Can't find her. I went to her cabin first, then the church, then here."

I kissed my new husband good night and asked him to look for Miss B. on his way home.

You gots to be a two-headed person. And what I means by that is you gots to think and see two things at once.

Where was Miss B.? She'd been at the wedding. She'd come to me afterwards, held my hands, her bony, familiar fingers whispering against my palms. She said she was tired, "Ain't no place for a blind old granny at a dance . . . my feet gets in my own way." I asked Charlie to walk her home, but she said she wanted to walk alone to enjoy the sunset and the warm evening. I kissed her cheeks. She whispered, "Mind her bones," and walked away. I thought it was a blessing for my wedding night. I was wrong.

The baby's shoulder stuck as it was coming down, and Sadie was getting tired. Where was Miss B.? If things didn't change soon, I'd have to break the baby's collarbone to get it out. *Mind her bones. Bring them bones down. Sing 'em on down.* I crossed my heart, found as many of Miss B.'s words as I could, spit on my finger and drew a cross on Sadie's belly, singing, "Mother Mary, bless this mother, bless her child, bless this house." I moved Sadie to the edge of the bed, so she was all but hanging off of it. Bertine sat behind her, holding her up, coaxing her along. "Come on, Sadie. A little while longer."

I gave a firm, slow twist, bringing the baby's shoulder to the soft of Sadie's skin. Bertine and I both called out for her to "Push, push!" and with that, the baby slid right out. A beautiful baby boy.

Dr. Thomas arrived, too late to catch the baby or the afterbirth. He took off his coat and paced around the house, grumbling about women not knowing what's best for themselves. "Since she chose to have the child at home, I'm afraid I'll have to limit the care I give her. I'll examine both Mrs. Loomer and the child, and then I'll have to be on my way."

Wes pulled the doctor aside, his two sleepy toddlers clinging to his legs. "You won't be back to look in on her again? We already paid."

"Yes, but the certificate clearly states that the mother's confinement and care are to be attended to at the Canning Maternity Home."

Bertine came into the kitchen where the men were standing. "Dora and I will see to her. And I'm sure when Miss B. comes around she'll look in on her too."

"Are you a relation of Mrs. Loomer's?"

"No, but—"

"As Miss Rare can tell you, I don't allow visitors of any sort at the maternity home. I don't recommend it for home births either. Health concerns, you understand." He turned to Wes. "I really must be on my way."

Bertine stood in the bedroom doorway, her large arms crossed over her chest, her foot tapping as she stared the doctor down. "Dora's done a fine job here. I don't know that Sadie or her baby needs you poking at them."

Dr. Thomas ignored her and pushed his way into the bedroom.

Sadie held her child tight. "Anyone can see, we're fine. No need to touch."

Dr. Thomas shook his head. "Good luck to you both, then." He looked at me. "Good night, Miss Rare."

Bertine said, "It's Mrs. Bigelow. Dora just got married tonight."

He tipped his hat as he walked out the door. "Well, I wish I could congratulate you under better circumstances." He looked me up and down, noticing my wedding dress, now stained with blood and afterbirth. "I'm sure you made a lovely bride. Good night."

Bertine and I made tea and porridge for Sadie, then tucked the other children in for the night. Wes was standing nearby as I got ready to leave.

"Sorry about your dress."

I smiled. "Why don't you go on in and see that new boy of yours. I'll be back tomorrow."

It was nearly dawn by the time I got to Spider Hill. My dear husband was snoring in our bed, still in his wedding suit, hog-tied. Hart was sitting in a rocker, his head lolled back in sleep and the weathered handle of a broadaxe cradled to his chest. He mumbled and stirred, his eyes opening to narrow slits.

"What's that? Dorrie, that you?"

"Yes, Hart." I motioned to the bed. "You trying to keep him in?"

"More like keeping Grace Hutner out." He yawned, stretching his legs out in front of him. "Now there's a girl who can't hold a drop. Boy, she put on a show . . . pounding at the door. She called Archie a yellow-bellied witch-loving coward, and kept going on and on, yelling about how this should have been her house."

"Oh dear."

"Don't worry. She won't be back. Her father came and dragged her off, swearing right and left that he was going to send her to live with his sister in Halifax."

I knelt down by the side of the bed and started to untie Archer's wrists.

"I wouldn't do that. He'll be some mad when he wakes up. Best just to let him sleep it off and wake up compromised."

If I hadn't smelled his stale breath and seen his face twitch, I would have thought he was dead. "Did he check on Miss B.?"

"No. He couldn't get himself home, let alone make his way to Miss Babineau's."

I left my soiled dress hanging on the back of a kitchen chair, changed into fresh clothing and walked to Miss B.'s.

~ July 12, 1917

I knew something was wrong before I even got to the door. A letter sat on the table, next to the Willow Book and five strands of rosary beads, all laid out and waiting.

> *Dear Dora,*
>
> *My, what good we've made of each other. I would never have known of Miss Austen without you, never had a notion of what it was like to have a home in this place. You made these humble walls sing.*
>
> *A long time's past since I made my way here from the Bayou. Now it's time to take a walk to my next place, my last place, my home-goin'. If I done it right, this life, then you don't gonna see me no more, that's all.*
>
> *You don't gonna cry, neither. You got to say a prayer instead. That's the way of the traiteur. We make our tears into prayers . . . not to beg or plead with God, but to remember the stuff we are made of. Same as Mother Mary, or your smart little Missy Austen, we're all the same, same as the moon, the stars and the sea.*
>
> *Offert ou pas, Dieu est ici.*
> *Bidden or not, God is here.*
> *Marie Babineau*

I believe it's possible Miss B. just vanished. Every day she had been getting closer to it, praying, calling out to heaven, raising her arms up to the sky, making herself lighter and lighter, her dress trailing after her like feathers, until she might have flown away.

There were many times that I thought to myself I'd do anything not to end up like her, to keep from being pushed aside like some sad have-not, forced to live alone in a leaning, aching, rundown shack. That was before I came to know her. Many times over these past few weeks, while everything seemed to be ending for her and beginning for me, I wished that the moon she worshipped each night would come and put some of Miss B. in me—that I'd wake up wise, with silvery prayers on my lips, saying whatever was on my mind (whenever I wanted). Next to Mother's sensibility, she seemed half an angel, half fright, somehow always knowing what I needed.

After reading her note, I felt more tired than sad. Tired of the day, of having to tend to Sadie's birth alone, of fighting with Dr. Thomas, tired at the thought that the time had come to leave this place behind and act like someone's wife. I lit candles all around the Blessed Mother, singing "Ave Maria" and praying that Miss B.'s soul would have a safe journey home. I twisted her rosaries around my neck and sat in her old rocker, pulling her quilt around me, crying until I fell asleep.

I dreamed of her laughter and the scent of coffee brewing in the morning, of the crooked handwriting that lined the pages of the Willow Book, every statue and likeness of the Holy Mother singing her prayers to me as I slept. I dreamed that I had come back to what was left of the place, set it on fire to burn to the ground, the flames bursting high up into the night. Shadowy men shovelled seaweed around the edges of the fire to make sure it didn't spread, bringing things they didn't want anymore, a broken-down buggy seat, rotten apple barrels, used-up lobster traps. Then the women came. They cried over Miss B. while they held their children tight. They stood next to each other, sharing stories of the births they had under her care. I held my mother's hand and rested my head on her shoulder while Miss B.'s ghost flew all around us, singing.

They gonna need you, Dora.

They need you. You gotta keep them safe.

The Midwife's Gift

from the Willow Book

Along the Bayou Blaize Le Jeune there lived a country midwife, a howdie or sage femme as some liked to call them. One night when she done got herself ready for sleeping, a swamp man came to the door. He was someone she'd never seen before and would never see again. He said to her, calling her name in almost a song, "Grann-ee Bonne, there's a woman down the river who's a-calling for you. She's a-howling and spitting, bringing her baby down soon." That granny, she tried to get a proper dress on, but the swamp man wouldn't let her. All he'd let her bring was a ball of cotton to tie the cord. He picked her up, right off the stoop, and carried her out to his flat-bottom boat that was waiting on the river.

Most times, Granny Bonne would know just where she was headed. She'd travelled all up and down that river to bring women's babies up, floating along in her canoe that she paddled for herself. But there weren't no moon that night, and the bayou was dark as blindness. She asked the stranger where they was going. He wouldn't say another word. When they got to the place, it seemed nice enough. A cozy cabin with a fire lit, and a lamp all bright and cheerful in the window. Granny Bonne went in and found the woman already "in the straw." Before long the baby came, a fine child indeed, causing his mama no trouble at all. The father of the house played the fiddle, the aunties gathered round and danced, and the mother sang sweet and low, sweet and low.

Granny Bonne was about to dress the child when one of the aunties came to her, carrying a little pot of salve. The auntie pulled the cork and the scent of magnolias came right out. She gave old Granny Bonne a rhyme to follow,

> I give to you this salve,
> As precious as a rose
> Anoint the child from end to end,
> From his wee fingers to his toes.

Now, before the auntie could say "don't," a moon moth was fluttering on Granny Bonne's cheek, leaving the dust of its wings in her eye. She brushed the thing from her face and rubbed the itch. What else could she do? And then, amazed she was . . . seeing with one eye what she always thought was there, and with the other something more like magic. It weren't no cabin she was took to. She'd been whisked away to a faerie hole, down under the willows, moss hanging all around, lights coming from fireflies and foxfire. Gathered all around her were the tiny folk. One on each shoulder, grinning. Three more was in her lap, tickling the baby's ears. Granny let go a squeak, dropping the pot to the ground. Right away, the auntie knew what had happened and told Granny Bonne that if she promised to never tell a soul where the faeries kept themselves, she could have any wish she wanted.

Granny Bonne thought and thought. She didn't want riches or desire fancy clothes fit for a queen. She didn't even wish for a grand house or better land, since she knew all these things could be taken away. She held out her hands to the auntie and said, "These are all I've got. Make my hands so's they'll always be of some use." The auntie blew into her hands comfort and goodness, tales and tears, and Granny Bonne got her wish.

 part two

20

THE FIRST THING I DID upon settling into the house on Spider Hill was to move every furnishing (even if it was only an inch)—the bed, the sofa, the kitchen table, every chair, lamp, plant stand, rug and vase— that the Widow Bigelow had placed "just so." After that, I made several trips to Miss B.'s, bringing back all the memories I could heap onto her old handcart. Archer complained, saying we didn't have room for hand-me-downs. When I tried to put Miss B.'s rocker in the parlour, he said, "At least put it where others won't see it. It's an insult to my mother's generosity."

He was especially mean when he found me filling a cupboard with jars of remedies and herbs. "I thought I told you to give it up."

"What if someone needs help?"

"That's what doctors are for."

"What if it's the middle of the night? Miss B. always had something on hand."

"Stop talking like the old woman ever made a bit of difference. I tasted the stuff she used to give Mother for her rheumatism . . . it was nothing but sugar-soaked wine. Half the time a person's sickness is all in the head, especially with women. Mother's always taking to bed with this or that. It's all the same. Just an excuse to get attention."

"If I get rid of it, then it won't be there for someone who might need it. What if they can't get to the doctor? What if a child has the croup, or a woman's got morning sickness? Miss B.'s not around to—"

When he saw that I was about to cry, he pulled me into his arms. "Alright, you can keep your little *potions*. Out of plain sight, though." He brushed the hair away from my neck, his voice convincing and low. "I hope you've made it clear to the other women around here that you're no longer in the baby business." He took my hand and slid it down the front of his pants. "You've got other duties to see to."

I knew little about my husband until I lay with him. It started the same every night, his lips finding mine in the dark, his hands groping their way around my body, but soon there was nothing gentle left between us, nothing to stop him from forcing his sweaty, cruel body against mine. "It's supposed to hurt the first time. This is how a man makes a woman his own: he 'breaks her in' and then she's all his." Archer feels a wife should be willing and happy to take her husband in any time he likes, that he's allowed to be demanding and restless, never giving me a day's rest for the pain or bleeding. I've tried offering him warm milk and a hot bath before bed, hoping he'll forget his *needs* and fall asleep, but he persists, saying it's his nature. "It's what gives me the rights to call myself a man." Nothing prepared me for this, for the shame that comes from not wanting to give him whatever he wants, not knowing how to be a wife, wishing he'd just leave me alone. I give in when I don't want to, until he has my hands over my head and my legs wide open, leaving me seasick and empty. When it's over, I search for roses in the shadows on the wallpaper while his snoring goes on and on, reminding me that he's been satisfied.

I tried talking to Mother about it, but it came out all wrong. Her cheeks turned red; she thought I was asking if it was possible for a woman to want marital relations too often. "Oh, Dorrie, dear, don't you worry about that. You might as well enjoy it while you have no children to tend to." Then she whispered, half hiding behind her knitting as she spoke. "Your father and I clung to each other every chance we got, some days it was everywheres but our own bed . . . the hayloft, in the belly of a worn-out skiff, out at Lady's Cove . . ." She stopped when I dropped several stitches and the cuff of the mitt I was working on began to unravel.

I began to put him off, staying awake until he was too tired to bother with me, knitting socks for the war effort, mending clothes, baking bread. I held on to at least one, maybe two nights a week that way, nights where I was free from my "obligations as a wife." It made the other days of the week bearable, even if it didn't stop his complaining.

One night became "excusable," especially if I said I was having my courses. Two nights was sometimes possible, but never in a row. Putting him off for three nights in one week has left me without a husband.

Not quite three months after our wedding day, he was waiting in the parlour, legs slung over the end of the couch, rolling an empty pickle jar on the floor with his lazy fingers. "Well, how-do-ye-do, there she is, Mrs. Dora Bigelow . . ." He got up and came towards me, grabbing at me, trying to kiss me. "Come on, Dorrie, how about I take you to bed and you act like a proper wife."

"Please, Archer, not when you're like this."

He pulled on my arm, and tore at the buttons on the front of my blouse. "Come on, you ungrateful little whore." He put his face close to mine, spitting the bitter, skunky smell of the Ketch brothers' overripe brew. "Wait, I forgot . . . you don't know how to be a whore, let alone a proper wife. I might as well have married Grace Hutner." He grabbed at my waist, pulling me into an awkward waltz around the room. "You remember Gracie, don't ya, Dora? Beautiful Gracie . . . now there's a girl who knew the way to a man's heart." I pulled free of him, but he came back at me, shouting, "Mother might have disowned me, and I'd have wound up poor, but at least Gracie would have let me crawl on top of her every night until I felt like a man." He made a fist and raised it high in the air. As he swung to hit me, he missed, punching a hole in the parlour wall.

I ran through the kitchen and locked myself in our bedroom, wedging the back of Miss B.'s rocking chair under the doorknob. He kicked and pounded at the door until the walls shook. "Just answer this, Mrs. Bigelow . . . how is it that a wife can't find one bit of pleasure in her own husband?" I could hear him pacing through the house, then coming back to the bedroom door, beating it with every word he said. "Let . . . me . . . in, and I'll give it *hard* to you, dear . . . then we'll see if you dare cry about it."

Finally I heard the door slam shut and the sound of a horse being whipped and whistled down the road.

Several people asked after Archer at church. Mother, the Widow Bigelow, Aunt Fran and Precious, even Reverend Pineo. I had considered missing services, but my absence would have sent Mother straight to the house looking for me. I had planned to say that Archer wasn't feeling well. (This was certainly the truth the last time I saw him.) But rather than going down the list of symptoms I'd rehearsed (sore throat, slight fever, night sweats and chills . . . probably just a cold), I concocted an elaborate tale from an advertisement I'd seen in one of Archer's copies of *Vaughn's Almanac*, telling them my dear husband had decided to travel across all of Nova Scotia, selling Bibles.

The BIBLE is still the world's best-seller

Because most people throughout the world have a great respect for this book, there is no need for high-pressure selling, and this is true more so with our new

ANALYTICAL BIBLE

The Bible salesman commands respect wherever he goes. People invariably ascribe to him ideals and virtues he may not possess.

"I truly feel it's the best thing he could do, a kind of service almost, rather than work, bringing people hope . . . in these troubled times."

Reverend Pineo gave a solemn nod, tucking his Bible under his arm so he could reach both his hands out to me in a gesture of comfort. "The Good Book is blessed balm for any soul. I'll be sure to pray for him, Dora. I'll pray for welcome, open doors and a safe return."

I'm bound for hell.

Still, the idea of Archer gone drumming isn't all that far-fetched. Not a week had gone by after the wedding when he started spreading the pages of the *Halifax Journal* and *Vaughn's Almanac* all over the kitchen table during mealtimes.

He'd point to this or that, soup dripping from his spoon, exclaiming, "There she is, Dorrie, the next big thing!" and whatever it was, from transistor radios, electric appliances or fire insurance to brooms and brushes, he was going to sell it. Every week another box would arrive, the samples and sales manuals piled high in a room at the top of the stairs, each one replaced with something else, soon forgotten. At least with my imagined excuse no one will expect to see him anytime soon, and when he does come home, I can be as surprised as anyone else.

Of course, Mother worries about my being alone. She asked if I might want to come home with her until Archer returns, but I can't see going from this quiet, empty place to being crowded between Father and the boys. *Why don't you pack your bags and come home, Dorrie?* She's given up. Thinks he's gone for good. Three days he's been gone, and she's supposing I expected too much, played at something I had no business with. I don't feel half as sorry for myself as I do for her. She had such hopes for this marriage. With every day he stays gone, there'll be another woman who will start to wonder, telling the person next to her—in the church pew, in a knitting circle, at the market—that she knew it was bound to turn out this way, that Dora Rare certainly wasn't pretty, or resourceful, or confident, or come-from-money-proud enough to be Archer Bigelow's match. Like Miss B. always said, *No matter what you do—somebody, somewheres, knew that you would.* Three months a wife and I couldn't be happy with what I had. Rest assured, by the time Archer comes home (if he comes home), I'll have it all figured out, and there'll be nothing more to worry about.

21

Bertine Tupper came to the house, pulling her youngest child along by the arm, the little girl dragging a rag doll behind, all three of them topped with red knit caps, looking like a lopsided chain of paper dolls. She came through the door without a knock, her loud, cheerful "hello" ringing into the kitchen ahead of her. She sat the girl and a lumpy, faded flour sack on the table and smiled at me as if I should have been expecting her.

"Was walking lunch out to Hardy, and little Lucy decided she couldn't go home until she'd been inside your pretty new house. Can't believe it's October already and I hadn't stopped by for a proper visit. Now's as good a time as any." She tugged the wool cap from her child's head, Lucy's hair sticking up all over. "Looks like I found her under a basket, doesn't she?" Bertine soon gave up on trying to smooth Lucy's wispy curls and turned her attention to the bag, bringing out a yeasty, sweet-smelling loaf of bread. "Good enough for tea, I'd say. Still warm, too." She sat down in the parlour and took Lucy into her lap. The child began to tug at Bertine's sweater, wanting to nurse. "Well, don't just stand there, Dora, how many hands you think I gots?"

"I'm sorry, I wasn't expecting . . ."

"That's not the right answer." She wrinkled her brow and grinned. "First I say, 'How many hands you think I gots?' and then you say, 'One less than you need, my dear. Let me make you some tea.' Didn't your mother teach you any manners?" She snorted, her hearty laughter shaking her whole body, Lucy's cheeks bouncing, her lips sucking hard to hold on to Bertine's breast. "Sweet baby Jesus, Luce— watch your teeth there, dearie."

I took the kettle off the stove and poured it into a fresh pot. "Raspberry leaf fine with you?"

"Mmmm . . . smells just like Miss B.'s." She slipped her pinky in the corner of Lucy's mouth, then tickled under the little girl's chubby chin. "I've got to get on with weaning this child, she'll be two next month." Lucy blinked back at her mother and smiled. "Of course, you know as soon as I do, the next one'll come along. Once the milk dries up, I'm ripe for the picking."

We sat in the parlour, taking our tea, Bertine knitting away on a pair of mitts, Lucy stealing back and forth between our laps, brushing behind the curtains. Before I could notice, she was standing on Archer's sitting chair, parading her rag doll across its high back, then sticking its limp arm through the hole Archer left in the wall. She laughed and giggled as she pushed the doll's head into the hole, as if they were on a grand adventure, searching for hidden treasure.

Bertine apologized, pulling at Lucy, trying to get her out of the chair. "Come down now, Luce. I think it's time Dolly had her nap." She settled Lucy and her doll on the chesterfield, curling them up together in the corner, then sat back down in her chair. "Never saw a mouse hole up that high. Some big too. You got a rat?"

I gave a nervous laugh and made an excuse. "The funniest thing happened, I was trying to hang a picture and . . ." I made a wide, grinning face at Lucy, hoping she would start giggling again and Bertine would forget what she had asked.

"And?" Bertine's foot started to tap under her skirt.

I pulled my apron in front of my face, popping my head above it occasionally to grin at Lucy. "And the hammer went right through the plaster."

Lucy kicked and squealed with laughter.

Bertine yanked my apron out of my hands. "No talk that starts with 'the funniest thing happened' has ever been the truth. Those words are meant for fishing tales and husbands come home late for supper. Besides, your father built this house, put these walls together . . . I know it would take more than a girl, a hammer and picture hook to undo his work." She tucked Dolly snug in the crook of Lucy's arm. "Hush now, girls." Lucy squirmed herself into a tight, obedient knot. Bertine gave me a stern look. "You've had your head stuck between a woman's legs, pulled out her baby and God knows what bloody else. You've seen more of a woman than their husbands dare to look at, so I figure that makes you more honest than not." She went back to her knitting, counting the stitches to herself before going on. "How about you try telling me what happened again . . ."

Bertine was always Miss B.'s favourite of the women from away. She'd made Marie laugh out loud the day Dr. Thomas came to deliver his lecture to the White Rose Temperance Society and the rest of the ladies of the Bay, sizing him up as soon as he walked through the door of the Seaside Centre. "I've never seen a man so clean. Looks like he doesn't believe in work. Almost looks sinful, doesn't it?" She's too young to be half as wise as Miss B., but she's just as fierce with her honesty. So, even though I'd decided that I wanted Archer to come home, that what had happened— his hurtful words, the hole in the wall, his needing to drink himself into a rage—was mostly my fault, I confided in Bertine, sobbing as I told her everything that had happened.

"I was tired of it, of him, I guess. I was cold to him, turned him away. He got angry with me. I don't blame him. I don't know. Maybe I'm not meant to be a wife. He's not happy with me. I'm sorry, I don't mean to cry. I don't blame him."

"That's terrible, just terrible." She handed me a hand-kerchief and put her arm around my shoulder.

"I know. I should've let him do as he pleased."

Bertine gave an angry snort. "If you say that again, I'll have to wash your mouth with tallow soap and vinegar."

"You think I'm right to feel this way? I tried to talk to Mother and—"

"My mind says you have every right to feel any which way you like. Not that a man's ever gonna understand, though."

"Was Hardy like this too?"

"Hardy's some sweet now, but he used to get all red-faced and mad over all kinds of things when we were first starting out, mostly burnt suppers or too much starch in the sheets. He changed his tune once there was a little one around."

"You think having a baby might settle Archer down?"

"Never know what might come between the jigs and reels. Of course, thinking you can change a man is thoughts wasted, but there's a bright side to everything, if you'll only look 'til you find it. Like my mother always said, *If your husband smokes, be thankful he doesn't chew; if he smokes and chews both, be thankful he doesn't drink; if he does all three, be thankful he won't live long.*" She started to bundle Lucy up for the walk home. "I'll come by next Thursday, say, seven o'clock?"

"That would be nice."

"What should I say we're doing?"

"Hmm?"

"Hardy gets his hackles up when I start doing things *for no good-God reason.* Seems to him that women have to have a *good-God reason* for everything."

"How about knitting socks for the war?"

"Perfect. That's what Dinah Moore says when she wants to sneak off with her cousin Hank, tells her father she's going to her sister's house to make care packages for the soldiers . . . it hasn't failed her yet. How's the Occasional Knitters Society sound?"

"Dinnie sneaks off with Hank?"

"Oh my gosh, yes, they've been at it since the war started. Everyone thinks she's pining after Emery Steele, but Dinnie has old Hank to keep her warm. I'll tell you the rest next Thursday, gotta get home and get supper on the stove."

Hart came by in the evening to say that he'd help keep things in order while Archer's away. At first I thought to say no, but I agreed to his caring for the team, mucking the barn and feeding the cow. I'll do the milking, since Archer nearly always forgot and poor Buttercup never liked his tardiness or the rough way he handled her teats. I'm afraid the sound of any man's voice might dry her up.

Sometimes it's hard to believe that Hart is the older of the two Bigelow brothers. Despite his crippled hand, and the fact that he's at least thirty, there's a willingness to his body, his step, his character that makes him seem younger than he is. He spends his days moving around the Bay, doing the work of two or even three men, helping wherever he sees a need. Most often a mess, with his curly brown hair full of hay dust, he's happiest when he's working, having no patience for "careless people and useless talk."

There was another visitor along with Hart: his collie, Pepper. "Would you mind taking a look at her? She's been limping for at least a week, and I can't figure why. She won't let me get hold of her to see."

I sat on the kitchen floor and looked her over. She had a small burr stuck between the pads of her paw, hidden under a tough mat of fur that she hadn't been able to gnaw loose, although she'd licked the rest of her foot raw, trying to get at it. The dog turned her head at me and tried to nip, but Hart kept her calm, and with one snip of my scissors I got rid of the troublesome thing.

He patted Pepper on the head. "Looks like I've witnessed Dora Bigelow's first miraculous healing at Spider Hill. Miss Babineau would be proud."

I laughed as I went to the cupboard under the china cabinet, looking through Miss B.'s things I had hidden away . . . the Willow Book was tucked alongside jars of remedies, bundles of herbs, tallow candles, figures of the Virgin Mary and a small wooden box filled with rosary beads, the pouch with my caul sitting on top. "Don't let word get out. I promised Archer I'd given up my witchery." I pulled out a jar of Miss B.'s marigold—honey salve and shut the door, tight. *Heals any burn or wound.*

Hart apologized for Pepper's growling. "Sorry she got a little testy with ya."

"I've seen worse." I bent down and rubbed the salve on her sore spot. "She may need to favour it for a few days. You should keep her inside until it heals up." Pepper hopped up and whimpered a bit as she made her way around the kitchen, sniffing for scraps.

Hart scratched his chin, combing his fingers at the roughness that comes with colder weather and his starting to grow a beard for winter. "Mother would have my head. She thinks Pepper's no better than a pig."

I set out a bowl of water and a soup bone for the dog to chew on. "She'll stay here, then. Doctor's orders."

Over tea, I showed Hart my most recent letter from Borden, forgetting that my brother had said a few unkind things about Archer.

> I told Albert about your marriage to Archer Bigelow. He said it better than I can. "Tell Dorrie she'd best be happy when we get home or we'll have to take Archer out to the woods to go hunting." I added that you should tell Hart he's in some hot water for not keeping his eyes on you!

Hart grumbled, "You tell Borden not to worry. It seems Archie's a new man now that he's got you for a wife. I never would have guessed he'd be making his way, selling Bibles to the good people of Kings County." He scratched Pepper behind the ears and looked at me. "It's Bibles, right? Isn't that what you said?"

I opened my eyes wide and tried to give a convincing stare. "That's right."

He put on his coat and went to the door. "God knows Archie could sell rain barrels in the desert."

"That's right."

I don't think he believed me.

~ *October 25, 1917*

Expecting that a woman might be with child after only a few months of marriage isn't unheard of. I got my hopes up when my courses were late, but despite my daydreams of a happy home, the blood has come.

Archer's been gone nearly three weeks. It can't be long before he runs out of money and needs to come home. Even if he doesn't care for me, his mother still holds the purse strings to the rest of his inheritance. This is one time when I'm glad she wants to keep Archer in her reach.

Bertine says, "He's not the first man to run away from his wife. He'll get tired of having to look for a place to rest his head, of having to explain who he is, of having to think about what comes next . . . he'll find his way home."

Whatever it is that brings him back, I'll welcome him with my affection, my love and my body. It's not that I expect that anything I do will ever change him; he can do as he pleases as long as I can have the one thing I've always wanted. Once there's a child inside me, nothing else will matter.

22

THE FIRST OFFICIAL MEETING of the
Occasional Knitters Society included not only
Bertine but Mabel and Sadie as well, each woman
bringing her children and a basket filled with yarn and needles. Bertine set out to teach us her grandmother's way of
knitting socks. She said it had come down through her family, first from the Orkney Islands, then to Newfoundland,
"and now to the Occasional Knitters of Scots Bay."

"Mum always called it the 'lover's hook,' other women
I know just call it *thrummin'*. Whatever you wants to call it,
it gives any sock, mitt or hat twice as much warmth. Mum
and my aunties made a batch for my brother's company,
and now the rest of the regiment's asking for them as well.
The boys on the front pay or trade whatever they can for
them." Bertine turned a finished sock inside out, the fleecy
thrums all fluffed out from her neat rows, her voice boast-
ing. "They've even been reported to have made their way as
far as Egypt. I'll bet no woman from the Bay can say that
much for her socks."

Mabel suggested we knit the initials O.K.S. into each
pair, "just to leave our mark." I added a band of white

around the cuffs of mine, a private prayer for peace. Between knits and purls the women from away became comfortable and wild with their talk, their thoughts moving from one thing to the next, fearless and far short of what Aunt Fran would consider proper. As the children settled in, the conversation shifted from bemoaning the wet autumn gales to the best and most effective way to "get with child."

"The trick is, don't get up 'til morning." Sadie was rocking her baby back and forth in a large round-bottomed basket at her feet. "Whatever you do, don't stand up until you have to or you'll lose the seed." Sadie's wiry and strong for such a tiny woman, always with laughter in her sea-grey eyes, her tongue as quick and wry as that of any sailor. With a wink and a grin she'll lead you to words you hadn't intended on saying, news you'd just as soon not share. "Speaking of lovers, how's that new husband of yours faring on the road, Dora?"

I bowed my head, pretending to have lost count of my stitches. "Fine. He's just fine."

"I guess you must miss him terribly." The baby's eyes fluttered and closed as Sadie clacked the needles between her fingers. "If I had a man that handsome, I know I would—"

Bertine frowned at Sadie and shook her head no.

"What's that face for, Bertine? I didn't mean anything by it. All I was saying is Archer Bigelow's a fair-looking fellow. Don't you act like you haven't noticed."

Bertine's face turned red.

"And ... I seem to recall hearing you say on more than one occasion that you'd guess he was clean enough to eat off of."

Mabel snorted, trying to hold back her laughter. "Stop it, Sadie, you'll have Dora in knots and fits, and me about to wet myself."

Bertine patted my knee to get my attention and then cupped her large breasts with her hands. "Don't worry, Dorrie. Sadie makes up for what she hasn't *got* by being rough as a cob, the little whore."

"Call me a whore all you like, Mrs. Tupper. My granny always said, *it's bad girls and whores that's the only ones who like it.* And I've been liking it just fine since I was fourteen."

Mabel stopped laughing and bounced her baby on her lap. "My mother took me aside the night before my wedding and told me, 'Mabel, dear, after the wedding's over, your husband's going to take you home. Something's going to happen to you, and you won't like it.' I didn't have the heart to tell her she was telling me a little too late."

Bertine sighed. "I don't mind it, I guess. But I've given up trying too hard at it. With Hardy, it's like one of those carousel rides—you get on and the minute you decide you like the music, it's a lovely ride, you'd like to go round again . . . just when I start to feel like I'm getting someplace, he's done."

Feeling bold, I asked, "But don't you have to *try,* if you want a child to come from it?"

"These days I only *try* when I want it to be over nice and fast. Like when I've got pots to scrub in the kitchen, or I think the babies will hear and I'll have to be up with them all night. But it doesn't matter what I do: once my courses come back, all Hardy will have to do is shake my hand, look at me sideways, and I'll have another little bun in the oven."

Mabel took a sip of tea and blushed. "God forgive me for saying it, but no man can do you better than you can do for yourself. If you think he's got to make you happy before you can have his child, you'll be stuck like Sarah, waiting for an angel. She was too picky, and old Abraham just couldn't seem to please her. That's the part of the story that doesn't get told, that's all."

Bertine nodded. "It's true. I knew a woman like that once. She went to some old howdie-witch who told her to tie three knots in a red string, wrap it around her waist and let her husband take her from behind, like a dog."

"Did it work?"

"Sure enough. She's long dead now, but not before she had three sets of twins."

Sadie shook her head in disbelief. "If you want to enjoy yourself, get up on top. Now there's a ride. Of course, if it's a baby you want, then it's best if you're on the bottom. Make yourself a nice firm pillow filled with buckwheat. Put it under your hips so when he climbs on top of you, he'll go in, right deep. Pull him to you when he groans. Think of dancing; think of reaching for him from the inside out. Think of the last time you were truly surprised—you might even find you like it. The trick is, don't get up 'til morning."

23

ONCE AUNT FRAN got wind of the Occasional Knitters Society, she decided to start hosting "family teas" on Sunday afternoons for Mother, Precious and me. As much as I try to refuse her invitations, Precious's fifteenth birthday fell on a Sunday and I couldn't stand to disappoint her sweet, fragile, china-doll heart.

I brought her my volume of *Heart Throbs, 1905: The Old Scrapbook*, a graduation gift from Miss Gertrude Coffill, the spinster schoolteacher of Scots Bay.

> Heart throbs—yes, heart throbs of happiness, heart throbs of courage, heart throbs that make us feel better. Those things that appeal to you must appeal to others; that note of inspiration laid aside—bring it forth and let us make a magazine that will speak the language of the heart as well as of the mind. I want you to send me these clippings to show me what kind of stories interest you, your mother, sisters, brothers, sons and daughters. I want to know just what kind of short, pithy articles you would select if you were sitting here with me at my editorial desk. You are

constantly reading stories and anecdotes in the magazines, books, newspapers or religious periodicals. Perhaps you have clipped them or pasted them in your scrapbook, or you may have remembered where you have seen such a story and said to yourself, "Well, that's about as bright as it could be." That's the kind of story I want.

I have placed on deposit with the First National Bank of Boston ten thousand dollars. This money to be held in trust until the time specified below, when it will be divided among those who help me. To ten persons sending in the best clippings, I will give each one

A PILE OF SILVER DOLLARS AS HIGH
AS EACH SUCCESSFUL CONTESTANT

Miss Coffill's sister Anabelle was one of the lucky ten that was measured for a prize. She married and moved away to New Hampshire some years ago, but no school year goes by without Miss Coffill telling some part of her sister's story. "Annabelle was a wee, beautiful girl. The day that telegram arrived was the one day she wished she were more like her tall, homely sister." It's through Annabelle's unfortunate lack of height that the children of Scots Bay have learned to figure sums:

If there are fifteen silver dollars to every inch,
And Annabelle measures four feet, three and
    a half inches
Then how much was her prize?

After we found the answer, we went on to measure each other, and after that we went home and measured our parents. Charlie went so far as to measure our fat old sow—ear to foot, snout to tail. Then he climbed on the roof of the barn and measured that too. Miss Coffill was too polite to say so, but we all knew what she wanted us to think . . . if we were worth more than Annabelle, we were doing just fine. At seventy years old, Gertrude Coffill still stands straight and tall—five feet, eleven inches. She's never had a husband, but at least she knows she's worth 1,065 silver dollars.

Heart Throbs is the only book I own that I know Aunt Fran won't object to and that I'm willing to part with. Among the many pages of "pithy" verse and endless tributes to Abe Lincoln, loyal hunting dogs and an "old canoe" are a few gems: Hamlet's soliloquies, George Eliot's "O May I Join the Choir Invisible" and Kipling's "Recessional." I have marked these and a few other passages with pieces of red string in hopes that Precious will find them. (The rest of the string is now tied around my middle, waiting for Archer to come home.) I also gave her a new sewing basket, one that Archer's mother had given me after the wedding. My old basket is fine, so I had no trouble giving up the new one to Precious. I wove a few lengths of pink ribbon through the lid and around the handle in hopes that the widow won't recognize it at a quilting bee or ladies social. I'm sure Aunt Fran didn't think much of my presents, but Precious made quite a fuss and was very sweet about the whole thing. I would have liked to have brought her something new, but with no word from Archer, and my still pretending all is well, I'm careful to save any extra I have in case I'll need it for the winter.

Aunt Fran was polite, but her kindness always comes at a price. She never says anything directly, of course. No, for

Aunt Fran there's a sickening joy that creeps into her voice from the just-so placement of *they say* and *or so I've heard.* Like iodine in a wound, her words are bright, painful reminders of whatever you lack, and whatever mistake she thinks you've made. "They say these days many of the men who go out drumming door-to-door are worse than sailors. They drink away their earnings, leaving their wives penniless and alone, or so I've heard. I certainly hope that your dear Archer hasn't run into any of that sort while he's selling Bibles. When will he be home next, dear?"

"Soon, Auntie Fran, he'll be home soon."

"Well, I hope so, for your sake. Cold weather's coming, and according to the almanacs, both *Belcher's* and *Ladies' Rural Companion,* it's going to be a difficult winter. More ice and snow than we've seen in years. Would you like to see? I finished reading the *Ladies'* already, I'd be happy to lend it to you." She reached into the sewing basket by her chair. "There's a helpful section on making salves and poultices . . . it reminded me of your dear friend Marie Babineau. And this year's recipe winners are listed here on the front. *Everything Apples: Apple Brown Betty, Applesauce, Apple Pie, Baked Apples and Pork Roast.* Maybe you'll find a new favourite dish for Archer. Take it with you when you go."

Precious yawned. "Can we have cake now? Or play a hand of whist?"

Mother interrupted, as if she had saved up all her questions so they could come out at once, one after another, buzzing in my ears so I couldn't think of what to say. "Reverend Pineo says he'd like to order new hymnals, prayer books and a Bible or two when Archer comes home. Do you know when that might be? I'd like to be able to tell the reverend something soon, so he can plan accordingly.

By Christmas, do you think? Did you say you'd heard from him? Has he travelled far? I'd expect people would need the comfort of the Lord's word in times like these. I suppose he's quite busy. Did you say that you'd heard from him?"

Aunt Fran put her hand under my chin and tilted my face towards the light. "Dora, dear, your face is flushed. Are you feeling under the weather? You could stay here tonight if you don't feel up to going home."

Precious clapped her hands together. "You could share my bed, just like we used to. We can tell secrets until dawn."

My face burned and my throat ached as I tried to keep from crying. "I'll be fine, Auntie, maybe a little cold coming on. I just need some rest. I should get home. Thank you for a lovely evening."

Mother whispered in my ear, "Did Archer leave you with a little bun in the oven?"

"No, Mama, it's not that."

"Are you sure?"

"Yes, Mama."

Aunt Fran announced, "I think she should visit Dr. Thomas. A woman can't be expected to look after herself when she's with child, even one who's lived with a midwife."

"But I'm not . . ."

Fran scolded me. "Not another word, Dora. I'm certain the doctor will see you at my request. Irwin has business in Canning this week. You'll ride with him. I'll take care of the rest, I insist."

She also insisted that Uncle Irwin hitch up the buggy to take me home. He took the longest route, whistling to the horses, talking to them about the weather. The long shadows of winter are coming on, the shoulder of the mountain stretching out, brooding and black, the god Glooscap asleep, his greatness turned away from the Bay and our little lives. The crescent moon lay on her back, floating between the darkness and the sea. An oil lamp, set near a kitchen window, cast a small yellow halo of light on two children as they begged their mother for one last treat. The smell of spruce fires, tended by watchful husbands, cut through the air. If I could steal these things and make them my own, I would.

Dr. Thomas diagnosed me as having neurasthenia, "a female disorder that presents itself through hysterical tendencies." He said it is not uncommon among the young women of today and that "the condition is treatable, but not always curable."

"I spoke with your kind aunt, Mrs. Jeffers. She's terribly concerned about an episode you had during a recent visit to her home. Are you certain you aren't with child?"

"Yes. Quite certain."

"But you'd like to have a child, of course."

"Yes."

After a brief examination and several questions, he announced, "Your premature exposure to the primitive and sometimes unseemly regenerative aspects of womanhood, coupled with your current desire to bear children, has left your body's systems in a constant state of nervousness. Your fragile psyche has forced your female organs to collapse, leaving you barren and gaunt with illness." He shook his head and sighed. "You haven't attended any more births?"

"No, not since Sadie Loomer's, on my wedding day."

"Good. See that you don't. There'll be no chance of your conceiving until we have your condition under control."

He got up and went to a closet on the other side of the room. Outside of the addition of several large diagrams depicting the human anatomy and various medical treatments, his office hadn't changed since the grand tour for the ladies of Scots Bay. While he was gone, I read from a large poster of women's health concerns that was tacked to the wall.

Feeling Anxious? Tired? Weepy?
You are not alone. The modernization of society has brought about an increase in neurasthenia, greensickness and hysteria.

Symptoms of Neurasthenia include: Weeping, melancholy, anxiety, irritability, depression, outrageousness, insomnia, mental and physical weariness, idle talking, sudden fevers, morbid fears, frequent titillation, forgetfulness, palpitations of the heart, headaches, writing cramps, mental confusion, constant worry and fear of impending insanity.

Talk to your physician. He can help.

A small stove in the corner of the room was knocking and ticking with heat. Its noises echoed the nervous pounding of my heart.

"Lean back on the table and I'll administer the treatment. It prepares the womb, leaving it ripe and waiting for a dear little soul." Dr. Thomas folded back the skirt of my dress.

I chose to remove only my stockings and undergarments, leaving my dress on for modesty's sake, hoping he wouldn't notice or ask after the red string around my waist. He pulled a small cart alongside the table and opened the large black box that sat on top of it. I could just make out the label—*The Swedish Movement Health Generator*—an odd, heavy-looking device, surrounded by a cushion of red velvet.

It was silver, new and shining, with a long black cord trailing from one end. Several attachments were nestled into depressions around the machine, each one resembling the mechanical snout of an animal or the polished, dark beak of an exotic bird.

"Truly a medical marvel." He twisted a large, rounded black nose to the other end of the machine. "I can administer the treatment in a matter of minutes, sending blood rushing to your congested parts, releasing inner stress, relieving you of your suffering. You'll leave here today with bright eyes and pink cheeks. You should sleep like a baby tonight, Mrs. Bigelow."

As Dr. Thomas flipped a switch on the handle, a loud buzzing erupted. He raised his voice over the noise. "Spread your legs and try to relax."

His face was steady, determined. I closed my eyes and tried to imagine being somewhere else. There was mending to be done at home. Had I knitted enough socks for Archer for the winter? There might be enough apples in the cellar for another batch of applesauce. I should see if they have started to go soft. I hope they haven't spoiled. The *Ladies' Rural Companion* suggests cinnamon: *It gives this winter favourite a kick, especially when served hot.*

Dr. Thomas circled the tip of the machine, reaching farther and farther past quivering pink folds of skin, opening, searching my womb. It caused my heart to race, making it difficult to concentrate. This was something more than I had ever felt in the arms of my husband, even more than I'd been able to give myself between the dark warmth of the blankets of my adolescent bed. Dr. Thomas was right; as I struggled to keep my brain occupied with innocent thoughts, my blood ran hot, gathering strength, pulsing with life. I thought of Sunday hymns, pages from worthy books, imagined Mother reading about the whirling dervishes of Constantinople, her hands pulling a large brown book from the shelf, its title gold and shining on the spine, *Good Words, 1866.*

The Dervishes themselves seemed low-bred and commonplace, with pale faces and a semi-sensuous, semi-nervous, and hysterical look about them.

Feverish and tense, my hips rose and fell, following his every movement. My knees trembled. The strand of Miss B.'s rosary beads I'd been wearing felt tight around my neck, as if they were pulling at me and I couldn't get loose, couldn't catch my breath. I bit my lip and the sweet, alarming taste of blood lingered on the tip of my tongue.

The tendency to express or relieve the stirrings and tumults of the soul by outward signs of joy such as singing, shouting, dancing or the like is natural, though these often pass into the hysterical.

"Good, Mrs. Bigelow. Fast, laboured breathing is what I like to see. It excites the nervous system, clears away disease."

The transition from mere animalism, unchecked by moral feeling, to what is grossly sensual is a very natural one.

If you want to enjoy yourself, get up on top . . . Think of dancing; think of reaching for him from the inside out. Think of the last time you were truly surprised . . .

"Release your pain, Mrs. Bigelow, cleanse the blood, release your pain."

My eyes startled open with a single, throbbing cry. The treatment was a success.

The buzzing stopped. The Swedish Movement Health Generator stopped. Dr. Thomas smiled; he had completed his work. I fell from my heavenly, spinning dance into giddiness and uncontrollable fits of laughter.

"Mrs. Bigelow? Mrs. Bigelow! Calm yourself. Get hold of your senses. Please, listen to me."

Tears streamed down my face. I couldn't stop trembling with laughter. Pulling my coat over my shoulders, I rushed from the office.

Secondary symptoms include: Yawning, itching, stomach upsets, muscle spasms and ticklishness.

Dr. Thomas followed behind, my Sunday silk stockings trailing from his hand. He shouted as he chased me down the street. "I would advise treatment on a weekly basis, Mrs. Bigelow. Your condition is very advanced. You risk complete emotional and physical debilitation if left unchecked."

Occurring most often in unmarried women and young widows, hysteroneurasthenic disorders are frequently manifest as attacks or "fits" of neurosis. Afterward, she is ashamed of her actions—even to the point of denying them or becoming offended when reminded of her behaviour.

Dr. Gilbert Thomas
124 Pleasant St.
Canning, Nova Scotia

November 6, 1917

Mrs. Dora Bigelow
Scots Bay, Nova Scotia

Dear Mrs. Bigelow,
Although my recent diagnosis of your present condition may
have come as a shock to you, I must urge you to heed my
advice and act promptly and appropriately. In our last visit, it
was made clear to me that your illness warrants close observation and care. As you have experienced, there is an effective
remedy for your ailments, and I am more than happy to take
whatever course of treatment is necessary for you to feel whole
and healthy again.

You need not worry about the cost, as I have spoken with
your kind-hearted aunt, Mrs. Francine Jeffers, and she has
agreed to see to your expenses. Be assured that she is not aware
of the delicate nature of your condition, but she is simply
concerned, as am I, for your happiness and well-being.

Again, I urge you, do not delay. This kind of situation
can quickly go wrong and leave even the strongest of women
wrecked, helpless and in need of hospitalization.

Sincerely,
Dr. Gilbert Thomas

~ November 8, 1917

Archer's been gone nearly a month.

Many of the symptoms of my neurasthenia have persisted: insomnia, melancholy, sudden fits of weeping and general weariness. Dr. Thomas has written several letters, all friendly reminders that his services are still available. While I understand his concern that my condition might worsen, "rendering me useless to my family and my community," I can't bring myself to face him again. Besides, I think I may have found a treatment of my own.

In the back of the *Ladies' Rural Companion* Aunt Fran lent me, I found an advertisement for the White Cross Home Vibrator. I will purchase it with some of the extra money I've been saving—the little Miss B. had gotten from generous mothers, what's left after my monthly receipt from Newcomb's Dry Goods, and the coins Father puts in my shoes every time I come home for supper.

The White Cross Battery-Powered Vibrator

Genuine Swedish movement and wonderfully refreshing effects, the same treatment for which you would have to pay at least $2.00 each in a physician's office.

Vibration is Life

It will chase away the years like magic. Every nerve, every fibre of your whole body will tingle with the force of your awakened powers. All the keen relish, the pleasures of youth, will throb within you. Rich, red blood will be sent coursing through your veins, and you will realize thoroughly the joy of living. *Your self-respect, even, will be increased a hundredfold.*

You can relieve pain, stiffness and weakness, and you can make the body plump and build it up with thrilling, refreshing vibration and electricity. *Just a few minutes' use of the wonderful vibrator, and the red blood tingles through your veins and arteries and you feel vigorous, strong and well.*

~ *November 25, 1917*
10 o'clock in the morning

A package came in the post today, the White Cross Home
Vibrator from Lindstrom-Smith Co., 253 LaSalle Street,
Chicago, Illinois, U.S.A. With the arrival of this "medical
marvel," I feel hopeful that I have put my savings to good use.

I will monitor and record the results of my using the
machine. If there is still no change in my condition, then I
will make a new appointment with the good doctor.

~ *Noon*

After some difficulty in connecting the machine to the large,
weighty battery, I have begun home treatments with the
White Cross Vibrator. I am pleased with the results thus far!
This may well be the answer to my prayers.

(This first attempt was much like my experience in Dr.
Thomas's office, although I was careful not to extend myself
beyond the heavenly spinning of the dervishes.)

~ *Half-past two*

I was feeling anxious and sad after lunch. All through my
daily chores, I was plagued with thoughts of loneliness,
thinking Archer might never come home. In an effort to help
myself and to test the true powers of the machine, I have
treated myself a second time today. Again, I was invigorated
to the point of great happiness. In fact, I am smiling to
myself with a sense of pride that this "physician's domain" is
so easily entered into by a lowly midwife such as myself.
Have I stumbled upon yet another exercise that is better
attended to by the fairer sex? Wouldn't the scholars and
journals of medicine be astounded to learn of my findings?

~ Ten o'clock at night

My third treatment left me glowing with exhaustion and a
bit feverish. It brings such joy to my heart, it is hard to know
what is the proper amount. (Perhaps three times in one day
is too much?) I was so tired that I lay down before supper
and didn't wake until nearly nine tonight! I feel splendid.
Ate a late dinner of breakfast. Bacon, stewed apples, heavy
cream and brown bread. I am confident that this, along with
my faith in Miss B.'s remedies, will have me ready (and more
than willing) when Archer returns.

24

Dear Dora,

I'm sorry to have left you for so long.
Will be home as soon as I can and with much to tell.
I'll be by your side by Christmas at the latest.

> *With affection,*
> *Your husband,*
> *Archie*

ARCHER'S POSTCARD WAS enough to send me back to the Willow Book, searching to see if I had missed any preparation or prayers that might help to bring a child into my womb. With each remedy I check off my list, I grow more anxious for his return (and selfish enough not to want to share the news with anyone else). I must have him to myself if this is ever going to work.

I am strict with my daily ritual: a good dose of Miss B.'s Moon Elixir four (or more) times a day—breakfast, lunch, tea, supper, and then a double dose along with a vibratory treatment before bed. I sleep on my back only, with a firm pillow under my hips, keeping my womb properly "tipped" until morning.

Miss B.'s recommended moon-bath was a cold and unsettling affair. I chose to lie in the cross where Three Brooks Road and the old logging road back to Miss B.'s meet. After no time at all, I was shivering.

Father always warned against sleeping with my head exposed to the moonlight. *Always keep the curtains closed on a full moon, and cover your head when you go out . . . especially when she's bright over the water. If it's light enough to make hay, then you might likely come down with moonstroke. Drives a person mad. Worse than sunstroke by far.* Several times I startled, thinking I'd heard footsteps in the road. It was only the wind stirring the dry dead leaves still clinging to the trees. Once, I even thought I heard the sound of Miss B.'s ghost calling to me, imagined the wispy trail of her skirts flying over my head, but it turned out that one of Laird Jessup's cows had gotten loose and was snorting its hot breath between the alders. Too much elixir that night, I guess.

I feel Miss B.'s remedies are working. The elixir seems especially helpful. When taken along with my treatment, I'm left feeling warm and wanting inside. I find myself waiting for evening, excusing myself from hymn sings and late suppers with Mother or the Occasional Knitters so I can be alone and have a healthy dose (or two), so I can dream of Archer coming home and the time when he'll be the one I want.

Hart came to the house after minding the animals for the night. Although Pepper's paw has been healed for a while now, he'd decided it was finally time to take the dog home. "There'll be snow soon, and I need her to help bring the cattle up from the pasture, closer to the barns." She'd been acting good as new, but was quick to put on a limp when Hart called to her.

Hart crouched down low and called again. "Come on, girl. Come on now, Pepper."

She hid under the table.

I sat on the floor and tried to coax her out with half a tea biscuit. "It's my fault she doesn't want to go. I've been letting her lick my plate after every meal, and she's gotten used to sleeping on the end of the bed."

He clapped his hands together once and commanded her, "Here."

Ears laid back, tail tucked under, she sulked over to him and lay at his feet, belly up. He laughed and rubbed her with both hands, cooing to her. "That'a girl, Pep. Let's go home. We've got a long day ahead of us tomorrow."

Pepper sprang up, tail wagging, all forgiven.

No sooner had Hart shut the door behind him when he rushed back into the house. He pulled my coat from its hook and held it out to me. "Come with me."

I slid on my boots and threw my coat over my shoulders. "What is it? Something wrong?"

He pulled me out into the dooryard. "We're not going far."

I looked out into the dark of the trees below the hill, thinking Pepper had run off after a raccoon or maybe a porcupine. I slapped Hart's arm and pointed to Pepper, who was lying patiently on the porch, her tail thumping on the steps. "She's right there. It's cold and I'm going back inside. Get the bucket off your head, take your dog and go home."

He held tight to my arm. "Look up."

Northern lights reached above the spruce at the top of the mountain's ridge, shimmering blue then green. They quivered and danced, every once in a while giving way to a stretch of deep pink. They're not often seen in the Bay, and I can't recall ever seeing them so brilliant and bright. Miss B. once told me that she believed the lights were there all the time, "like rainbows or an honest friend, they's there, but we's only blessed enough to see their remarkability when we needs to. The secret of how the earth was made is caught up in their dance, in the tune you hear 'em whistlin' sometime. Them lights tell the story of the world, it's just that God ain't let us find the words how to say it out loud. But if he ever sees fit to tell me, I'll let you know."

For all their differences, there's something similar between Hart and Archer, the heaviness of their breathing, the catch that comes down low, in the deepest part of the voice, the way they both, without meaning to, leave me feeling nervous. If I fear them both, it's because one always leaves me not knowing if he's happy, the other not knowing where I stand. They are different, of course, and not to be confused.

"He doesn't know what he's doing. He'll come back and when he does, he'll laugh at anyone who tries to tell him he was gone far too long."

"I know." I was going to tell him about Archer's recent note, but he went on before I could say anything. As soon as he began to speak, I thought better of it.

"If you want me to go out and find him, bring him home, I will."

"No. Better he comes home on his own."

25

M Y GREAT-GRANDMOTHER Mrs. Mae Loveless used to say, *When you fail to cure, the maggots set in.* If you didn't know her, you'd think she was talking about shad, or herring, or mackerel, but Granny Mae liked to spout off that phrase whenever she had the chance. More often than not, she was meaning to talk about the proper way to raise a child, or the way age sets too many lines in a young mother's face if she's got a hard life. If you fail to cure, if you neglect what's important, if you don't take notice . . . *mind your manners, watch the pot, keep an eye, careful now with your husband or he'll get away from you.* Granny Mae also liked to mention that her mother, Mrs. Dahlia Woodall, was a legend unto herself and the *true* reason the Great Shad Seine of Scots Bay went down. "Those men were forced to meet with Dahlia's hand, and that was that."

When a few wealthy men from Halifax got wind of the amount of shad that was to be caught in the Bay, they came in, making all sorts of promises, and founded the Great Seine Company at Scots Bay. Some say it was as grand a venture as the railroad that runs from Halifax to the Annapolis Valley, and as much talked of in every town between. Men from the Bay were eager to sign on to work. The women gladly took on the task of knitting large pieces of net, their hands skilled at working birch needles and making seine knots. In the spring, each house brought their section of the seine to be laid against the next, the women sitting in the road, weaving the thing together.

They set up a mighty seine, as well as a bunkhouse for the foreman and the workers. But rather than paying the men a fair wage, the boss thought it better to pay them in hogsheads of rum, often times "passing around" their wages as the catch was being made. Before long, the men would be helplessly drunk, some having to be thrown into the skiffs along with the fish. Others staggered about, getting lost in the fog or falling down on each other, splashing and yelling like schoolboys. In the end, much of the catch would be lost, uncured and left rotting on the shore.

While the men were floundering about, tipping over their shad-filled skiffs, not knowing the tail end of a fish from its ugly gaping mouth, Dahlia rounded up the women and marched out to the seine. With wash baskets and handcarts, they collected all the fish they could and took them home to clean and salt for their own use. Granny Mae would always say with great pride, *In all that madness, those women weren't about to let their children starve.* As this went on, talk started to make its way down the mountain about the lazy, drunken, *nearly related* fools that lived in Scots Bay. The women fast grew tired of having to make such incredible efforts to save the shad and their husbands' reputations. Dahlia knew it wouldn't be long before the men of the Bay would start losing their lives as well as their livelihoods to the "Old Demon Rum."

On the evening of August 1, 1800, the women of Scots Bay met at the Woodall family homestead. Dahlia was waiting. She told the women that the time had come to put an end to "Satan's elixir of idleness," that "tonight we'll bring our husbands home, we'll bring them back to the fold." She locked their children safely in the cabin and handed each woman a torch, as they marched out the door. On that warm, summer night, armed with fire and broadaxes, the women went down to the seine, circling the bunkhouse, singing "Jerusalem." When the men came out to see what was happening, the ladies rushed in, smashing each and every noggin of rum, letting the amber liquor flow through the cracks of the floor and into the earth. Now, in their turn, *they* whooped and hollered, while their torches set flame to the walls. The roof caught light, crumbling into bright blossoms of orange and red, then falling away to ash.

If I wanted my husband back, I'd have to bring him home myself.

"I seen him at the Burnt Nickel two nights ago. I didn't think anything of it, since most men stop in for a meal or something to drink on their way to somewheres else, but when Archie got himself in a bit of trouble, I thought I'd better let you know." Jack Tupper was sitting at my kitchen table, shoving what was left of a generous piece of apple pie in his mouth. Almost fifty, thin as a rail and with no wife, Jack begins most conversations with a simple cup of coffee, but never makes his point until he's eaten away half your icebox. "I suppose you know as well as anybody that Archie likes his share of the brew. If he's had just a nip or two, he's not so bad, but this time he had an empty bottle in one hand and nowheres near a full house in the other. What's worse is that he didn't have enough in his pockets to pay what he owed to old Georgie Wickwire. Archie begged for a second chance, double or nothing, but Wickwire doesn't give second chances, and he don't put up with welshers."

"Was Archer hurt? Where's he now?"

"Wickwire hired someone to take him out and 'make good on the debt' . . . the man can afford not to get his hands dirty like that. Archie took a good beating: broken fingers and ribs, his ears all boxed and bloody, and his eyes are right black. Mr. T.L. Gordon, the apothecary, you know him? He said he'd bandage Archie up, sober him up and let him stay in the room above the shop 'til he's fit to come home."

I put the pie plate in front of him, still three-quarters full. "Have as much as you like, Jack. There's fresh bread on the counter and cream in the icebox to go with it. Thanks for taking the trouble to come by. I'll take care of the rest."

"Okay if I eat it right out of the pan?"

"That's fine. Leave the plates on the counter when you're done." I packed a few things in Miss B.'s birthing bag and headed for the door. "Just keep Archer's whereabouts under your hat for now, alright?"

Jack looked up, nodded and smiled, his mouth bulging with pie.

Charlie was kind enough to take me down to Mr. Gordon's shop in Kentville. It takes a half-day's ride to get there, so it was late when we arrived. Archer was asleep in the bare-walled room upstairs.

Miss B. often spoke of Mr. Gordon but never met him. He'd send the things she needed (castor oil, Jayes Fluid, cotton thread and other supplies) up by post, most of the time not charging her much, if anything, for it. There were three other pharmacists closer to Scots Bay, but she wouldn't hear of going to anyone else. "It's got to come from a believer. Did you know what the T.L. spelled out is? That man's given name is Mister *Trusted Lord* Gordon. Praise the blessed Virgin, it's *Trusted Lord*! Say so right on his scripts. If his mama thought enough to call him that, then he ain't got no choice but to believe."

Archer was still moaning a bit over his bruises, but was full of charm and remorse. "Ah, my darling wife. Couldn't stand another day without me, could you, dear?"

"After two months, you'd think she'd almost forget she was married." Charlie crossed his arms over his chest, looking tired and angry.

I sat on the bed next to Archer, adjusting his bandages. Although I shared Charlie's thoughts, I couldn't help but feel sorry for Archer's sad state, even somewhat responsible. I would have said anything to make sure he was coming home. "He's been through enough without your scolding him, Charlie."

Mr. Gordon was kind enough to put us all up for the night. "No sense in your going back home in the dark. Plenty of room right here."

26

THERE WAS MUCH COMMOTION in Mr. Gordon's shop the morning of December 6. A man ran in from the street saying that a terrible disaster had fallen on Halifax. Others said the same, but no one could say exactly what had happened or what had been the cause of it all. Two local physicians came in, asking that Mr. Gordon give them all the supplies he could manage to do without. All doctors, nurses, midwives and other help were to report to the train station before noon. Charlie was quick to tell them "My sister, Dorrie, is a midwife, she's a healer. She'll go."

"I don't know, Charlie. I should get Archer back home. How much help could I be?"

One of the doctors urged, "They need every pair of hands they can get. If you have any experience at all, dressing wounds, caring for the sick . . ."

"I'll go," Charlie volunteered.

"Charlie, no."

"I'm going, Dora, even if you won't."

Charlie looked at Archer as if he expected him to say he would come along as well, but Archer just shook his head and held up his bandaged arm. "I've got wounds of my own to tend."

Mr. Gordon packed several boxes, putting them on the counter for the doctors. He handed a small medical bag to me. "You go on and help. I'll look after him."

Autumn gales can strip away an entire wharf from the shore, a storm of snow and ice can break the roof of a cattle barn, but those are things brought by nature. I have never been so frightened or humbled as when I saw the wreckage left behind by the Halifax Explosion, miles upon miles of waste brought on by man's devotion to war.

It took a few hours to reach Halifax. (My first time on a train. My first time that far from home.) Before we came upon any signs of the disaster, we stopped along the line in Falmouth and then Windsor, where we saw masses of wounded men, women and children headed for hospitals in Truro. At least one doctor and a nurse from our party left to join them, as there were so many who were sobbing, bleeding or nearly dead already. I remember holding Charlie's hand as we moved closer and closer to the city. I clutched it tight as glimpses of crumbled chimneys and piles of debris turned into an endless stretch of blackened homes and ruined lives. Grey clouds hung low to the ground. Bits of tarpaper floated in the sky, first dancing light and joyful like dandelion fluff, then landing here and there, becoming part of the dirty landscape. When the train could go no farther, we walked into Richmond, where the tracks loop around along the Narrows and the east end of the harbour, passing visions that I had imagined as being only a part of hell. Houses were torn in two, wide gaping holes left where walls once stood. I saw a mother and her children huddled in the corner of their home, holding their hands over a pile of burning coals, trying to hang on to what little comfort they could find. As we made our way to Camp Hill Hospital, we came upon the dead, their limbs or heads caught between floorboards, jagged pieces of metal poking through their flesh. Their bodies, their homes, their lives had gone black. Death burned and stank in the heavy, greasy air and grabbed at my lungs. Worse off than the dead were those left to wander . . . those looking for someone or something they could recognize. Clothes torn, their faces covered with blood and soot, they had become part of an army of grief, each one looking as ruined and lost as the next.

The hours came to nothing as the bodies moved in and out of Camp Hill. There was never a time when I could wait to see what was coming, or stop to count how many were dead. My corner of the second floor was open to everything else, doctors sawing off tattered, bloody limbs, nurses pulling sheets over bodies, voices calling out from the rows of stretchers. *Please, help. I'm alive. Mama* . . . We did what we could to comfort those around us, but it was never enough.

They sent the pregnant women back to me. They came, clutching at their bellies or holding a hand between their legs like it was all they could do to keep the child in. The sound and force of the explosion had sent them into labour, and there wasn't much I could do to turn it back. Child after child born too soon, a dozen or more like Darcy, dying in their mothers' arms, and even more that were born barely human, already dead. A reporter from the *Halifax Journal,* collecting names for the daily death roll, told me that half-ton anchors had gone sailing out of the harbour, flying over houses and crashing into factories and schools. It was a miracle any of these babies or their mothers survived. For every baby that was lost, there were just as many who would live, only to become orphans when their mothers died from shock.

The reporter said, "It's important that you get their names, especially if you think they won't make it. The bodies are piling up in the morgue, and we don't know who's who. Go through their pockets if you have to." In all the confusion it had never occurred to me to ask. This wasn't like anything I had experienced at home, where everyone knows everyone else and there's never a question of who you are, or where you belong. He took an envelope from his pocket and handed it to me. It contained several paper tags, like the kind you'd attach to a parcel for delivery. "When you lose one, fill this out as best you can. It will save time in bagging the bodies and moving them to the morgue. There's so many dead that there's no good place to put them all. They're using the school down on Chebucto Road for now."

Several times a day I directed people there, people who had come searching for their loved ones at Camp Hill only to learn they were dead.

Lara, or Laura? Light brown hair, blue eyes. About 20 years. Pink waist with brown skirt, blue petticoat, black wool stockings and patent leather No. 4 laced boots. Wearing a gold locket with soldier's picture inside. Died in childbirth. Male infant, also deceased. Stillborn.

Mrs. Hannah Jones. Brown hair, brown eyes. Approximately 25–30 years of age. Blue housedress, and brown overcoat with black armband. Wearing wedding ring and house slippers. Died in childbirth. Female infant is alive and was taken to the Halifax Infants Home. Please look for father or other relatives of Mrs. Jones. Formerly of 1245 Gottingen Street.

One birth was sadness and hope all at once. Charlie and a young soldier brought the mother to me on a stretcher, her face covered with bloody bandages, her arm strapped to her side. Colleen O'Brien was the one thing that saved me from wanting to run from that hospital and throw myself into the dirty, wrecked waters of the harbour. For all that had happened to her, she was joyful over the birth of her child. She moaned and even laughed through her labour, complaining more of the wounds to her eyes than of bearing-down pains. The baby was coming fast, so there wasn't time to look at the dressings on her face. I told her she would have to wait.

It was a pink and healthy boy. Colleen was doing well, even chatting some with me as she worked and pushed to deliver the afterbirth. When we were finished, I propped her up in a bed in the corner so she could better hold her child.

"Can you uncover my eyes?" she asked. "I think the blood might have dried them shut." I held warm towels to her face and gently removed the bandages. Through the blood I could see several pieces of glass buried in her swollen skin. Her eyes were barely recognizable, beyond repair. "I'm never going to see him, am I."

I was glad she couldn't see my tears. "You have each other, and that's all that matters."

"Tell me what he looks like."

I took her hand and led it over his soft, dark hair. "He's got quite a shock of hair . . . it's black as coal."

She went from one part of him to the next, counting his fingers with her hands, rubbing her cheek against his. "Go on," she pleaded. "Don't stop."

"His cheeks are ruddy and his chest is broad. You can tell he's going to be some strong."

"Just like his papa." Her voice caught in her throat. "I wish he were here."

"Do you know where he is?" I was almost afraid to ask, afraid he might be dead.

"He's in France. Who could have guessed that the trenches would be safer than Halifax?"

~ *December 26, 1917*

Christmas was weary. I feel lonesome, even with Archer's homecoming, even in our warm, cheery house. I might blame it on my thoughts of Halifax, but in my heart I know that, with or without those memories, December is a month shadowed in darkness and fear. With every lamp blazing, with oranges and stockings, ribbons and holly, whether Christians rejoice or not, this is the truth of the season. As a young girl, I felt the shock of the annunciation, my belly sinking into hurt every time I listened to Gabriel standing winged and menacing over Mary. *The Holy Ghost shall come upon thee and the power of the Most High shall overshadow thee . . .* Not once did sugar plum faeries dance through my window on Christmas Eve. Instead, my dreams were filled with the hiss of Gabriel's whisper bringing the terrible message that heaven had made a mistake and *I* was to take the Blessed Virgin's place. With a blanket over my head, I would wait for the dawn, knowing that poor Mary must have suffered more than anyone ever knew. That *in that hour,* she swallowed the spirit of the Christ Child down into her belly, crying into the night, knowing He would have to die. Aunt Fran, or even Reverend Pineo, might call it blasphemy, but when I told Miss B. about it, she said, "That's a sacred dream. The blood you share with the Holy Mother is what sets you to achin' like that. The same blood she shares with all women."

This year, I gathered up everything I could afford and sent it to those still suffering after the explosion. The strains of the Coventry Carol seem darker than ever; candlelight and church bells cast lonely doubts on my efforts. Still, I have read in the newspapers that the children in the orphanages of Halifax are singing Christmas carols and making wishes for the New Year. Perhaps the stories Mother tells this time of year are true; perhaps the dark-masked mummer has lost the fight. Archer has promised to keep his habits in moderation, I have promised to be more devoted. I am still hoping for a child.

27

I HAD ARCHER READ Dr. John Cowan's thoughts concerning sexual congress, hoping to bring about the best possible conditions for conception.

Dr. John Cowan's Law of New Life
The husband and wife—lovingly united, in perfect health and strength—mutually desire to generate a pure, bright, happy, healthy love-child, having implanted in its organization the qualities of genius, chastity and holiness. If they never have heretofore exercised the spiritual of their natures, let them this morning, on bended knees, before the throne of grace, give earnest utterance to their thanks and desires.

An enjoyable walk and saunter, of an hour or more, into the pleasant morning sunshine. Breakfast at about eight o'clock—a breakfast of plain, unstimulating food. Again into the open air and bright sunshine; and for a couple of hours the husband and wife should lovingly and enthusiastically exchange thoughts, hopes and desires. Keeping their natures as is the bright sun, with not the smallest cloud intervening to darken their chamber, and in the clear light of day the New Life is conceived and generated—a new soul started into eternity.

Of course, he has his own thoughts on the matter . . .

Archer Bigelow's Law of Persistence
"Say you go to the county exhibition.

"You decide to try your luck at a barker's booth, the one with the grinning, round-bottomed carnival dolls. The object of the game is to throw the ball and knock the dolls over, right? Knock one off, you get an extra try. Knock two off, you get to take the doll home. Knock three off and you've won your choice of any number of fine prizes—from whirligigs to spinning tops, from teapots to china dolls. Three balls for a penny. A whole bucket of balls for three pennies. The more balls you throw, the better your chances. You're bound to put the pigeon in the hole eventually.

"So, it stands to reason . . . if you, dear wife, allow me to give you the punch more often than not . . . we'll have it licked. They don't call it 'getting knocked up' for nothing."

He isn't scientific in carrying out his theory. During the run of a week, I'll be hiked up against the door frame in the parlour, rolled in the cold of the hayloft, climbed upon first thing in the morning and taken from behind any number of times. If it works, red string and all, I'll never be able to say exactly the how, when, or why of it.

I can't see turning him away while I'm willing. Besides, it doesn't hurt so much anymore. Maybe it's my evening double dose of Miss B.'s elixir, but I find that, while in the act, if I think about the chance that it might bring forth a child, that it might change me into a mother, I forget about the pain. I can forget about almost anything that way: Archer's leaving, his never explaining why, my never asking for a reason. I lie there and imagine him as an honest, kind, Bible-selling man and myself as a large-bellied, round-bottomed, smiling mama. I close my eyes and try to make things seem better than they are in the hopes that my persistence might make it true.

Sometimes I even get to the point where I'm tempted to pray, to ask the Virgin Mary to see fit to bring me a baby, but since I've never had a talent for remembering psalms, I make little conversations with Miss B. in my mind instead. Praying twice removed, asking her to call on Mary to call on God on my behalf, is the only sort of prayer I imagine might be appropriate during intimate relations.

28

THE NEWS THAT SOMETHING was wrong with Ginny Jessup came from Sadie at the first Occasional Knitters meeting of the New Year. "I stopped by the house to leave off some apples. The baby was under the kitchen table, whimpering, his little face covered in soot. Ginny wasn't doing anything about it . . . she was just sitting at the table, holding her head, her eyes all dark and sore. When I asked her what was the matter, she said 'Don't know' and started to cry. I tried to help, but she threw me out, said she didn't want my apples or my pity, so I turned around and went home . . . I left the apples, of course."

By the time I paid Ginny a visit, things had only gotten worse. The kitchen table was coated in flour with a mass of tough, past-risen bread dough stuck in the centre. Three baskets were sitting in the corner, two overflowing with laundry, the other cradling her baby boy as he napped. Half-bundled in one of his father's shirts, he smelled of soiled diapers and sour milk.

Poor Ginny acted glad to see me and embarrassed all at once. She was quick to invite me to sit, offering tea, flitting around, shoving the morning's breakfast scraps into a large pot already crusted with boiled-over porridge. She stood with the cupboards open, staring at the shelves, searching for something more to offer. "I'm afraid I don't have any biscuits made, but if you'll stay awhile, I'll bake molasses cookies."

The little boy yawned and opened his eyes. I smiled at him, and he started to teeter his way towards me. "Well, look at that, not quite a year old and Baby Jessup's walking! Aren't you a big boy? I had no idea." I held out my arms and he climbed up on my lap. "I guess it's been awhile since I've seen you—not since before Christmas? He sure can get around, Ginny. How long has he been doing that?"

"Since before Christmas, I guess." She took a tea towel and began to dust the flour off the table, frowning as most of it drifted to the floor. She shuffled her feet through it, trying to make it disappear. "You'd think his learning to walk would make things easier, but it doesn't."

"Ginny, is there anything I can do for you? Sadie Loomer said . . ."

"Sadie? What's she got to say about anything? Just 'cause she's got three babies at home, she thinks she knows everything about everything."

"I don't think she meant anything by it. She wanted to help, that's all."

"She can mind her nosy apple-picking self. Those apples she brought were half rotten, you know." Slow tears fell from her cheek, wetting the front of her stained dress. "She's got no right to judge. She's no better than anybody else. Those apples won't make more than three quarts of sauce, and it'll probably turn and bust the lids right off the jars before spring. She's got no right."

I brushed the hair away from her eyes and wiped her face with my handkerchief. The clean white cloth caught smudges of dirt from the dark creases around her eyes. She's not much older than I am, but she holds the look of a used-up wife. Still having the form of a girl, but holding her chin down, her shoulders slouched, as if she believes it's not proper or worth the effort to smile. "How long has it been since you've had a good night's sleep?"

She hid her face in her hands. "The baby's underfoot all the time, wanting to nurse or be held. I swear, when he's not in my arms or sleeping, he's crying."

"What does Laird say about all this?"

"Of course, he's some sore at the baby's fussing all the time. Usually he takes it as long as he can and then goes out the door, but not without saying he might as well go off to war so he can get a little peace and quiet. Then he kisses me and says he's only teasing, that he's only going down to Jack Tupper's place for a bit and would I wait up for him, since he'd like to have another boy before he gets too old to bounce them on his knees. Another boy . . . like I can order it up from Eaton's. Another baby. He wants another baby."

"Could you send for someone from your family?"

"I come to live with my aunt in Fredericton when I was just a baby, but Auntie's gone crippled the last few years, she can hardly get up and down her own stairs."

"What about Laird's mother? She's not far from the Bay. I'm sure she'd be happy to help."

"Oh, no . . . not on your life. She comes in here and takes hold of that little boy like he was hers, calls him *my baby, my sweet boy*, like she did all the work of carrying him and birthing him. Let him bite and tug at her tired old nipples and keep her awake all night and see how she feels about *her* baby, then."

"But he's old enough now, she could watch him from time to time. Just so you could have a rest, come to my house for tea?"

"And give her reason to call me a bad mother, a bad wife? She'd like that, the spout-mouthed biddy. I'd rather let this house fall down around me before I asked her to lend a hand. Laird goes on and on about her virtues: *Mother made the world's best shepherd's pie, I can almost taste it right now. And she kept five children, a husband and her house in order; why's it so hard for you?* You know that man smells like cow dung, even after his bath? No wonder the first Mrs. Laird Jessup ran off." She laughed and cried all at the same time.

"Don't worry, Ginny, we'll work this out. I'll be your family."

From what Ginny told me, and what I could remember from Miss B., I figured the baby had colic. *Most times, if a baby's losin' sleep it's cause he gots a fire in his belly. A colicky child can lead even the sweetest mama to curse. Make sure she thinks on everthin' she puts in her mouth.* Ginny had been fixing Laird's favourites: cabbage soup, sausages with sauerkraut, liver and onions. *There's to be no cabbage, garlic, onions or hot spices while she's nursin'. Rub the babe's belly with dill seed oil. Arrowroot cookies and applesauce for the child after the first little pearl of a tooth. Fennel tea, smoked mackerel and milk toast for the mother until you get that baby's tight little belly straightened out.*

I put Ginny to bed and the baby in the washtub for a bath. Cleaned the house, made a pot of potato soup and a batch of molasses cookies, rushing to get it done before Laird came home for dinner. I put on my best Miss B. when

I said goodbye, telling Ginny she needed "tea and rest, then more tea and more rest" and that I'd be back the following day to help her again.

Mrs. Dora Bigelow
Scots Bay, Nova Scotia

January 10, 1918

Mr. Borden Rare
Ship's Carpenter
The Just Cause
Sydney, Cape Breton Island

Dear Borden,
We all missed you and Albert over Christmas. However, I am grateful that you aren't so very far away from home. I'm not sure if Mother has written to tell you, but Charlie has gone away. He had been travelling to and from Boston while helping in the relief efforts after the explosion in Halifax and has since decided to stay. (I'm not certain, but there may be a girl involved in his decision?) I guess I'd much rather lose a brother to a woman than to the war.

With this letter you should receive enough socks and mitts to get you and the crew through the winter. They are compliments of a new ladies' organization in the Bay, the Occasional Knitters Society. I am the secretary at large.

I am hoping to see you soon.

Your loving sister,
Dora

29

THERE'S A HUNGER THAT comes with long February nights, a wanting for warm sweet things, laughter and biscuits . . . a pot of lavender tea alongside a plate heaped with Miss B.'s sugary beignets. With Ginny Jessup, the Occasional Knitters are now five, still gathering at my house, but on Wednesdays only, since that's the Sons of Temperance night for cards and darts, our husbands otherwise occupied. In the middle of this hungry, cold winter, I've become a friend, nursemaid and sometime gypsy (as Mabel calls me), reading tea leaves and holding other women's children in my arms. Most Wednesday nights end with trails of icing sugar scattered through the parlour and kitchen, each one making its way to a plump, sleeping child curled up under the counterpane on my bed.

When we aren't knitting socks for the soldiers, we make efforts at other noble causes, sewing rag dolls for the children of Halifax, or taking mid-winter boxes of cheer to those who are shut in or in need. Preserves, bread, apple-sauce, butter, salt pork, salt herring, wool scarves, socks and mitts, and a bottle of Miss B.'s coltsfoot cough syrup. We leave the gifts on the step, rap on the door and run away.

Mabel suggested that we keep our giving a secret, "as being poor never means being without pride."

No matter how virtuous our deeds, our conversations are something altogether different. Loud, and low enough to make a sailor blush. Hot like a fist full of fire.

Having exhausted all we could say about the best way to "get with child," Bertine decided she'd like to discuss how *not* to get with child.

"Lucy's all but done with her weaning . . . I guess I'd better get ready for baby number three."

"Can't you count your days? Put him off when you're in the middle?"

"Never been able to count on my blood. I'm all up and down. Besides, Hardy doesn't put up with being put off."

Sadie smirked. "Make him wear a rubber."

"Once again, Sadie, you mention something reserved for whores. What husband's going to wear a skirt on his willie when he's with his wife? When there's no chance of slippin' the syphilis? Do you have Wes wear one?"

"No, but I'm not the one complaining about having babies all the time. Just take a good-sized bit of sea sponge, soak it in pepper juice, dip it in honey and shove it up your—"

Mabel looked down at her knitting. "There are other ways . . ."

Bertine snickered. "You know what Hardy's mother once told me to try? *Tong water tea,* made from the nasty stuff that's left in the bucket after the smithy's spent all day dipping his lead tongs in it to cool. *From one blacksmith's wife to another,* she said, like it was a precious little secret. No wonder that poor woman's tongue always looked all purple, like it was about to fall off. She also said you could *loose the bud,* if you thought you might already be with child, by rubbing gunpowder all over your breasts." She put her hands together like she was praying to Mabel. "If you've got something that works, I'd love to know."

"The only way I know that works for certain is for after the fact. My cousin Penny took Madame Drunette's Lunar Pills, she'd seen them advertised in *Ladies' Rural Companion* . . . said she thought she was going to die. She wound up with a terrible headache and anything she ate went right out of her again, both ends at once. It worked, but in the end she said she'd have rather taken her chances in falling off a horse."

Ginny dropped two sugar cubes into her cup and stared at it as she stirred. "My cousin sent me something she calls a fisherman's knot. It just looks like a wad of tangled line to me, but she swears if you put it far enough up inside you, it'll keep the babies out."

Sadie questioned her. "You tried it yet?"

"No, Laird says he wants another boy soon."

"It's you who's got to carry it and then care for it," I reminded her.

"I was afraid he might notice or, worse, that I couldn't get the thing back out."

Bertine took another beignet from the plate and brushed away the sugar that fell in her lap. "Oh, we might as well stop talking about it. Poor Dorrie here is so bent on having a baby, I'm afraid we'll jinx her if we keep it up. Praying's gonna do me as much good as anything." She looked up to the ceiling. "Just a few more months, Lord. Maybe a year if you can spare it?"

I went to the cupboard under the china cabinet and pulled out the jar Miss B. had gotten out when Grace Hutner came to her, her jar of Beaver Brew. "Miss B. had something that might work for you, Bertine, although I can't say that it will taste any better than Hardy's mother's tea."

Bertine scolded me. "Why didn't you say something before?"

"Miss B. had a rule about having to be asked. It's silly, I know, but . . ."

Mabel looked concerned. "I thought you weren't midwifing anymore."

"I'm not. Just doing a friend a favour."

Bertine looked at the jar as if she was a little afraid of its contents. "But I didn't ask."

"You put your hands together and prayed; that's enough for me."

I poured the brew into Bertine's teacup. "Here, take it with your tea. It'll go down easier."

Bertine sniffed the cup. "Whooo, Dora. There's some hooch in there. What's in it?"

"You don't want to know. Besides, Miss B. would come back and haunt me if I told. But I can tell you this . . . it'll keep you from getting a bun in the oven for at least a month."

Sadie held her cup out to me. "Barkeep, I'll have one of those."

Mabel held out her cup and grinned. "Me too."

I filled their cups and turned to Ginny. "Some for you?"

Ginny hung her head. "I don't take anything with alcohol."

Sadie elbowed Ginny. "It won't bite you . . . too much. Besides, it's not like you're taking a bottle of rum to bed with you. It's just tea with mitts, that's what my granny always called it, *tea with mitts*. Are you really wanting to have another little one keeping you up all night?"

Ginny bit her lip and pushed her cup forward.

As soon as hers was filled, I poured myself a cup of Miss B.'s Moon Elixir and held it high in the air. "A toast. To ye who want for nothing, and me who wants for one."

"To tea with mitts!"

"Tea with mitts."

"Tea with mitts!"

The following Saturday, I saw Dr. Thomas at Newcomb's Dry Goods down in Canning. He was standing between pickle barrels and the meat case, declining an invitation from a rather wealthy-looking woman. "As lovely as it sounds, I'm afraid we'll have to wait. I've got to make an unexpected trip out to Scots Bay, and Sunday's the only day I can manage it."

The woman tsked as she pointed to a wheel of cheese, motioning for Mrs. Newcomb to cut a wedge of it for her. "Half pound, please. Yes. That one will do." She pointed to a ring of bologna. "Same here, too." She put her finger to her chin, unsure as to what else she wanted. "That's really too bad. Another time, I suppose." She tapped on the glass, this time pointing to a platter filled with pork chops. "Scots Bay, on a Sunday in the middle of winter. How unfortunate."

Dr. Thomas drummed his fingers on the top of a barrel. "If I could avoid it, I would. Except for a chosen few, there's not much sense or civility to be found in that place. Too many marriages with too few names, I guess . . ."

The two of them laughed, heads bobbing together, bodies quaking. The woman was barely able to make her name as she signed for her bill. Dr. Thomas took her arm as they turned towards the door.

"Hello, Dr. Thomas."

"Hello." He stared at me, not looking into my eyes but keeping his gaze steadily moving between my neck, my breasts and my shoes, as if he hoped to forget that he knew me. "Mrs. Bigelow, yes, how nice to see you. It's been quite a while—November, was it? I gather you're feeling well?"

"Fine, just fine. And your wife and child, are they well?"

"Yes, yes."

The woman tugged on the doctor's sleeve.

"Oh, I'm sorry. Mrs. Bigelow, this is my neighbour, Mrs. Florence Hatfield. Mrs. Hatfield, this is Mrs. Dora Bigelow of Scots Bay."

Mrs. Hatfield smiled and extended her hand. "Scots Bay? Why we were just talking of it, weren't we, Gilbert? Do you have much wind and snow there this time of year? I can't imagine spending an entire winter up there— you're a braver soul than I. Lovely spot for a summer picnic, though."

Dr. Thomas interrupted Mrs. Hatfield's nervous chatter. "If you'll excuse me, Florence, perhaps I can deliver my business with Mrs. Bigelow and accept your invitation, after all."

"Wonderful! Let me get out of your way, then." She waved, bustling her way out the door, jangling the bells that hung over the knob. "So nice to meet you, Mrs. Bigelow. See you Sunday, Gilbert."

Dr. Thomas took my arm and pulled me behind the dry goods shelf. He lowered his voice. "Stay away from Mrs. Jessup."

"Ginny is a friend."

"Mrs. Jessup is my patient, and you've no business handing out questionable home remedies to her. Especially the kind that sends her husband to my door, ready to have my head. I think I should warn you, Mrs. Bigelow, that any means of preventing conception, even the mention of such means, is illegal. You really must stop putting yourself in trouble's way."

"What is it, Dr. Thomas, that's got you so interested in the women of the Bay?"

"I care about the well-being of all my patients, of all women. It's my duty to give them the best care modern medicine can provide, the care they deserve."

"You care so much that you abandon them as soon as they get more than a mile away from your office? I'd say it's more that you care to line your pockets with their money, and you don't think twice of what it costs them to give it to you."

Dr. Thomas straightened himself up. "A man's means is no one's business."

"And the secrets a woman chooses to keep between her sheets are not your business."

He glanced back at Mrs. Newcomb, who was now staring from behind the counter. He smiled, talking through his teeth. "Maybe it's time that a hysterical, reckless woman who encourages women to deceive their husbands should be everyone's business." Mrs. Newcomb disappeared through the door of the meat locker. Dr. Thomas leaned close to me, his lips touching my ear as he spoke. "Are you feeling well, Mrs. Bigelow? I only ask because you're looking a little flushed." He stroked my cheek with his hand. "You feel a little feverish. Isn't Mr. Bigelow seeing to your well-being? Isn't he working at giving you the child you've been wanting? I could speak to him about that, Mrs. Bigelow. I could tell him what you require. I could tell anyone, really."

Hysterical Woman
Attacks Local Doctor

This writer has learned of an unfortunate event that occurred some time after noon, this Saturday last. According to witnesses, a woman who had gone into Newcomb's Dry Goods to purchase goods and essentials for her family became suddenly and inexplicably agitated. In her hysterics, she proceeded to empty a 2-gallon jug of "Sure Sweet Molasses" on the head of Dr. Gilbert Thomas, of Canning.

No other customers were assaulted during the incident.

Mrs. Lila Newcomb, wife of the proprietor of the establishment, had this to say: "I can't say what happened exactly. All I know is, one minute they seemed to be having a friendly conversation, and the next, Dr. Thomas was standing there, wiping the stuff out of his nose, gasping for air, looking like he'd been tarred for feathering."

Dr. Thomas, a well-known doctor of women's hygiene and obstetrics, added, "I see no reason to involve the authorities in the matter. Sadly, this kind of behaviour is to be expected from a woman in her condition. Nervous disorders of the female system are more and more common these days. Let this be a lesson to all, showing what can happen when a woman's emotions are left unchecked. I only hope that she will see fit to return to my doorstep so that I might assist her in her time of need, before something dreadful happens, before it's too late."

The woman, who quickly fled from the store to return to her home in Scots Bay, was unavailable for comment. Dr. Thomas paid 25 cents for the molasses. A kind and generous gesture, indeed.

The Canning Register,
February 19, 1918

30

WE HAD SUNDAY DINNER at the Bigelow house, Archer, Hart, the widow and me. The widow took great pains to make it clear that she's happiest when both of her "boys" are home. As always, she held court in the parlour and left all the serving to me. I never minded when it was just tea and biscuits for the widow and Miss B., but now that I'm married to Archer, I'm disappointed to find that my mother-in-law still looks on me as more of a housekeeper than a daughter. Her coldness towards me must seem justified in light of the gossip that's come up from Canning, attaching my name to the "crazy-molasses-woman of Scots Bay." Most of the White Rose Ladies could barely look me straight in the eye at church this morning, Aunt Fran saying only, "Honestly, Dora—how could you?" Bertine, of course, passed me a note: "Here's to molasses on doctors, and tea with mitts!"

I accepted all the widow's requests without argument, her voice trailing after me all evening. "Oh, and don't forget the gravy, dear, still in the kitchen, dear, and in the proper boat, please, the Royal Albert with the gold rim and lovely blue flowers, the gravy? *S'il vous plaît?* Oh dear, do you think she heard me? Dora?"

I brought the gravy, in the right dish, and served her first, even before my husband. This was a small kindness, one I supposed I owed her after having made such great efforts to avoid her during Archer's absence. She never called on me, not once, and for that she deserves a kindness or two . . . the all-too-easy graciousness one woman gives to another when she's guilty of having kept a secret, or the tight-lipped smile that's most often exchanged between young wives and their dear mother-in-laws.

Archer more than made up for the both of us, doting on his mother the entire time, going on and on about how lovely she looked, the fine new dress she was wearing, the quality of the roast she had chosen, the deliciousness of every bite. (You'd think it was his first decent meal in months.) He's never that thoughtful during our dinners, even on nights when he's determined he'll be having his way later on. I'm just hoping that once I'm expecting a child things will change, that he'll become attentive and kind, hovering with worry and care. Certainly a first grandchild will give the widow cause enough to wait on me.

Dinner was almost finished when the true reason for Archer's flattery came to light. When his mother asked him his plans for the spring, he spooned the last of the potatoes on his plate and replied, "I'm glad you asked. There's something I'd like to talk over with you."

Hart picked up the empty serving bowl and ran his thumb around the edge, scraping off the last bit of potatoes still clinging to the rim. "How're you gonna swindle money from the pockets of the hard-working people of Kings County this time, Archie? Can't imagine you've found anything more honest than peddling the Lord's word, unless, of course, you're planning on selling tickets to the other side of the Pearly Gates . . . and in that case, be sure and save one for yourself, you'll be needing it."

Archer ignored Hart's remarks and began moving the plates around on the table, puckering the tablecloth into soft, wrinkled mountains and valleys. "Say this serving tray is the Bay, and this ridge over here is the mountain . . ." He motioned along the gap between the two. "Most of the houses are built along here." Then he ran his hand along a smooth slope of cloth leading to the top of the peaks. "And these fields here, the ones that are cleared, they're used for what, grazing cattle, growing hay? You can't grow anything worthwhile on them."

Hart interrupted, "Laird Jessup grew some cabbages back there this past year, and they did just fine."

Archer laughed. "Cabbages? How much cabbage does one little town need? How many people really like cabbage anyway? The stuff stinks. The only other things that'll eat it is pigs, and it leaves them bloated. For all the work it takes to grow it, you're left with a few cents and a bunch of angry swine."

Hart shook his head. "Well, it's too windy there to grow much else."

Archer snapped his fingers. "Exactly! Wind's the one thing we have plenty of here in the Bay, so why not farm that instead? We can build windmills, lots of them. Instead of praying each spring that a freshet doesn't come and wipe out the lumber mill you've got built over Ells Brook, you could have a wind-powered mill. And better than that, we can use the windmills to generate *electricity*. The townsfolk of Canning have been trying for years to get electric for their street lamps, let alone their homes, so it's certain the county won't be bringing it up the mountain anytime soon. Why should we wait? With a few windmills here and there, we'd have enough electricity to power all this side of North Mountain." He made a proud sweeping gesture, like a rainbow had just formed over his head. "The Bigelow Electric Company of Scots Bay . . . then, Halls Harbour, Arlington, Blomidon, Medford, Ross Creek, Delhaven . . ."

Confused, I pointed to his tabletop landscape. "I'm not sure what you have in mind, but the church cemetery and our house look to be right in the middle of your wind farm."

He patted my hand. "Those folks are dead, my dear, I'm sure they won't mind." He circled his finger around the gravy pitcher. "We'll build the windmills *around* the house. It'll be like living in a field of giant twirling daisies, and *you*, my dearest wife, will be the first woman to have electric, right in her home."

Hart scowled. "What exactly do we need electric for? A small windmill or hand pump brings enough water for a house, and oil lamps give off plenty of light. Seems to me we do just fine without it."

Archer sighed and looked at his mother with pleading eyes. "This is why I've had to come to you. Hart's not the only man in the Bay without a sense of vision. I've tried to talk to some of the other men about my ideas, and have gotten much the same response." He took her hand. "Hens will only lay eggs in the sunny months of the year. Once autumn comes and the days grow short, they're through until spring. But, if we had electricity, we could give them the light they need and they'd lay all winter long." He grinned at his mother. "You always said the hens were smarter than the roosters."

With that, the widow agreed to give Archer the rest of

his inheritance and anything else she could spare. She also promised to make arrangements for Archer to speak at the spring meeting of the White Rose Temperance Society. He is over the moon. I'm left wondering if, once again, he's making a promise he can't keep.

~ *February 26, 1918*

For centuries, farmers have harnessed the wind for its power.

Majestic windmills

have long dotted the European landscape, and in the past few years the prairies of North America have been made lush by sturdy, towering wind machines that ceaselessly pump water from the earth. The wind turns our grain to flour and our forests into lumber, all for our betterment.

Now it looks as though the wind may once again hold promise for mankind. In 1892, the Danish inventor, Poul la Cour, first produced electricity from a windmill. In 1903, he established The Society of Wind Electricians, and by 1904 he began publishing the *Journal of Wind Electricity*. This enterprising fellow then went on to build a test turbine in his hometown of Askov, Denmark. In this year alone, Mr. la Cour will successfully be running over 100 wind generators, thereby providing power to the rural areas of his homeland.

 *Vaughn's Almanac* is pleased to offer a set of plans *so that you can build your very own replica* of Mr. la Cour's amazing wind generator. They are available exclusively through Vaughn's by sending **$13.75** to our offices in Plaistow, New Hampshire.

A large package arrived for Archer today from *Vaughn's Almanac Inc.* He has been holed up in the barn since after lunch. Despite the cold, damp weather, he is determined to keep at his task until it's finished. I took a plate to him at dinnertime and an extra sweater as well. He motioned for me to set the food on an apple barrel in the corner and then continued his work, circling around a makeshift table he had made from two sawhorses and a few wide boards. Tacked to the side of Buttercup's stall were three large sheets of blue paper, crowded with figures, diagrams and numbers. As of my last visit to the barn at midnight, his table was still empty.

~ *February 27, 1918*

Went to take Archer some breakfast and found the barn doors barred shut. His voice grumbled from inside. "Just leave it, I'll get to it in a bit."

I pressed my lips to a knothole and said, "Don't forget to milk the cow."

Not long before lunch I heard the angry sound of Buttercup, deep in protest. I looked out the window in time to see Archer whipping the poor, bawling creature out to the pasture. He stomped back to the barn, threw out the milking stool and pail and slammed the door.

I took the cow by her harness and pulled her to the south side of the barn, where the roof hangs over the woodpile. I stroked her side, milked her swollen, red udders until they were dry and walked her down to the Widow Bigelow's barn to see if Hart might have room for her.

Once she was settled, Hart offered to bring me home in his buggy. When I refused, he insisted I at least let him walk with me so he could get a look at Archer's handiwork. Pepper scampered along as we walked, sniffing in the ditches and along the fencerows. She smelled the food still sitting untouched in the lunch pail outside the barn door and raced ahead to gobble it down. I didn't scold her. Archer's breakfast had long gotten too cold to be any good. I did scold Hart, however, for his teasing and saying that he was going to "kick in the doors to make certain Archer was still alive." Instead, we snuck around to the back of the barn and stared through the cracks between the boards.

The way Archer had paced the floor waiting for its arrival, you'd have thought this thing, this grand invention, was going to be as big as a church. When Jack Tupper brought it to the house, Archer wrapped his arms around the large wooden crate, his face peering over the top, eyes lit up like Christmas morning. From the size of the box, I had expected something at least as tall as my husband, something formidable, and strong enough to hold up against the winds off the Bay. Hart went on and on, whispering and laughing, "That's some small. But I suppose the mice could have a nice little tea party under it."

Archer leaned over his workbench, one arm braced on the roof of a dollhouse, tinkering with his toy-sized creation. He whistled and hummed, occasionally talking to the thing, proclaiming his skill with nuts and bolts, praising the ingenuity of man, promising to "show her off, some good."

For the first time I had ever seen, my husband was truly devoted to something. Yes, there is our marriage, but compared to this, it's clear that his effort and his desire have never belonged to me. With a baby or not, I'll never inspire the sweet, hypnotic words of Shakespeare's lovers or the winning smiles and delicious conversation of Jane Austen's heroes. I'll never be cause enough for shivering in the cold or going without supper.

~ *February 28, 1918*

Just before dawn he came through the door, calling to me. "Dorrie, come on, she's up!" He carried me from the bed to the barn, blankets trailing down between my legs. "You sit right here." He dropped me in a pile of hay and ran to push the barn doors apart as wide as they would allow. "Keep your eyes on the dollhouse." Cold gusts of wind rushed through the barn, kicking up stray bits of hay, rattling the blades of the windmill into a whirl of motion. Lights flickered from inside the rooms of the small house. A chandelier, a lamp on the staircase, a light in the front window. "Let there be light!" he said, as he pulled me into his arms and twirled me around, everything spinning, our breath hanging in the air in the first warmth of the sun.

31

The Ladies of the White Rose Temperance Society
Invite you to their spring tea
Sunday, March 3, 1918
At 2 p.m.
The Seaside Centre
Our special guest will be Archer Bigelow
Presenting the lecture
Electricity: A Woman's Best Friend

WE SET UP THE TINY windmill at the Seaside Centre after church. I borrowed one of Aunt Fran's tablecloths and some of Precious's dolls and furniture to help make the presentation complete.

For all the troubles Archer had last year with his temper and drinking, one thing hasn't changed: he can still turn any woman's attention to anything he wants. Even with the windows wide open, the ladies never complained (not even his mother). They huddled around the dollhouse, their faces peeking into the brightened little rooms, their mouths open with wonder. Once the windows were shut and they were settled in their seats, Archer told them of his magnificent wind farm and the superiority of hens to roosters. It wasn't long before they were clucking for more.

This is the time of year when spring is a tease in the air. The sun warms the ground, the snowdrops have appeared, but as soon as two people start talking about blue skies and planting peas, it begins to snow and there's another inch or two of "poor man's fertilizer" covering the ground. Archer had every head nodding in agreement when he proclaimed that this year's winter must be the longest on record. "Some cold, too, I'd say." He walked over and took his mother's hands in his own. "Cold hands, warm heart—they must have been thinking of dear ladies like you when they came up with that phrase." Even Aunt Fran blushed at that.

He opened the pages of a Sears catalogue and pointed to the large black lettering across the top of the page.

"Electricity can do more for the women of the Bay than just getting your hens to lay eggs." He smiled and asked the women, "How many times have you wished for more hours in a day? Or dreamed of having an extra pair of hands?" He snapped his fingers. "If you had electricity, you might just feel as if those wishes had come true." He passed the catalogue to my mother and me. "Look at that page and tell me there isn't one thing there that wouldn't make your life easier."

Aids That Every Woman Appreciates

Very attractive with its bright copper lining, and polished nickel-plated steel.

Majestic Electric Radiator.
Fine for that cold bedroom, small office etc.

Home Motor.
This motor shown above will operate a sewing machine. Easily attached; makes sewing a pleasure.

The many attachments (not shown) may be operated by this motor to help to lighten the burden of the home. (Household mixer, churn and mixer attachment, beater attachment, fan attachment, buffer and grinder attachment, as well as the portable vibrator attachment.)

Make sewing easy with an

Electric Sewing Machine Motor.
Quickly attached to your sewing machine without marring machine in any way. Can be run fast or slow. Speed easily regulated. You can do a great deal more sewing without being worn out from running the machine. Cannot be used in homes that do not have electricity, for it is not constructed to operate from dry batteries.

"I promise you, if you support this venture, I'll deliver electricity straight to each and every one of your doorsteps before the days turn short and the nights turn cold."

By morning the porch was crowded with pickle jars, filled to the rim with coins. After breakfast, Archer carefully packed his miniature wind farm in an old steamer trunk, taking great care to make certain that every bit of it was padded and safe. He said he was off to put all the money in the bank in Kentville—the money from his mother and the money from the ladies. Then he'd be off to Halifax to seek out investors. "I need real money, city money, to make this work."

"You have to leave today?"

"I can't wait around any more to get this thing started, and I certainly wouldn't want people to think I can't provide for my dear little wife. You don't want women to start coming here to have their babies in our parlour, giving us cabbages and beans because they feel sorry for you. Do you?" He kissed me and gave a firm pinch to my bum. "Anyway, if I wait around for you to decide that you want me to go, I'll never get out of here."

"How long will you be gone?"

"Can't say. But if I don't get going . . ."

I felt the tears coming to my eyes. "I think I might be—"

He ignored my sadness, giving me a broad smile as he went through the door. "Now don't make me worry over you, Dora. That's what selfish girls do, and I never guessed you to be like that."

~ *April 15, 1918*

Bleeding today. No baby, again.

Archer's been gone over a month, the war is still on, and it feels like darkness is winning at everything. By all reports, March 1918 was taken by the Germans. Many soldiers captured, many more killed.

Mother has heard from Albert and Borden. They are fine. I do wonder about poor Tom Ketch, wherever he may be. He never sent word after I wrote to him. It seems so long ago.

I did get a package from Charlie in today's post and there *is* (as I suspected) a girl involved in his move to Boston (or woman, I should say, from the photo he sent). Her name is Maxine Cabott, and she's as beautiful and sophisticated a thing as I've ever seen. Charlie is standing next to her, grinning like the cat that came in with a mouse in his teeth. Although he claims he's in her employ, it looks to be much more than that.

He even sent me a book of poetry by Emily Dickinson . . . his thoughtfulness makes me wonder if he isn't in love!

I hope you like this little book of poems I've sent along to you. It was Max's idea. I told her how much you love to have your nose stuck between the pages, and she said, "She'd probably prefer something racier, like Balzac or Lawrence, but some postal clerk would confiscate it in the name of Comstockery and virtue, and then where would we be? Send my regrets. Miss Dickinson will have to do for now."

32

THE PINK MOON, April's moon, pulls the green of the earth right up from the roots. The pink moon, the Lady moon, gives wide silver rings to the sky, her sudden, bright face coming over the spruce, singing, *Three days of rain, day and night. Three days of rain and unexpected houseguests.*

Precious came down for supper. I fixed boiled ham with potatoes, cabbage and carrots. Had to keep a fire in the kitchen at night, just to hold the chill off. After dinner, we sat at the table, dunking brown bread in thick cream and maple syrup. Sucking at the tips of her fingers like a child, Precious begged to have her tea leaves read. "Please, Dora, I won't tell my mum. I won't tell a soul."

At fifteen, she's in a sweet and terrible spot. On Easter Monday, Sam Gower went off to war. He's decided to "do his part." For her part, Precious has promised to write, to place his letters under her pillow and to keep his mother company until he returns. It's nothing short of painful to watch her give her heart away for the first time. We are all standing guard, Aunt Fran, Uncle Irwin, Mrs. Gower, Reverend Pineo, everyone who knows and loves her. There is something in her waiting, in her sad patience, that warns us, "If this girl's heart should happen to break, the whole world will be broken along with it."

"Watch carefully now . . . I hold the cup in my left hand, left is closest to the heart, see? Turn it over and let the last drops drip out past the handle." Precious was watching, squirming in her seat with anticipation. "Upright the cup and place the saucer over top. Then, fast as you can, turn it the other way around so now the cup is on top."

"Now, Dora? Can we look now?"

"Shh . . . No, now we wait." I placed my hands piously on the cup, slowly turning it, just as Miss B. had always done. *One, two, three times 'round the clock.* "Always pick it up with the left hand, always the left."

She peered between her fingers as she held her hands over her face. "I'm afraid to look, Dora, is it any good?"

"I can see . . . a hand. Someone you know will need your helping hands. Be sure you give them your assistance, and good luck will come back to you."

Precious sighed with disappointment. "I always help others, that's easy enough. Isn't there anything else in there?"

"Wait . . . oh yes, a ribbon and an ear. Someone thinks highly of you, and soon you will get news from far away."

Precious smiled and closed her eyes. She whispered, "Sam."

"Maybe so."

"I think I should marry Sam when he comes home."

"I think you're too young to think about getting married off."

"But you were only eighteen when you married Archer. That's not so different."

"It's not the same."

"Why not?"

"When you come from a house with six brothers and no money to speak of, a marriage proposal is a gift, not a choice. Count your blessings, dear cousin. You're an only child from a well-to-do family. You have plenty of time to decide who you'll marry."

Precious retied the ribbon at the end of her braid. "Aren't you anxious for Archer to come home? Don't you love him like mad? Don't you wish he were here?"

"Wishing doesn't make it so, and no matter how badly you try to help her along, Love always makes it plain that she can take care of herself. Here, let's clear the table."

She sat pouting, with her hands folded in her lap. "Not until we look in your cup too."

"Oh, alright." I turned the cup, not looking to find anything important. *One, two, three times 'round the clock. Then with the left, always the left, it's closest to the heart. There, see?* "Blackbird flying. Two hands shaking. A treasure box."

Before I finished, we heard horses and voices in the dooryard. Too late for Hart to come by, too soon for Archer to be home. I tried to hide my worry from Precious as I opened the door.

A man was pushing a young girl ahead of him, their bodies moving together, then apart. It was difficult to judge if it was fear or illness that was causing their cumbersome gait. The man called out, "You Judah Rare's girl, right? Oh—I should say, Mrs. Archie Bigelow . . ." Brady Ketch's speech was crippled by drunkenness, his clothing and face soiled.

"Yes, but—"

"Here ya go, My Wild Iris Rosie . . . Mrs. Bigelow'll know what to do with you." He shoved the girl up the steps and through the door, causing her to fall into my arms, whimpering. "Take her."

"If she's sick, you need to take her to Dr. Thomas. I can't help her."

"This little bitch? She'll cost more to keep than she's good for. No amount of money's worth the trouble she's caused."

The ragged wool scarf on her head fell down around her neck, showing that her tender face was bruised over one eye, that the corner of her mouth was swollen with blood. I put my arm around her to steady her. "Did he do this to you?"

He began to make his way back to a dilapidated wagon on skids, pulled by a mismatched team of horses. "Damn right I give her that. Fix her or kill her, I don't care."

I called after him, but he was already on his seat, whipping his team, his senseless muttering turned into song as the rig lurched down the road.

We were so happy 'til father drank rum
Then all our sorrows and troubles begun . . .

The girl's body slumped heavy against mine. She was crying now, moaning with pain. Precious stood behind me, staring, waiting. "Set the rocker by the stove in the kitchen. Let's see if we can get her to sit up," I said.

Precious moved quickly, her hands shaking as she dragged Miss B.'s heavy oak chair across the floor. "What's wrong with her?"

"I'm not sure yet. Here, help me get these wraps off of her."

A jumble of patchwork pieces, coat remnants and old blankets surrounded her sobbing, frightened body. "Can you tell me what's the matter, dear?" I whispered gently, hoping to coax her into telling me what had happened. She bent her head into her chest and clutched her arms around her belly. The weeping became a long, tortured wail. I slipped my hand under the remaining blankets. Her middle was tense, knotted with contractions. Precious stood near, whispering in my ear.

"I know this girl. Iris Rose Ketch. She lives on the mountain. Mother says her father hires her out, sells her body, for money."

How long had it been since I'd seen her tired, little-girl face worrying over her mother at Deer Glen? A year? No, more than that. It was autumn, my first birth with Miss B., when I'd seen those same wide eyes, watching through a crooked staircase, waiting for a miracle. This child, who'd been set aside by a mother who was always short on food, clothing and love, wasn't long from becoming a mother herself.

I knelt at her feet. "You're safe here, Iris Rose. I'll take care of you now."

Frightened and breathless, Precious was quick to offer to fetch Aunt Fran. "Please, Dora. I'll bring her right back. Let me go get my mum."

There's been talk going around the circle of card-party girls of a "midwife curse," or a witch's mark that's been passed from Miss B. to me. According to this tale, I can blame the curse for driving my husband away and leaving me barren. Any girl who is unmarried is liable to "catch it" if she drinks my tea, walks through my door, sits at my kitchen table, sits next to me at church, touches wool that I've spun, eats food I've prepared and so on. On other occasions, Precious and I have laughed over the thought of it, settling on the idea that she was free from the curse by virtue of loving me. Now she was looking as if she wanted to run out the door, as if witnessing a birth by my side was the one thing that might do her in. *The longer words spill around, gettin' caught between knittin' needles or clothespins, the easier it is to believe them, even when you know you shouldn't.*

"I'll go get Mother. She'll know what to do."

"No, Precious. I need you to stay here. I'll open the doors to the bedroom off the kitchen and get it warmed up in there. You run upstairs and get a dressing gown from my wardrobe and as many sheets as you can carry out of the linen closet." Iris Rose sat trembling in the rocking chair. I took her hand in mine. "You're in the eye of the storm, dear; try to relax when you can—we have some work ahead of us."

I dressed her in a clean, white gown and helped her onto the bed. Precious flitted around the kitchen, putting the kettle on for tea, tearing sheets into strips, lining a basket with lamb's wool and flannel. Iris Rose fell in and out of a restless sleep, weary from the pain that took hold of her body every few minutes.

Scissors, needles, sewin' cotton, crochet hooks, scorched muslin. Calendula salve, peroxide, cayenne, witch hazel bark, castor oil, ergot, Jayes Fluid, Stop Bleed, Mother's Tea. Mandrake root—balm of the bruised woman. Stand with your back to the wind. Draw three circles, clockwise, around the plant with a knife. Douse it with Mary Water. Turn west to uproot. Salve nos, Stella Maris. Save us, Star of the Sea.

Iris Rose wailed as another wave of pain swept over her body.

"It's almost time to bear down and bring your baby into the world. During the next calm, I'll help you get on your knees." I pulled a chair from the kitchen table. "We'll put this chair in front of you so you'll have something to hold on to ... Precious, slide that quilt underneath her legs so it's right soft when I catch the baby."

The clock on the mantel in the parlour struck twelve times when we started. At two she was still struggling, practically faint from exhaustion. Soon, mother and child would be in danger. "Precious, get me the crow's wing from over the door, then fetch the cayenne pepper off the table."

Quilling was something Miss B. had told me about but I had never witnessed, let alone practised. She said she learned it from what was left of the Chitimacha Indians who lived near the Atchafalaya Swamp. *Her face will done turn red and hot, and she'll think her head's on fire, but when she lets it go, she lets the babe go too. Sometime it's the only way. Porce'pic quills is best, but crow or even a gull's feather'll do.*

Precious watched as I pulled a feather from the wing and scraped the quill clean. I dipped the end of the quill into the pepper, its redness filling the hollow tip. I held the quill close to Iris Rose's face, gently brushing her cheek as I explained, "Hold steady; as soon as we feel the next surge, I'm going to blow. This should do the trick."

She was too weak to respond. Her fingernails clawed into the ladder of the chair, anticipating her pain. With a shot of breath the pepper flew through the quill and into her nose. Her eyes widened as her face turned scarlet. A violent episode of sneezing caused her body to thrust and heave, her voice wailing with tears and half-words. *Cryin' like she'd got the Lord, like a repentant, glory-be soul bringin' the Spirit straight down from heaven,* Iris Rose delivered her baby into my waiting hands.

Time of birth, 2:30 a.m.

A baby girl.

33

Every birth's a lesson.

 I imagined all the care and love I would offer Iris Rose and her baby. Days of rest, clear soup, gruel, soft-boiled eggs and groaning cake. Days of a mother sleeping with her baby nestled soft against her breast. Days of talk, and singing and bliss. With Archer gone, there was more than enough room for at least a week of these days, nine or ten, maybe more if she wanted.

She was thirteen.

Whether it was her father, one of her brothers or some other man, this was not her doing.

Rough winds do shake the darling buds of May.

Before the narcissus, before the pebble buttercups, before the wild rose, bleeding hearts and delphinium, she died . . . leaving silence in the wake. Summer will not warm her face again.

The white cotton nightdress and the bedding surrounding her were soaked in blood. Her face had gone pale. I tore through the pages of the Willow Book, searching for something I might have missed. *Salve nos, Stella Maris. Save us, Star of the Sea.*

When you see a woman who thinks prayin' won't do her no good, you know her blood's gonna flow like a river. She can't hang on to it. She's had hope beaten right out of her. To ease childbirth and expel the placenta— basil, honey, nutmeg.

The afterbirth had delivered as difficult as the child, and Iris Rose had little strength left for it. She was tired, inside and out, before the birthing even began. I had tried to get her to drink blackberry root tea laced with Mary's Tears and Stop Bleed, but she spit it back at me as if I'd given her poison. I tried to explain to her that it was for her own good, but she had already given her reason over to the pain. One minute she'd push me away, the next she'd cling to my neck, hanging on to me, crying, "Mama, Mama, help me. Mama." *A woman's mind makes all the difference during a birth. She's either with you, or she's not. Heaven help her if she's not.*

Precious tended to the newborn, swaddling her in flannel, then placing her in a laundry basket and setting her in the warm halo of the stove. She stood in the doorway, staring, watching Iris Rose struggle, her eyes wide with fear. I knew I'd have to keep her busy if I wanted her to stay calm. "Precious, I need you to go get a large bowl for the placenta and some fresh towels."

With the afterbirth came the blood. Slow at first, then steady and dark, pooling in my hands, through my fingers. Precious tugged on my arm, her voice quaking. "Is she going to die?"

I gave her a stern look, hoping she would realize that, although Iris Rose was not responding to my coaxing, she could still hear what was being said. With a cheerful voice, I assigned Precious another chore. It was a simple task, one of Miss B.'s old tales, but I thought at least it might make her feel useful. "Let's give the secundines their proper end. We have to 'burn the blood away' in a case like this." I handed the bowl, now heavy with membrane and blood, to Precious. "Sprinkle coarse salt on the placenta, wrap it in newspaper and throw it in the fire. It helps slow her bleeding down."

While Precious was distracted with her task, I tried to get Iris Rose to drink more tea. She wouldn't have anything to do with it. I put my hand on her belly, hoping to find that it had begun to tighten back into place, but it was boggy under my fingers, a sure sign that her womb was refusing to close. *Unless her body puts an end to it, she'll bleed 'til she's dead.* "I'll have to push down your belly to try to stop the bleeding. Lie back and relax. Imagine your insides making a nice, firm fist." *You've got to start kneadin' it, push away, hush away, Mother Mary bring it down, push away, hush away . . .*

She closed her eyes, her heartbeats slow and faint, then silent. I shook her, called out her name. *Alls you can do is keep her safe until her angel come.* I prayed to God, to Jesus, to Mary, to Miss B., making the sign of the cross all over her body, all over myself, but Iris Rose had given up long ago . . . before her baby's first breath, before she was forced to my door, before the pain of birth had made her weep. She'd been hurting since the first time she was bruised by her father's angry hand, since the day she learned to pretend at being innocent. Iris Rose had started her life with a soul that wanted to die.

I took the needle jar out of the china cabinet. Holding a handful of sewing needles up to the lamplight, I chose the brightest one. I stood over her body, praying that she would be alive, wishing I didn't have to force myself into what came next. Precious joined me for the morbid ritual.

"I've never seen the dead needle before," she whispered solemnly. "I guess you have to do it, just to be sure. My

Grampy Jeffers said once that you could get the sleeping sickness, and if they didn't needle ya, you might get buried alive. Sometimes it's the only way to tell."

I nodded. I was sure Iris Rose was gone, but the needle would make things easier. If the story of her death somehow got out, got passed from house to house, questions would follow. We would all be held accountable unless I made sure. "If it's tarnished, she's alive; if it's polished, she's dead." I pushed the needle into the softness of her arm, and then recovered it. There, in the palm of my bloodstained hand, it shone, silver-white.

34

I SENT PRECIOUS HOME at first light with strict instructions. "Go to Bertine Tupper's and tell her that she and the other Occasional Knitters are needed at my house. And you mustn't tell your mother any bit of what has happened."

Within an hour, every member of the O.K.S. had arrived. Once I explained the grim tale of Iris Rose's death, we set to working out the details. Sadie and Ginny were both still letting down milk, and they were glad to share in nursing our dear little girl. My breasts feel weepy whenever I hold her. I even tried putting her to them while waiting for help, but there wasn't enough of anything there to keep her happy for long.

Sadie teased as she pulled up her blouse and held the child close. "The milkmaids of Scots Bay, at your service, my dear."

She can't possibly know the relief I felt in seeing that child suckle, her face turning pink and content.

Before long, Precious returned to the house, a large basket on her arm. "I told Mum you were feeling under the weather and needed company." She gave me a sly wink.

"Don't worry, I explained it away as your having a slight cold, and that I suspected it was more of a case of you missing Archer than your needing medical attention."

I tried to turn her away at the door. "Maybe it would be best if you went back home. It was such a long night, you must be exhausted."

She pushed her way into the house. "Please, Dora, let me stay. I haven't been able to stop thinking about everything that's happened. Isn't there something I can do to help? I could hold the baby, sing to her, make tea and biscuits. Even if I went home and marched straight to my room and fell asleep, which I'm certain I couldn't, I'd probably start talking in my sleep and give it all away. You know how I'm prone to giving up secrets when I'm anxious." She handed me the basket, tied an apron around her waist and began breaking eggs for brown bread. "Don't forget to take a look at what I brought."

I sat in a chair and laid the contents of the basket on the kitchen table. Hidden under a layer of the *Ladies' Rural Companion* was a parcel wrapped in tissue paper. When I pulled it open, I found a fine, delicate dress made of lavender silk and lace. It was Precious's new Easter frock, shipped all the way from Eaton's in Toronto. She'd only worn it once since it arrived, skimming through the pews at church, looking heartbroken and lovely as she bid Sam Gower farewell. Precious stroked the wide ribbon that had once been tied snug around her waist. "I want Iris Rose to have it. She should have a proper dress." I turned my head and wept as Ginny held it up for everyone to admire. "It's perfect. Just perfect."

We pulled the sheets from the bed, the stained gown off her body, and cut them to pieces to be burned. Then we laid her out. I washed her, wiping the blood from her skin, watching the water turn red each time I rinsed the cloth in the basin.

Precious helped to dress her and then sat by the edge of the bed, combing her hair in long, steady strokes. "Isn't she beautiful, Dora? She's like a princess going to a grand ball, or a bride with one more sleep before her wedding day."

Mabel picked what flowers she could find and made a bouquet for Iris Rose's sweet, reverent hands to hold. Purple crocuses and star of Bethlehem, a few early tulips, branches of forsythia and pussy willow. "It seems like such a little thing to do, to give her beauty in death."

We swore as sisters to keep this a secret, a prayer tied to our hearts with half-blood knots. We cried, every one of us, whenever the baby cried. We sang tearful lullabies for mother and child. It wasn't that we'd never had death in our lives, it was more that we'd all had too much of it.

Bertine was brave enough to ask, "What can we do with her?"

Mabel made a suggestion. "There's the Ells family burial ground. No one goes there anymore. It won't be too grown over this time of year."

Bertine shook her head. "We can't get there without someone seeing, and even if we could, it was a long, cold winter, and the ground's still pretty hard. It'd have to be a pretty shallow grave."

Ginny spoke quietly. "My granny died in early spring, so Father built a brush pile over her plot and let it burn until the ground was right soft."

Sadie interrupted her. "And everyone won't come running when they see a bonfire?"

"Oh," Ginny replied.

I stopped their bickering. "I have a place. But we'll have to go after dark, and I'll need help getting her there."

Precious and Ginny stayed behind to look after the baby. Bertine, Mabel, Sadie and I shrouded Iris Rose in a blanket, then bound her with sailcloth and rope and dragged her into the woods.

"Take off your shoes."

Sadie laughed. "You feeling alright, Dora?"

Can't let no outside world touch Mary's ground.

"Here, bring her over by the tree. There's room to put her body under it."

"Jesus, Mary and Joseph, that's some deep."

"Looks like she's not the first to go down there."

"What is this place?"

"Don't say anything more. Just do what I ask."

In le jardin des morts, *the garden of the dead, the garden of lost souls, they shall have their rest. Sweet, blessed rest. A home-goin'. A meetin' with the angels.*

"Holy Mother, Star of the Sea, take this little soul with thee. *Salve nos, Stella Maris.* Save us, Mary. Save her, Darcy. Come and save her. Come and take your sister home."

Three days after Iris Rose's death, I bundled the baby girl up and took her down to Deer Glen. Determined to do what was right, I went there thinking I would have to give her up. I had rehearsed what I would say: *I'm so very sorry. There was nothing more I could do. At least we have a part of Iris Rose with us.* As far as burying Iris Rose in the woods . . . there was nothing else to be done. It was more out of respect than secrecy since the Ketch's couldn't afford a proper grave-stone, and the church has rules about who is and isn't worthy to have their bodies rotting away in sacred ground. *I could take you to the spot where we laid her if you like, so you can say a proper goodbye.* None of my speeches ever came to pass. When I got to the loose, stuttering door, Brady Ketch was waiting, squinting at me with his hard, cruel eyes.

"What you want?"

"I came to see Mrs. Ketch."

"What for?"

"It's about Iris Rose."

"Ain't never heard the name."

"But I have her baby here and—"

"That's your business, now, ain't it?" His face turned red as he started to yell. "Get on out of here. Get the hell off my property, or I'll shoot ya dead!"

I took the child home, spinning a tale in my head as I went, a tale of the full moon, a lonely wife and an abandoned baby.

Under the full moon in April, while Precious and I were sharing tea and brown bread, I heard a faint cry at the door. I went to the porch with a bowl of cream for the barn cats. Instead, I found a sweet little babe. She was bundled in a wool blanket and tucked inside a crippled old lobster trap. Of course I took her in, warmed her up and looked her over, head to toe, worried she might be sick from the cold and wet of a spring evening. A perfect child. Apple-cheeked with rosebud lips and a mess of red curls on her head. I don't know where she came from or to whom she might belong. It was as if the faeries had fetched her from the woods and set her on my doorstep, my little moss baby. The peepers have been singing every night since she arrived, and she sings along with them, more like a bird, opening her mouth in a round, hungry O. I have named her Wrennie.

The sisters of the O.K.S. all agree it's a fine tale. They take great pleasure in telling it, over and over, Sundays after church, in front of the Ladies of the White Rose Society, and most especially to anyone who might be visiting from away. They wiggle and coo, putting on quite a show, acting out the spare details.

Why, Dora was so shocked at what she found, she spilled the cream all down her front and into her shoes!

She called out to the dooryard, looked up and down the road. Never heard or saw a thing. Honest to God.

That baby, she's some sweet, some good.

A real, live moss baby.

Honest to God.

We are careful not to change the story, keeping what happened plain and simple, but as with all the other mysteries of the Bay, one story sprouts another, and another, and another, until, like a curse of alders, *that's not what I heard* has grown up all around it.

I heard Archie Bigelow sent the child home to her, special delivery.

I heard she stole it from a woman over in Delhaven.

I heard it was brought by the spirit of Marie Babineau, creeping over the water with the fog. A ghost baby, a moss baby. She'll wake up one morning and find it's gone.

35

A RCHER ARRIVED ON A SUNDAY morning at the church. As the last hymn ended, I spotted him, standing in the back of the sanctuary, Grace Hutner clinging to his arm. They looked like a picture, the kind I've seen in Aunt Fran's magazines or on picture postcards down at Newcomb's Dry Goods. One of those smiling, haughty couples that parades down city sidewalks, thinking everything in the world was meant for them.

Members of the congregation made their way from the pews. The ladies whispered, the men looked puzzled, and several girls stopped in front of Grace to wonder at the showy, expensive cut of her dress. Bertine's girl, Lucy, reached out and smoothed her hand along Grace's hip. The little girl sighed, as if nothing she had ever touched, not the airy down of a new chick or the softness of Wrennie's cheeks, could compare.

Archer grinned as I approached. "Look what I found under a rock in the Halifax harbour."

I gave a polite nod. "Hello, Grace."

She let go of Archer's arm as if she hadn't expected to see me. "Hello, Dora."

Wrennie was a bit restless in my arms, so I pulled the blanket away from her face.

Grace stared at Wrennie. "What a beautiful baby. Still catching them for everyone else, I see. Who does this one belong to?"

I smiled at her. "She belongs to me."

Archer gave Grace a pleading look, his face turning red. "I didn't know. I didn't think I'd been gone that long. You didn't say anything before I left, Dorrie? Honest-to-Pete." He turned to me and grabbed my arm. "Why didn't you send word?"

I pulled away from him and started out the door. "You're a hard man to find."

Archer followed at my heels all the way home, scratching his head, cursing. When I explained how Wrennie wasn't really ours by birth, how she was left at our door, he fumed and huffed and told me I was cruel to have teased him and Grace about such a thing.

"And it wasn't cruel of you to waltz right into the church, the same church where we were married, sporting Grace Hutner around like she was some sort of prize?"

He sat at the kitchen table, head down, picking at his fingernails. His voice wavered as he stumbled and back-tracked over his words. "I'm sorry about Grace, but she needed a way home, and I . . ."

"Never mind about her."

"Then I'm forgiven?"

"No."

"Why not?"

I kept my voice low so I wouldn't wake Wrennie from her nap. "Don't come here, where people have next to nothing, where families have lost their sons to war and their lives to hard work, holding yourself up as better than everyone else." I picked up his new hat from off the table and flattened it between my hands.

He grabbed the hat from me, poking and preening at it, trying to get it back to its original shape. "I just wanted to show everyone that I'm doing well."

"You just wanted to put on a show."

"I wanted to let people know that I'd made good on what they gave me."

"Then give them something real, give them what you promised, not some half-bit burlesque starring you and Grace Hutner."

"I met a man, in Halifax, he's from Delaware, or was it New Jersey? Anyway, he said he'd get me everything I need and ship it straight to Scots Bay. I'm surprised the supplies for the wind machines didn't get here before I did. I have a bill of goods . . ."

I started to walk away.

"Goddammit, Dorrie . . . come back here and listen to me."

"I'd better check on the baby."

"I thought you were smarter than the rest of the slow-brained people in this place."

"Well, I guess when it comes to you, I'm not."

Support for Archer's wind farm soon went cold with everyone here. They counted the days, and when they saw no signs of his great plan coming to pass, they blamed him for falling in with "drummers and charlatans," for taking their money and changing it for air. He says he's not certain what's happened, why nothing has appeared. *Any day now. I'm sure it will be here soon.* I can only say that, no matter if it comes or not, my husband will always be a man who's never happy with what he's got, who's always wishing he had more. He never stops saying how he wants to bring the world to the Bay . . . electricity, railroads, telephone wires, balloon rides. With Wrennie to care for, I find I have little patience left for his talk. We've not been married a year, and already the words he says and the things he does no longer sound fair or true.

He sleeps upstairs now. I told him he'd be better off, since Wrennie still wakes up in the night. The truth is, I'm not ready to give up the quiet, twinned breathing she and I share as we settle in for bed. I cook his meals, pick up after him, wash his clothes, always feeling like he's an uninvited guest. How is it that Mother still smiles at the boyish things Father does? When he's as forgetful as my brothers about wearing his muddy boots in the house, when he sneaks around from behind the barn and scares the laundry right out of her basket. Her squeals and screams always turn to laughter, inviting him to pull her into his arms.

Our playful moments (the few we've had) have ended for Archer and me. Even Grace Hutner seems to have given up on him. Word is she's vanished back to Halifax again, leaving my marriage alone just a little too late. Now the only smiles, the only blushes he raises, come from the young girls who sit in the last pew of the church, the ones that twitch and giggle when he brushes their ears with the brim of his hat, girls who are not quite seventeen.

Father and Hart come stomping through the house at sunrise each day. They drag Archer downstairs, bleary-eyed and half-dressed, their conversation always sounding the same.

"I'm some tired today . . . maybe it'd be best if I waited at home until the shipment comes for the windmills." He pulls up his trousers and fills the pot for coffee. "Any day now, you know, it'll be coming, in wagonloads up the mountain, or a ship coming into the wharf . . . how about a cuppa before you're on your way?"

Father stands with his hand on Archer's shoulder, looking my sallow-faced husband up and down. "That's fine news, son, but right now I have work that needs to be done, and you're gonna help me do it."

Archer begs, "How about you give me until tomorrow? A man's gotta have one day to rest."

Father chews at the inside of his cheek and grumbles, "That's what Sundays are for . . . I'm three boys short with a three-masted schooner that won't get built on her own. Besides, you can work off *my* share of the money you spent on that spankin' new suit of yours."

Hart picks up Archer's boots and throws them out the door. Father shoves Archer right along behind them. "Pick it up now, let's keep you honest." He turns to me and smiles. "I'll have him home for supper, Dorrie."

I've stopped trying to converse with him. I offered him his meals and little else. *More potatoes? Supper's ready. Father needs a hand with the horses this morning.*

He's gone back to his drinking, only this time he keeps it away from the house. He comes home late most every evening and acts as if it's an insult for me to question him about where he's been. The back of my arm is green with bruises from where he leaves his disappointment. He kisses it after he pinches it raw, as if to say he didn't mean to go so far.

But he never says he's sorry. I know how it is when boys play, how they don't always know what they've done . . . I've scars on my shins from every trip and shove my brothers didn't mean to happen. I understand his weakness, his disappointment in me, but poor Wrennie, she needs a father. Whenever I point out her awkward attempts to smile, or her first bites of porridge, he ignores my words and passes her by.

This evening after supper, he tossed the rag doll I've been sewing for her onto the floor, soiling its tender, empty face by his carelessness. When I called it to his attention, he slapped my face. "Just keep your mouth shut." He dug his fingers into the waist of my skirt, hitting at me again, pulling at me as I tried to get away. "Did you hear me? You need to learn to keep your mouth shut."

I can't say how long he might have kept at me if his brother hadn't come to the door, asking if Archer could lend a hand down at the wharf.

Hart stood in the kitchen doorway, waiting. "Hey there, Mrs. Bigelow. How's that niece of mine? How's the prettiest baby in the Bay?"

I pretended to look for something in the china cabinet. "Some sweet as always. You know our Wrennie." I could see in the glass of the door that Archer's hand had left a bold striped mark. I pulled my hair loose from its bun and let it fall in my face.

"You still got a piece of that caul of yours somewhere, Dorrie? You ought to give it to Archie there; he's got neither the stomach nor the head for water."

Archer stomped into his rubber boots. "Shut your bucket-mouthed yap."

"See there, Dora? You'd better hand it over. Pride cometh before a fall."

I took the locket Widow Bigelow had given me for our wedding, hung it around Archer's neck and tucked it under his collar. "For luck."

He kissed my cheek where it still felt hot and sore.

"Good God, Archie, stop peckin' at your wife and let's get to it." Hart waved a cheerful goodbye, as if he hadn't noticed a thing. "Give Wrennie a squeeze for me."

"Will do."

36

FULL MOON, CLEAR SKIES. The Dulsin' tide. By day the men go out to the split, dulsing, their skiffs trailing with red ribbons of seaweed. Laid out on the rocks or the roofs of fishing sheds, it will crinkle and dry. *Puts salt in the veins, keeps the blood strong for another year.* By night they torch for herring in the Bay. The skiffs dance over the water, torches tied to the dragon of the bow, glowing with fire, nets sparkling like they were spun and knotted from silver. Mother used to say that, along with the fish, the light of the dulsing moon called up mermaids. *Watch careful now, Dora. If you look real hard, you'll see them jump right out of the water for a kiss.* This is the tide of haying, of wild blackberries and mussel bakes down to Lady's Cove. The tide of my marriage. The tide of happiness. The sound of the waves comes through the kitchen's open window, the tide marching, marching, marching away. The voice of the moon. The Dulsin' tide.

Once you're a mother, your waiting must be patient. Only after supper's gone cold, the baby's asleep and the lantern's been lit in the window can worry be allowed to settle in. I should have been worried, should have paced the floor, wondering where he was, but I didn't think of it. Didn't think better of the dogs barking into the night, complaining of the south wind in their mouths. Of the rattle at the door, so loud I called out Archer's name. Three times. *It come three times in the night, shakin' a soul right out of its body. A shadow man, a foretellin'.*

"Archer? Is that you?"

The side door had come open. Any other night I would have barred it, but I didn't want Archer left out in the cold if I happened to fall asleep.

"Archer?"

A tall shadow loomed in the doorway. His clothes hung heavy-wet, salt water dripping in a large puddle around him, seaweed caught in his boots.

"Archer? No—Hart? My God, you're soaked to the bone. Here, come in, sit down." I sat at his feet, tugging off his boots, pulling away layers of wet newspaper and wool socks. "How far behind is Archer? Didn't you come in together?"

"Dora, I—"

"Let me guess. He didn't fall in, but you did. Did he stop at Jack Tupper's place for a nip of brew? He should have walked with you. Oh well, you know Archer. Talk comes before the wife, especially after dark."

"Dora . . ."

Three times. *A foretellin'.* The door had rattled three times. I looked him over. "Looks like your eye took a good beating. You really should get out of those wet overalls. I'm sure I have something of Archer's that will fit. The legs will be short, but—"

He grabbed my hands and held them still. "Archer's gone, Dora. He was messing with the torch, his clothes caught on fire, he jumped in the water, must have hit his head on the bottom of the skiff."

"You couldn't save him?"

"I reached over and grabbed for him. I had his hand a couple of times, but he slipped away. You know how the Bay is at night. It's black as pitch to look down into it. I lost him. He just disappeared."

Man Drowns at Scots Bay

It is with great regret that we record the disappearance of Archer Bigelow of Scots Bay. He left his home the evening of June 24 to go out with his brother, Hart Bigelow, to torch for herring. He fell overboard and could not be saved. Searching parties have been out every day, on the shores and in the Bay, trailing for the body, but no trace has been found. The deceased leaves a wife and one daughter, who have the sympathy of the whole place in this shocking fatality.

The Canning Register,
June 30, 1918

I called off the search.

After nearly a week, I couldn't ask any more of my family, my friends or the good people of this community. Archer did nothing for them, always talking behind their backs, saying they were fools to be smiling and content with their "hopeless little lives." In the end, I was left to make the decision, to consider what his life was worth, to say our efforts had been enough.

Mother brought nearly every meal to the house. Auntie Althea came each day with fresh eggs and brown bread. The other aunties made cookies and pies (even Aunt Fran), and Precious was a great help with Wrennie. My dear sisters of the O.K.S. cooked and cleaned and kept me company all through the day and night, engaged in the work of those who are left but not grieving. This is part of a woman's nature—knowing how to busy herself around a death that isn't in her heart.

Every man in the Bay went searching, rowing skiffs in and out of the coves along the shore, afraid of what he'd find. Every man wondering if his own life would be considered a life worth saving. One by one, they came back to shore, traced his name on stones with bits of charcoal and laid them in a heap, *a sailor's grave.*

His body has been recorded as "unfound." No morbid, waterlogged reminder to account for. God forgive me for saying it, but somehow I am relieved. His death was a passing I had already rehearsed. Each time he left me alone, I played at being a widow, taking up his side of the bed, putting his clothes in the bottom drawer, his shoes in the cellar, setting flowers next to his tombstone in my head. *Archer Fales Bigelow, beloved husband.* Now he's gone again, this time for good.

37

WIDOWED AT THE AGE of nineteen.

Already I've grown tired of wearing black to church and town. It makes me feel useless and old. Aunt Fran constantly reminds me that Archer's mother has suffered the greater loss. "She never complains—may the good Lord bless her—Simone Bigelow lost two husbands and now her oldest child. That poor woman will have to wear black, day and night, rain or shine, for the rest of her life." While I'm no authority on fashion, I'd guess that the Great War will leave those who insist on bowing to etiquette no choice but to change their standards. There can't possibly be enough crepe and Henrietta cloth to cover the doors of the homes that have been touched by death, let alone the grieving wives and mothers who have been left behind. The world is dark and weary enough as it is. My parading around like a ghoul won't make it any better.

For once, Mother agrees with Aunt Fran. She scolded me when I asked for her help in sewing a new Sunday dress. "It's too soon. If you trade in your mourning dress for something new, you'll lose the support of the Bay. There would be talk. You have to mourn for at least a year and a day, no less. After that, you can start looking for a new husband. Maybe then you'll have children of your own."

Wrennie *is* my own. No matter how I got her. My moss baby. *A blue moon child,* as Miss B. would say. *Blue moon babies don't cry, don't mind nothin'. They're sent by Mary herself to poor mamas who ain't got room in their heart for any more sour. I know one as soon as they's borned, it's as if they come down with one finger still touchin' heaven.* When she's older, when she's learning to stand on her own, when she clings to my legs, hides her peek-a-boo face in my skirts, she should find herself wrapped in the colour of sunshine, the blue of cornflowers. She should see that her mother isn't afraid to laugh, that she's not afraid of anything. This is how to raise a child to be happy, to be the girl that everyone loves.

Mother and most of the other women treat me as if I will break, always shushing me and patting my knee, then bringing me another cup of warm milk. Bertine understands, having known of Archer's outburst last autumn. Sadie and Mabel and even Ginny might listen, but to speak ill of a dead man, to any woman who has a husband, is to tempt fate.

Hart's the only person I have shared my true feelings with since Archer's passing. He comes to the house, feeds the horses, mucks the stalls, stacks firewood in the cellar for the coming winter, just as he did when Archer was away. Wrennie adores him. He folds his long arms around her and sways from side to side, singing, *"You're the prettiest girl of them all,"* then she nods off with her face buried in his neck. After she's asleep, we sit together for tea and sometimes a late supper. It's such a relief to be able to admire the beauty of a sunset, or to curse the stubborn purple raspberry stains under my fingernails, and not feel guilty for living.

"I didn't give him my caul."

"You gave him your locket. I remember you putting it around his neck."

"There wasn't anything in it." I was feeling guilty, my hands shaking. "Maybe if I had . . . do you believe in that sort of thing?"

"Archie always got more than his share, Dorrie. Especially from you."

"It's all I have that's worth anything. At least that's what I was thinking when he left to go to the wharf. I thought I might need it. More than I needed him."

"And some would say you were right. Or at least they'd think it."

"But that's a horrible thought. It's as if I wished him dead and then it happened."

"That's not what happened." He looked me. "I let him go. I could have jumped in after him. I could have saved him . . ."

"Or you both could have drowned."

"I saw what he'd done to you, Dora. And I couldn't stop thinking about it. The last time he grabbed at my hand, the last time he gasped for air—I thought of you. I let him go."

part three

38

IT WAS THE FIRST OF August when Mrs. Ketch came to the house. Seeing her at my door made me catch my breath. More than three months after Wrennie's birth, had she come to say she wanted the baby, to raise her as her own? Even if she had the means (and I'm certain she's never had two nickels to rub), her husband has the Devil in him. No doubt he beats them all, right down to the littlest one.

She was standing on the porch, her face showing what was left of Mr. Ketch's latest outburst, one eye drooping, swollen red ears, her nose bent to one side. She bore all the trademarks of a rum-induced left hook. If it was Wrennie she was after, she'd have to kill me first.

"Mrs. Bigelow?"

"Come in, and call me Dora, please."

"Thank you, Dora . . ."

Her voice was small and flat. She sat straight to the back of the kitchen chair, hands folded tight in her lap. I watched her scared, watering eyes blinking behind her ratty brown hair.

"Have a cuppa? The pot's on the stove, already hot. Did you walk all the way here?"

"Yes, I didn't want . . . I mean, yes, I walked."

"Quite a hike, so late in the day."

"Yes."

She held the teacup in both hands, her chapped thin fingers turning red. Putting the cup to her face, she breathed in the sweet steam of raspberry leaves and rosehips between her dry, peeling lips.

I carried on with the conversation, hoping to get rid of the sick feeling in my stomach and my guilt that I had somehow stolen something from her. "How's your family? How's Tom? Have you heard from him?"

"Tom's dead."

"Oh. I—"

"Blown right up in the trenches. Nothing left of him. They sent his pay, his second pair of shoes . . . and some letters he kept in his locker . . . one from you in there, I think."

"Yes, I wrote him, once. I'm so sorry. I didn't know."

I went on, not sure what to do with the silence.

"Would you like to see the baby? She's napping right now, but I could—"

"No, don't bother. Anyway, it's you I come to see." She drank down her tea in fast, nervous gulps. When she finished, she wiped the corner of her mouth with the frayed cuff of her sleeve, then stared at the empty cup. "I'm in the family way."

"Oh." I busied myself with pouring more tea in her cup, trying to think of a way to get out of helping her. Nothing good had ever come from my knowing her or her family. Nothing except Wrennie. "Perhaps you should see Dr. Thomas, then. I'm sure Mr. Ketch would prefer it. Besides, I'm not really midwifing anymore."

"Brady don't know. I tried a few things already to lose it—all those things grannies say ain't good for a woman that's with child. Raisin' my hands above my head, spendin' too much time at the spinnin' wheel. I even tried slippin' off the porch the other day, but none of it's worked. I gots enough children to feed and care for, and you know Brady can get some angry, has a real bad temper. I know most people would say I should be grateful, that if it's a girl I could name her Iris Rose, and if it's a boy, I could call it Tom, that it's only right, that it's God's way of makin' up for the ones I've lost.

"My mother had three baby girls named Experience— Experience Ruth, Experience Esther and Experience Hope. Experience Hope, that's me; I'm the only one that stuck . . . she said it was the *Hope* that did it. Well, whatever it was, it don't make any difference now. I gots my hands full." She looked at me with tired, pleading eyes. "You can make it go away, right?"

Mrs. Ketch had more than any woman's share of children. *That woman's got more babies than she can count on her fingers; she's got so many babies, she's got toesies.* I couldn't blame her for not wanting to have another child, but more than feeling sorry for her, I wanted to tell her there was nothing I could do and just turn her away.

"Like I said, I've given up—"

"With or without your help, I ain't gonna have this baby."

Without my help she'd turn to throwing herself down the cellar stairs or poisoning herself with yew bark tea. If mother and child survived, what then? One more mouth to feed, one more body to keep warm, one more like Darcy, or Iris Rose, or Tom . . . one more for the back of Brady Ketch's hand. *Only the heart knows what it's got to lose, one way or another. I'm here to deliver women from their pain. Simple as that.*

I breathed deep, Miss B.'s beads feeling heavy around my neck. "Well, then, we should see how far along you are. Why don't you lie down on the bed and let me take a look at you?"

She obediently followed me into the bedroom and propped herself against the head of the iron bed, her legs spread out, hands folded on her chest. I began searching across her middle with my fingers, feeling for the ridge of her womb. She sank into the quilts, her nervous body hung with bruised, pale skin, her breasts pulled low by the constant strain of too much mothering and fear.

"When did you last have your courses?"

"Let's see . . . it's August now. So, the end of April, I think . . . yes, April, there was fiddleheads pokin' up in the woods behind the house."

She was further along than I had hoped she might be. Not like when Aunt Fran had come to Miss B., wanting to just move things along. I excused myself to get the Willow Book, looking for the page that explained how to make an angel come down early.

It was laid out clearly.

One moontime past—she gets the Mary Candle and
     High Tide Tea.
Two moontimes past—she gets the Mary Candle and
     Angel Water.
Three moontimes past—she's too late.

She was nearly three times late, but desperate enough that I couldn't say no. I went through Miss B.'s steps, coating the long, slender taper in slippery elm oil and pushing it slowly up inside Mrs. Ketch. She winced, but didn't complain.

When I tried to explain that she needed to pray with the candle, keeping it lit for the next three nights, she just shook her head and frowned. "I don't need the witchery. I just need it to work. Is that all?"

I thought about the ingredients listed beside Miss B.'s Angel Water. *Pennyroyal, black stick, a pinch of borax . . .* "I can give you something, but it's pretty powerful. You'll have to stay here tonight so I can watch over you."

She sat up, her legs dangling over the edge of the bed. "I can't leave the little ones alone with Brady. Especially not at night. He's not right most evenings. They'd get no supper and if they complain, he'll whip 'em 'til there's no tears left. Just mix it up and I'll be on my way."

"At least let me have Hart Bigelow take you home. He'll be by soon to feed the horses. He can leave you off at the the end of the road to Deer Glen if you like." I followed Miss B.'s recipe, poured the mixture into a brown bottle and handed it to Mrs. Ketch. "You can put it in your tea. A tablespoon every four hours. Take it all, every last bit. The bleeding will be heavy at times, cramping too. Send word if it doesn't stop or you don't feel right."

She nodded, still looking nervous. "You won't tell anyone why I was here?"

"If anyone asks, we'll say you came to see if I had some of Miss B.'s cough syrup left for the children."

My dog, Daisy, had her first litter of pups when I was ten. Five fat-bellied collies with the sharp bark of Laird Jessup's best hunting beagle. Father kept two for himself, Nip and Tuck, to chase after pheasants and help bring in the cows. The others went off to live with three of Father's brothers,

Uncle John, Uncle Homer and Uncle Web. Daisy's second litter came the morning after my eleventh birthday, when I spotted her weaseling her round, wobbly body through a hole in the lattice under the side porch. Frightened she might get stuck, I tried to crawl in after her, but she snarled and nipped at me, letting me know I shouldn't come any closer. I checked on her through the day as she whimpered out six squint-eyed babies, their pink noses and bodies all struggling and worming over each other for Daisy's milk.

When Mother called me for supper, I was still lying flat on the ground, staring under the porch. Father was on his way in from the shipyard, hot, dusty and tired. He shook his head as he approached, knowing what was holding my attention. "Don't go wantin' to keep those pups, Dorrie."

Over dinner I did my best to plead my case, promising that as soon as they were weaned I'd stand up in church and announce that we had six beautiful puppies to give away . . . every Sunday until they all had a home. But Father wouldn't hear it. He said that, if he recalled correctly, it was Charlie's fault we had too many puppies in the first place, that Charlie had been the one to let Daisy loose while she was in heat, that Charlie should be the one to "take care of it." Charlie gave a solemn nod. Mother said she'd make sure he did his job first thing in the morning. We all knew what that meant. I cried into my pillow that night, but I knew better than to say another word about it.

In the morning, after breakfast, Mother coaxed Daisy out from the porch with a steaming bowl of stew meat still clinging to the bone. Charlie crawled through the hole, clutching an empty potato sack. Mother shut Daisy in the barn, and Charlie emerged from the porch with the sack hanging heavy, squirming with muffled cries. "Dora, you go back inside now. Charlie and I will be home soon."

I waited, staring out the window, until I could see that they were halfway down the path to Jess Brook. Then I crept through the alders, following behind.

Mother watched as Charlie knelt down by the deepest part of the brook. She grabbed the sack before Charlie could plunge it into the water. I could hear the tears in her voice as she told him, "Go away, Charlie, just go on home." She didn't turn to watch him run away. She just sat and waited until she couldn't hear his footsteps, then she closed her eyes and pushed the sack into the stream, leaning in up to her elbows, holding it down with sadness and duty.

I never understood why she had to do it, why she felt Father was right to want to kill those pups. I went on after that day believing that my mother was not who I'd always thought she was, that her face was less beautiful, that her arms gave less warmth than before.

I wonder if Wrennie can feel the coldness in me that comes when I think of Mrs. Ketch, the chill that runs right through me, to my fingers and down to my toes. *It don't matter one way or another. I ain't God. Only the woman knows if she's got enough love to make a life.* No matter how many of Miss B.'s old quilts I wrap around me, I can't seem to keep warm.

39

Family Mourns Loss of Mother

Mrs. Experience Hope Ketch died in her home, Tuesday, August 2. She leaves behind her husband, Mr. Brady Ketch, as well as many loving children. She was predeceased by her oldest son, Private Thomas H. Ketch, who was lost in the battle of Cambrai. Mrs. Ketch was laid to rest in the Union Church Cemetery at Scots Bay. The service was carried out by the Ladies of the White Rose Temperance Society, followed by a gathering of fellowship at the Seaside Centre. Food, clothing and other donations for the Ketch family were gratefully accepted at that time.

The Canning Register,
August 6, 1918

I DIDN'T ATTEND THE FUNERAL. I did, however, leave Wrennie with Mother so I could sneak into the kitchen at the Seaside Centre and leave food and a few small things for the Ketch children. It would have been best if I'd stayed away, but I couldn't help myself, I needed to find out anything I could about Mrs. Ketch's death.

"I've never seen a man so quick to get his wife in the grave." Mrs. Trude Hutner was standing in the meeting room with Aunt Fran, folding a pile of Grace's old dresses, putting them on the table with the rest of the donations. "No viewing, no visitation. It seems so odd. I'm wondering if she didn't run off somewhere. That could very well be an empty coffin we buried today."

Aunt Fran began to set out plates for those who might want something to eat. "Oh, there's no doubt she's dead, but just *how* it happened is another story."

Mrs. Hutner lowered her voice. "You think *he* did it?"

"It's possible. All I know is that Irwin was down to Canning, and when he came home he said he heard Constable McKinnon was on his way to visit the Ketch place, to *talk* to Brady."

"He sure isn't acting like he feels guilty for a thing. Did you see? He's got his wagon out back, handing cups of brew to his friends and cousins, making toasts to his dear wife's name, getting drunk as a skunk while we ladies feed and clothe his children."

Mrs. Newcomb had joined them, bringing boxes of supplies from the dry goods store in Canning. "I think she probably just wore out. How many children did she have? Fifteen? Sixteen? It takes its toll after a while. A woman can kill herself with a life like that."

Aunt Fran nodded. "You're probably right. The poor thing . . . at least she's better off now."

Mrs. Hutner smoothed the hair on one of Grace's old china dolls. "God bless her."

I had been thinking of Experience Ketch ever since she left my house, hoping that she would remember to follow my instructions and that things had gone easy for her. I had no doubts about Miss B.'s notes, or even about having helped her, but when I heard that she was dead, I couldn't help but feel that I was to blame. Standing behind the kitchen door, I wept silent tears, thankful that this time the women's gossip didn't include my name.

Before I could leave, Bertine bustled into the kitchen, carrying two large baskets of food. I tried to stifle a groan as the door jammed against my toes. She peered around and spotted me. "Dora Bigelow, playing hide-and-seek at your age! Get out from there and lend a hand. Those poor little Ketch children are lining up, and they need something more than your auntie's dry tea biscuits."

"I should go. I only stopped by to leave some things. Wrennie's at my mother's . . . she's got plenty of work to do without taking care of a baby. I—"

She handed me the tea towel that had been covering the food in one of the baskets. "Sad thing for those poor little ones. Here, wipe your eyes and let's get some food in their bellies."

I stood with the rest of the ladies, passing plates down the line, as we served up our sympathy alongside mashed turnips and slices of brown bread. Before long, Brady and the rest of the men in his family came in, reeling from too much brew. When he got to my place in the line, he started talking and didn't stop.

"None of that for me, there. And I'd say no one else should take what this girl has to offer—you can't be so sure it ain't poison."

I tried to calm him down. "Mr. Ketch, I'm so sorry about your wife, we all are. I know you don't mean what you're saying. It's a difficult time—"

"Brings death to everything she touches. She's the reason I ain't got my wife—and I told the constable that very same thing. Now he's got the truth."

Laird Jessup, who is a cousin to the Ketch brothers and who had also had more than his share of brew, was right behind him. "About time someone did somethin' about her. She's caused nothin' but trouble in my house. From the time she was a little girl, always sneakin' around my place, puttin' the witchery on my cattle. I lost a perfectly good calf because of her, had to put the cow down too. Couldn't breed it again after somethin' like that. I'd have been callin' on the Devil."

Down the line the women began to whisper, some wondering if someone should go and fetch my father or one of the other men down at the wharf. Others started to wonder if maybe Brady Ketch was right and if something hadn't better be done.

Mrs. Hutner turned to the women around her. "Her own family doesn't know what to do with her. I've lent a sympathetic ear to her poor aunt on more than one occasion." She opened her eyes wide, looking half-crazy. "She's been diagnosed with hysteria, you know."

"Hysteria? Really."

"She was always such a strange little girl."

"And it only made things worse, her mother letting her live with that witch."

"He's right, you know—everything she touches."

"Seems like it."

Laird continued his ranting, holding up the line. "And she's always puttin' thoughts in my Ginny's head. You think I don't know what you done? Here I blamed it on a good man. I should have known Dr. Thomas wouldn't give my wife so much as a drop of water without telling me first. Nearly made her barren, just like herself, with some potion she mixed up. Ginny'll tell you. Go on, tell 'em, Ginny, these people need to know." Ginny hung her head and looked at her feet.

Mr. Ketch leaned over the table, sneering at me. "You'd better pack your bags and say your goodbyes. It won't be long before they comes up here to drag you off." He put his hands up to his neck, grasping at it, his face turning red. "Before they puts your pretty face in the noose."

Bertine had started tapping her foot the minute Brady opened his mouth. She practically kicked over the table now, shouting at him. "You best be glad I don't hitch your feet to the back of my buggy and drag *you* through the Bay and down the mountain." She straightened the lace collar on her dress and stood firm. "Of course, being the good Christian woman that I am, I wouldn't do such a thing on the day your wife's gone into the ground. God rest her soul. But come tomorrow, Brady Ketch, you'd better watch where you step."

Aunt Fran came to my side and pleaded with me. "You need to leave. It's for your own good." She pulled on my arm and led me to the door, Brady Ketch's words following behind.

"Go on and leave, but they'll be comin' for you. They're comin' right to your door, with the noose."

I started to turn in the doorway, to say to Brady and everyone else that he was nothing but a lousy drunk who had no trouble selling his daughter away or beating his wife to death, but Aunt Fran stopped me. Seeing the anger in my face, she put her lips close to my ear.

"You don't want to do that just now. Things will seem better if you go home and get some rest." She kissed my cheek and closed the door.

40

I RAN ALL THE WAY to Spider Hill, only to find Dr. Thomas sitting at my kitchen table with the Willow Book laid open in front of him. Several bottles of Miss B.'s remedies were clustered on either side.

"Mrs. Bigelow, you look unwell. Is everything alright?"

"Get out of my house."

"I'm afraid I have some matters to discuss with you. They are quite urgent."

"Please leave."

"If it were my own business it might wait for another day, but I've been asked by Constable McKinnon . . . here, sit down."

"I'll stand, thank you."

"Very well, then." He ran his fingers across the writing in the book. "Interesting reading. Is this your hand?" He picked up one of Miss B.'s bottles of cough syrup and held it up to the light. "You've a nice collection of herbals and other remedies. Any apothecary would be envious." He put the bottle back on the table. "From what the constable told me of Mrs. Ketch's death, I can see that you've gotten yourself in quite a lot of trouble. You stand to lose everything . . . this house, your family's good name, your child."

I thought of Miss B. and the way she'd handled things when Dr. Thomas came out to her cabin after Darcy died. When I'd asked her why she'd lied to him, saying she didn't know anything about Mrs. Ketch's giving birth, she said, "Sometimes it's best to play possum with a man . . . until you finds out what he's after."

"I haven't any idea what you're talking about. I've done nothing wrong."

"With what I've seen here, I think it's clear that you have. But I can help you . . . if you're willing to admit to your hand in Mrs. Ketch's death, then I could say, as your physician, that you were under great stress, that your uninformed use of 'home' remedies, along with your history of hysterical illness, caused this sad, irreversible error. Think of it not only as a way to free yourself from guilt, but as a way to do a favour for so many women—putting the problems of midwifery to rest, setting the record straight. Of course, you'd have to be sent away for proper observation and rehabilitation. There's a beautiful women's sanitarium in Saint John, New Brunswick. They'll pamper you, feed you wholesome foods, help you put your mind at ease. Think of the better person you'll be in the end, returning home a better woman, a better mother. You really have no choice."

I started to wonder if what he was saying wasn't true. *Anything's the truth, as long as enough people believe it.* I'd have given up anything, all of Miss B.'s secrets—called everything I'd learned from her a lie—as long as I could keep Wrennie. "I could take my daughter with me?"

"Well, no. You'd have to leave the child with one of her relatives." He frowned. "Oh dear, but that causes another problem, doesn't it? She isn't yours by birth, now, is she?" The corners of his mouth quivered, as if he was trying not to smile. "And according to the incredible accounts I've heard about how she came to you, you've no idea who her *real* family is. The Orphans Home in Kentville is a perfectly suitable institution. With no records to say she's yours, I suppose you'd have to leave her there until things could be sorted out."

"How long would I have to stay?"

"As little as a month, or perhaps as long as a year. Occasionally it takes longer. It's hard to say . . . however long it takes for you to be declared fit, sound and well."

With that kind of help, I might as well be dead. "I'll manage on my own."

"Think about what you're saying, Mrs. Bigelow."

"No, thank you, I've made up my mind."

He put on his hat and walked to the door. "You may think you have friends here, people who care about you, but I assure you, with every day that passes, there will be more and more who turn their heads away when you call their names, acting as if they never knew you."

"Goodbye, Dr. Thomas."

What Mother had to say

"Fran told me what happened between you and Brady Ketch down at the Seaside Centre. I wouldn't worry yourself over it. He's drunk half the time and was nothing but terrible to his wife. Everyone knows it. You're a good girl, and you haven't done anything wrong. God sees what you do. He wouldn't have given you dear little Wrennie if you weren't a good girl, a good mother. She's been the sweetest thing all afternoon. You want to stay here for the night?

No? Are you sure? I suppose you're right. Best to get her to her own cradle by her mama's bed. I'll check on you tomorrow. Sweet dreams for my sweet girls."

What Hart had to say

"I don't believe a word of it, but you know as well as I do that people outside the Bay have never paid us enough respect to let us do things our own way. Seems to me that doctor's got all kinds of things going on in his head that don't belong there, but his mind's made up that you're the one who's got to pay. Until we can set it straight, you're better off on a little holiday to see Charlie. We've got to get you out of here. I'll row you out to the *Bluebird*. When the tide goes out, she's headed for Boston."

What Bertine had to say

"Of course I'll take care of Wrennie, and I'll take care of things with Brady Ketch too, the rum-sucking pig. Don't worry, I won't let a soul lay a hand on her head. I'll write down every little sound she makes, every grin and coo."

"I'd leave her with Mama, I know she'd say yes, but she's so busy with the boys."

"I'll make sure she sees Wrennie whenever she likes. Anything else I should do?"

"I've never seen you back down from a fight, Bertine. Just be who you are, and I know she'll be fine."

"Wind in your sails, Dora. Wind in your sails."

41

THE JOURNEY FROM SCOTS BAY to Boston was uneventful as I stayed below deck most of the time, huddled at the edge of a bottom berth, my head between my knees and a bucket at my feet. Father would have laughed if he'd found me in such a state, no doubt remarking that I had proved (once again) that women aren't fitted with sea legs.

The first mate was familiar with the North End, and although unable to accompany me to my destination, he was kind enough to give me some direction as to how to reach Charlie's residence at 23 Charter Street. "Fleet Street across North to Hanover. North on Hanover to Charter. West on Charter to 23."

It was evening when I started from the docks, lonely and tired, clutching one of Miss B.'s old carpetbags. The Willow Book weighed down the bottom of it, along with the few things I'd brought with me—a second skirt and shirtwaist, my Sunday dress, one of Wrennie's crib blankets (in hopes that it would still smell of lavender soap and her) and a purse full of coins that Hart had given me before he put me on the ship. As I looked ahead to the puzzling streets and the faces streaming by, it was all I could do not to grab the nearest lamppost and hold on for dear life. Faced with Boston, my youthful dreams of running off to a city now seemed painfully misguided, and I wondered how I would ever find my way. I breathed in, hoping to find the same salty breezes I was used to in the Bay, but the air was moist and much hotter than at home, even for August. My clothes and the braid down my back felt heavy and dirty, clinging wet to my body.

The sunset was nearly filled right up to the top, the orange-red sky sharing its glory with endless crowds of ships' masts and row after row of houses, buildings and church steeples. The cobbled streets stretched out in every direction, never quiet or still—delivery trucks honking and sputtering as they pushed their way around people on bicycles, children playing ball, horses struggling to pull carts full of fish or fruit.

As I moved away from the harbour, the streets became narrow and dark. I picked up my pace, trying to seem as busy as everyone else, hoping not to be noticed, wanting nothing more than to get to Charlie. The heavy brick buildings that stand shoulder to shoulder were still letting off the heat of the day, holding close the smell of the wharf, of dung, of work, of sweat, of nighttime, and the garlic-laden scent of a hundred mothers cooking. Here and there street lamps came out from the walls, hanging yellow over the sidewalks. Each door front and corner brought clusters of children kicking at crumpled sheets of newspaper and tin cans that had been tossed to the curb. There were more sweet, dirty faces than I'd ever seen in one place; the girls skipping rope or playing jacks, the boys chasing one another or cluttering the stoops, laughing and teasing while they chewed on licorice whips.

Although everything about them seemed poor, from their worn shoes and soiled clothing to their arguing over a half-eaten apple, I still felt simple and naive compared to them. Even the littlest ones looked at me with curiosity and confidence, as if it would be rude for me to feel any sort of pity for them. Above the street, mothers called out to each other from the windows of the tenements, most often in what I guessed (from what I could remember of Aunt Fran's gramophone recording, *The Languages of Europe*) to be Italian. Even with *o*'s and *a*'s singing through their conversations, they are much like Mama and all the other mothers I have ever known. The rhythms of their talk and their lullabies seem the same, but when they hang their laundry, it is strung between buildings, over sidewalks and gutters. When they call their children or gossip with a neighbour, it makes no sense to my ears.

For the first time in my life, I've gone to a place my mother's never been. She visited Halifax, once, when she was young, to help Aunt Fran pick out her wedding gown, but never went any farther. The longer I walked, the more I longed to touch Mother's face or to hear her sing to Wrennie. It was as if I'd become a child again, feeling the chill that comes when you step outside of your mother's voice, too far to hear her calling, gone so far you're sure you've disappeared.

By the time I got to the corner of Fleet Street and North, I couldn't remember if the first mate had said "North to Hanover" or "North on Hanover." Regardless of what was correct, there was so much noise coming from North Street that I chose to follow it. Trumpets and drums drowned out the other sounds of the city, heralding a march in the middle of the street. Steam rose from cart after cart along the sidewalks, sausage vendors and candymen singing and whistling songs of their wares. Flags striped in red, white and green hung over nearly every door and window. Lights dressed with tinsel had been strung in garlands overhead. Hundreds of people were crowded together. Too tired and confused to think better of it, I let myself be taken right along with them as they pushed and edged as close as they could to the object of their adoration and celebrations—a statue of the Blessed Virgin Mary.

She was more brightly adorned than any of Miss B.'s figurines and nearly as large as Sadie Loomer. The dark-haired statue was draped in robes of gold and white and seated within a gaudy, brilliant throne, a gilded, carved canopy over her head. Yards of white and blue ribbons trailed down around her as twenty or more men moved slow and steady, carrying her on their shoulders. The calmness of her painted expression, the kindness of her eyes made me feel safe, made us all the same.

Before long, the crowd seemed to have reached Mary's destination. They stood, waiting, in front of the steps of a large building. All went silent as two young girls dressed as angels came forward, standing on the steps, giving prayers and *Ave Marias* to the Virgin Mother. As they finished, people began to look up. Mothers held their hands to their hearts, and fathers with small children on their shoulders pointed to a window on the third storey of the building.

Standing on a sill was another young girl, her head crowned with candles, her angel's robes of white satin rippling in the breeze. Without warning, she stretched out her arms and leapt, her body slowly flying down to greet the statue, while two large men stood on the rooftop, working the ropes and pulleys attached to her. She hovered over the crowd, singing blessings to Mary before being hoisted back up to her perch. With that, the trumpets again began to play, the crowd cheered, and confetti showered down all around me.

Standing there, surrounded by unfamiliar voices and bodies, I began to feel dizzy and weak. Having come off the boat, going too long without food, finding myself frightened, amazed and breathless in such a strange, crowded place, I began to tremble. Afraid I might fall and be trampled, I reached for the person nearest to me, a young, dark-eyed boy, who looked to be around the age of thirteen, maybe fourteen. He held me up, speaking to me in Italian at first, but when he could see that I didn't understand, he said, "Only English?" I nodded. He then led me to the steps of a nearby storefront. "You lost?" I nodded again and pulled a postcard out of my bag and pointed to Charlie's address. He smiled and took my hand. "I take you there."

For a moment I thought it might not be wise to follow this stranger, but there was something in his face that made me think of my brothers and of home. Honesty. Goodness. Laughter.

We walked down Hanover Street. The buildings were decked with awnings and large lettered signs, and window after window was filled with baskets and barrels . . . fish, bread, rounds of cheese, pickles, plump ripe tomatoes and peaches, long thin noodles strung on racks to dry. My guide pointed to the sign over a large grocer's shop: PASTENE'S. He pointed to himself, his oversized pants hanging loose from his suspenders, the fuzzy hint of what would one day become a moustache turning upward as he grinned. "Lorenzo Pastene." On our way to Charter Street, he explained (in deliberate, thoughtful English) that I had stumbled across the Fisherman's Feast of the *Madonna del Soccorso,* Our Lady of Help. Miss B. would have loved her. Not only are the fishermen of Sciacca, Sicily, devoted to her, but she also carries a large wooden club in her right hand, the weapon she used to beat a devil away after it tried to steal a little boy from his mother. The Madonna then hid the boy in her robes, and together they stood on the beast until it was dead.

Number 23 Charter Street was something of a puzzle: an ample, grand, ivy-covered home with stained glass window-panes in the door and three magnificent dormers across the top; not where you'd expect a fish-throwing boy like Charlie to land upon arriving in Boston. In its own way, the house seemed out of place as well. It was neat, seeming to be freshly painted and unlike any other home I'd seen on my way. A gracious, well-dressed beauty, settled between tall, wanting tenements and storefronts.

The woman from Charlie's picture, Miss Maxine Cabott, greeted us at the door. She is a marvellous, brazen-looking woman, and even more remarkable in person than in Charlie's picture. She was dressed in a fine vest and the tai-lored trousers of a man, and her sleek auburn hair had been cut short and tucked behind her ears. She's older than Charlie by far—thirty, at least, I'd guess—and next to Wrennie's, her eyes are the most beautiful I've ever seen. They are sometimes grey, sometimes blue, but always search-ing, as if she's trying to look right inside you. She kissed the boy on both cheeks. "Ah, Lorenzo! What have you brought to my door?" She laughed as she teased him, running her finger across his top lip. "What, no peaches anywhere but there?"

He blushed as he took the cap from his head and addressed her. "She's Dora, for Charlie. I help her find her way."

Maxine slipped a handful of coins into his shirt pocket. "*Grazie*, Lorenzo. Tell your mama hello for me."

He waved as he jumped off the steps, holding his other hand over his pocket to keep his money from falling out. "*Grazie*, Maxine. *Ciao, bella!*"

Maxine ushered me through a large, open foyer and into the parlour. She took my hands and now kissed me on both cheeks. "Welcome to our humble home. So good to have you here, Dora."

A young woman was seated on a sofa, reading. Her skin was brown, but not dark, more like the colour of Miss B.'s, café au lait. Black hair braided and piled on her head, hands graceful and reverent as she studied her open book, she looked like a queen, or the likeness of Nefertiti that serves as the handle for one of Aunt Fran's silver spoons.

Maxine introduced us. "Judith, my love, this is Charlie's Dora."

Judith stared over the top of her book just long enough to say "hello." Her mouth made the polite shape of the word, but her voice was so shy and faint that I had to imagine for myself how it sounded. Other women's voices echoed through the house, laughing, singing, calling back and forth from room to room.

Maxine motioned for me to sit next to her on a green, velvet-covered settee. "We received a telegram yesterday—from a Mr. Hart Bigelow—announcing your arrival. Charlie is more than anxious to see you. Not a day goes by when he doesn't mention your name."

I looked around the room for traces left behind by my brother. "Will he be here soon?" The parlour walls were lined with bookcases and paintings, the windows framed with the finest fabrics and lace. Not a spot of dirt had been trampled into the rugs or left on the tiles in the hallway. Nothing I had seen so far gave any clue that Charlie, or any man, was living at 23 Charter. "I know he works for you, but he lives here, with you?"

She threw her head back and laughed. "Don't look so surprised. Charlie's a gentleman and a great help. He's the man of the house, you might say. Wouldn't you say that, Judith?"

Judith looked up again from her reading. "Hmm?"

Maxine gave her a slow, knowing wink. "Charles Rare is definitely the man of this house."

Judith moved the book in front of her face. "Yes, Max. Yes, he sure is."

Maxine puffed on the end of a cigarette holder, then hollowed out three smoke rings over her head. "Would you like something to drink? I think we have some lemonade in the icebox, or something a little more *stiff* if you need it." This time, she winked at me. "And who could blame you if you did . . . you've come a long way from Nova Scotia, love."

Maxine and the other women in the house were all quick to serve me. A tall, lanky young woman with paint-spattered overalls placed a plate of cold cuts and a bowl of peaches with clotted cream in front of me. She wiped her hand on the edge of the tablecloth. "Rachael. I paint." She extended her hand to me. "Judith, Charlie and me live full-time with Max. The others come and go as they please."

Maxine corrected her. "Judith, Charlie and *I*. And the tea towel over the sink is for your hands, love." Maxine took the towel off its rack and set it on the table. "I like to think of the house as a community of artists. Writers, painters, photographers, musicians, even an actress or two have come here in pursuit of their art."

"Oh, I'm afraid I'm not an artist of any sort. I don't want to get in anyone's way . . . I can stay in Charlie's quarters."

"There's more than enough space here for you to have your own room. Stay as long as you like. I insist. Every woman must have a sanctuary."

My room is on the third floor at the back corner of the house. Roses climb up a trellis to my window, and their sweet, heavy scent comes right into the room, even at night. If not for the building next door, Paddy Malloy's Playhouse, I'd have almost forgotten that I was in the city. Rachael calls it the Trap. *It's silent during the day, but once the street lamps are lit, the music rolls through the windows and pounds under the floors. It's pretty entertaining once you get used to it.* I pulled the corner of the shade away from the window facing the alley. The buildings are so tight together that I could eat supper and shake hands with the patrons at the same time.

"Don't open the shade on the Trap side of the room or you'll get an eyeful."

I let the paper blind slap against the frame. "Why is that?"

Rachael popped her finger against the inside of her cheek and whistled. "The upstairs rooms are reserved for Saturday Evening Girls gone bad. Those honeys will do anything, for a price. Old Paddy Malloy sweet-talks 'em into being his chorus girls. A few extra trips to the back-rooms each week, and she thinks she's got it made. It's faster money than fighting war widows for a spot at a set-tlement house." Rachael ran her hands up her sides and under her breasts with provocative flair. "Who needs to learn to make pottery and show proper etiquette when you've got your *trade* built right in?"

A newspaper article had been framed and hung on the wall. The headline read, "Woman Bares All for the Vote!" A photograph hung next to it. Maxine was standing naked in front of a grand building with nothing on but a "Votes for Women" sash.

"Max likes to get people talking. That was just last month, at the state house. You'd never guess her family's a bunch of high-society snobs."

I smiled, wondering exactly what kind of woman Charlie had gotten involved with.

"Max might be a little crazy sometimes, but she's alright, you know. Me and Judith could've been over there at the Trap if it wasn't for her. One day she came down to the Baldwin Place Orphanage and said, 'I'd like your two oldest girls, please. Make it snappy now, before it's time for you to let them loose on the streets.' No one argued with her, they just handed us over, no goodbye or nothing, just sent us out with a wave and a kick in the ass. We didn't know who she was or what she was going to do with us, but we'd had nothing for so long, we didn't care. Thank heavens for Max."

Mrs. Dora Bigelow
23 Charter Street
North End, Boston,
Massachusetts
U.S.A.

August 11, 1918

Mrs. Bertine Tupper
Scots Bay, Nova Scotia
Canada

Dear Bertine,

I know that you have taken my dear little Wrennie into your home without question or a second thought. Thank you.

I miss home. I miss resting Wrennie on my hip, the scent of talc on the nape of her neck, the grasp of her tiny hand around my finger.

Most mothers would send a reminder, a list to say these are the things my baby needs, these are the things you must do. But I can't bring myself to make such requests. You are a good friend, you are a good mother. You'll give her all that she needs and more.

These are the things you mustn't do:

- Never take her out on the porch to feel the mist of the fog on her face.
- Never tie lavender over her bed.
- Never waltz with her, singing, "And the Band Played On"
- Never kiss her cheek after she's asleep and say, "Sweet dreams for a sweet girl."
- Never tell her, "Mommy's coming home."

I don't know if I cared for her long enough to say I was a good mother, or even the right mother for her, and I don't know if I'll ever come home. But I'm hoping if you leave these things alone, in a matter of days or however long it takes, she'll learn not to look for me. If you love her enough in your own way, she'll learn to do something that I cannot—forget that I was her mother.

If Miss B. were here, she'd scold me and say this isn't a time to feel sorry for myself. She'd tell me it was time I got on my knees and prayed. "Kissin' the dirt's the only way you'll see heaven." But I'm so far from home and everything I know that even my prayers feel like sinning.

Take care of Wrennie.

I know you will.

Yours,
Dora

~ August 12, 1918

In the middle of the night, I went to Charlie's room and curled up next to him like we used to do when we were children. I touched his sweaty, boyish hair and counted the freckles across his nose, waiting for him to wake up. Asleep, he looked like the dear little boy who was always my playmate, my friend.

Charlie used to tell me that we were twins, only Mother had to carry me a year longer than she did him, because I needed more baking to make me sweet. I'm thankful he ran only as far as Boston and that he stopped chasing after thoughts of going off to war. He'd be dead right now, I know it. His heart is too big, his smile too bright to have survived it.

I whispered to him that I couldn't sleep, that whenever I closed my eyes I saw the faces of the dead in Halifax, Archer's body sinking under the dark of the water, the trail of Iris Rose's blood on my arms, my sheets, my bed.

They're looking for me Charlie. Brady Ketch, Laird Jessup, Trude Hutner, Dr. Thomas. . . . They're all saying I killed Mrs. Ketch.

The worst part is, I don't know if I did or not. I couldn't save any of them, not Darcy, not Iris Rose, not Mrs. Ketch. I've gone over it in my mind, closed my eyes and watched myself reading Miss B.'s Willow Book, boiling down the tincture, asking Mrs. Ketch to let me watch over her until she was right again. I never imagined it might kill her.

I finally fell asleep, Charlie's arm snug around me. "Whatever came after wasn't your fault. You did just what Miss B. taught you. It wasn't your fault. You have to believe that."

Mrs. Bertine Tupper
Scots Bay, Nova Scotia
Canada

August 18, 1918

Mrs. Dora Bigelow
23 Charter Street
North End, Boston,
Massachusetts
U.S.A.

Dear Dora,
We hope this letter reaches you in Boston and finds you safe and sound.

>   *Of course we are sick that you aren't here with us.*
>   *Of course we are sick over the things that have been said.*
>   *Of course we will find a way to bring you home,*
>   *And give Dr. Thomas a whack on his crazy head.*

That said, here is what we have been able to discover thus far from the gossip and reports that have come our way. It seems that when Experience Ketch took a tumble down the stairs, Mr. Ketch sent one of the boys down to Canning to fetch the doctor. When Dr. Thomas arrived, poor Mrs. Ketch was already dead.

Brady Ketch (the drunken bastard) claims you gave his wife some "concoction or brew" that made her "some crazy-dizzy." He said she couldn't help but fall. Supposedly, he has produced an empty bottle for all to see. (Nothing unusual for him.)

Dr. Thomas has been quoted in the Canning Register as saying, "This is a tragic loss for our community and the whole of womanhood. We must bring the guilty party to justice before she causes harm to countless other women and children. This is the kind of sad, inexcusable tragedy that comes when we dismiss scientific theory and cling to the ignorance of the past."

Ginny has volunteered to visit Dr. Thomas's office under the guise of seeking care for her unborn child. Yes, that's right, she's got another bun in the oven. Seems her confessing her sins to Laird were for nothing. She only swallowed half her cup of tea with mitts and spit the rest into her napkin. Sadie's told her for all the trouble she made she'd better come up with something that will help your cause.

Wrennie is some sweet as ever. No need to worry about her.

Tell us what more we can do. We are anxious for your reply.

Bertine and your sisters in the O.K.S.

Mrs. Dora Bigelow
23 Charter Street
North End, Boston,
Massachusetts
U.S.A.

August 28, 1918

Mrs. Bertine Tupper
Scots Bay, Nova Scotia
Canada

Dear Bertine and honourable members of the O.K.S.
Thank you for your letter.

I'm not sure what to make of Mr. Ketch's tale. The truth
of the matter is, I did give Experience Ketch a bottle of
tincture. An infusion of herbs to make her lose a baby she
didn't want. I advised her that she should stay with me to make
certain it had the desired effect, but she insisted on returning
home that same day. What is confusing to me is that I can't
imagine the tincture would make her dizzy enough to take a
fatal spill. She'd be prone to bleed to death before she'd fall
down the stairs. A quick check between her legs would've
proved if I am the one to blame, but it's too late for that.

This is all I can give you. Judging by the way my words
look guilty on the page, I guess I won't be home anytime soon.
Do not put your names or families in harm's way over this. If
someone comes to your door, you might be better off to
"forget" I was your friend.

Kiss Wrennie for me.

Yours, Dora

42

THE DAY AFTER MY ARRIVAL, Maxine declared that I should have my very own "Independence Day, Dora's day to meet Boston." First, I was treated to a long soak in the most luxurious tub I have ever seen. It is a smooth white porcelain creation that curves out longer than my toes can reach and seems to sit atop four golden scallop shells. Running water from a tap. French milled soaps of lavender and rose. These things made me forget, if only for a little while, that I ever had a care in the world. Rachael cut my hair, leaving it bobbed just below my ears. Judith lent me a dress in the most modern style, a floral, sheer thing. It has a straight skirt, with long slits on either side. Maxine says they're for dancing. "You never know when you might want to do the Turkey Trot!" She put a smart new hat on my head and rouged my lips, and we all went "out on the town" with Charlie.

My brother's reaction to all this fuss was just as I'd expect, teasing and funny as ever: "Why, Dorrie, you look like a *real lady*. I hardly knew ya."

Maxine responded with her own wit. "That's the point, dear Charles. Today your sister's whomever she decides to be." She held my chin in her hand and looked me up and down. "Please make it anything besides Bigelow, you've far too curious a face for such a dower name."

Judith chimed in. "I think you mean to say *dowdy.*" Maxine winked at me. "No, I believe I'm right in saying it's *dower.* Perhaps you'd like to follow the Boston tradition and be known by the name of your birth? I find the name Rare suits you perfectly." And so I was introduced as Miss Dora Rare all through the streets of Boston. From the steps of Christ Church to St. Stephen's Church, up one side of Hanover Street and back down the other. Maxine has thrown my faded dress and black stockings into the trash. I wonder what Mother would say?

I wish I were half as confident as Max. It's clear that she has no doubts about who she is. It's in the way she dresses, in the cut of every word she says. She carries the city inside her, and the city, in return, carries her. Perhaps Boston will give some of its swagger to me. So far, it's just insisting I stay afloat.

It's been a few weeks since then, and the more I hear my old name said, the more I wonder if it even belongs to me anymore. Except for having the Willow Book under my bed and Charlie in a room down the hall, everything that was ever mine is gone (or so far away that it might as well be). In my first few nights here, I lay in my bed, the windows open wide, listening. Once, I thought I could hear the tide, the kind, familiar voice of the moon, but it was only the constant hum that echoes between the buildings and the mechanical roar of the elevated train.

This afternoon, we all went to Copps Hill for a picnic. It is a pretty place, filled with trees and well-groomed lawns, one of the oldest burial grounds in Boston. Its beauty is not the same as at home, where the green of everything (the grass, the woods, the moss on the rocks) gets its way. Even the fields that are plowed in the Bay aren't anywhere near square. We plant around the trees and let the brooks mind their own business. Houses are built to sway with the wind, the women dance with the moon. Here, the harbour has walls and the buildings grow faster than the trees. People run place to place, always busy, always brisk. They are the tide.

At first I thought it an odd thing to take our lunch among epitaphs and stone angels, but Maxine explained it as a long-standing tradition: "It's lucky to visit the dead, so long as you bring merriment and libations." With that, she pulled a large silver flask out of the picnic basket, poured a few drops on the ground and clanked it against a faded, leaning tombstone. "To the wee Thomas Copp, may he rest in peace."

Thomas
Son to David Copp & Obedience his wife
Aged 2 years and 3 quarters
Died July ye 25
1678

She took another drink from her flask and passed it on to Rachael. "Between temperance teetotalers and the Watch and Ward Society, poor old Beantown has all but lost its sizzle. *Gött in Himmel,* I never thought I'd see the day you couldn't get a decent bottle of beer in this town." She gestured to a large building in the distance. "Here's to Mr. Burkardt's brewery . . . shut down in the name of patriotism."

She turned to me. "Has Charles told you the story of how he came to be in my employ?"

I shook my head. "No, but I've been wondering about that."

Maxine grinned. "See, I *knew* she had a curious face." She turned to Charlie. "Will you tell it, Charles, or shall I?"

Charlie had his mouth full of bread. "You can."

Maxine sat herself between Charlie and me, one hand on Charlie's knee, the other holding my hand. "It was February, and my dear friend Helen Ruth, knowing it had been far too long since I had been anywhere outside of the snow-crusted streets of the city, invited me to spend the weekend in the woods. Just as we were communing with the ghosts of Emerson and Thoreau, Helen's husband, Babe, and a half dozen of his closest drinking buddies joined us at the cabin on Willis Pond."

Max winked at Charlie. "Charles came shortly after, delivering a secret cache of Mr. Burkhardt's Red Sox Beer. Mr. Ruth, being the gracious host he's known to be, invited Charlie to stay. As the night wore on and the bottles were tipped, I was asked to honour the party with a song or two.

"The next thing I knew, Babe picked me up, plopped me on top of the player piano and set the crank to spinning. Just as I launched into 'Somebody Stole My Gal,' four of his cohorts began to roll the thing out the door, carrying me away to the middle of the frozen pond." Maxine closed her eyes and swayed back and forth. "What a beautiful night it was. My voice was clear, and I remember the full moon shining white through the trees. A few other guests slipped out around the piano to dance while I sang, 'Good-bye Broadway, Hello France.'"

Charlie interrupted Maxine's tale, grinning. "It was 'Take Me Out to the Ball Game,' and I wouldn't call it singing."

Rachael laughed, spitting whiskey all over the ground. Judith slapped her arm while Rachael elbowed her, and said, "Well, he's right, she can't sing."

Maxine rolled her eyes and continued with dramatic flair. "Just as we reached the chorus, Charlie cried out, 'Everyone off the ice, she's gonna go!' It was madness—people were scurrying and slipping their way to the edge of the pond, while I was stranded on top of the piano."

Charlie whispered in my direction. "She didn't even notice—she just kept on singing."

Maxine cleared her throat and went on. "Your dear brother Charles came to my rescue and skated me away in his arms, gliding along in his boots as if he were Hans Brinker. The piano, however, met an unfortunate end and sank to the murky bottom of Willis Pond." She kissed Charlie firmly on the lips. "I owe this man my life. The least I could do was give him a job and a place to stay. He's my lucky star."

As we left for home, Maxine pointed out three children who were dancing around a wishing stone in the corner of the graveyard. We watched them as they skipped, merrily singing, *Wish I may, wish I might, have the wish I wish tonight.*" When they were done, they each took a turn sitting on top of the stone, eyes closed, one finger to the sky, one finger to granite.

Maxine insisted we do the same. "Nine times 'round, widdershins, and then sit on the stone and make your wish."

Charlie wished for another kiss from Maxine.

Maxine wished for a kiss from Rudolph Valentino, but Charlie kissed her anyway.

Rachael wished for Mr. Ruth and the Red Sox to win the World Series.

Judith wished for more days like today.

I wished for Wrennie to always be happy.

Mrs. Bertine Tupper
Scots Bay, Nova Scotia
Canada

September 5, 1918

Mrs. Dora Bigelow
23 Charter Street
North End, Boston,
Massachusetts
U.S.A.

Dear Dora,

We'd be more than willing to dig up Mrs. Ketch if it's the only way to prove your innocence. Our ears are to the ground, waiting to hear whatever else we can learn. Anything for you, dear sister.

Ginny came back from Canning with a funny story, I'll hand the pen to her to tell.

Hello Dora,

How is life treating you in steamy old Boston-town? I am missing you terribly and have the highest hopes that you will be home in time for my new baby's arrival. I have found that Dr. Thomas relies on books and charts more than he relies on his heart. I went in last week to tell him that I have been suffering from ongoing bouts of morning sickness. (It had gotten to the point where I was unable to keep much of any food down.) He said he'd have me cured in no time using "the latest in obstetrical theory," something called "the suggestive method."

He came to the house and ordered everyone out, even Laird. Then he did the strangest thing . . . he brought the soup *tureen from my grandmother's china set (the only thing of value I brought with me when I married and moved to the Bay) and placed it in the middle of the bed. He ordered me to use it as my sick bowl. Well, I certainly wasn't going to get sick all over my granny's china. Can you imagine what it might do to the gilding? I turned to the side of the bed and got sick on his shoes instead!*

He says that morning sickness is neurotic in nature, the pregnant woman's way of gaining attention from a husband who is uncomfortable with his wife's condition. "Very common and nothing to worry about."

Laird told him "a pregnant wife ain't nothing compared to a pregnant cow." I'm not sure what he meant by that.

Anyways, not to worry, I'm feeling much better. My only complaints now are swollen ankles and hands, as well as an occasional headache. "Very common and nothing to worry about. Eat more bread and less meat." So says Dr. Thomas.

By the way, even if the doctor turns out to be right in all things medical, I'm still sane enough to figure out that he and Brady Ketch are thick as thieves. Laird's mentioned in the past that Brady's taken Dr. Thomas hunting, but I didn't think anything of it until the last time I was down to Canning and Mrs. Thomas invited me to their home for tea. To my shock and sadness, the head of Miss B.'s beloved white doe had been stuffed and mounted, and was staring at me from above the mantel in the parlour. We are wondering what Brady got in return.

Much love to you,
Your sisters in crime, Ginny and Bertine

~ September 12, 1918

The news of the white doe brought tears to my eyes. I guess Dr. Thomas won't be happy until he's taken every last thing that mattered to Miss B. My heart aches tonight as if I've lost her all over again.

Ginny's comments about the doctor's care also concern me. I can't see how his advice will help. In fact, I think it's likely to make things worse. Still, she's prone to fretting and my telling her my thoughts on the matter may set her off. I'll send happy words and a little advice from Miss B. and leave it at that for now.

Miss Dora Rare
23 Charter Street
North End, Boston,
Massachusetts
U.S.A.

September 14, 1918

Mrs. Bertine Tupper
Scots Bay, Nova Scotia
Canada

Dear Bertine and my sisters in the O.K.S.,
Thank you for your recent letter and for standing by me through my exile. A special thanks to Ginny for her account of Dr. Thomas's "suggestive method." Just the thought of the good doctor's surprise at Ginny's "reaction" to his treatment was enough to bring a smile to my lips. I have a feeling that he's left quite puzzled when the results are not as he expected them to be. Let's hope this mishap leaves him wondering. Curiosity in medicine (and life) is

essential . . . it nobly takes up where doctrine leaves off. Tea and rest, Ginny, and don't forget to put your feet up.

Life in Boston is bursting with activity. The other women in this house are somewhat wild with their lives (and their words), especially the woman who runs the place, Miss Maxine Cabott. She is supported by family wealth and treats the rest of us with more than our share of whatever we might need, filling the house with glorious bouquets, our bellies with food, our hands and our minds with literature. How Charlie came to be her errand boy is a tale in itself that I could only do justice by telling you in person. While I can't say exactly what it is she does, I can tell you that she's had her heart broken at least once in her life, that her beauty is glamorous and brooding and that she always has her hand in something, "stirring the pot" as Miss B. would say.

Tonight, Maxine is hosting a suffragist meeting. We are preparing hundreds of postcards to be sent to those senators who still oppose women getting the vote. I'll admit, I carry some pride in knowing that women are already persons of consequence in Nova Scotia. Sadly, though, I can see now that I never did enough to take any credit for our victory. Why is it that I have often thought to myself how unfair life has been for women, or for the men who are made to fight in the trenches, but have never been strong or bold enough to protest? Women have been imprisoned, have died for these rights, while I was complacent, happy enough to sit at home and knit.

Even with children in our arms, there is always more we can do. Kiss Wrennie for me.

Your sister, Dora

P.S. As you may have noticed, I have decided to change my name to its former state, Miss Dora Rare.

43

A GROUP OF WOMEN, including Rachael and Judith, read from the Greek play *Lysistrata* for an "Evening of Letters at 23 Charter Street." Maxine read poetry from Walt Whitman's *Leaves of Grass*, and I chose to read from Judith's copy of *Tess of the D'Urbervilles*. It is horrible to think that we must hide these books away and limit our sharing of them to an intimate, secret group of friends. They have been "banned in Boston" by the Watch and Ward Society, and those caught with such works in their possession are subject to fines and even imprisonment. Maxine has taken to rescuing whatever books, plays and art she can get her hands on. Tonight's selections came from a raid of her mother's estate, where she and Charlie recovered several boxes of literature that had been collected for a book burning.

"We thanked Mother for a lovely evening, slipped out to the carriage house, loaded up the goods and sped away in my trusty Hupmobile coupe. It's the least that woman owed me for having to sit and listen to her rattle on about the evils of *modern* music. She thinks that anyone who's out to have a bit of fun is headed straight for hell. No wonder

Daddy takes his leisure in the dark of the billiards room (he and more than a few snorts of rum). I wish I could be a little bird sitting on her shoulder when she finds the fuel for her bonfire's gone missing."

Most evenings I'm happy to sprawl out on my bed and write letters, or make notes in my journal. Last night there was a wet breeze pushing the blinds in and out as if it were breathing against the window frame. The shade on the Trap side glowed red. As Rachael first advised, I've made it a practice to always keep the blind down on this side of the room, especially since the spindles at the head of my bed rest against that window. Maxine loves to tease me about it. She often sneaks into my room of an evening and tries to get me to lift the corner of the shade like a peeping Tom. I always refuse. I find it's enough just to lie on top of the covers with the mist of the rain coming in, bringing hints of perfume, music and Miss Honey.

Since my arrival, Miss Honey has been a busy woman. She has, by far, the most visitors at Paddy Malloy's Playhouse, and from the sound of things, it's a different man nearly every night. Last night's guest had a low, appreciative hum to his voice. "Honey, you always know what I need . . ."

She answered, in her bright, sassy way, "That's right, I do, and don't you forget who's in charge here . . . it's *Miss* Honey to you."

"That's right, baby, that's right."

Echoes of the rest of Paddy's Saturday Evening Girls drowned out Miss Honey's musky conversation, their heels grinding and stomping on the downstairs stage, the piano rolling, talking back in heavy strides of the blues.

A good man is hard to find
You always get the other kind
Just when you think that he's your pal
You look for him and find him foolin' 'round some
    other gal
Then you rave, you even crave,
To see him laying in his grave

The wind lifted the shade to reveal that Miss Honey had left the light on. Her shadow danced over the mister's body with heady sweet perfume. He lifted her hips, tugging at her garters and lace.

"Mmmmm, Miss Honey, that's right, that's right."

So if your man is nice, take my advice
And hug him in the morning, kiss him every night
Give him plenty of lovin', treat him right
'Cause a good man nowadays is hard to find.

Most nights for her are like this, *she* being in charge of *him*, taking her time, along with the repeated sway of glass beads calling gentle and sweet around the fringe of her bedside lamp. In these past few weeks of listening to her conduct her affairs (far more knowing and better than any of the other girls), I have wondered, is it so terrible to be in her postition? She seems so pleased, so proud of herself, and as far as I can tell, she does it all with no regret. Maybe it's the women who are quick to be married off for the sake of marriage, the station of a name, a supposed life or even a house . . . maybe we are the ones who have sold ourselves for far too little a price.

In other matters of love and the fairer sex, I have recently noticed that Judith and Rachael are a pair. I came upon them in the bath while they were washing, enjoying each other with more than the laughter of two sisters. Seeing them kiss and touch one another with such tenderness was enough to keep me there, watching through a crack in the door, holding my breath, until Maxine pulled me away.

"Let them have their 'Boston Marriage,'" I say. Even the mother of temperance, Miss Frances Willard herself, had a constant companion in her dear friend Anna. I guess that bicycle she was always going on about couldn't afford her a good enough ride." The sounds of splashing and laughter spilled out into the hallway. Max raised her eyebrow and grinned. "No matter what form it takes, love is always a glorious thing, wouldn't you say, Miss Rare?"

I smiled and nodded, wishing I hadn't wasted myself with Archer. Although I can't stop my heart from wanting it, I hold little hope that I'll ever find love or even true affection now that my white dress days are gone.

Miss Dora Rare
23 Charter Street
North End, Boston,
Massachusetts
U.S.A.

September 16, 1918

Mrs. Bertine Tupper
Scots Bay, Nova Scotia
Canada

Dear Bertine,
As you may already know, influenza is making its way

through Boston and spreading to other places in America. I
suppose it will come to Nova Scotia as well, if it hasn't already
arrived. I'm worried, especially for the children of the Bay, for
Wrennie. As soon as you hear of it being anywhere close,
please take care in following my advice:

~ Close the road to the Bay.

~ Don't allow visitors from away.

~ Make gauze or muslin masks for the men to wear at the
wharf and for anyone who must go down the
mountain to Canning.

~ Have the men strip off their clothes before coming in
the house.

~ Wash hands with hot water and soap.

These measures may seem foolish, but if you could see
how many shrouded bodies are brought out of houses each day,
you would understand. If someone does come down with it in
the Bay, open my place as a sick house. No sense in a whole
family suffering from this terrible disease.

Yours,
Dora

44

A CASE OF INFLUENZA brought me to Miss B.'s, once. It came on with a fever too stubborn for even Mother to cure. She tried everything to bring on a sweat to break the fever, including Father's suggestion of wrapping salt herring around the back of my neck (a tradition passed on to him by a peg-legged sailor from Inverness County). When the herring didn't take and the fever threatened to go higher, Mother bundled me in blankets and gave me up to Miss B.'s care.

"First, she done need a cold bath—to shock the fever—then a dose of onion syrup and a right good rubbin' with castor oil." Miss B. sent my mother away and told her to come back in the morning. "A mother's worry don't do no good. She has your love, that's all she needs. Go home." Mother wrung her hands, kissed my burning forehead and left.

Miss B. dragged a large tub in from the dooryard and placed it in front of the woodstove. I watched through drowsy eyes as she fetched bucket after bucket of water, her shoulders tight and rounded with age, the grip of her fingers crooked and determined. "This ain't nothing, you know, your illness." She smiled as she poured Epsom salts in

the water. "You turned fourteen this spring, no?" She circled the salt through until it dissolved, shaking her hands,
flipping drops of water on the milky surface.

I nodded and answered, "Yes, my birthday was—"

"First of May," she finished for me. "I remember . . . I
gathered the May dew the day you was born. You carried a
caul on your eyes as you passed through. Such a beauty you
was! Dark hair, pink skin, not wrinkled and ugly like most.
There was no mistakin', you were blessed with something
that day . . ." She motioned for me to get into the tub. "A
fever's just a gift, tapping you on the shoulder. It's when you
don't pay attention that it sets out to kill you."

I lowered myself into the bath, body shaking, skin bub-
bling with gooseflesh. She dowsed my head and face with
bowlfuls of water until I was spitting and gasping for air.
Painful and cold, I felt my heart opening and shutting, getting smaller and smaller, turning into a tight, frozen fist.
Eyes wide, mouth open, I wheezed out any heat that was
left inside. She tilted my head back and spooned two large
doses of onion syrup down my throat. The taste was
wretched, but I was too weak to spit up the thick, dark mixture of molasses, onions and garlic. She took my hand and
led me to the bed, her voice singing soft and low as her
hands worked the warm oil into my clammy flesh.

My hands are His hands,
My hands are His hands,
Palma Christi,
Palma Christi,
The Hands of Christ.

When she was done, she spit on her finger and traced the sign of the cross on my chest. She fed me brown flour coffee and wrapped me in a thick dark quilt made from worn pieces of wool and velvet, her goose-footed stitches holding together the nooks and crannies. Like a map to heaven, it was covered with flowing patterns of roses, doves and hands pointing their wise fingers to God.

~ *September 19, 1918*

Boston is being laid to waste by the Spanish Influenza. Each day there are more doors bearing warning signs or a hopeless, sad curtain of black crepe. As with the Halifax Explosion, people are quick to place the blame on the Germans, spreading rumours that secret agents are roaming the city and turning influenza germs loose in theatres and dance halls. They are looking for the source of their fear and grief, for a place to point a finger. The truth is worse than their imaginings—there is no one to blame, no way to stop it and no way to tell who will be next. Official statements are in the paper every day. "Avoid crowds, especially movie houses, dance halls and pubs. Avoid anyone with a cold or cough. Avoid nervous and physical exhaustion. Avoid tight clothing and shoes. Do not dance. Cover face when coughing or sneezing and do not spit in public. Chew food carefully."

It's been spreading through the girls at the Trap. Three days ago the sign was nailed to the door:

INFLUENZA

WARNING!
This card must not be removed without authority.
Milk Dealers must not deliver milk bottles.

Today I heard Miss Honey coughing through her open window. I lifted the blind to look for her and noticed blue smoke curling out under the screens. I called to her, worried that the place had caught fire. "You need help?"

She opened the window, and more smoke billowed out. "Yeah, send somebody to shoot me."

"Why's there so much smoke, is there a fire?"

"Naw, just ole Paddy. He heard if you put sulphur and sugar in the ash bucket while the coals are still hot, it chases the flu away. I don't know if it'll work, but he might as well try. Half of us feel dead already, and the doctor refuses to call."

"You can't get anyone to help you?"

"We sent for two or three different ones, and they all say the same: '*Those* kinds of places with *those* kinds of girls are the worst offenders in spreading it around.' Ain't nobody care if a whore like me gets her six feet."

I told her to tell Mr. Malloy to stop his smoke treatment and let in some fresh air. From the obituaries that have been running in the paper, I can see it's not the influenza that does people in, it's the pneumonia that settles in their lungs after. This afternoon I made a pot of chicken soup and handed it to Miss Honey through our windows. It's the only safe way I can think of to help right now, as I can't risk any sort of exposure.

I will continue to give advice and send what I can in hopes that they are all strong enough to pull through.

~ *September 23, 1918*

Maxine is bedridden. She came down with it two days ago after having spent the evening at a suffrage meeting in the Back Bay. I have insisted that I be the only one to attend to her, since neither Judith nor Rachael has any experience in caring for the sick. Charlie will be the one to go out and get whatever we might need, following my rules of always wearing a mask, never shaking hands and stripping off his clothes on the back porch and knocking for a bucket of hot, soapy water before he comes in the house.

The ladies of the Trap are recovering. One girl was lost; her heart practically burst in her chest after the fever had passed. I'm happy to report that Miss Honey has mended. She came to call today, bearing a small bouquet of asters and brown-eyed Susans. I couldn't let her in, but she stood under Maxine's window, singing her song after song. "Sugar Blues" was Max's favourite, and despite feeling weak and feverish, she managed to whistle and applaud Miss Honey's efforts. Charlie comes home each evening carrying a new-found cure from the pharmacy. They are useless, made mostly of soda water and boric acid.

I'm sticking with Miss B.'s advice: *Aspirin if the fever gets to where they's gonna have fits. You can always tell it too . . . theys skin gets hot and dry, feelin' thin like paper. If that don't work, then dunk 'em in cold water.* So far, Max is getting by. She goes back and forth between fever and chills, and she can only hold down tea and broth. She says her whole body aches "like I was run down by the 6:15 train." I asked her if she'd rather have a doctor, but she refused. "Charlie says you were born a healer; that's enough for me." I've sent him off to Pastene's to get a jug of castor oil. *It's gotta come from a believer. Don't get it no place else.* "Tell Mrs. Pastene you need cold-pressed oil, *Palma Christi,* not the stuff you spoon down the throat."

~ September 25, 1918

She's suffering today. Once we got through the worst of the fever, she started coughing, struggling for air, her chest heaving and tight. I've been putting mustard plaster on her throat and chest, oil packs on her body, and have even started singing Miss B.'s old songs and prayers. Charlie's face is desperate when he asks after her. I think he loves Maxine more than she knows. I can't lose her.

Mrs. Bertine Tupper
Scots Bay, Nova Scotia
Canada

September 21, 1918

Miss Dora Rare
23 Charter Street
North End, Boston,
Massachusetts
U.S.A.

Dear Dora,
Come home! Come home to Wrennie! Come home to us! We are going to ring the bells in the church tonight in celebration of your innocence. Hart came to the Bay tonight with the good news from the fire hall down in Canning.
It seems that after all this time of trying to take care of his brood without a wife, Brady Ketch gave up his sanity. He

packed the children up (the ones he could find) and took them down to the town square in Canning and tried to sell them off, asking $25 for the ones who could do hard labour and $10 for the little ones. This made quite a scene and soon after he started people began to gather. Hart, who was down the mountain delivering barrels of smoked herring, was among those in the crowd. Well, as soon as he figured out what was going on, he quickly went to fetch the constable, the same Constable McKinnon who has been looking for you. The two men managed to shackle Brady's hands and feet and carried him away to the fire hall so he could dry out. Once the children had some warm food in their bellies and saw that their father wasn't able to lay his hands on them, they spoke right up, telling the constable and anyone else who would listen the truth about what happened to their mother. (I put in a clipping from the Canning Register *so you can read it for yourself.)*

Here's a note from Ginny:
Dora, I hope you'll be home for my baby's arrival. Mrs. Sarah Deft's cousin, over in Halls Harbour, had baby number three under the care of Dr. Thomas at the Canning Maternity Home last week. He said her labour was taking too long, so he cut her and gave her ether! She required quite a few stitches, and the ether made her sick. The baby's fine, a boy, some big, but she said she'd rather have had her baby at home. They'll have to sell their best milk cow to pay the bill. (Sound familiar?) My figure is changing every day, and the wee one is making his presence known by kicking quite vigorously, especially in the middle of the night. I say "his" because when Hardy came to shoe the horses he guessed I was carrying a boy. Said, "He's travelling right low." You know as well as I, a blacksmith's never wrong at guessing babies.

I will admit I've been feeling rather strange. More swelling, even in my face. Headaches and a few flashes of light whenever I stand up too quickly, but Dr. Thomas says it is normal. "Get more exercise and stop reading so much." Is there anything else to do?

So far we have no cases of the influenza to report in the Bay, although Jack Tupper's brother down in Kentville passed over from it just yesterday. We have been taking your advice and are being cautious. Send word of your homecoming so we can put clean sheets on your bed and flowers on your doorstep.

Come home soon! Bertine and Ginny

Children Freed from Murdering Father

This writer has just learned of shocking news from Canning. Ten children, who have been held captive in their father's house for over a month, have told authorities of their harrowing experience. The father, Mr. Brady Ketch of Deer Glen, has been charged with the murder of his late wife, Experience Ketch.

On August 2, the dear little souls looked on as their father brutally beat their mother and then pushed her down the stairs. Mr. Ketch had formerly explained his wife's untimely death as due to poisoning from a tainted home-remedy administered by a midwife, a Mrs. Dora Bigelow of Scots Bay.

The children are currently residing at the Methodist orphanage in Kentville. However, this writer is happy to report that an offer of adoption has been made by Reverend and Mrs. Joseph Pineo. They hope to take all ten children into their home as soon as the proper arrangements have been made.

The Canning Register,
September 22, 1918

Miss Dora Rare
23 Charter Street
North End, Boston,
Massachusetts
U.S.A.

September 29, 1918

Mrs. Bertine Tupper
Scots Bay, Nova Scotia
Canada

Dear Bertine,
What news from the Bay! While I am sad that the Ketch children were made to suffer for so long, I am happy that they will have a new family and a new life without the abuse of their father.

As much as I'd like to come home, I must stay in Boston for now. Maxine is holding on, but I cannot leave while she is confined to her bed.

Tell my mother not to worry. Charlie is fine, and I am somehow immune to this thing. Tell Wrennie I miss her terribly and her mommy's coming home!

Will write soon,
Dora

~ September 29, 1918

I've put bricks under the posts at the head of the bed and propped Maxine up with pillows. She's still having trouble breathing, and the only time she stops coughing and seems to get any rest is when I distract her with stories of the Bay.

She begs every day to hear more about my growing up in a house full of boys, my "scheming dead husband," and Miss B.'s wise advice. Today it was the story of my dousing Dr. Thomas with molasses, followed by the death of Experience Ketch. She was wide-eyed with concern when I finished, like a child who can't wait to hear how the story ends. "You have to get back there, to fight for your place— your house, for Wrennie."

I pulled the ties of her nightshirt open and rubbed mustard plaster down her back. "I need to stay here and take care of you."

It was all she could do to stifle her coughs as she argued with me. "What about the women of the Bay? What will they do without you?"

"They took care of themselves before me, they can take care of themselves now." I fluffed her pillows and settled her back against them. "Besides, who'll lick all the stamps for the suffragists if I leave?"

Maxine pulled at my sleeve as I tucked the blankets around her body. "Never let someone take what's rightfully yours. You can give all you want in life, but don't give up."

I gave her a smile and a kiss on the forehead. "I won't, and don't you give up either."

~ September 30, 1918

This morning Maxine spit blood into the towel she uses to cover her mouth. I could hear the rattle of pneumonia in her breathing when I put my ear to her back. *Beware the death rattle creepin' in.*

Miss B. told me of her pulling a man named Xander Lightfoot back from the death rattle. She gave him *bain d'oignon et orge*, the onion and barley bath. For three days she kept him buried in raw onions and fermented barley and fed him heavy doses of onion syrup.

Charlie has gone back to Mrs. Pastene for as many bags of onions as she'll give him. Barley's hard to come by, so he's off to Mr. Burkhardt's to see if he's willing to part with a few bottles of beer. When I told Maxine what she's in for, she gave my hand a squeeze and said, "Can I wash down the syrup with the beer?"

~ *October 3, 1918*

We've been weeping for three days straight, each day Maxine breathing a little easier. I can tell she's feeling better because she's been complaining, "This house will smell like a sausage stand for months. All that's missing is the sauerkraut." She laughed and shook her fist in the air. "Damn your Cajun witchery, Marie Babineau!" She told me that last night Miss B. came to her in a dream. "She was standing under a willow tree, with teacups dangling from every branch. She said the same thing over and over: *Don't you wanna know what done come next?* I wasn't sure if the message was for you or me, Dora, or exactly what she meant by it. All I know is that I feel like climbing on the roof and doing the Bunny Hog."

~ *October 10, 1918*

The amendment that would allow votes for women in the U.S. has been defeated yet again. "Maybe I should take Miss Honey and the rest of Paddy's Saturday Evening Girls out to D.C. and do a little dance for the boys in the Senate. I bet that'd open their eyes to women's rights." Maxine is in full health and back to being a ranting suffragist. She has been writing letters to every congressman and member of the U.S. Senate from morning until night.

I scrubbed the house from top to bottom. I'll admit, it's much easier to do all the household chores when there's running water and electricity. As Maxine says, "How on earth did you ever survive without electricity, fine art, low-heeled finale hopper shoes and the blues?" I could do without the shoes and, to be honest, while I find the steady jangle of music from Paddy's Playhouse to be exciting, I have grown far more attached to sitting in the back of St. Stephen's Church and listening to the choir practice. In recent weeks, most all churches and temples have closed their doors. Authorities fear that any public gathering might encourage the spread of influenza. Although they have cancelled Sunday services at St. Stephen's, the choir hasn't stopped singing. Thursday evenings, at half past seven, they gather in the choir loft and sing out over the all-but-empty pews. It's as if they can't keep themselves from it, from sending their voices and their hope out into the air.

Tonight, as I sat at St. Stephen's, I fell asleep. The city whispered to me in a dream, telling me to start a new life. Boston's voice was tempting and sure, thinking I'd choose to stay, barely believing me when I told her I couldn't and that it was her own fault for making me strong enough to think for myself. Then I dreamed of the Bay, Mother's smile, Bertine's laugh, Spider Hill, the voice of the moon.

I'm worried about Ginny, and I miss my sweet Wrennie. It's time to go home.

45

HART HAD THE HOUSE open and ready for my arrival. Bertine, Sadie and Mabel had clean sheets and food waiting. Wrennie seemed happy to have me home. She's content to be propped up in a basket or to scoot around my feet in the kitchen. She loves to show off with a smile and giggles for everyone she meets. Last night she fell asleep while Mother rocked her in front of the stove, and, of course, Mother shed more than a few tears of relief at "having her girl home." I thought I might feel at least some regret for having left Boston, but these two places are worlds apart. Now that I am here, I find it difficult to remember the city, even when I close my eyes. There is much for me to do . . .

I knew as soon as I saw her that Ginny was well on her way to trouble. She's swollen all over, suffering from crippling headaches and nearly blind each time she tries to stand up. There's no fever with her sickness, so I'm certain it's something other than influenza. Her face is puffed up, features gone coarse. I think it's what Miss B. called *visage d'etranger*, the stranger's face. *When you don't know the woman no more by lookin' at her, then she gots the mask of death come on her . . . after that, there's not much can turn her back.* The advanced state of Ginny's condition worries me. I will do everything I can, but her symptoms should have been attended to weeks ago.

> *Stranger's Face:* I seen it in a woman over Blomidon way. By the time I got to her she was gone out of her mind with convulsions. I had to cut the baby out, losing the mother to save the child. The baby died anyways. Was too early to have enough strength to survive.

Miss B.'s sprawling script wanders across the pages of the Willow Book, her amendments and successes turned sideways, rhyming in the margins.

> Skullcap tincture—good for any variety of anxiety. Potato skins and beets will put her back on her feet. Raspberries and nettle, sweet as can be, perfect for a Mother's Tea.

Ginny will stay at Spider Hill until after the baby is born. Mother, Precious and the rest of the Occasional Knitters will help look after Wrennie. If I can bring Ginny's swelling down and keep her strength up for the next couple of days, then I should be able to bring the baby along without any trouble. (Albeit three, possibly four weeks early.) We cannot afford to wait.

~ October 17, 1918

I'm having trouble keeping Laird away from Ginny and my house. He's worried about her, and has mentioned more than a few times that he'd be glad to fetch Dr. Thomas. It's as if he still doesn't trust me, despite knowing the truth about Mrs.

Ketch's death and the fact that I attended the birth of his last child. I've done my best to calm him down and then send him away again. It's clear that the hard-earned money Laird paid for Dr. Thomas's obstetrical theory hasn't done Ginny any good. *You must understand, Mrs. Jessup: like you, the majority of pregnant women are neurotic.* The last time the doctor saw her, he told her that if the swelling in her ankles and hands didn't go down he'd have to perform a bloodletting. If he shows his face at my door, he may be in for a bloodletting of his own. I know it can be difficult to get a straight answer out of Ginny, but no woman, no person, deserves such thoughtless care. *More exercise, less meat.* No wonder her blood's gone weak. At least she had sense enough to put herself to bed.

~ October 18, 1918

A long day.

At first I was afraid that nothing was working. The swelling wasn't going down and Ginny was getting quite agitated, but thankfully, she started to come around after supper. Tonight she is looking better and resting well.

Two Epsom soaks, one in the morning, one before bed.

Teas that work:
Juice of half a lemon plus 2 teaspoons cream of
tartar, twice a day for three days
Skullcap, one to two cups per day
Raspberry-nettle tea
Steeped hops, once a day (this seemed to do
the trick)

Also:

> Shad (coming from cold waters, they are dark
> and greasy)
> Greens of chive and garlic (they are just letting
> go, hope I have enough to last)

Homeopathy: Apis, phosphorus, sulphur, colchicum

~ October 19, 1918

Checked Ginny this morning. She's forward and soft.
Both good signs. I will try to coax the baby along today.
Hopefully, it will be a slow, gradual birthing. The moon's
on my side. It's the Harvest moon tonight, perigee tide too.
Clouds moving in from the northwest. A thunderstorm
certainly wouldn't hurt. I'll put my laundry on the line, to
invite the rain.

> Castor oil, two large spoonfuls
> A finger slip of evening primrose oil
> Basil tea
> Soak her feet in milk up to her ankles, then rub
> them, especially behind the heel.
> Instruct Ginny to pinch and pull on her tits, five
> minutes on each side, every half hour.
> Homeopathy: Caulophylum, cimicifuga, gelsinium

Of all things, I'm out of castor oil. Will have to walk to
Bertine's after breakfast. Laird and Ginny's place is closer,
but I don't want him nosing around until after the baby's
born. Ginny's face is calm and smooth, cheeks rosy, eyes
bright. A visit from her husband might break her cheerful
mood, something I cannot allow to happen. She's been

gazing out the parlour window, watching children play and the ships moving in and around the wharf.

"Dora, can't I please take a walk today? The trees are turning such beautiful colours, and I'm feeling much better."

"No, dear, you must stay in bed until after the birth. If all goes well, we might see your little angel as soon as tonight."

"But . . ."

"Don't fuss. We have a lot of work ahead—all three of us—and you need to be ready for it. We'll have a nice breakfast and then a long Epsom bath."

"Not shad again, I hope."

"Yes, shad again, and steeped hops too."

Ginny pouted, sticking her tongue out. "Those hops are the most dreadful thing I've ever tasted, like boiled dish-water and mouldy bread."

I laughed at her childish protests. "Well, aren't we feeling impatient today?"

I fluffed up her pillow and tucked it behind the small of her back. "That's a good sign. Looks like you're ready to have this baby."

She sighed, her hands caressing the sides of her belly. "I don't know if I can. Isn't it still early? Can't we wait a few more days?"

"You musn't think that way." I sat next to her on the bed. "There's no danger in bringing the baby now, but there will be if we wait much longer. Think how you'll feel when you see your baby's face, when you hold him for the first time."

"But what if he dies, or I die?"

"What if you don't? What if both of you are healthy as spring chickens? You'll have a lot to think about, a lot to do once he arrives."

Ginny looked uncertain and scared, like a girl trying to dance for the first time or reading a poem aloud at school.

"You've done this before, Ginny. You can do it again."

"But I remember so little of it."

"You trust me, don't you?"

She nodded. "Yes."

I cradled the roundness of her belly in my hands, looking into her frightened eyes. "We can do this."

All was going well . . . Ginny felt ripe, and her bearing-down pains were getting closer together, only twenty minutes apart.

Just after supper, Dr. Thomas came pounding at my door. I tried to ignore him, but he raised his voice and called out to me, "Mrs. Bigelow, open the door. Laird Jessup says you have his wife in your house. She's my patient, and I must attend to her."

Laird had met me in the road when I was coming home from Bertine's. I didn't make any effort to hide the large bottle of castor oil I was carrying, but I did let him know that he needed to stay away for one more day. He seemed understanding at the time, but I guess he wasn't. He must have gone straight to town to enlist Dr. Thomas's help. I opened the door a crack and smiled innocently at the doctor. He attempted to look past me and into the house. When it was clear that I didn't want to let him in, he stuttered with frustration.

"Mrs. Jessup needs to be under my constant supervision. I'm not leaving until I see her."

"I think she's had enough of your *supervision.*"

He tried to push past me. "Mr. Jessup says you've had her locked up here for days. He's concerned for the welfare of his wife and child."

I grabbed the frame of the door and held tight, refusing him entry.

Ginny called out from the birthing room, "Dora, who's there? Is it Laird? Everything alright at home?"

I called back to her, "Stay in bed. I'll take care of—"

Before I could stop him, Dr. Thomas was through the kitchen and standing in the birthing room. He placed his bag on the end of the bed, pulled out several medicine bottles and brandished a pair of forceps. He grunted in my direction. "She looks well." He yanked the sheet back and began to grope at Ginny's ankles. "Swelling's gone down. Remarkable."

Ginny was squirming, trying to get loose from his hands. "Dora, you said *we* were going to do this. What is *he* doing here?" She doubled over, groaning with pain.

Dr. Thomas grabbed her wrist, attempting to take her pulse. "I see she's still neurotic. A dose of Pituitrin should speed things along. This should take no time at all."

Ginny began to scream, her face turning red. "Get him away from me!"

I pulled on his sleeve, leading him out of the room. "I'd like to speak with you . . . outside."

"I really don't think that's necessary, Mrs. Bigelow. I have things under control now. If you'll agree to assist, I think we'll have this done in no time . . ."

Ginny was still ranting. "I don't want that man anywhere near me. Get out, get out, get out . . ."

He whispered to me, "Don't worry, I have chloroform if she insists on keeping this up."

I dug my fingernails into the back of his hand, and led him out of the house. "Do you want to kill her?"

"Mrs. Bigelow . . . I tip my hat to you. She looks much better than last time I saw her, but let's get this over with, shall we?"

"She's feeling better, no thanks to you. And now that you're here, she's getting herself all worked up again. You know as well as I that any aggravation to her condition could put both mother and child in danger."

"I told you, I have chloroform—"

Hart walked out from behind the barn, a pitchfork in his hand and Pepper at his heels. "Need a little help there, Dorrie?"

I took the pitchfork from him. "I think this will do."

Hart whistled his way back towards the barn, turning every so often to see that I was alright. Pepper stayed at my side.

I held the points of the fork to the doctor's chest. "You're going to do exactly as I say from here on out." I gestured with my head towards the door. "We'll go in the house. *You* will wait in the parlour. If I hear one word—or I find you're trying to leave to fetch Laird—we'll have a late haying season in Scots Bay."

I circled around him and prodded him in the back. He stumbled up the steps. "Mrs. Bigelow, may I remind you that the Criminal Code of 1892 states—"

"I don't think you're in a position to say much of anything right now, Dr. Thomas."

Once inside, Dr. Thomas sat down on the settee in the parlour. Pepper sat guard in front of him. Returning to Ginny, I tied the curtains between the parlour and the birthing room shut.

"Is he gone?" Ginny asked.

"He's nothing to fret over. Time to concentrate on having this baby."

By dawn, mother, baby and Dr. Thomas were all sleeping peacefully.

Eli Jessup, born October 20, 1918.
Some small, but holding his own.

46

WHEN WORD OF THE ARMISTICE came, we met at the church, said our prayers of thanks and rang the bells all through the night. The papers have been filled with stories of people all over Europe and North America greeting the troops, singing and dancing. They are safe enough to smile again. My favourite of all the photographs I have seen is one that was taken in San Francisco, California. Although they are still battling against the Spanish Influenza, the residents of that city ran out into the sidewalks and streets, hugging and kissing each other through handkerchiefs and gauze masks.

Albert and Borden arrived November 15. They are the first boys home. They never did get any farther than Cape Breton Island. In some ways, I think Albert feels a bit guilty for the simple nature of their service on *The Just Cause,* but whenever he seems too humble, Borden is quick to remind all of us that several of the Royal Navy's mystery ships were lost at the hands of the Germans.

Albert has brought something home from the war that none of us could have guessed. Her name is Celia. She's a lovely girl from Sydney, and it's plain to see that my brother adores her. No wonder he barely sent two words to Mother when he was on shore: he was too busy getting himself a wife! They will live in Uncle Irwin's hunting cabin until he can build her a house in the spring. Right now, poor Celia seems homesick and overwhelmed by the smallness of this place, but we are all doing our best to make her feel welcome. Precious has been especially kind to her, inviting her for tea, going on at length about life in the Bay. I suppose it keeps her from counting the minutes until Sam Gower walks through her door.

The schooner *Huntley* was launched a week after Armistice. The four-masted 520-ton beauty will sail from Newfoundland to England. She has been the pride of the Bay for almost two years; nearly all the men in the village worked their sweat into her bones. The names Thorpe, Macdonald, Steele, Tupper, Munro, Rogers, Corkum, Legge, Bigelow, Shaw, Coffill, Brown, Irving and Sandford all stood shoulder to shoulder with my father and my uncles to bring her up. She sighed, leaving a trail of steam as she slid down the slip. It was hard for the men to watch her go. Some say she's the last of the great vessels to be built in the Bay. Old men stood patting one another on the back, singing:

> *Come all ye old comrades,*
> *Come now let us join,*
> *Come join your sweet voices*
> *In chorus with mine,*
> *For we'll laugh and be jolly*
> *While sorrow refrain,*
> *For we may and may never*
> *All meet here again.*

That evening, we gathered at the Seaside Centre for one of the White Rose Temperance Society's charity pie auctions. Dozens of cakes and pies were crowded together on a long table at the front of the room. Each dessert was dressed with a gaudy bow or a spray of crepe paper flowers. I laugh to myself every time I see such a display, knowing that the original purpose for these decorations is a tradition that has long since faded. My mother and father were one of the last couples to have started their courtship "at auction."

The rules state that each baked good is to be presented anonymously, the young male bidders not knowing which young lady made what. The girls of the Bay, being honest but wise, agree among themselves how they will adorn their creations, signalling their preferred bidders accordingly. Father's final bid won Mother's daisy-crowned sugar creme pie as well as her heart. The activity, a favourite of most everyone in the Bay, was suspended during the war, mostly due to there being so few young men to bid against one another for the young ladies' wares. Last night, almost all the women, young and old, brought something to share. Even I came with pie in hand, apple with a lattice crust, a simple verse wobbling on a toothpick sticking out of the top: *The morning air is so refreshing when one has lost one's money.* It was homely compared to the others, but appropriate for a young widow, I guess.

Borden and Hart bid against each other for my offering. It was all in fun and I was glad to watch them fall all over themselves to keep me from feeling left out. My dear brother bid nobly, digging in every pocket to see if he could add one more penny. When he got to "three dollars and fifty-two cents," his pockets were turned inside out. Hart put him out of his misery by responding with "four dollars."

Then he jangled the change in his hand and added, "and fifty-two cents." Tradition dictates that the gentleman who wins the pie gets to share it with the lady who baked it. Hart followed me home, whistling and teasing, with my pie tin balanced in his hands.

Long after his stomach was full and Wrennie had gone to sleep, he sat in the kitchen, poking at the wood in the stove. I watched him, wondering why he'd never had a wife, and never gotten angry or sour enough to want to leave this place. If anyone had a right and the means to do so it was Hart.

"Here." I handed him a silk purse filled with money, the same one he had given me when I left for Boston.

"What's this? It's still full. Didn't you spend any of it?"

Maxine had given me enough to repay Hart, and a little extra as well. "Didn't need to."

He put it on the table and shoved it towards me. "You have it."

I gave it back to him. "Haven't you ever wanted to see what's outside the Bay?"

He opened the door to the stove and pushed another log into the flames. "I've seen enough to satisfy me."

"The rest of us would care for your mother. I could look in on her. You wouldn't have to worry."

"Why—you trying to get rid of me?"

"No, that's not what I meant. It's just, with the war over and all, I thought you might—"

He stood up as if he was going to leave. "Don't you go worrying about what I might and might not do."

I pulled on his shirt sleeve, trying to get him to look at me. "I'm sorry. You've been nothing but the greatest of help to me. I suppose I shouldn't have anything to say to you except thank you." I stood on my toes and kissed his cheek. The beginnings of his winter beard brushed heavy against my face, along with the smell of sweet, stale hay made from last summer's clover.

We failed to say goodbye until morning. And even now that he's left the house, his breathing is still here, in the shallow between my breasts, the wrinkle of my pillow. He has left me with a quiet, sure happiness that will not go away, and I don't think it matters if he ever says he loves me. I know him, have always known him. Same as I know he doesn't like too much sugar, not in his coffee, not in a girl. Same as I know he's never had patience for lies. *Sin has many tools, but a lie has a handle to fit them all.* Same as I know that tonight at midnight, or half past one, or whenever he sees that the rest of the Bay is asleep, Hart Bigelow will make his way up the road to Spider Hill and lay his body next to mine, again.

Miss Maxine Cabott
23 Charter Street
North End, Boston,
Massachusetts
U.S.A.

January 30, 1919

Miss Dora Rare
Scots Bay, Nova Scotia
Canada

My dearly departed Miss Rare,

We are still missing you at 23 Charter Street.

I am sending this letter so that you might not worry when you hear of the great tragedy that came upon the North End a few days ago. I know it is not of the magnitude of the Great War, or your terrible Halifax Explosion, but it was so shocking that I am still shaking over it.

The North End was about to welcome home our brave boys who had served in the Great War. Be it in their honour, or because of the impending doom of prohibition, a house-sized fermentation tank had been topped off for a higher than usual yield of the Old Demon Rum.

It was a warm day, too warm for January. As the mercury rose, the molasses gurgled and bubbled, expanding inside the already bloated tank. No one suspected . . . not young Peter Murphy leaning against the warmth of the tank, not the sweet Catholic schoolchildren walking home for lunch, not the women doing their daily run to the market, not the fine men working in the warehouses along Commercial Street. No one heard it stretching . . . ticking . . . and then . . .

*BOOM! The scariest thought is that I was one of those
unsuspecting persons walking down the street that day. I was
innocently strolling, holding hands with Charlie, when the
great thirty-foot wave of brown came oozing down upon the
North End, crushing the elevated train tracks, heaving into
buildings, smothering twenty-one people to death.*

*If it weren't for our dear Charles climbing up the terrace
wall above the street and pulling me to safety, why I'd have
been number twenty-two, I'd have been a molasses cookie.
I think I may have to marry your brother for this one.*

*Are you back in the business of catching babies? Charlie,
the girls and I have started a new venture, a "transport
business," delivering beverages of spirit from the back of my
good old Hupmobile. If I could just keep my shoes from
sticking to the molasses in the sidewalks, I'd be happy.*

> *Kisses to you and Wrennie,*
> *Max*

*P.S. I came across something of George Sand and it made me
think of you: "The world will know and understand me
someday. But if that day does not arrive, it does not greatly
matter. I shall have opened the way for other women."*

Miss Dora Rare
Scots Bay, Nova Scotia
Canada

February 10, 1919

Miss Maxine Cabott
23 Charter Street
North End, Boston,
Massachusetts
U.S.A.

Dear Maxine,

I am relieved to have gotten your letter. There was a photo-graph of your great molasses flood in the Halifax paper just this past week. What a mess it must be! The article said that the Boston fire brigade has gone to spraying salt water from the harbour in an attempt to clean it up. At least for now you're having winter weather. I imagine whatever remains of it might freeze and be broken off the buildings like giant pieces of molasses candy? Charlie always loved it as a child.

My dear little Wrennie is growing so fast. She has two teeth already, and she thinks she's ready to walk. Her legs, however, do not wish to accommodate her just yet. Her hair is as red as ever, only she has much more of it. I guess she takes after her Auntie Max.

Life on Spider Hill is grand, as I have had a bit of extra happiness these past few months. It seems I have found myself a lover. Please don't scold me for not mentioning it before now, but I thought it best to keep it to myself to make sure it would hold. I know you won't think it as scandalous as most people of the Bay find it to be, but the man I've been sharing my bed with is none other than Hart Bigelow, the brother of my scheming dead husband. Do not worry, he's not a bit like his brother. (Charlie can attest to it.) He has broached the subject of marriage, but I'm content to leave things as they are for now, despite the shock we are giving to the community.

Come visit in the spring, and perhaps we'll have a double wedding.

> Here's to love!
> Dora

"I ask the support of no one, neither to kill someone for me, gather a bouquet, correct a proof, nor go with me to the theatre. I go there on my own, as a man, by choice and when I want flowers, I go on foot, by myself, to the Alps."
—George Sand

47

B Y SPRING, HART WAS coming up to Spider Hill almost every day. He stays late; neither of us caring what anyone else has to say about it. His mother can hardly stand to look at me. She shuts her eyes and pretends to pray whenever I walk by her pew at church. Hart says she's still grieving over Archer and not to worry over it, but I feel that it's something more, that she's got it in her head that I'm somehow to blame for Archer's death and that I'll be the end of Hart as well. Mother hasn't said a word, but she beams whenever she sees us together, and I've heard Father mumble to himself on more than one occasion, "He should just make an honest woman out of her and be done with it."

My dear sisters in the O.K.S. can't stop talking about it, teasing me at every meeting. Precious is now a "junior" sister, and the worst offender of all when it comes to trying to get me to talk.

"Aren't you afraid of the Bigelow curse? All the men in that family die young."

Sadie laughed. "All the more reason to have him now . . ." She was cutting my hair with my kitchen shears, snipping off what had grown since I came back to the Bay. "Stop giggling,

Dora, or you'll wind up looking like Bertine's girl, Lucy, cut it for you. You saw what she did to her dolly."

Mabel looked me over, tilting her head to the side, circling around the back of the chair. "It suits you, Dora." She folded her hair up by her ears, turning her head for advice. "What do you think, you guess it might suit me too?"

After we'd all had a round or two of tea with mitts, I took the scissors and bobbed every one of the Occasional Knitters' tresses. Aunt Fran's sure to come after me for taking off her daughter's lovely curls, but Precious insisted she join in the ritual. It certainly makes her look sophisticated. Maybe even old enough to get engaged to Sam Gower.

While I was cutting Bertine's hair, she told me the news that her sister-in-law, Irene, was now with child. "They don't have enough for her to go down to Canning to have it, not that she'd want to anyway. You think you could help her, Dora? I'll come and lend a hand. Even with two months to go, she's getting some big and starting to fret over what she'll do. It's her first one."

Ginny was holding up my hand mirror so Sadie could see her hair. "She should come here and stay with you at Spider Hill. It's just you and Wrennie in this big house; there's plenty of room. It's not like you have a husband to worry about."

Sadie snatched the mirror away from Ginny. "Maybe Dora likes it that way. Maybe she doesn't want another husband and she's tired of catching babies. Don't you ever think before things come out of your mouth?"

"I wasn't finished with what I was saying," Ginny pouted. "I meant to pay Dora a compliment. If it weren't for my staying with her, I wouldn't have my little Eli, and I might not be here myself."

Mabel was sitting in Miss B.'s rocker, knitting. "It would make things easier for you—if you decided to go back to midwifing, I mean. You'd be right here at home, and we'd be close at hand to help."

Bertine now held the mirror, peering at my face as I concentrated on keeping her hair straight. "You're not saying anything, Dora. What's wrong?"

I looked into the mirror. "I'm not sure it's the right thing to do."

"Irene's place is pretty small, but she could come to my house if you don't want to have her here. I understand. It's your home, after all."

"It's not that."

"What is it, then?"

"It's . . ."

Bertine scowled at me. "Brady Ketch is sitting in jail. You saved Ginny *and* her baby. What can the doc say against you now?"

I brushed the stray hairs from the back of her neck. "He didn't say a word the morning after Ginny's birthing. He just got in that car of his and drove off. I haven't heard from him since."

Sadie laughed. "Maybe he's scared you'll come after him again with a pitchfork."

I nodded. "I probably shouldn't have done that. The longer he's silent, the longer I feel like he's planning something. I wouldn't be surprised if I don't wake up tomorrow to see my old friend Constable McKinnon at the door."

Ginny smiled and nudged me in the arm. "Then we'll all have to take up our pitchforks and run him out of the Bay."

"Ginny's right: let's go after him before he comes after

you." Bertine was smiling, her foot tapping. "Let's do something about Dr. Thomas, once and for all."

~ *April 20, 1919*

Bertine and Sadie delivered letters to local women, asking for their support at a Mother's May Day march in Canning. Precious and Mabel have sewn a large banner for the women to carry, and I have agreed to speak (to anyone who'll listen).

If women lose the right to say where and how they birth their children, then they will have lost something that's as dear to life as breathing.

I'm tired of being afraid.

Hundreds March on Canning

Women and Children First!— This was the banner that led the way through the streets of Canning, Nova Scotia, this past Wednesday afternoon. Over two hundred women from communities all along North Mountain came together to raise their voices in support of rural midwives. They did not come alone. Each woman had at least one child in tow, some still babes in arms. Their chanting and singing made quite a stir in our little town, stopping all business for the rest of the day.

Mrs. Bertine Tupper had this to say about the gathering: "Men have the right to tell their wives what they expect for breakfast, lunch and dinner, but they want to refuse women the privilege of saying where they're going to have their babies. Anyone who believes that's right hasn't got the sense God gave a goat."

Mrs. Kathleen Jess of Baxter's Harbour told the harrowing tale of her sister, Ellie's, untimely death in childbirth. "The midwife, Mrs. Sommer, came to see if she could lend a hand. Then Ellie's husband brought the doctor. That Dr. Thomas, he pushed the old midwife right out. She begged at the door, telling him she knew the baby was breech, that she could help, but he turned her away, saying he could take care of it. He took care of it alright. By morning both my sister and her baby were gone. He just stood there, wringing his hands, telling us that he'd done all he could."

Mrs. Ginny Jessup told of her recent birthing, a healthy baby boy born at the Scots Bay home of midwife Dora Rare. "She just knows what to do. She had the tradition handed down to her. Just like a master shipbuilder, or a farmer who knows his family's land, she knows what to do. Any doctor could learn a thing or two from her."

Miss Rare gave an eloquent speech to a crowd gathered in front of the Canning Maternity Home. She spoke of her experiences as a midwife, as well as the dangers rural women face in travelling down the mountain while in the last stages of labour. She called for "co-operation and trust" between doctors, midwives and the women they serve. Her final thoughts gave way to a roar of cheers and praise. "When a ship is sinking, the men all cry, 'Women and children first!' Sisters and mothers of North Mountain, of Scots Bay, Blomidon, Medford, Delhaven, Halls Harbour, Ross Creek, Gospel Woods and Baxter's Harbour, do not let them forget: Women and children first, women and children first!"

The Canning Register,
May 2, 1919

~ May 30, 1919

Bertine took this clipping from the *Canning Register* and passed it down the pew during church, stuck between the pages of a hymnal.

Canning Maternity Home to Close

The Farmer's Assurance Company has announced that they are shutting down operations of the Canning Maternity Home, effective immediately. Dr. Gilbert Thomas made this statement: "On behalf of myself and the Farmer's Assurance Company of Kings County, I would like to thank all of the mothers and families who have sought care at this fine facility. I regret to report that I cannot find good reason to maintain my practice in your fair town at this time. The need is simply not great enough to support such an endeavour."

Those women in the area still holding a Mother's Share are welcome to seek obstetrical care at Dr. Thomas's new practice—in Halifax.

I've decided to offer up Spider Hill as a birthing house for the Bay. These are the only things I will ask of the women who come here:

· No woman or child shall be turned away.
· No payment shall be required.
· No idle gossip or cruel words shall cross the threshold.
· No one may attend a birth unless requested by the mother.

· Mother and child (or children) shall stay in confinement for at least nine days after the birth, or until the mother's been churched.

· Well-wishers may not enter unless the mother approves.

· The mother's home must be clean and tidy, her household chores looked after, and supper enough for a week must be waiting for her when she returns home.

When I finished my tea tonight, I turned the cup over. One, two, three times round. *I sees a pretty little house, right full with babies.*

epilogue

Electricity Comes to Scots Bay

Twenty-two years after the first electric street-lights were lit in Canning, power poles have finally found their way up North Mountain to the last community on the line—Scots Bay. Mr. Joseph Berch of Kings County Electric said, "It's been an enormous undertaking and we are grateful to the people of Scots Bay for their patience and understanding." Many homes, as well as the Union Church, the Seaside Centre and the Scots Bay School can expect to have electricity by the end of the month.

The Canning Register,
July 4, 1944

THERE WASN'T MUCH CALL for three-masted schooners after the war. The shipyard went to waste, and Father spent his days knocking on other men's doors, looking to help them with "whatever needs doing." It wasn't so much that he needed a job, it was just that he couldn't stop moving. Right up to his death, I never saw him sitting with his hands folded in his lap, quiet.

People came and left the Bay, more leaving than staying, feeling there was something better out in the world for them, something bigger. Those of us who stayed behind still can't say this place is on the way to anything else, we just call it home.

My home on Spider Hill, this birth house, has seen her share of life and babies. Of course, there's fewer of them now that every other place has a car parked out front and every other young man has gone to war again. Most of those boys were born in my house; they are my sons too. Still, women come to me for "whatever needs doing," a bottle of Miss B.'s cough syrup, a cup of tea with mitts, a few minutes' rest with her feet up and my hands on her belly to say, "Everything's fine, just fine." Some of them, when the time comes, have gotten quite good at waiting too long to go to the hospital, their husbands roaring them up the road and to my door. I never mind it.

Mabel had two more here . . .

Bertine had a boy.

Precious married Sam Gower . . . and was soon carrying twins.

Pregnant or not, the Occasional Knitters never miss a Wednesday night.

No woman or child shall be turned away.

There have been those who have stayed here a day, a week and even a month or more. *Every woman needs a sanctuary.* Judith left Boston and ran away to Paris with a poet, leaving Rachael heartsick. The poor girl came to Scots Bay and hid herself up in the ell chamber, filling it with her sadness and painting after painting of the dark, brooding sea.

And Wrennie, my little moss-baby, grew up caring for the women as much as I did. She was happy to sit by the bed, holding a young mother's hand, or to share her dolls with two little girls who had lost their home in a fire. Always a beautiful girl, she's outgrown her honest eyes, not quite sure how to tame the fire that sits in her heart, a fire that can send any man begging at her window. At twenty-eight, she's gone to Boston and back so many times I've lost count.

Every summer, Charlie arrives with Maxine, smiling and happy to have his wife by his side. I always expect them about this time of year, when the weather gets hot in Boston and "the goddammed molasses has started to ooze from the cracks in the sidewalks of Beantown again." When Max is in the Bay, you can be sure the rum and talk won't stop flowing 'til she's gone. She always comes bearing gifts. "What kind of auntie would I be if I didn't bring plenty of books for Wrennie and plenty of hooch for Mommy?" And so Wrennie was raised on healthy doses of Virginia Woolf, Katherine Mansfield, James Joyce and F. Scott Fitzgerald, as well as brown bread, black raspberries and shad.

When Wrennie was five, Max brought her a hand-cranked Victrola. Wrennie giggled and laughed, "Auntie Max, that's the funniest flower I've ever seen!" But when Max made it go and the music started, Wrennie fell in love. She spun around the room, holding out her arms, eyes closed. Tangos, waltzes, the Charleston, she loved them all. Long summer nights all through July and August, we'd drag Wrennie's "singing flower" out to the porch, and people from all around the Bay would come and listen, sometimes dancing in the dooryard.

Hart has remained my dancing partner. Always my lover, never my husband. He still asks for my hand from time to time, but never complains when I say I prefer it this way. Even as the Widow Bigelow lay in bed dying, she scolded me and blamed my refusals on my being born different, on my having lived with Miss B. or on my being "the girl who went to Boston." I should have told her it was more that I didn't want to end up like her—having married and lost two husbands, two brothers, two Bigelow men. I think Miss B. would have a good laugh over it all. *That Missy Austen always seemed to be endin' her books with a weddin'. Catherine marryin' Henry, Miss Bennett marryin' Mr. Darcy, then* fin, *the end. Seems to me what she's sayin' is that once you're hitched, it might as well be the end.*

I plan to stay just far enough from Hart to keep it all from ending. He can have his mother's rattly old house of rooster red. I'll stay perched up here on Spider Hill, catching a baby or two when they come, singing Miss B.'s lullabies, writing poems on old grocery receipts and keeping Hart company when he happens by.

Tonight he'll make his way up the hill, tired but wanting, home from the Dulsin' tide. In the dusk I can see people gathered together, some in skiffs on the water, others in a large circle around the church. They are waiting for a twinkling, a rapture. They are waiting for the lights to go on in the Bay.

Notes from the Willow Book

The Moon owns the willow

The Midwife's Garden

A is for anise, sweet relief for the bowels
B is the butcher's broom to shrink the womb down
C is for cayenne; its heat stays the blood
Dandelion greens should be boiled some good

E is for eggs, one a day cooked 'til hard
Fennel brings mother's milk and a woman's blood
G's the gooseberry, for pie or for jam
Hyssop, tansy, and mugwort for taking a bath
I's the Irish Moss for blanc mange and stew
Juniper without berries is for making tea too
K is for kelp, when it's dried it will keep
Labrador tea if you're needing some sleep

M is for mustard, on her belly makes her bleed
N's for the nettle, just the leaves, not the seed
Onions to the feet will bring down a fever
Pennyroyal's tincture makes a tiny baby leave her

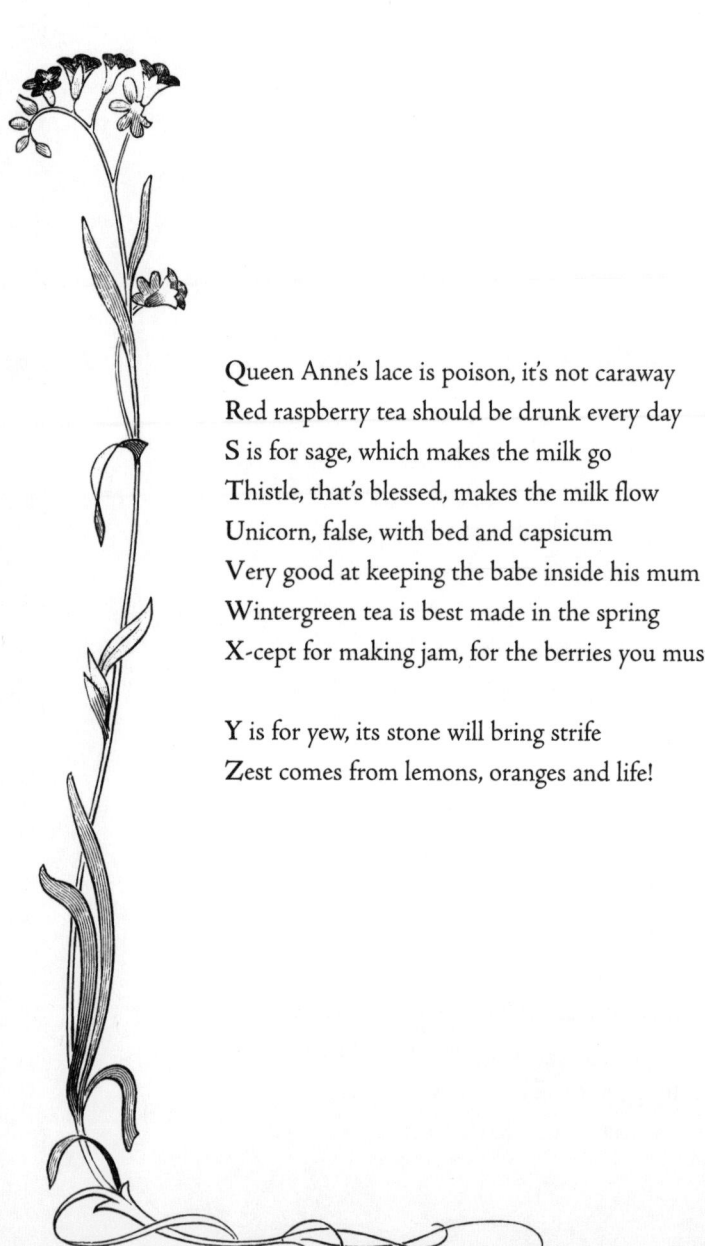

Queen Anne's lace is poison, it's not caraway
Red raspberry tea should be drunk every day
S is for sage, which makes the milk go
Thistle, that's blessed, makes the milk flow
Unicorn, false, with bed and capsicum
Very good at keeping the babe inside his mum
Wintergreen tea is best made in the spring
X-cept for making jam, for the berries you must bring

Y is for yew, its stone will bring strife
Zest comes from lemons, oranges and life!

Alder

To clear the liver and cut the hives. Brew up a pot of weak red alder tea. Give in drops to the newborn. Keeps a babe from turning yellow.

Althea

(*mortification root*) A spirit puller. Calls good spirits into the home.

Angel Water

For calling an angel down when a mama's two moontimes late. Boil up: black stick, pennyroyal, wild carrot seeds. Add a pinch of borax, a pinch of gunpowder. Mix with whiskey, drink, and wait.

Barley

Scatter by the door to keep evil away. If you want love, drink a cup of barley water every day. *Barley and onions in a bath will surely bring a person back.*

Bay

Write your wishes on leaves of bay, burn them and they'll come true the same day.

Beans

Three blue beans in a blue bladder. Rattle, bladder, rattle. Sing three times in one breath to chase the haints away.

Beaver Brew

A dose (straight or with tea) keeps a woman clear from babies for one moontime. Steep the oysters of beavers in gin. Set out in the light of three full moons.

Birthwort

Holds a mother against illness. Take a bath with its juice and a snake's bite will never do you harm.

Borage

The seeds and leaves make a mama give more milk. Cures a broken heart.

Breech

Means trouble to mama and child. Best to get the babe to done turn on its own. Try: tipping the mama, having her do the elephant walk, giving her a cold belly, singing the babe a sweet song, Mother's Tea with pasque flower.

Brown Flour Coffee

Turns sickness. Set a pint of flour on the stove until it gets right dry—stir and roast it down dark, like coffee. Put two tablespoons in a pint of boiling water. Scald in milk. Make sweet with honey.

Cabbage

Takes soreness out of hot breasts. Steam the leaves. Let cool. Place on a mama's tits. Plant cabbage first after a marriage to bring luck and love.

Camphor

Use as a rub for croup or aching skin. Mix with the wash to scare off fleas and bedbugs.

Caul

A babe with a caul sees more than us all. Brings the gift of sight. Saves a man from drowning.

Castor Oil

(*Palma Christi*)
Brings healing wherever it's given to the body.
My hands are His hands
My hands are His Hands
Palma Christi
Palma Christi
The Hand of Christ

Cayenne

(*capsicum*)
See also *Quilling*. Brings strength to the womb. Useful for yellow babes.

Childbed Fever

Brought on by unclean hands. *Always wash before you pray.*

Coltsfoot
(son-before-the-father)

Nothing works better to tame an angry throat. Don't plant the coltsfoot in your garden  unless that's all you want there. You'll see yellow buttons peeking out between rocks and ditches long before the leaves come on, the son-before-the-father. Make note of where you saw it in the spring so you can come back to it. Cook leaves down, strain, add sugar, then boil until a drop of the syrup turns hard in cold water.

Comfrey
Cures the whites when put in a douche.

Dead Needle
To make sure of death. Push a clean needle in the flesh of the left arm. If it comes back dark, they's alive. If it comes back polished, they's dead.

Devil's Bit
(scabiosa)

Brew the flowers to keep her courses regular and clean. Smells like honey. *So sweet the Devil bit off the root of the first plant to try to take it away from us.*

Dill
For colicky babes, rub the child's belly with dill seed oil. Makes them sweet again. For hiccups, boil seeds in wine and breathe in the scent.

Dulse
(Neptune's girdle)

Puts salt in the veins. Keeps the blood strong for another year. *Careful! Can arouse a man's desires.*

Fennel
Brings milk to a mama's breasts. Boil leaves with barley and drink as tea. Makes the flow creamy and good.

Feverfew
(*maydeweed*)

Make tea with the leaves. Good for a lady who frets. Simmer plant and flowers in water for a sitz bath for a lady's private parts. Gives strength to the womb. Best to keep it on its own in the garden. Bees don't have nothing to do with it. Good for a *Moon Elixir*.

Fiddlehead Fern
Break the first frond you see in the spring. Keeps a toothache away for a year.

Flax
Make tea with seeds, lemon and honey—for coughs and sore throats.

Groaning Cake
(*kimbly, gateau a la mélasse*)

2 cups molasses
1 cup boiling milk
1 tsp baking powder
3-1/2 cups flour, sifted
4 eggs
1 cup butter
1 tbsp ground ginger
1/4 tsp ground cloves
1/4 tsp ground cinnamon
1/2 cup raisins (or grated apple)

Headache
Simple—Walk backwards half a mile, slow as a snail.
Sick—Take catnip tea. Make a plaster of cayenne pepper and vinegar, apply to brow, then sleep it off.

A rumour is about as hard to unspread as butter.

High Tide Tea
To ease menstrual pains and keep the courses regular. Three days before her courses are due, a lady should begin to drink this tea:

> One part burdock
> One part seaweed
> Three parts fennel seed
> One part wild carrot seed

Tie herbs into a muslin pouch and steep in boiling water. Twice daily, preferably at the high tides. Not to be taken by ladies wanting to get with child.

Irish Moss

For blanc mange and quieting a troubled belly. Boil one tsp dried plant in a cup of water. Drink twice a day.

Lady's Mantle

Our dear Lady's mantle give her tears between the dawn and the dew. Kneel before her between your courses, sip them up with your tongue, and a child she'll bring to you.

Lavender

Flower of the Blessed Virgin Mother. Tea: for truth, faith and love.

Lemon

The juice of a ripe lemon will clear the head. Squeeze into your hand and *sniff!*

Lobelia

A flower what knows. If a mama's gone to cramps and letting go of blood, lobelia will tell her body what to do. If it can save the child, it will. If not, it helps her let it go. Cleans her out. Tea: lobelia, feverfew, red raspberry, catnip. *Tea and rest.*

Mandrake Root

Balm of the bruised woman. Stand with your back to the wind. Draw three circles, clockwise, around the plant with a knife. Douse it with Mary's Tears. Turn west to uproot.

Marigold
(calendula)

Marigold honey salve heals any burn or sore spot.
The maid what dances barefoot with the marigold will know the language of the birds.

Mary Candle

To loose an angel from her seat. See *Slippery Elm.*

Mary's Tears

On May-eve, stretch a sheet between the trees. Place a stone in the centre so the dew will run down. Put your bowl underneath to catch the drops. At dawn on the first of May, gather it up in a bottle, singing this little song:

On the first of May
Before the sun shines
Mary gives up her tears
For healing divine

Moon-bath

Lay naked in a crossroads in the light of the full moon. Makes the womb ripe.

Moon Elixir

Readies her for making babies. Steep licorice root, feverfew flowers, and bee balm in wine at the full moon. Cook it down slowly, never boil. Add cinnamon, nutmeg and sugar to taste. Makes a woman sweet and her man sweet on her.
Drink through the day to be sweet, ripe and gay.

Moss

From a good woman's grave will bring you luck.

Mother's Tea

Raspberry leaves, nettle, Melissa, dried apple, fennel.

Mouse Ear

Mouse ear tea will save your life. Cures bold hives when they've gone around the heart. Grows on rocks at the edges of fresh water.

> No matter what you do, someone always knew you would.

Navel Cord Care

Grease a piece of fine muslin with tallow, place on a shovel over a fire and scorch until brown. Cut small hole in muslin and pull the navel cord through. Pin bands around it to keep it snug, to prevent ruptures in the belly caused by crying. Leave for 3 to 6 days or until the cord stump dries and falls off. Goldenseal powder is good for drying.

Onion

To cure a cold, rub feet with onions. Bury them when through. Onion syrup (garlic, onions, molasses): Three times a day, makes all sickness go away. *Bain d'oignon et orge:* A bath of onions and barley will turn the worst illness. *Throw an onion after a bride and you'll throw away her tears.*

Pasque Flower

(*meadow anemone, pulsatilla*) See also *Breech.* For a woman what weeps one minute and is sunny the next. For a woman who's scared to be alone, who changes her mind with the wind. Warms the blood and makes her sweat. If that woman's baby done turned breech, a dose in her Mother's Tea can turn it around. Wrap the first blossoms in spring in a red cloth and tie it to the arm. Keeps away disease.

Patience Dock

Tie to the left arm of a woman who's wanting a child.

Placenta

Bury the afterbirth with a scallop shell. Gives a woman at least a year before she gets with child again. Bury under an apple tree and the child will never know hunger. If a mother's bleeding won't stop, salt the thing, wrap it up in paper and throw it to the fire. Burns the blood away.

Quilling

Brings a child out when a mama's gone tired. Take a quill, push pepper up in it. Blow up her nose when she's hurting, and she'll push the babe right out.

Quince

Heals sore, cracked nipples and is quite pleasant. Warm quince seed in a little cold tea until the liquid gets glutinous. Apply to nipples.

Raspberry

God's gift to all mothers. Gives strength to her whole being. Her heart, her womb, her bones.

Sage

Helps with after pains. Careful! Dries up milk. Toads love it. *She who would live for aye, must eat sage in May.*

The most horrible curse you can put on a woman is to kiss her on the cheek and tells her that things couldn't get any worse. The minute you say it, they surely does.

Stop Bleed

Brew Mother's Heart with bayberry bark to make a tea.

Stranger's Face

Beware the stranger's face. If a mama's got it come upon her, get her to bed and get the baby out.

Slippery Elm

Brings the angel down. Anoint the Mary Candle three times round with the oil of slippery elm. Slip the end into her sweet spot. To stop gossip: Tie a yellow string around a branch. Feed it to the fire.

Weaning

Sage tea in the waning moon. To dry up the breasts after weaning, have her pull some of her milk onto a hot stone.

Willow

Knock on the willow three times three, no evil will follow thee.

Salve nos, Stella Maris,
Save us, Star of the Sea.

author's note

During the First World War, news from the front dominated newspaper headlines. Stories of the women's suffrage movement became back-page items of interest. Other issues such as fertility awareness, birth control and the science of obstetrics were only briefly mentioned in large city papers (unless it was to report that Margaret Sanger had been arrested, yet again, for distributing information about family planning) and rarely, if ever, covered by small-town press.

A woman's struggle to gain the right to choose what happened to her body was a silent issue, recorded in personal journals or through letters, one woman to another. Traditions, information and ideas about childbirth, as well as women's health and happiness, were shared in the sisterhood of knitting circles and around the kitchen table. In small, isolated communities, the keeper of this wisdom was the midwife.

When I was young, I used to watch my mother so I could learn from her. I loved sitting with her while she cooked, sewed or gardened, and even while she was putting on her makeup. One thing I remember well was her end-of-day ritual of emptying out her pockets onto her vanity.

A spool of thread, a note from a friend, bobby pins, a recipe card, a pine cone I'd handed her as a gift, a torn-out picture from a magazine—these treasures would sit on a mirrored tray, looking like they were ready to be presented to a queen. A reflection of her day, her art. When I sat down to write *The Birth House*, I realized that this was how I wanted to arrange my words, as well: by making a literary scrapbook out of Dora's days.

I drew from many books and sources while writing, including *Shattered City: The Halifax Explosion and the Road to Recovery* by Janet F. Kitz, *A Midwife's Tale: The Life of Martha Ballard, Based on Her Diary, 1785–1812* by Laurel Thatcher Ulrich, *Giving Birth in Canada, 1900–1950* by Wendy Mitchinson, *The Technology of Orgasm: "Hysteria," the Vibrator, and Women's Sexual Satisfaction* by Rachel P. Maines, *Hygieia: A Woman's Herbal* by Jeannine Parvati, *Herbs and Things* by Jeanne Rose, *Edible Wild Plants of Nova Scotia* by Heather MacLeod and Barbara MacDonald, and the wonderfully arcane *Science of a New Life* by Dr. John Cowan. Most invaluable of all were my conversations with residents, past and present, of Scots Bay.

acknowledgments

Thanks to the Province of Nova Scotia and the Department of Tourism, Culture and Heritage for their generous support in the form of a Creation Grant.

For hands-on training, I send special thanks to my angel of a midwife, Louise MacDonald. For many hours of walking, talking and tea, I send gratitude to my midwife in friendship, determination and laughter, Jen White.

For her constant interest and guidance (and for never settling for anything less than spectacular), I am grateful to my tireless and wonderful agent, Helen Heller.

Profound thanks go to Louise Dennys for including my work in her passionate, trail-blazing advocacy of new Canadian fiction; to my publisher, Diane Martin, for her belief in my work and her keen editorial eye; to my editor, Angelika Glover, for her strong sense of vision and impeccable literary intuition; and to designer Kelly Hill for finding the true essence of my words and dressing them more finely than I could have ever imagined. Special thanks to the ladies who lunched, Marion Garner, Deirdre Molina, Kendall Anderson, Mary Giuliano, Constance MacKenzie and Jan Sibiga, for being such marvellous readers and for championing my work. Thanks also to Sue Sumeraj for her copy-editing assistance.

This book could not have been written without the support of wonderful mentors along the way. My undying respect and thanks go to Dick Miller of CBC Radio for his encouragement and sense of creativity. My friendship and admiration go to Richard Cumyn for hours of conversation and guidance. I will always be grateful to Jane Buss and the Writers' Federation of Nova Scotia for their proving ground of a mentorship program.

Helpful guides in research included Dan Conlin at the Maritime Museum of the Atlantic, as well as the wonderful volunteers at the Kings County Historical Society and the Fieldwood Heritage Society. Additional inspiration for this work came from many wonderful kitchen table conversations and afternoon visits with Mrs. Mary Rogers Huntley, the Tupper sisters—Pat and Sharon, Calvin and Joy Tupper, Mrs. Fran Steele and Mrs. Irene Huntley. I thank you all for your generosity and your stories. Thanks also to Mrs. Rhea P. McKay for her encouragement and for sending me her copy of *The Science of a New Life*.

Although I spent many hours scribbling away in the quiet of my room, the psychic hum of my family and friends could always be felt. Thanks to my siblings, Skip, Doug and Lori, for letting me spill milk and monopolize dinner conversations. Thanks to Mom and Dad for always reading to me (and to each other) before bed. Thanks to Dawn and Marta, my daisy sisters, for lasting friendship. Thanks to Mitzi at Box of Delights for always asking, "How's the book?" Thanks to Doretta and the other full-moon hikers (Chris, Holly and all) for hikes, picnics and fires on the beach, and for proving that moms make art. Thanks and hugs to my sons, Ian and Jo, for giving me time to make my art. Dearest thanks of all to my beloved, Ian, for taking my hand on a stormy November day and bringing me home.

the birth house

SPECIAL FEATURES

THE REAL BIRTH HOUSE

A week after *The Birth House* was first published I received a call from an interested and eager news reporter in Halifax. "We're thinking of coming out to Scots Bay for an interview. We can film the spot in the birthing room. Do you have any relics from the midwife?"

"Relics?"

"You know, an old cradle, a rocking chair, midwifery things."

In that moment, I realized that the house fared much better in fiction than it looked in real life. In my writing, the house is new and at the centre of Dora's world. In my life, the house is under continuous reconstruction and filled with toys, boys and noise. In my life, I wear overalls, garden clogs and a bandana on my head. In my life, I'm usually listening to my five-year-old pontificate to his big brother about the fundamental differences between belches and farts and whether or not they can exist in a black hole. In my life, I'm constantly battling my dog's mysterious skin condition (one which causes her hair to fall out and her skin to smell as soon as the grass turns green in the spring). In my life, the reason I get any writing done at all is because I've given up on housework and embraced the "clutter fosters creativity" way of life.

"I have some medicine bottles that I found while digging in my garden and I have some old newspapers I peeled off the crumbling plaster walls in an upstairs storage room."

"So, you haven't restored the birthing room or anything like that?"

I sighed, thinking of the messy bookshelves and computer desk that now inhabit that space. "No, I'm afraid we haven't gotten to that yet."

"How about the kitchen?"

I sat at the kitchen table looking at the mishmash of wall coverings various residents had used to hold up the crumbling plaster—faux panelling, a patch of faux brick wallboard, the ugly wallpaper I'd been meaning to remove. Were the chubby white farm geese speckled on a blue background mocking me?

"Haven't gotten to that yet, either."

We settled on my travelling to the studio instead.

Since then, people have made their way to Scots Bay, asking, "Where's the birth house?" Cars creep down my road, rolling to a long stop at the end of my driveway—and on several occasions there's been a knock on the door. Sometimes I have time for tea, sometimes, (as much as I wish I did) I simply don't.

I always wonder how the house had been pictured in their imaginations. It's a question I've never had the courage to ask. Besides, my visitors have questions of their own: What happens to Wrennie? How did Miss B. wind up in Scots Bay? Do Rhett and Scarlett ever get back together? (Oops, that's Margaret Mitchell's question). I nod and smile. I'd like to know these things as well. Maybe one day my cluttered, wonderful old crone of a house will tell me.

RECIPE FOR A GROANING CAKE

The tradition of the groaning cake, or *kimbly*, at (or following) a birth is an ancient one. Wives' tales say that the scent of a groaning cake being baked in the birth house helps to ease the mother's pain. Some say if a mother breaks the eggs while she's aching, her labour won't last as long. Others say that if a family wants prosperity and fertility, the father must pass pieces of the cake to friends and family the first time the mother and baby are "churched" (or the first time they go to a public gathering) after a birth. Many cultures share similar traditions—a special dish, bread, or drink, spiced with cinnamon, allspice and/or ginger. At one time there was even a "groaning ale" made to go with it!

I made groaning cake the day of my son's home birth and my neighbour brought me "health bread" the day after the birth. This recipe is a combination of the two. It has apple, molasses, orange juice and spices and can really help to see a woman through a long labour, or give her strength after the birth!

2 1/2 cups	flour
2 tsp	baking powder
1 tsp	baking soda
2 tsp	cinnamon
1/2 tsp	cloves
3	eggs
1 1/2 cups	apple, peeled and grated
1/2 cup	vegetable oil
1/2 cup	orange juice
1/4 cup	molasses
1 1/3 cups	sugar
1 tsp	almond extract

Preheat oven to 350°F.

Line the bottoms of two 9″ x 5″ loaf tins with parchment. Oil the sides with vegetable oil.

In a large bowl, whisk together flour, baking powder, baking soda, cinnamon and cloves.

In a separate bowl, beat eggs. Add apple, oil, orange juice, molasses, sugar and almond extract. Blend well.

Add wet ingredients to dry ingredients. Mix well.

Divide batter between two prepared loaf tins.

Bake 35 to 40 minutes, or until a toothpick tester comes out clean.

Modify to make it your own by using about a cup of raisins, dates, dried fruits or nuts.

INTERVIEW WITH A BOOK DESIGNER

Ami McKay interviews Kelly Hill, the designer of The Birth House's *book cover*

Q: Can you explain the process you went through in designing the cover for *The Birth House*? What were you trying to convey to the reader?

A: For every book I design, I first sit down with the editor, who describes the general themes and the storyline, the audience for the novel and offers comparable books or authors. I also like to read a portion of the manuscript to get a feeling for the writing and to look for "images" within the text. What I always want to do with a cover is present something that is true to the book with just enough intrigue, and hopefully beauty, that whoever picks it up will want more. In the case of *The Birth House*, I used the image of a pregnant woman (Who is she? Is she going to be okay?) and the label and botanical print, which hint to the Willow Book and the "scrapbook" style of the novel.

Q: *The Birth House* also includes many design elements within the text of the book, including advertisements, invitations, old news clippings and an herbal notebook—all circa World War I. What sorts of challenges did these elements present?

A: These were fun to work on. I used some actual ads from that time period as inspiration and did my best to mimic the fonts and graphic style. Since some of the authentic ads were not well designed I was allowed to break some of my own rules for the purposes of authenticity.

WRITING UNDER THE INFLUENCE

As an author, I've gotten used to answering the question "which writers have influenced your work?" I thoughtfully list off my favourites—Austen, Hardy, Dickens, Nabokov, Toni Morrison, Carol Shields—the assumption being, books beget books. While this is a valid assumption, I have to admit, there's another artistic medium that shares an equal part of the light when it comes to inspiration and my writing.

Before I took up writing as a career, I was a full-time music teacher. I started piano lessons at the age of five and by the time I was seventeen, music school seemed the natural next step. (My sister always predicted I'd wind up being an opera diva, jazz singer or a punk rock star.) Lucky for me, being a musician and being a writer have much in common. The best way to get to publication (and to Carnegie Hall) is to practice, practice, practice.

Before I sit down to write, I often take a few minutes to noodle around on the piano or listen to a favourite piece of music. When I was writing *The Birth House*, folk and acoustic music played large into my musical taste—I spent hours listening to Pete Seger, Kate Wolf, Alison Krauss, Sarah Harmer, Joni Mitchell, Mary Jane Lamond and sacred harp singing. Truth and heart are at the core of those songs, and that was exactly what I was after when I was trying to find Dora's voice.

Now as I turn to new projects (another novel, as well as my first play), I find myself going back to the well of music for inspiration. Here's some of the music that's been the soundtrack behind my scribbling as of late.

Flamenco music

This is music that is mind, body and soul all at once. There's passion and heartbreak, there's spirit and movement. It's a rich mix of cultures and history with a fair bit of mystery thrown in—making it irresistible to me.

Sketches of Spain

Miles Davis is an innovative jazz genius. I've gone back to listening to *Sketches of Spain* because it's a beautiful example of what can happen when various forms of music collide. Gil Evans pulled inspiration from classical pieces of music inspired by Spanish folk music, and Miles then placed himself inside the music, bringing it to a whole new place. I can only hope to do this with my writing . . .

Madeleine Peyroux

Her voice is past and present all at once. This is what I've been after with the voice of my narrative as well—writing that feels very present and intense, yet holds a tone that comes from somewhere in the past. It's the stuff of fairy tales, ghost stories and myths.

Danny Elfman

He isn't only the wacky songwriter behind the group Oingo Boingo and the composer of the theme music for *The Simpsons* and *Desperate Housewives*; he's also scored most of Tim Burton's movies. The soundtracks to *Edward Scissorhands* and *Sleepy Hollow* are my favourites. I love the way he brings dark and whimsy side by side. I'd love my next novel to "read" like an Elfman score sounds.

AMI MCKAY's work has aired on CBC Radio's *Maritime Magazine*, *This Morning*, *Outfront* and *The Sunday Edition*. Her documentary, *Daughter of Family G*, won an Excellence in Journalism medallion at the 2003 Atlantic Journalism Awards. She lives with her husband and two sons in an old birth house on the Bay of Fundy. Visit Ami's website at www.thebirthhouse.com.